"The dean of émigré literature . . . a superb stylist and the most brilliant representative of the school of Turgenev and Chekhov in contemporary Russian letters."

—MARC SLONIM, *Modern Russian Literature*

Bunin began his literary career as a successful poet, but his greatest fame came from his achievements in the short story. Master of an opulent, lyrical prose style, his plots are often less important than the moods he evokes. His most important themes are love and death, which frequently are intermingled with despair and the futility of life.

This aura of tragedy in Bunin's work is a direct reflection of his personal experiences after fleeing Russia in 1918. Living in exile from his beloved Mother Russia, he intensely yearned for the past glories of aristocratic Czarist times. His last years were eked out in almost total obscurity in Paris. Until Boris Pasternak was awarded a Nobel Prize in 1958, Bunin was the only Russian author to have been so honored.

The Gentleman from San Francisco

and other stories

Ivan Bunin

With an Introduction by Thompson Bradley

Translated by Olga Shartse

WASHINGTON SQUARE PRESS, INC. • NEW YORK

THE GENTLEMAN FROM SAN FRANCISCO AND OTHER STORIES

1963

A new edition of a distinguished literary work now made available in an inexpensive, well-designed format

L

Published by
Washington Square Press, Inc.: Executive Offices, 630 Fifth Avenue;
University Press Division, 32 Washington Place, New York, N.Y.

WASHINGTON SQUARE PRESS editions are distributed in the U.S. by Affiliated Publishers, a division of Pocket Books, Inc., 630 Fifth Avenue, New York 20, N.Y.

Printed in the U.S.A.

Contents

Introduction

In January 1891, Anton Chekhov received a brief letter, written with painful clarity, from a young provincial journalist in Elets. It opened with the self-conscious statement that "since you are my favorite contemporary writer and since I have heard from some of my (Kharkov) friends that you are a straightforward and good person, my 'choice fell' on you." There then follows an embarrassed, humble request: "If you have a spare moment to take a look at the works of a person such as I, please do and let me know for heaven's sake if I might send you two or three of my (typed) stories and if you would read them sometime for lack of anything better to do and let me know some of your criticisms." It ends with an apology for the importunity. With this letter Ivan Alexeevich Bunin began a close and lasting friendship with Chekhov. Their friendship was to have a profound and dominant influence on Bunin's writing throughout his life.

Born on October 22, 1870 in Voronezh to an impoverished gentry family of ancient lineage, Ivan Alexeevich Bunin spent his youth on the family estate in the Elets district. This district and its environs, situated southeast of Moscow in southern Russia, figure most frequently as the setting of the author's stories. There he studied at the local high school through the fourth year and completed the remaining two years at home under the tutelage of his favorite brother, Yulii. After a short stay in Kharkov with Yulii, Bunin moved to Orel where he worked on the local newspaper for four years (1889–92). At this time he first wrote to Anton Chekhov. Here too he first began to manifest his restlessness and desire to travel. Following the Orel period, the young writer moved to Poltava in the Ukraine and served in the Zemstvo, first as a statistician, and later as librarian. This episode and the years in Orel form a significant part of the more autobiographical passages in *Lika*.

Fame came early to Bunin, when in 1887 his first verses were published in a Petersburg journal. He was only seventeen. Four years later the first volume of his poetry came out and in 1893 his first prose work *Tanka* was published. On moving to Petersburg in 1895, the young writer became acquainted with the major publishers and literary figures in Russia. He stayed there ten years, until he once again moved, this time to Moscow. A collection of his stories came out in 1897 and met with unanimous praise. The Russian Academy awarded him the Pushkin prize in 1903 for his excellent poetic translation of Longfellow's *Song of Hiawatha*, which had been extremely popular and was republished in numerous editions, and in 1909 the Academy elected him a member. In

Moscow Bunin joined the literary circle *Sreda,* to which such well-known writers as Maxim Gorky, Leonid Andreev, and Alexander Kuprin, among others, belonged. Chekhov had also been a member before his death in 1904. At this time most of the young author's works were published in literary journals under Gorky's editorship or in which the latter participated.

Bunin was infected with a chronic desire, perhaps even need, to travel and did so extensively in Russia, Europe, and Asia during the years before the First World War. The bizarre strangeness of Asia caught his fancy most of all. This deep fascination with the East is prominently represented in his poetry and to a lesser extent in his prose, but in neither case are his efforts any way near as successful as his strictly Russian works. Soon after the Bolshevik Revolution Bunin emigrated to France and took up residence in Paris in 1919. Throughout his self-imposed exile the aging writer suffered an acute longing for his native land. His writing even in emigration is almost totally devoted to Russian themes and life. Death came to Bunin soon after he had completed editing his collected works for its first Soviet publication. He died in Paris on November 8, 1953.

A wide variety of literary movements and groups flourished in Russia during the two decades preceding the 1917 Revolution. Amidst the highly mystical lyricism of the Symbolists, the neoclassicism of the Acmeists, the frankly political and often sociological journalism of Maxim Gorky and his *Znanie* group, and the morbid pessimism and sensationalism of Leonid Andreev and Mikhail Artsybashev, Ivan Bunin cut an odd figure. Just as these movements coexisted independently, seemingly uninfluenced by one another, so he wrote in his own peculiar style, untouched by the literary debates taking place around him. He simply did not fit and did not try to. He was not, however, totally isolated from contemporary events and other writers. In fact, along with Alexander Kuprin and Andreev, Bunin was for a time a contributor to the journal *Znanie* and a close friend of its editor Gorky. Both had shared a deep friendship with Chekhov and had been helped and influenced by him in their writing. That experience and the fact that Gorky and his journal followed more closely the nineteenth-century tradition of realism momentarily drew the two men together. Certainly, there is no mistaking Gorky's inspirational role in the short novel *The Village* which appeared in 1910 and firmly established Bunin as a major writer of the day. He had at last found his "voice" in prose and almost overnight ceased to be treated as a poet who also wrote lyrical stories. The novel was widely acclaimed and Gorky was unqualified in his praise. In return Bunin attributed the work's completion and success to the former's persevering interest.

The Village is admittedly a social novel, but of a special sort. It is not political, offers no solutions, and points to no specific conclusions. Here, as in almost all his works, Bunin is indifferent to the political and social "Right" and "Left." Written at a time when the journals and papers were glutted with idealistic portrayals of the peasant and his life, the work shocked the public with its unadorned characterization of the muzhik's spiritual poverty and barren existence. It was followed by a succession of first-rate works which are now recognized as Bunin's masterpieces: *Sukhodol* (1912); *The Cup of Life* (1914); *The Gentleman from San Francisco* (1916). *Sukhodol* is an obvious companion piece to *The Village*, considerably more terse and controlled, forming a perfect stylistic and structural whole. This time, however, Bunin turned his unsparing eye to the spiritual emptiness and peasantlike savagery of the landed gentry. He often returned to this theme in shorter pieces such as *The Last Rendezvous* and *Light Breathing*. Yet, the most perfect stylistic and thematic synthesis of Bunin's prose is found in *The Gentleman from San Francisco*. He is unsparingly laconic and controlled. His language is bald and compact as the plot unfolds with a ruthlessness as insistent and unceasing as the pounding waves. It is, in addition, especially significant that here Bunin turned his attention from the familiar and personal to treat spiritual poverty and sham on a universal scale. It is a morality play without a moral. Its effectiveness lies in the author's detachment, and although it is slightly more than a long short story, it must be treated as a novel because of the density of the descriptive detail and characterization.

Thus, in a brief eight-year period, beginning with *The Village*, Bunin was more prolific than at any other period in his life. During it he wrote his most lasting works which secured him a prominent place in Russian letters. After his emigration to France in 1919, he never quite regained his full literary powers, but unlike many of his émigré compatriots he continued writing and editing his works until his death.

Bunin's prose clearly distinguishes him as a direct descendant of the mainstream of nineteenth-century Russian literary tradition. His forbears are Tolstoy, Turgenev, Goncharov, and Chekhov. As Mirsky suggests in *A History of Russian Literature*, ". . . Bunin's language is 'classical,' sober, concrete. . . . Bunin is probably the only modern Russian writer whose language would have been admired by the 'classics,' by Turgenev and Goncharov." The early lyrical stories written before 1903, and especially *Antonov Apples*, may be traced back to Turgenev's *A Sportsman's Sketches*, to Goncharov's *Oblomov's Dream*, and to the lyrical mood of Chekhov's mature works and clearly to his extended lyrical song to nature, *The Steppe*. One encounters not only a similar lyrical mood in the works of Chekhov and Bunin, but furthermore, a similarity of themes and even a resemblance of titles. There is more than a coincidental resemblance between Chekhov's *The Peasants* and *The Literature Teacher* and Bunin's *The Village* and *The Teacher*, to cite but two examples. To be sure, Bunin entered literature by means of the already popular short story which Chekhov had done so much to develop and perfect. He continued to work in this genre throughout his life as witness the large collection of short stories written in the 1930's and 1940's, of which *Dark Paths* (1938) and *The Raven* (1944) are among the best. Even his longer works, often called novels because of their poetic density, must be considered extended short stories by virtue of their compact plot structure and length. Once again the similarity to Chekhov is striking.

If Chekhov's imprint is most clear, then other often contradictory influences are also readily discernible in Bunin's work. *Sukhodol* recalls two dark and moody masterful novels dealing with the decay of a gentry family, Goncharov's *Oblomov* and Saltykov Shchedrin's *The Golovlev Family*. Throughout *Sukhodol*, moreover, there is the rich fabric and mood of the Russian "byliny" (legends), magic and incantation curiously interwoven with saints' lives which had so fascinated Dostoevsky, Tolstoy and Remizov. Here, as in their works, is presented the characteristic Russian mixture of pagan animism and Christianity with a predominantly pagan comprehension. *The Gentleman from San Francisco*, on the other hand, is spiritually of a piece with Tolstoy's *Death of Ivan Ilich* as it relentlessly lays bare the sham and insignificance of even the most protected and richest life under the shadow of death.

Later, in *Lika*, the narrative abounds with references and quotations from Pushkin, Gogol, Tolstoy, and Chekhov. In it Bunin attacks and overcomes an earlier infatuation with the anti-intellectual, simplistic tenets of Tolstoyanism. We find, in addition, not only extensive lyrical passages from Gogol about the Ukraine, but echoes of his peculiar humor whereby the distinction between animate beings and inanimate objects is blurred and reality is rendered in an hilarious surrealistic confusion.

Lika is quite exceptional in this respect, for here Bunin, writing in emigration, torn from all that was familiar, from the very source of his inspiration, immersed himself in every aspect of the Russian literary heritage from the legends and fairy tales of the Middle Ages to the nineteenth-century classics in an effort to summon up a now distant Russia and keep alive his "Russianess." The work is more self-consciously Russian in mood and substance than any of his others. It is a veritable index of Russian literature skillfully interwoven with a haunting love story. In sum, Bunin emerges as the last major Russian writer who encompassed and continued the literary traditions of the nineteenth century. With his death the direct line of continuity was broken. He is most definitely the last classical writer, both in his language and motifs. Political events and literary currents had so changed the face and mood of Russia by the turn of the century that Bunin was destined to be treated as somewhat an oddity despite his popularity.

The industrial revolution came late to Russia, but by the first decades of the twentieth century considerable development had taken place through growing internal interest and foreign investment. Bunin was not alone in his concern about the ramifications of this change and its effect on the traditional gentry way of life. But, unlike his contemporaries, he had a vision of the close spiritual relationship between the landed gentry and the peasantry, as between kindred souls immediately attached to the soil, embraced in nature, and immersed in, in fact reared on the bountiful legacy of legends, superstitions, and traditions passed down through the generations. His vision extended even further, seemingly to an eventual union of the peasant and landowner freely and equally joined on the land in nature. Yet, it was the depressing disintegration of this life and its hopeful future which Bunin witnessed and in its wake the rise of an insensitive, brutish middle class bereft of tradition, cut off from the land, and motivated solely by the drive for pecuniary advantage. *Sukhodol* and *Antonov Apples* portray the far-reaching effects of industrialization and inner decay of the gentry while *The Village* and *The Good Life* directly confront the impact on the peasant. Even *The Last Rendezvous* has elements of this theme in its early depiction of the pathetic seediness of Streshnov and especially his parents. With a characteristic wistfulness Bunin remarks in *Antonov Apples* that "the fragrance of Antonov apples is disappearing from the country houses. Those days were such a short while ago and yet it seems to me a whole century has passed since then. . . . The reign of the small-estate owners, impoverished to a state of beggary, has now taken over. But even the beggarly life of the small estates is good."

Despite his rather idealistic vision of this carefree life, Bunin was not blind to the irresponsibility, ignorance, and lack of energy manifested by the gentry. They had long been living on borrowed time, at least since the abolition of serfdom and even before, yet they did nothing to adjust to or take advantage of the change. If *Antonov Apples* may be seen as a lyrical portrait of the passing order, then *Sukhodol* offers a sensitive, melancholy though unsparing account of its decline. The blame is justly attributed to causes both external and internal. With a profound sense of nostalgia Bunin chronicles the end of this idyll, albeit imperfect, perhaps self-destructive, but in his eyes preferable to what has come to replace it. He by no means seeks a return to the past, but it is his sad contention that the natural and spontaneous, the real values, are being thrust aside by an artificial and complex force.

But love preoccupied Bunin above all else. Of the nine tales in this book, six are wholly devoted to the motif of thwarted love, and the same theme figures prominently in *Sukhodol* and incidentally in *The Gentleman from San Francisco.* All these works are united thematically and structurally by this somber theme of doomed or lost love. Despite the intensity of early joy and hope there ever hovers a tragic sense of irrevocable impending failure. Within such a framework, Bunin treats a variety of different loves. In *The Raven* we witness the pathetic brief awakening of adolescent love frustrated by a callous father and in *Sukhodol* its cruel nonfulfillment leading to hopeless alienation or, as in the case of Aunt Tonya, flight into insanity. *The Last Rendezvous* portrays a love consummated too late, while in *Dark Paths* its earlier realization is comprehended only when the past can no longer be reversed. *Sunstroke* clearly parallels *Dark Paths* in its depiction of a real, spontaneous love momentarily cloaked by sensuality, and revealed once again too late. Failure and disillusionment prevail, deriving from the characters' lack of initiative or self-destructiveness. Death and alienation follow in the wake of each failure and this tragic attitude strongly suggests that of the early nineteenth-century romantics. *Lika,* the longest of the stories, is a study in destructive and almost willful self-destructive passion and finds its counterpart in the terse bleak account of Olya Meshcherskaya's grotesque precociousness and senseless death, in *Light Breathing.*

Yet, transcending all considerations of morality and guilt, there recurs throughout these stories an insistent sense of loss, loss of purity, spontaneity, and, most significantly, loss of love. It is fused with a longing to recall the moment, the object, and relive the experience, if but for the briefest time. Therefore, even when narrated in the present, Bunin's works are permeated with an autumnal mood of nostalgia, as if they had been written at a temporal distance and were in fact a kind of recollection. In the early part of *The Last Rendezvous* the narrative is momentarily interrupted by a brief lyrical digression: "The moon hung to the right over the desolate, hazily silver meadows. . . . Oh, the melancholy beauty of autumn!" We might take this feeling, at once aesthetic and emotional, as the emblem of Bunin's narrative style. It is precisely that moving apprehension of the "melancholy beauty of autumn" which mediates the sensuality and cruelity. The nostalgia it inspires sets the narrative mood and ultimately emerges the dominant theme.

The peculiar mood and substance of Bunin's prose, distinguished him from his contemporaries; the originality and distinctiveness of his prose derived from his own stylistic innovations. His early works in the period from 1892–1903 are, strictly speaking, not short stories at all. They are short, but for the most part tell no story, for they lack both plot and narrative structure. Bunin simply isolated one element, the *paysage*, as it is called in Russian, which is a sketch or description of nature and usually figures as a lyrical digression or setting, and developed it into an independent prose form. Within this form he strove to evoke a particular mood and a myriad of related emotional associations through vivid sensuous imagery and description. The result was a lyrical sketch or an extended mood piece, barely held together by the mood. The narrative is suffused with an overpowering variety of smells, colors, and sounds through which the reader is directly, almost forcibly, drawn into a total sense experience. (In the later, maturer works it is this sensuous perception of the external world which is often blurred and leads to Bunin's highly sensual portrayal of love.)

One is immediately reminded of the Impressionist painters of roughly the same period. *Antonov Apples* is the most perfect realization of this approach. In one sense it is nothing more than an evocation of a particular scent and fragmentary sketches of the world it has come to represent. Nothing happens, yet the reader comes away from the story virtually steeped in every facet of the life depicted. Kornei Chukovskii tells us that when Bunin and Alexander Kuprin were together, "they would play an intense and lively game to see who could most exactly describe the smell of a Catholic church during the early Easter mass or the smell of a circus arena . . ." Besides the ever-present redolence of the Antonov apples, the story abounds in intoxicating sensations. In describing his aunt's house the narrator brings the reader right in with him: "When you walked into the house you first noticed the fragrance of apples, the smell of mahogany furniture and of dried lime blossom that had lain on the window sills since June . . ." At another point during the hunt ". . . suddenly the whole forest was in an uproar, ringing like glass, with a furious barking and baying." And finally, consider for a moment the brilliant visual image in the following description of the house: "I always fancied its façade was a living thing, an old face that seemed to look at you with deep-sunk eyes from under a huge hat—and its windows iridescent like mother-of-pearl from the rain and the sun."

Precisely this sensuous descriptive approach accounts for the poetic density of Bunin's style. The actual narrative scope of a particular story is in inverse proportion to the mass of evoked sensations. Originally a poet and continuing on in both poetry and prose, Bunin was well versed in the severely limiting poetic form. He then transferred the necessary compactness and connotive metonymic imagery of poetry to prose. Therefore, despite the length and complexity of individual periods (and there are many such complex, long sentences), the style is laconic. The language is neither hyperbolic nor ornamental, for Bunin strives to find and fix the exact word or shade of meaning to fit his purpose. In successive clauses he will experiment with various aspects of a color, for example, as if he were sharpening the focus of a projector lens, until he achieves the desired clarity and exactness.

There is no analysis or psychological characterization. Bunin was concerned with the physical aspect of things and the emotional responses they evince. His was a physical lyricism, a lyricism of objects. This peculiar perception accounts for the preponderance of emotionally charged and extremely sensuous description and characterization and the relative lack of dialogue. In his mature works after *Antonov Apples* when Bunin had found a basically social direction and developed a definite subject, the *paysage* was reintegrated into the narrative and plot structure, but continued to play an extremely important independent role. The formerly loose structure became more controlled and tighter. His language assumed a distinctive laconic and austere quality. Nowhere is this more apparent than in *The Gentleman from San Francisco* or *Sunstroke*. Yet, finally, one is left with a parodox: Are Bunin's longer works novels or short stories. Depending on the point of view, they are both, and it is a tribute to his fine talent that he could so artfully unite the two genres.

Almost thirty years have passed since Ivan Bunin won the Nobel Prize for literature. With the exception of a few Russian editions published in Paris and New York, until quite recently, time and the war had apparently doomed him to oblivion in the West. In the Soviet Union he remained unpublished until 1955. Bunin then has been rediscovered and fully deserves this renewed interest. Neither his style nor his subjects have lost their freshness and originality for the contemporary reader. The present collection offers a superb selection of his finest literary achievements.

THOMPSON BRADLEY
Swarthmore, Pennsylvania
October, 1962

Bibliography

WORKS BY IVAN BUNIN

The Elaghin Affair and Other Stories by Ivan Bunin, selected and translated by B. G. Guerney, New York, Knopf, 1935.

The Gentleman from San Francisco and Other Stories by Ivan Bunin, translated by D. H. Lawrence, S. S. Koteliansky, and Leonard Woolf, New York, T. Seltzer, 1923.

Memories and Portraits, translated by Vera Traill and Robin Chancellor, New York, Doubleday, 1951.

Reminiscences of Anton Chekhov by Maxim Gorky, Alexander Kuprin, and I. A. Bunin, translated by S. S. Koteliansky and Leonard Woolf, New York, B. W. Huebsch, 1921.

The Village (authorized translation from Russian by Ivan Bunin), translated by Isabel F. Hapgood, New York, Knopf, 1923.

The Well of Days, translated by Gleb Struve and Hamish Miles, London, Leonard and Virginia Woolf at Hogarth Press, 1933.

The Gentleman from San Francisco
and Other Stories

Antonov Apples

I

I REMEMBER a fine, early autumn. August was a month of soft, warm rains that seemed to fall specially for the sowing—rain just when it was needed, in the middle of the month, about St. Lawrence's Day. And the saying is that autumn and winter will get on well together if the waters are still and there's rain on St. Lawrence's Day. After that came an Indian summer when gossamer settled lavishly on the fields. That's a good sign too. I remember a crisp, clear morning. . . . I remember a big, golden orchard, rather dry, with thinning trees. I remember the walks lined with maples, the subtle fragrance of fallen leaves and the smell of Antonovka apples

—a smell of honey and autumn freshness. The air was so pure it hardly seemed to be there, and the whole orchard echoed the call of voices and the squeak of cart wheels. That was the *tarkhane,** the trading gardeners who, with the help of hired peasants, were loading apples on to the carts to send to town that very night—at night it had to be, when it was so pleasant to lie on top of the load, gazing into the starry sky, smelling the tar in the crisp air and hearing the soft creaking of the long train of carts along the dark road. A peasant loading apples would eat one after another with a juicy crunch, but that was one of the unwritten laws—the employer would never cut him short; on the contrary, he would say:

"Go ahead and eat your fill, there's nothing I can do! Everyone drinks mead on barreling day!"

All that disturbed the cool stillness of the morning was the complacent chirp of thrushes in the coral-red rowans down the orchard, the call of voices and the hollow thud of apples as they were poured into the measures and barrels. Through the thinning trees you could see far down the straw-strewn road leading to a large tent, and the tent itself which the peddlers had made quite a household during the summer months. The smell of apples was strong everywhere, particularly here. Inside the tent there were some camp beds, a single-barreled gun, a moldy-green samovar, and some kitchen utensils in the corner. Mats and packing cases, rags and rubbish lay in a heap beside the tent and a hearth for the fire had been dug in the ground. At midday a delicious stew was cooked there and in the evening the samovar was warmed up, and a long ribbon of bluish smoke would spread between the trees in the orchard. But on holidays there was a regular fair round the tent and bright Sunday finery would flicker behind the trees. There would be a crowd of pert girls, the daughters of small holders, dressed in *sarafans*** that smelled strongly of dye; the gentry's servants would come too, in their beautiful though coarse, strange dress, and the young

* *Tarkhane*—tax-free traveling peddlers.—*Tr.*

** *Sarafan*—a sleeveless Russian peasant dress.

pregnant wife of the village bailiff, with a broad, sleepy face and the sedateness of a cow. She wore a headdress known as "antlers." Her hair was parted in the middle, plaited and pinned up on each side, with several kerchiefs worn over it, making her head look enormous. Her feet in half boots with steel-tipped heels were planted firmly, the toes turned in; her sleeveless jacket was of velveteen, her apron long, and her skirt of deep mauve with brick-red stripes had a wide gold braid trimming.

"That's the right sort of little woman!" the tradesman would remark, slowly shaking his head. "They're getting rare nowadays. . . ."

Little boys in white twill shirts and short trousers, with their white bleached hair uncovered, kept coming up. They would come in twos or threes, tripping along on their bare feet with short, quick steps and darting wary glances at the shaggy sheep dog tied to an apple tree. Only one of the group would be a buyer, of course, for all the wealth they possessed was a kopek or a fresh egg to barter; but there were plenty of customers anyway, business was brisk, and the consumptive tradesman in a long frock coat and yellow top boots would serve them gaily. He and his brother, a lively half-wit of slovenly speech whom he kept out of charity, joked and clowned, and sometimes even played a tune on a Tula accordion as they sold their wares. And until late in the evening there would be a crowd of people in the orchard, there would be laughter and talk and sometimes the tap of dancing feet close to the tent. . . .

In fair weather it got very cold and damp toward nightfall. After a day out on the threshing floor, where you had breathed your fill of the scent of threshed rye and chaff, you briskly walked home to supper past the orchard boundary ditch. Voices down in the village or the creaking of a gate rang with extraordinary clearness in the frosty evening air. Darkness would fall. And then there was a new smell, that of a woodfire being lighted in the orchard and the fragrant smoke of the burning cherry branches. The picture you saw at the bottom of the dark orchard was like a scene from a fairy tale: in the surrounding darkness, the crimson flames blazing close to the tent were like a corner of hell, with black shapes that seemed to be carved of ebony moving around the fire, while their monstrous shadows wavered across the apple trees. A black arm, several yards in length, would lie across the whole of a tree, or suddenly a pair of legs, like two black pillars, would be etched clearly. And suddenly, all these shadows would slip down from the tree and in one long shadow fall on the path, from the tent to the very gate. . . .

Late at night when the lights had gone out in the windows and the brilliant stars of the Great Bear shone high in the sky, you would run once again into the orchard. With the dry leaves rustling underfoot, you would grope your way blindly to the tent. It was a little lighter there in the opening, with the Milky Way overhead.

"Is that you, young master?" someone's voice would call softly from the darkness.

"Yes. Aren't you asleep yet, Nikolai?"

"We're not supposed to sleep. But it must be late, eh? There's the passenger train now, I think."

We would listen hard and then make out a tremor running along the ground. The tremor would become a noise, it grew and grew until it seemed that wheels were beating time loudly and hurriedly just beyond the orchard ditch; knocking and clamoring, the train rushed on . . . closer and closer, louder and angrier. . . . And suddenly the sound grew fainter and muffled as though it were vanishing into the ground. . . .

"Where's your gun, Nikolai?"

"Why, here, beside the box."

You would fling up the gun which was as heavy as a crowbar, and fire at random. A crimson spurt of flame would shoot up into the sky with a deafening report, blinding you for a moment and snuffing out the stars, and a cheerful echo would roar and roll toward the horizon, fading in the pure and keen air, far, far away.

"My, that was a good one!" the tradesman would say.

"Give them a scare, young master, give them a scare! The trouble they're giving us; they've shaken down all the pears by the wall again. . . ."

Shooting stars streaked the black sky with fiery trails. You would gaze so long into its dark blue depths thronged with constellations, that you felt the ground slipping away from under your feet. Then you would get up and, hiding your hands in the sleeves of your coat, run home quickly along the path. . . . How cold and damp it was, but how good to be alive!

II

"If the apples are good, the year will be good." All's well in the village if the Antonovkas are good: it means the grain harvest will be a good one too. I remember a year of abundant crops.

At the break of day, when cocks were still crowing and black smoke was pouring from the chimneyless huts, I would throw open the window into the cool orchard, cloaked in a lilac mist, through which the morning sun flashed brightly here and there, and the temptation would be so strong that I would order my horse to be saddled at once, while I hurried down to the pond to wash. The willows dipping to the water were almost stripped of their tiny leaves, and the turquoise sky showed through the bare branches. The water beneath the willows had grown transparent and icy, so that it seemed heavy. It dispelled your drowsiness and lassitude at once, and when you had dressed and eaten your breakfast of hot potatoes and black bread sprinkled with damp coarse salt in the kitchen with the farm hands, you reveled in the feel of the slippery leather saddle as you rode out hunting through the village of Viselki. Autumn is the season of patron saints' days, and the people look trim and happy; the village itself has quite a different, festive air. If the crops were good that year and tall castles of gold rose from the threshing floors, while the geese gabbled shrilly and clearly on the river of a morning, then life in the village was not bad at all. Moreover, our Viselki had always been known as a prosperous village since the beginning of time, since Grandfather's day. Viselki people lived to a ripe old age—which is the first sign of a prosperous village—and all these old people were tall and big-boned, with hair as white as snow. You were always hearing someone say: "Look at Agafya there, she's eighty-three if she's a day!" Or conversations like this:

"And when are you going to die, Pankrat? You must be nearly a hundred by now?"

"What's that you say, my dear?"

"I'm asking how old you are?"

"That I couldn't tell you, my dear."

"D'you remember Platon Apollonich?"

"Of course I do, I remember him well."

"You see! That means you can't possibly be less than a hundred."

The old man, standing rigidly before his master, would smile a humble and guilty smile. What could he do? He had outlived his day, he felt. And probably he would have outlived it even longer if he had not eaten too many onions on St. Peter's Day.

I remember his wife too. The old woman was always sitting on a bench on the porch, her back hunched, her head shaking, her hands clutching the edge of the bench, her breath coming in short gasps, and her mind busy on something. "Thinking of her wealth, I expect," the women used to say, because she really had a lot of "wealth" in her trunks. But she seemed not to hear; with fading eyes, she gazed from under her sadly raised eyebrows into the distance, shaking her head and trying to remember something. She was a large woman, and everything about her was dark. The skirt she wore looked a hundred years old, her cloth slippers were the kind they put on the dead, her neck was yellow and scraggy and her blouse, inset with dimity diamonds, was always very, very white—"good enough to bury her in," they said. There was a large stone slab lying close to the porch:

she had bought it herself for her gravestone, as she had her burial robe—a splendid shroud with angels, crosses and a prayer printed round the edges.

The houses at Viselki were in keeping with the old people. They were mud cottages built by their grandfathers. But the more prosperous peasants, like Savely, Ignat and Dron, had big cottages of double or triple lengths of timber, for in those days Viselki did not go in for property division. Families such as these kept beehives, took a pride in their steel-blue stallions, and looked after their property well. Hemp fields, thick and lush, stretched beyond the threshing floors; the sheds and barns were neatly thatched; storerooms and lofts had strong, heavy doors, which guarded rolls of linen, spinning wheels, new sheepskin coats, silver-chased harness, and measuring casks, hooped with copper. The top of the gates and the sledges had a cross burned into the wood. I remember there were times when I thought it must be fascinating to be a peasant. As I rode through the village on a sunny morning I kept thinking how good it was to mow and thresh, to sleep in the strawstacks by the threshing floor, and on holidays to rise with the sun to the deep, melodious pealing of church bells in the village, to wash beside a water barrel, put on a clean twill shirt and trousers and a pair of indestructible hob-nailed top boots. And if, to top all this, you had a wife—handsome and robust, dressed in her holiday finery—then a drive to church followed by dinner at your bearded father-in-law's, a dinner of sizzling mutton served on wooden platters, fine white bread, honey from the comb and home-brew, one's dreams could not go further!

Until very recently, already in my time, the mode of life of most of the country squires bore a very strong resemblance to that of the wealthy peasants in the thriftiness and its rustic old-world prosperity. Such was the estate of our Aunt Anna Gerasimovna, for example, which was some twelve versts from Viselki. By the time you got there it would be quite light. You would be riding slowly if you had your dogs on leashes, and indeed, you would not want to hurry, for it was so splendid to be out in the open on a cool, sunny morning. The plain was flat and you could see far into the distance. The sky was so light, so spacious and fathomless! The sun cast its brilliant slanting rays on the road, which had been rolled smooth by the carts after the rains and shone with the greasy sheen of steel rails. Lush, green winter crops stretched far and wide. A young hawk would soar up into the crystalline air and hang poised there, fluttering its little pointed wings. You could see the telegraph poles running away into the bright distance, their wires like silver strings, gliding along the clear sky. Swallows perched on the wires—little black signs on a sheet of music.

I had neither known nor seen serfdom, but I remember I could sense it at Aunt Anna Gerasimovna's. The moment you rode through the gate you felt that here it was still in full sway. The estate was not large, but all of it was old, sturdy, and surrounded by century-old birches and willows. The outbuildings, though low-raftered, were convenient and numerous, and they all seemed to have been cast in the same mold—dark old logs and thatched roofs. Only the smoke-blackened kitchen stood out among them because of its size, or rather its length, with some ancient men and women, and a senile retired chef who looked like Don Quixote, peeping out of the door—the last of the Mohicans of the house serfs. As you rode into the yard all of them would draw themselves up and bow very, very low. The gray-haired coachman, coming toward you from the coach house to take your horse, would take his hat off at the coach-house door and walk across the yard bareheaded. He used to be Aunt's postilion, but now he drove her to church in a covered sledge in winter and in summer in a sturdy little cart reinforced with metal hoops, the type of cart popular among the priests. My aunt's garden was famous for its state of neglect, its nightingales, turtledoves and apples, and her house for its roof. The house stood at the entrance to the estate, with the garden close around it and the branches of lime trees caressing it.

It was squat and rather small, but its unusually steep, thickly thatched roof, blackened and hardened with time, gave it such a solid appearance that it looked as if it would last forever. I always fancied its façade was a living thing, an old face that seemed to look at you with deep-sunk eyes from under a huge hat—and its windows iridescent like mother-of-pearl from the rain and the sun. There were two old, large, pillared porches—one on either side of this face. Plump, self-satisfied pigeons were always sitting in the gables, while thousands of sparrows scattered in a torrent from roof to roof. And a guest was snug and comfortable in this nest, beneath the autumn skies of turquoise blue. . . .

When you walked into the house you first noticed the fragrance of apples, then the smell of old mahogany furniture and of dried lime blossom that had lain on the window sills since June. . . . All the rooms—the hall and the drawing room—were cold and dark; that was because the house was surrounded by trees and the top panes of the windows were of colored glass—blue or mauve. All was quiet and clean, though, I believe, the armchairs, the inlaid tables and the mirrors in their narrow, fluted gilt frames had never been moved from their places. And then you would hear a light cough and Aunt Anna would come in. She was not a tall woman but, like everything about her, she looked sturdy. A large Persian shawl was draped round her shoulders. She entered the room with an air of solemnity but with a smile of welcome, too, and while keeping up an unstemmed flow of conversation about the old days, wills and inheritances, she would at once begin to treat her guest to various delicacies such as pears and apples of four sorts, to be followed by a wonderful dinner: pink boiled ham with green peas, stuffed chicken, turkey, pickles and red *kvas*,* strong and very, very sweet. . . . The windows into the garden would be left open so that the bracing coolness of autumn flowed into the room. . . .

* *Kvas*—a drink made, in this case, of fermented beetroot.—*Tr.*

III

In recent years the only thing that kept up the waning spirit of the landowners was hunting.

Estates such as our aunt's were no rarity in the old days. There were also those which, though going to rack and ruin, still clung to the standards of high living, maintaining their vast properties and fifty-acre orchards. And though some of these country seats have managed to survive to this day, all the life has gone out of them. There are no troikas, no Kirghiz horses, no hounds, no serfs and even no owners of all this—hunting country squires like my late brother-in-law Arseny Semyonich.

From the end of September our orchards and fields began to take on a desolate look, and the weather would change suddenly. The wind blustered and tore at the trees for days on end, and rain drenched them from morning till night. Occasionally the tremulous golden glimmer of the setting sun broke through the gloomy, low-hanging clouds in the west, the air turned pure and clear, and a ray of sunlight would flash blindingly on the leaves and branches as they moved in an animated network against the sky, stirred by the wind. The watery-blue sky gleamed coldly and brightly in the north above the dark, leaden clouds, while white clouds like snow-clad mountain ridges rose slowly behind them. You would stand by the window and think: "Let's hope it clears up." But the wind would not abate. It worried the garden, rent the column of smoke curling in an uninterrupted stream from the kitchen chimney, and drove the ominous, shaggy gray clouds together again. They sailed low and fast and soon enveloped the sun in a smoky shroud. Then the sunshine dimmed, the little window looking out of the blue sky closed, and the garden became desolate and bleak; the drizzle started again, softly and gently at first, but growing in intensity until at last it became a downpour with raging winds and darkness. Night would fall, long and uneasy. . . .

After a drubbing like this the garden emerged practically bare, subdued and humble, and scattered with wet leaves. But then how beautiful it looked when fair weather set in again, in those first days of October, transparent and cold —autumn's parting glory! And the leaves which had not fallen would remain upon the branches until the first frost. The black trees, transparent against the cold blue sky, would meekly wait for winter now, finding what warmth they could in the reflection of the sun. But already the patches of tilled ground were standing out blackly in the fields, and winter crops sprang up in a bright green carpet. Hunting time had come!

And now my memory takes me back to the country seat of Arseny Semyonich, to the hall of his large house, filled with sunlight and the smoke of many cigarettes and pipes. There were many people there—all sunburned men with weather-beaten faces, dressed in *poddyovkas** and top boots. They had just finished a very rich dinner; they were flushed and excited with their loud-voiced discussion of the coming hunt, and although dinner was over they did not forget to refill their glasses with vodka. A hunting horn blared in the yard and hounds wailed in various keys. A black borzoi, Arseny Semyonich's favorite, climbed on to the table and started guzzling away at the remains of the roast hare. Arseny Semyonich, coming out of his study armed with a hunting crop and revolver, suddenly fired with a deafening report, and the dog, squealing horribly, bounded off the table, overturning plates and glasses. Smoke hung thicker than ever, but Arseny Semyonich just stood there laughing.

"Pity I missed," he said, his eyes flashing.

He was tall and lean, broad-shouldered and well-built. He had the face of a handsome Gypsy and a savage gleam in his eyes. He looked very smart in his raspberry-red silk shirt, velvet trousers and top boots. Having given the dog and the

* *Poddyovka*—a long, collarless coat, gathered at the waist, worn with a sash or belt.—*Tr.*

company a scare with his gun, he recited in a baritone with comic solemnity:

The time has come to mount your eager steed,
Across your shoulders sling the sweet-voiced horn. . . .

Then he shouted:

"Well then, don't let's waste our precious time!"

I remember to this day how greedily and deeply my young lungs drank in the coolness of the clear, damp air of the late afternoon when I rode with Arseny Semyonich's noisy crowd, thrilling to the hounds' melodious yelps in the thick woods somewhere in Krasny Bugor* or Gremyachy Ostrov,** whose names alone were exciting enough to the huntsman. I used to ride a stocky Kirghiz hunter, fierce and strong, and as I strained to hold it in I felt I was almost one with it. The horse snorted, impatient to go into a gallop, its hoofs rustling noisily through the deep, brittle carpet of dead black leaves, and every sound echoed hollowly in the emptiness of the damp woods. A hound yelped far away, another one responded plaintively and passionately, a third joined in, and suddenly the whole forest was in an uproar, ringing like a glass, with a furious barking and baying. A shot rang out sharply above the din—and the chase began, rolling and rumbling away into the distance.

"Tally-ho!" The forest rang with someone's desperate yell.

I'll hold it! the heady thought would flash through your mind. Whooping at your horse, you broke away and tore through the woods, no longer conscious of anything on the way. There was nothing but flickering trees before you and clots of mud, kicked up by the horse, flying into your face. You leaped out of the wood to see the variegated pack strung out across the green fields, you spurred your horse on even harder to cut off the quarry, speeding across the fields,

* Krasny Bugor—Red Mound.
** Gremyachy Ostrov—Rumbling Island.

across ploughland and stubble, until at last you rushed into the further copse and the pack in full cry disappeared from view. And then, wet through and shaking with excitement, you reined your foaming, panting hunter and thirstily gulped in the icy dampness of the wooded dell. The shouts of the huntsmen and the baying of the hounds died away in the distance, and perfect silence dropped around you. There was no movement in the shrubless tall pine forest, and you seemed to be in some forbidden realm. The strong, dank smell of mushrooms, decayed leaves and sodden bark came from the gullies. And the dampness rising from the ravines could be felt more keenly, the forest grew colder and darker. . . . It was time to go home. But it was not easy to get the pack together again. The huntsmen's horns rang through the forest with a hopeless wistfulness, for a long time you would hear shouting, swearing and the whimpering of the hounds. Finally, when it was quite dark, a crowd of huntsmen would invade the bachelor home of some gentleman, little known to any of them, and the whole yard, lighted by lanterns, candles and lamps, brought out of the house to welcome the guests, would be full of the noise of many voices.

It sometimes happened that the hunt would stay for several days at some hospitable neighbor's. We would ride out into the woods and fields at the break of day, in the damp early frost and the icy wind, and toward nightfall we would be back again, our faces flushed, covered with dirt and our clothes drenched through and through with the stench of horse sweat and the hide of the run-down beast; and the night would be spent in drinking. The bright, crowded house seemed very warm after a day out in the icy air. Everyone wandered from room to room with their coats open, eating and drinking in a disorderly sort of way, discussing the day's run noisily over the body of the big wolf, which lay sprawled in the middle of the hall, dyeing the floor with pale congealed blood, its teeth bared and eyes rolled up, its fluffy tail flung out. After the vodka and the food you felt so deliciously tired, so sweetly drowsy, that the hum of voices seemed to come through a wall of water. Your chapped face stung, and if you closed your eyes the ground seemed to slip away from you. But when you retired and lay back in a soft feather bed in some old-world corner room with an icon stand and a sanctuary lamp before it, visions of fiery-colored hounds would flash before your eyes; your whole body would ache with the sensation of galloping, and before you knew it you would plunge into a sweet and healthy sleep, forgetting all your visions and sensations, without even remembering that the room had once been the chapel of an old man around whose name sinister legends of serfdom days were woven, and that he had died in that very room and probably in that very bed.

If you happened to oversleep next morning, your rest was particularly enjoyable. When you woke up you would lie in bed for a long time. The whole house would be locked in silence. You could hear the gardener treading carefully about the rooms lighting the stoves, and then the logs crackling and shooting. Ahead of you lay a whole day of leisure in a house already muffled up for winter. You dressed unhurriedly, wandered through the garden, found a cold, wet apple which had been overlooked among the wet leaves, and for some reason it seemed extraordinarily tasty and quite unlike other apples. Then you would settle down to the books of Grandfather's day, volumes bound in thick leather, with golden stars on their morocco backs. There was a nice smell about those volumes which looked like prayer books with their thick, yellowed pages, a smell of old perfume and a pleasant tang of mustiness. I liked the notes which had been made in the margins with a quill in a soft, rounded hand. I would open a book and read: "A thought worthy of ancient and modern philosophers, the light of reason and deep feeling." And you could not help becoming engrossed in the book itself. It was the *Nobleman-Philosopher*, an allegory, published some hundred years before at the expense of a "cavalier of many orders" and printed by the charity board printing press. It was the story of a "nobleman-philosopher who, having the time and aptitude for reflection, to which the mind of man might be elevated, one day conceived the desire of making a map of his spacious lands." Then you would come across "the satirical and philosophical works of M. Voltaire," and for a long time you would revel in the charming and pretentious style of the translation: "Sires! It pleased Erasmus to compose a praise to buffoonery in the sixteenth century (an affected pause—semicolon); while you, sires, are commanding me to extol reason for you. . . ." After that, from the ancient times of Catherine the Great you would pass on to the day of romance, to almanacs, to novels —sentimentally pompous and long. . . . The cuckoo would hop out of the clock and in the empty house, somewhere above your head, you would hear its sadly mocking call. And little by little a strange, sweet sadness crept into your heart.

Then you opened *The Secrets of Alexis* or *Victor,* or the *Child in the Woods,* and you read: "The clock struck twelve. Inviolable silence replaced the noise of the day and the merry songs of the villagers. Sleep spread its somber wings over the surface of our hemisphere; it scattered darkness and dreams. . . . Dreams. . . . How often are they simply the continuance of the sufferings of the wretched!" And beloved old words would flash before your eyes: rocks and groves, a pale moon and loneliness, ghosts and wraiths, Cupid's darts, roses and lilies, "the playful pranks of naughty little boys," lily-white hands, Lyudmilas and Alinas. . . . And there were the periodicals with the names of Zhukovsky, Batyushkov, and Pushkin, the young Lycée student. And you'd wistfully recall Grandmamma, the polonaises she played on the clavichord, the languid way she read verses from *Yevgeny Onegin.* And the old, dreamy world rose before you. . . . How lovely were the girls and women who once used to people these country seats! These beautiful, noble women with old-world coiffures looked down on me from their portraits on the wall and dropped their long eyelashes meekly and gracefully over their sad and gentle eyes. . . .

IV

The fragrance of Antonovka apples is disappearing from the country houses. Those days were such a short while ago and yet it seems to me that a whole century has passed since then. The old people of Viselki are all dead; Anna Gerasimovna is dead too, and Arseny Semyonich has shot himself. . . . The reign of the small-estate owners, impoverished to the state of beggary, has now taken over. But even the beggarly life of the small estates is good.

I see myself once more in the country in late autumn. The days are dimly blue and overcast. In the morning I would mount my horse, take but one dog along and ride out into the open, armed with a gun and a huntsman's horn. The wind sings in the barrel of the gun and blows hard into my face, sometimes bringing dry snow with it. I would roam the desolate plain all day long. . . . Toward dusk I would ride back to the house, hungry and frozen through, but what a warm and happy feeling I had when I saw the lights of Viselki flickering in the darkness ahead and caught the smell of smoke, of home, wafting toward me. I remember, our family was fond of the twilight hour, they would sit and converse softly without putting on the lights. When I went in I would find that the double windows had already been put back into place, and that, more than anything else, would attune me to the peaceful drowsiness of winter. One of the servants would be lighting the fire in the servants' hall and, just as I did when I was a child, I would squat beside a heap of straw which smelled strongly of what was now a wintry crispness, and gaze into the blazing fire or at the windows beyond which the twilight was sadly waning in the darkening blue. And then I would go into the kitchen, brightly lit and crowded: kitchen maids would be chopping cabbage for salting, and I would listen to the vigorous, rhythmic tapping of their flashing knives and their voices harmoniously blended in the wistfully gay village songs. . . . Sometimes one of the neighboring small-estate owners would call on us and take me away for a long stay with him. . . . The life of a small-estate owner was good too.

He would rise early. After a good stretch he'd get up and roll himself a thick cigarette of cheap black tobacco or simply of *makhorka.** The pale light of an early November morning revealed a plain study with bare walls except for a couple of brittle yellow foxskins over the bed, a stocky man in Cossack trousers and a loose unbelted shirt, while the mirror reflected a face with a Tatar cast, heavy with sleep. Dead silence reigned in the warm dusky house. The old cook snored softly in the corridor; she had served in this house since she was a little girl, but this would not stop the master from shouting huskily at the top of his voice: "Lukerya! Samovar!"

And then, putting on his top boots and throwing his coat over his shoulders, without buttoning the neck of his shirt, he would go out on to the porch. The entrance hall, which had been shut all night, reeked of dogs; they stretched lazily, yawned with little squeals and, smiling, clustered close to him.

"Go away!" he would say slowly in a loving, low-pitched voice, and walk through the garden out into the fields. He would breathe deeply of the biting early-morning air and the fragrance of the bare garden, chilled by the night. Autumn leaves, curled and blackened by the frost, rustled underfoot in the birch-lined walk, of which half the trees had already been felled. Ruffled jackdaws sleeping on the ridge of the barn roof stood out in sharp relief against the somber, low skies. "A good day for hunting, today," he would think and, pausing in the middle of the walk, would stand and gaze for a long time at this autumn scene, across the bleak fields of green winter crops with some calves wandering over them. Two hounds were already whimpering at his feet, while Zalivai had gone beyond the garden, and as he bounded across the prickly stubble field, he seemed to be calling to his master and begging to be allowed to run out into the open. "But what can you do with hounds now? The beast is out in the open, it is on black fields, frightened of the woods because the

* *Makhorka*—coarse, peasant-grown tobacco in Russia.

leaves rustle in the wind. . . . Oh, if only I had some borzois!"

Threshing was under way in the barn. The threshing drum hummed and droned as it slowly worked up speed. Horses walked, swaying, round and round the drive gearing, tugging lazily at their traces and thrusting their feet into a manure-strewn path. The driver sat on a little stool fitted on to the driving bar, and as he revolved round the drive he shouted monotonously at the horses, his whip falling on the brown gelding alone, the laziest of the lot, sleeping as it walked, since its eyes were blindfolded anyway.

"Come on, girls, get a move on!" the drum-operator, a sedate man, would shout sternly at the girls as he put on his loose hempen shirt. The girls would hastily sweep the threshing floor and rush about with barrows and brooms.

"Godspeed!" he would say and the first trial cluster of rye would fly through the buzzing, squeaking drum and be tossed up in an untidy fan. The droning of the drum grew more and more insistent, work went on apace and soon all the sounds merged in the one pleasant sound of threshing. The master would stand at the barn door and watch the red and yellow kerchiefs, the hands, the forks and the straw flickering in the darkness within, all of it moving rhythmically and busily to the roaring of the drum, the monotonous shouts of the driver and the cracking of his whip. Clouds of chaff came flying to the door, and the master stood there getting covered with this gray chaff. He kept glancing out into the fields. . . . Very, very soon they would be white, very soon they would be covered with the first frost. . . .

The first frost, the first snow! He had no borzois to go hunting with in November, but winter was coming and then he could put his hounds to work. And once again, as in the old days, the small-estate owners would go visiting one another, drinking away the last of their money, spending all their days in the snow-clad fields. And at night, in the darkness of winter, a light would shine out afar from the hunting box of some remote little estate, where in a room, filled with clouds of smoke, lighted with dimly burning tallow candles, a guitar would be tuned up. . . .

A blizzard fierce arose at night
And threw my gates wide open,

a deep tenor would begin, and the others would join in discordantly with sad and hopeless bravado, pretending this was nothing but a joke:

It threw my gates wide open
And buried roads in snowdrifts white. . . .

1900.

Sukhodol

I

WHAT HAD always amazed us about Natalia, was her attachment to Sukhodol.

She was the daughter of Father's wet nurse and was brought up in the house with him. She lived with us at Lunevo for eight years; we treated her as one of the family and not like a former serf at all. And all those eight years, as she herself used to say, she was recuperating from Sukhodol and from all that the place had made her suffer. But evidently, what is bred in the bone never gets out of the flesh: when she had raised us to adolescence she went back to Sukhodol once more.

I remember snatches of conversation we had with her when we were children.

"You're an orphan, aren't you, Natalia?"

"Yes, I take after my masters in this. Your grandmamma, Anna Grigoryevna, she closed her lovely eyes ever so early, too. No worse than my father and mother."

"And they—why did they die young?"

"Their death came and so they died."

"But why so young?"

" 'Twas God's will. The master punished my father by sending him off to be a soldier, and my mother didn't live her time on account of the turkey-poults. I don't remember, of course, I was too young, but they told me afterward. She was a poultry maid, and looked after ever so many turkey-poults, and then out in the meadow one day they got caught in a hailstorm and every one of them was struck down dead. . . . She rushed out to the meadow, took one look—and gave up the ghost from fright."

"Why didn't you ever get married?"

"My betrothed hasn't been born yet."

"But really, why?"

"They say that the young lady, your auntie, ordered it so. That's why they christened me 'miss,' too."

"Oh, go on, what sort of a 'miss' are you?"

"A real and proper one," Natalia replied with a thin smile, pursing her lips and wiping them with her dark old hand. "You know I'm Arkady Petrovich's foster-sister, a second aunt to you. . . ."

As we grew older we listened more attentively to everything that was being said in our house about Sukhodol, and whatever we had failed to understand before grew clearer now, so that the queer peculiarities of life at Sukhodol stood out more sharply. Who if not we should feel that Natalia, who had been brought up with our father, almost sharing his life, was really one of us Khrushchovs, nobles of ancient lineage! And now it appeared that these same gentlefolk had driven her father into the army and her mother into such terror of them that her heart had burst at the sight of the dead turkey-poults.

"But then a misfortune like that might kill anyone," Natalia said. "She'd have been packed off to some Godforsaken hole."

And then we learned something even stranger about Sukhodol: that "in the whole wide world there were no masters kinder and simpler than theirs," but we also heard that none were more "hot-tempered" than they were either; we learned that the old house had been dark and gloomy, that our insane Grandfather Pyotr Kirillich had been murdered there by his illegitimate son Gervaska (our father's friend and Natalia's cousin), that our Aunt Tonya had gone out of her mind long ago because of an unhappy love affair and was now living in one of the old servants' cottages close to the impoverished manor house, rapturously playing *écossaises* on a piano which droned and jingled from old age; we learned that Natalia, too, had once been insane, that as a very young girl she had fallen in love with our late Uncle Pyotr Petrovich once and for all time, but that he had banished her to the farmstead of Soshki. . . . We were justified in weaving our exciting dreams about Sukhodol. To us it was nothing but a romantic memorial to the past. But what did it mean to Natalia? It was she who once uttered with great bitterness, as though in answer to some thought of her own:

"Well, there it is! At Sukhodol they even sat down to dinner armed with Tatar whips. Just thinking of it makes you shudder."

"You mean hunting crops?" we asked.

"It's all one," she said.

"But what for?"

"In case they quarreled."

"Did they all quarrel at Sukhodol?"

"Heaven save us! Never a day went by without a fight. They were all hot-tempered—downright gunpowder."

We all but swooned at her words and exchanged ecstatic looks. And for a long time afterward we would dream of a huge garden, a huge estate, a house built of oak logs with a great thatched roof blackened with time; and then the dinner in the dining hall where everyone sat round the table glaring at one another, eating and throwing the bones down to their hunting dogs, each man with a whip across his knees. We dreamed of the time when we, too, would be grown up and would also dine with whips across our knees. We understood well enough, though, that it was not Natalia who got any pleasure out of those whips. And yet, she left Lunevo for Sukhodol, she went back to the source of her sinister memories. She had neither a corner of her own there nor any family ties, and it wasn't her former mistress Aunt Tonya she served there, but Klavdia Markovna, the widow of the late Pyotr Petrovich. But there it was, Natalia could not live without Sukhodol.

"I can't help it, I'm used to it," she said humbly. "Where the needle goes, the thread must follow. Where you're born, there's your home. . . ."

Neither was she the only one to be obsessed with this love for Sukhodol. All the other Sukhodolians were as ardently devoted to it, as passionately fond of its memory.

Aunt Tonya was living in misery, in a hovel. Sukhodol had deprived her of happiness, sanity and human dignity. But she never even entertained the thought of leaving her birthplace and settling at Lunevo, however much Father reasoned with her.

"Why, I'd rather break stones in a quarry," she'd say.

Father was a carefree man; he seemed to be above any kind of attachment. But his stories of Sukhodol, too, rang with a deep nostalgia. It was years and years since he had left it and settled down on our great-aunt Olga Kirillovna's estate at Lunevo, yet he brooded on it almost to the day he died.

"The last, the only Khrushchov left in the world! And even he is not at Sukhodol!"

And after saying this he would often become thoughtful and stare through the window at the fields, but suddenly he would chuckle and, taking down his guitar from the wall, add just as sincerely as he had spoken but a minute before:

"Sukhodol's a fine one too, damn and blast it!"

But then his soul belonged to Sukhodol—the soul over which the sway of memories was so immeasurably strong, the sway of the steppe, its sluggish way of life, that ancient clannishness that united the village, the servants' hall and the manor house into one. Of course, we Khrushchovs come of an old lineage; our name is entered in the *Sixth Book of Noblemen,* and many of our legendary ancestors were noblemen of old Lithuanian stock or Tatar princelings. But then, since time immemorial, the blood of the Khrushchovs was mingled with that of the servants and the villagers. Who fathered Pyotr Kirillich? History differs on this point. Who was the father of Gervaska, his murderer? Ever since we were little we always heard that it was Pyotr Kirillich. What caused the characters of our father and our uncle to be so sharply dissimilar? There were different explanations for this, too. And then Natalia and Father were suckled at the same breast, while Father and Gervaska changed baptismal crosses. . . . It was certainly high time for the Khrushchovs to reckon up their relations with the servants and the villagers!

For many years my sister and I were entranced by our longing for Sukhodol and the attraction of its history. The servants' hall, the village and the manor house there formed one family. Our forefathers ruled the family, and the consciousness of it lingered long in their descendants. The history of a family, a clan, is deep, complex, mysterious and often gruesome. But its very strength lies in its dark depths, its legends and its past. As for written records or other memorials, Sukhodol is no richer in this than any *ulus** in the Bashkir steppe. In Russia, legend takes their place. But legends and songs are poison to the soul of a Slav. Our former serfs were desperate idlers and dreamers—where, if not in our house, could they have found such spiritual satisfaction? The only remaining representative of the Sukhodol masters was our father. The first language we learned to speak was Sukhodol talk. The first stories and the first songs that moved us were Sukhodol ones, too—Natalia's and Father's. And I doubt if

* *Ulus*—a nomad tent village.—*Tr.*

anyone could possibly sing the way our father, taught by the servants, sang of "his true and haughty love" with that carefree sadness, that tender reproach and weak-willed sincerity. Could anyone tell stories like Natalia? Was anyone closer to us than the Sukhodol peasants?

Like any other family which has long been living in close and isolated unity, the Khrushchovs were known since the beginning of time for their wrangles and their quarrels. The quarrel which took place between Sukhodol and Lunevo in our childhood was so bitter that our father never crossed the threshold of his home for ten years. That was why we did not really know Sukhodol when we were little; we had only been there once and even then it was in passing on our way to Zadonsk. But sometimes dreams are apt to be stronger than reality. And that long summer day left an indelible though vague memory of undulating fields, a wide, neglected road which fascinated us with its spaciousness and the old, hollow willows which had survived here and there; we remembered a beehive on one of these willows far from the road, amid the grainfields—a beehive abandoned to its fate in fields bordering a desolate road; we also remembered a wide turning up a long slope, a huge, barren common surrounded by wretched chimneyless huts, the yellow of the rocky gullies behind them and the white of the pebbles and broken stones lining the bottom of these gullies. The first event which struck terror into our hearts took place at Sukhodol, too, when Grandfather was murdered by Gervaska. And as we listened to the stories of this murder, we wove endless fancies round the yellow gullies which led we knew not where, believing that this was the way Gervaska had escaped, "dropping like a key to the bottom of the sea," after he had done his gruesome deed.

The reasons that sent the Sukhodol peasants to call on us at Lunevo were different from those of the Sukhodol servants. The peasants mostly wanted a plot of land, but they, too, treated our home like their own. They would bow low to Father, kiss his hand and then, tossing their hair, kiss him thrice on the lips, after which they would kiss Natalia and the two of us. They brought us gifts of honey, eggs and homespun towels. And, reared as we were in the open, as conscious of scents and odors as we were of songs and legends, we forever remembered that peculiar and agreeable smell, reminiscent of hemp, when we kissed the Sukhodol men. We remembered, too, the smell that clung to their gifts, the smell of an old village in the steppes: the honey smelled of buckwheat in flower and rotting oakwood beehives, the towels smelled of hempen sacking and the smoky huts of our grandfather's day. The Sukhodol peasants told us no stories. What did they have to tell? They had no legends to pass down. Their graves bear no names. And their lives are so like one another, so destitute of riches, that they leave no trace. For the fruit of their labor and endeavors is bread, just ordinary bread which we eat every day. They also tried digging ponds in the stony bed of the little Kamenka River, long since dried up. But ponds provide no security—they dry up, too. They built dwellings. But their dwellings were not long-lived: they would burn down to the ground at the merest spark. . . . Why then did all of us feel drawn to the barren common, the huts, to the gullies, the ruined Sukhodol estate?

II

We were already in our teens when we got the opportunity of staying at Sukhodol, the estate we had heard so much about, which had shaped Natalia's soul and ruled her entire life.

I remember it as if it were yesterday. Rain came pouring down in torrents, thunder crashed in deafening claps and lightning flashed blindingly in swift fiery snakes when, toward the end of the day, we drove up to Sukhodol. A dark mauve thundercloud slumped heavily down toward the northwest, arrogantly blotting out half the sky. Against its vast background the green carpet of the crops looked flat, clear and deathly pale, and the short wet grass on the highroad seemed bright and extraordinarily lush. The wet horses, which suddenly seemed to have grown lean, sloshed through the blue mud, their horseshoes sparkling, and there was a moist sound in the swish of the wheels. . . . And all of a sudden, as we turned in toward the house, we saw a tall, peculiar figure, which might have been either an old man or an old woman, in a dressing gown and hood, standing in the tall wet rye and whipping a hornless, skewbald cow with a switch. As we came closer the switch struck more fiercely, and the cow, twitching its tail, ran clumsily out on the road. Yelling something, an old woman made for the coach and, coming up close, strained toward us with her pale face. Staring, terrified, into her black, mad eyes and feeling the touch of her sharp cold nose and a strong musty smell, we exchanged kisses with her. Could it be Baba-Yaga, the witch herself? But this Baba-Yaga had a tall hood made of a piece of dirty rag on her head, and her naked body was wrapped into a ragged dressing gown, wet to the waist, that left her withered breasts uncovered. She screamed as though we were deaf or as though she were trying to start a vicious brawl. And from her screams we understood: this was Aunt Tonya.

Klavdia Markovna screamed too, but her scream was jolly, with a schoolgirlish delight in it. She was a small fat woman with a little silver beard and unusually eager eyes. She was sitting at the open window of the house which had two imposing porches, knitting a sock and, her spectacles pushed up on her forehead, she looked out over the common which had become one with the yard. On the right-hand porch Natalia, wearing bast shoes, a red woolen skirt and a gray blouse cut low round her dark, wrinkled neck, welcomed us with a low bow and a soft smile on her kindly sunburned face. I remember thinking as I looked at her neck, her jutting collarbones and her wearily sad eyes, that it was she who grew up with Father a very, very long time ago; and that it was here, on this very spot, where all that remained of Grandfather's oak-built house, burned down time and again, was this ugly building. All that was left of the old garden were some shrubs and a few old birches and poplars; all that remained of the outbuildings and the servants' quarters was a hut, a granary, a mud barn and the icehouse, overgrown with wormwood and goosefoot. . . . We could smell the samovar being kindled, questions were showered on both sides, crystal jam jars began to appear from the century-old sideboard, along with little golden spoons worn to maple-leaf thinness and some sugar biscuits, kept specially for unexpected guests. And while the conversation warmed up, intensely friendly after the long quarrel, we went wandering through the darkening rooms in search of a terrace or a door into the garden.

Everything was dark with age, plain and crude, in these low empty rooms, the arrangement of which was the same as in Grandfather's day, and which were actually built of what remained of those same rooms where he used to live. In the corner of the hall hung a large dark icon of St. Mercury of Smolensk, whose iron sandals and helmet repose on the dais in front of the iconostasis in the ancient Smolensk Cathedral. We heard it said that St. Mercury had been a distinguished man, to whom the voice spoke from the icon of the Holy Virgin the Guiding, summoning him to the rescue of the lands of Smolensk from the Tatars. When he had defeated the Tatars, the saint fell asleep and his foes beheaded him. And then, carrying his head in his hands, he came to the town gate to tell the people of the happening. . . . We had a creepy feeling as we looked at this ancient Suzdal painting of the decapitated man, holding in one hand his deathly livid, helmeted head and in the other the icon of the Holy Virgin. This painting of St. Mercury, cherished by Grandfather, so we were told, which had gone through several frightful fires and had split in the flames, was encased in heavy silver and bore on the back the genealogical table of the Khrushchovs, written in Slavonic. As though in keeping with the icon, the heavy folding doors to the dining hall were secured with heavy iron bars at top and bottom. The floor boards were inordinately broad, dark and slippery, and the windows had small sashes.

Though half the size, this was a replica of the dining hall where the Khrushchovs had once sat down to dinner armed with hunting crops. In the drawing room, opposite the doors opening on to the terrace, had stood the piano, which Aunt Tonya used to play when she was in love with Voitkevich, Pyotr Petrovich's officer friend. As we went on, we saw the open doors into the sitting room and the corner room where once our grandfather had his apartments. . . .

It was a gloomy evening. Summer lightning flashed in the thunderclouds beyond the edge of the felled orchard, the half-dismantled barn and the stand of silvery poplars, and for a moment revealed mountains of a roseate gold in the clouds. The downpour had evidently passed by Troshin Wood, darkening behind the garden on the hills beyond the gullies, for the dry, warm smell of oaks was wafted up, mingling with the fragrance of verdure and of the moist, mellow breeze that ran through the tops of the remaining birch trees, the tall nettles, the burdock and the shrubs around the terrace. And the profound silence of the evening, of the steppe, of the depths of Russia reigned supreme. . . .

"Tea is served, if you please," a voice called to us softly.

It was she, the participant and witness of all this life, its chief bard, Natalia. Her mistress appeared behind her, peering intently with her mad eyes, bending slightly forward and gliding ceremoniously across the dark smooth floor. She had not taken off her hood, but instead of the dressing gown she now wore an old-fashioned *barège* dress with a silk shawl of faded gold thrown over her shoulders.

"Où êtes-vous, mes enfants?" she screamed with a prim smile, and her voice, clear and strident like a parrot's, echoed strangely in the dark, empty rooms. . . .

III

The impoverished estate held the same charm as did Natalia in her peasant simplicity, in all the beauty and pathos of her soul, born of Sukhodol.

There was a smell of jasmine in the old drawing room with its slanting floor boards. The grayish-blue terrace crumbling with age, from which you had to jump down because there were no steps, was submerged in a wild growth of nettles, elders and priest's-hood. On hot days, when the sun blazed hard upon the terrace, when its warped glass doors were flung open and the merrily sparkling glass panels were reflected in the dim oval mirror on the opposite wall, we could not help thinking of Aunt Tonya's piano which had once stood under the mirror. There had been a time when she had played the piano, looking into her yellowed music with vignettes decorating the titles, while *he* stood behind her, his left hand on his waist, his jaws clamped tight and a frown upon his brow. Beautiful butterflies wearing bright cotton frocks, or Japanese kimonos, or black and mauve velvet shawls, flitted into the drawing room. And just before he left, in a fit of anger he slapped one of them down as it alighted tremulously on the piano lid. Only a little silvery powder remained. But when a few days later the housemaids, in their stupidity, dusted it, Aunt Tonya had a fit of hysterics. . . . We would come out on to the terrace through the drawing-room doors, and sit down on the warm boards, and think and think. The wind running through the garden carried up the silky rustle of the birches—their trunks white satin inlaid with niello, and their branches green and spreading. It blew across the fields, rustling and swishing, and a green and golden oriole darted like an arrow over the white flowers with a shrill and joyous cry in pursuit of the chattering jackdaws that dwelt with their numerous relatives in the tumbledown chimneys and the dark attics that smelt of old bricks and were heaped with grayish-purple ashes shot with streaks of golden light coming in through the dormer windows. The breeze died down, bees crawled sleepily over the flowers near the terrace performing their leisurely work—and in the silence all you could hear was the silvery poplar leaves murmuring softly, with a steady, dripping sound, like the incessant patter of a thin rain. We wandered through the garden and made our way into its remotest corners. There, where it merged into the cornfields, stood our great-grandfather's bathhouse, the bathhouse where Natalia had once kept the mirror she had stolen from Pyotr Petrovich. White rabbits lived there now. They leaped out on the threshold so softly and, twitching their whiskers and their split lips, squinted queerly with wide-apart goggling eyes at the tall thistles, the henbane and nettles that choked the black-thorns and the cherry trees. The half-dismantled barn was the home of a brown owl. Haystack poles stood up in a corner, and on the very top perched the owl, choosing a spot as gloomy as possible, sticking up its ears and bulging its blind yellow eyes so that it looked wild and fiendish. The sun sank far beyond the garden on to a sea of corn, and evening fell, mellow and tranquil; a cuckoo called in Troshin Wood, and the old shepherd's pipe rang plaintively far out in the meadows. . . . The brown owl sat and waited for night to come. Everything slept at night—the fields, the village and the house. But the brown owl sobbed and hooted. It rushed noiselessly round the barn and across the garden, it flew to Aunt Tonya's cottage, alighted softly on the roof and gave an agonizing shriek. . . . Aunt Tonya, sleeping on a bench by the stove, would wake with a start.

"Gentle Jesus, save me," she whispered, sighing.

Flies buzzed sleepily and resentfully close to the ceiling of the hot, dark cottage. Something disturbed their sleep every night. It was either the cow rubbing her flanks against the side of the cottage, or a rat scurrying along the piano keys to make them ring with staccato notes until it lost its footing and fell with a clatter into the pile of broken crockery which Aunt Tonya stacked carefully in a corner; or else it was the black, green-eyed cat coming home late from his prowls and lazily begging to be allowed in; or again the brown owl would alight on the roof, presaging disaster with its screams. And Aunt Tonya, overcoming her drowsiness and beating off the flies which swarmed at her eyes in the darkness, would get up, grope over the benches, slam back the door and, standing on the threshold, fling her rolling pin at random into the starlit sky. The brown owl would tear off the roof, rustling the straw with its wings, and drop down into the darkness far below. It almost touched the ground as it flew smoothly to the barn, and, soaring up, perched on the ridge of the roof. And once again the wind carried its sobs to the house. It sat there as though trying to remember something and, suddenly, it would let out a wail of amazement; then silence, and abruptly it started hooting hysterically, laughing and screeching; it would grow silent again for a moment and then burst out with groans, whimpers and sobs. . . . But the nights, warm and dark, with little mauve clouds in the sky were extraordinarily serene. The slumbering poplars murmured on sleepily and monotonously. Summer lightning flashed warily over Troshin Wood, and the air was filled with the dry, warm smell of oaks. In a gap between the clouds, over the sea of oats, close to the forest, the Scorpio shone in a triangle of silver, like a gravestone with a little roof over the cross. . . .

We used to get home late. Having breathed our fill of the dew, of the freshness of the fields, of the wild flowers and grass, we would make our way quietly up the porch steps and enter the dark hall. And often we came upon Natalia saying her prayers before the image of St. Mercury. She would stand before the icon—slight, barefooted, her hands folded—and whisper something, cross herself and bow low in the darkness to the invisible saint. And all of it was done so simply as if she were talking to one of her family, to another simple, kind and gracious soul.

"Natalia!" we would call.

"Yes?" she would answer softly, breaking off her prayer.

"Why aren't you in bed yet?"

"I expect we'll sleep our fill in the grave."

We would then sit down on the window seat and open the window, while she stood before us with her arms crossed. Summer lightning flickered mysteriously, brightening the dark rooms. Far away in the dewy steppe a quail was clucking, and on the pond a duck, awakening, quacked warningly in alarm. . . .

"Been for a walk?"

"Yes, we have."

"Oh well, you're only young once. . . . We used to stay out all night too. . . . Sunset would send us out and sunrise drive us in. . . ."

"Was life good in the old days?"

"Yes, it was good."

And a long silence followed.

"Tell us, nanny dear, why does the brown owl scream so?" my sister would ask.

"He bodes no good with his screaming, bother him. Perhaps we should give him a scare with the rifle, it makes you creepy, thinking some disaster might be coming. And it frightens Miss, too. She's scared to death of everything."

"How did she fall ill?"

"The usual way—crying and crying and grieving. . . . And then she took to praying. . . . And she grew fiercer and fiercer with us servants, and angrier and angrier with her brothers. . . ."

And remembering the hunting crops, we asked:

"You mean they didn't get on?"

"Heavens, did they get on! Especially after Miss fell ill and Grandfather died, the young gentlemen grew up and the late Pyotr Petrovich got married. They were a fiery lot—real gunpowder!"

"And did they often flog the servants?"

"No, that has never been the way here, never. Look what I did for instance. And all the punishment I got was Pyotr Petrovich ordering my hair to be cropped with sheep shears, a shirt of ticking put on me and have me packed off to the farmstead. . . ."

"But what had you done?"

A quick and straight answer did not always follow. At times Natalia would tell her stories with amazing frankness and punctiliousness, but at others she would stutter and pause, thinking something over, then she would sigh and, although we would not see her face in the dusk, we could tell by her voice that she was smiling mirthlessly.

"I did what I did. I've told you before, you know. . . . I was young and stupid. . . . 'To her woe and grief sang a nightingale. . . .' And, of course, being a young girl . . . "

My sister would beg her sweetly:

"Nanny dear, please tell us the rest of the verse."

This would embarrass Natalia.

"It's not a verse, it's a song. . . . And I can't remember all of it now. . . ."

"It's not true. You can."

"Oh well, have it your own way. . . . Now how does it go?" and she finished off rapidly: " 'To her woe and grief sang a nightingale in the garden dark, and its song of love kept the foolish maid wide awake all night. . . .' "

Fighting down her shyness, my sister would ask:

"Were you very much in love with Uncle?"

And Natalia whispered curtly and dully, "Very."

"D'you always remember him in your prayers?"

"Always."

"They say you fainted when they took you to Soshki?"

"That I did. We house servants were ever so delicate . . . thin-skinned when it came to punishment . . . no comparing us with those coarse small holders. When Yevsey Bodulya started off with me, I went all numb with sorrow and dread. . . . First time in town the dust all but choked me. But once we were out in the steppe, I felt so weak and woeful. And suddenly there was an officer driving toward us who looked like the Master. I cried out and fainted dead away! And when I came to, I lay in the cart and thought: I'm so happy now, like I'm in heaven."

"Was he strict?"

"Heaven preserve us!"

"But still, Auntie was the most willful, wasn't she?"

"She was, she was. But I'm telling you, they even took her to the saint. Oh, the time she's given us all! She ought to have been well and happy now, but she scorned him and so she went off her head. . . . And Voitkevich, he loved Miss so. But there you are."

"Well, and Grandfather?"

"Grandfather was different. He was feeble in his mind. But, of course, it happened with him too sometimes. Everyone was hot-tempered in those days. . . . But then, the old masters were not squeamish about the likes of us. . . . Sometimes your father would punish Gervaska at dinner—and he well deserved it too—and in the evening you'd see the two of them feasting in the yard, thrumming their balalaikas. . . ."

"Tell us, was he handsome, Voitkevich, I mean?"

Natalia would grow pensive.

"No, I wouldn't tell a lie: he was like a Kalmyk. But he was serious and stubborn. He kept reading poetry to Miss and scaring her that he'd die and come after her. . . ."

"But it was love, too, that made Grandfather mad, wasn't it?"

"That was because of your grandmother. Quite a different thing. And then our house was so gloomy—it was never a cheery place, bless it. Well, listen to my foolish words if you please. . . ."

Her voice low and unhurried, Natalia would begin her long, long story. . . .

IV

If legend is to be believed, our great-grandfather, a wealthy man, only moved to Sukhodol from Kursk toward the end of his days: he did not care for the place with its remoteness and its woods. But then, it has come to be a saying now that "woods were everywhere in the old days." People walking our roads some two hundred years ago had to make their way through dense forests. Everything was lost in the forests then —the River Kamenka, the country upriver, the village, the estate, and the undulating fields around it. But in Grandfather's time it was no longer the same. The scenery had changed—rolling steppe, bare hills, fields of rye, oats and buckwheat, straggling hollow willows lining the road, and nothing but white pebbles on the rise where the house now stands. All that remained of the forest was Troshin Wood. The garden had been beautiful of course. There was a broad walk lined with seventy spreading birches, cherry trees submerged in nettles, a wilderness of raspberry, acacia and lilac bushes, and what was almost a grove of silver poplars at the bottom where it merged into the grainfields. The house was roofed with thick, dark, sturdy thatch. The windows faced a courtyard surrounded by outbuildings and the servants' quarters in long, many-sectioned timber buildings; and beyond the courtyard stretched a boundless green meadow and then the spreading village which belonged to the estate, a large village, poor but carefree.

"Took after the masters, it did," Natalia would say. "The masters were carefree, too, not good managers and not greedy either. Semyon Kirillich, your grandfather's brother, divided the property: he himself took the bigger and better part, the patrimonial estate he took, and he left us only Soshki, Sukhodol, and four hundred souls thrown in. But of the four hundred almost half ran away. . . ."

Grandfather Pyotr Kirillich died when he was about forty-five. Father often said that he went out of his mind after a sudden hurricane had hurled a torrent of apples down upon him as he lay sleeping on a rug under an apple tree. In the servants' hall, Natalia told us, Grandfather's insanity was explained differently. They said Pyotr Kirillich went off his head from being lovelorn when our beautiful grandmother died, and that on the evening before, a great thunderstorm had swept Sukhodol. And so Pyotr Kirillich—a dark, round-shouldered man with a tender, intent look in his black eyes, a little like

Aunt Tonya, had ended his days in a state of mild insanity. According to Natalia, they had had more money than they could spend in those days, and Grandfather, wearing morocco-leather top boots and a colored housecoat, would wander anxiously and soundlessly from room to room and, glancing about him warily, thrust gold pieces into the cracks in the timber walls.

"It's Tonya's dowry I'm thinking of," he would mutter when caught in the act. "It's safer, my friends, much safer . . . but on the whole—it's up to you. If you don't want me to, I won't. . . ."

And he would start thrusting them in again. Or then he would begin to move the heavy furniture about in the hall and in the drawing room, for he was always expecting visitors, although his neighbors hardly ever came to Sukhodol at all. Sometimes he would complain that he was hungry and would make some hash for himself, awkwardly chopping and mashing some green onions in a wooden bowl, shredding bits of bread in, pouring thick frothing *surovets** over it and sprinkling it with such a quantity of gray, coarse salt that it was bitter and quite unbearable to the taste. And when there was an after-dinner lull in the house and everyone trailed away to his favorite corner for a good, long nap, Pyotr Kirillich, who slept very little even at night, would not know where to turn in his loneliness. When he could stand it no longer, he would go peeping into the bedrooms and living rooms and quietly call the sleeping:

"Arkasha, are you asleep? Sleeping, Tonya dear?"

And, rewarded with an angry shout: "Oh, leave me alone, for heaven's sake, Papa!" he would mumble hastily and placatingly: "Well, sleep, my dear, sleep. I shan't disturb you. . . ."

And he would continue on his way, only giving a wide berth to the servants' hall, for the footmen were a very rude lot. And within ten minutes he would be back at the bedroom

* *Surovets*—a beverage made by pouring warm water over flour and letting it ferment.—*Tr.*

doors again, calling the sleeping with more caution than ever, inventing news of someone driving down the village road with jingling stagecoach bells—"It couldn't be Petenka coming on leave from the army, could it?"—or of great hailclouds gathering in the sky.

"The master, bless him, was ever so scared of storms," Natalia told us. "I was nothing but a pigtailed kiddy at the time, but I remember it, too. Our house was so black somehow . . . a cheerless place, so help me. And the summer days were so long. We had so many servants—footmen alone we had five. Well, the young masters would naturally go to sleep after dinner, and we, faithful servants, good serfs, would do the same. And then Pyotr Kirillich had better not come near us, especially, Gervaska. 'I say, footmen, are you asleep?' he would ask. And Gervaska would raise his head from the coffer and say: 'D'you want me to stuff your pants with stinging nettle right now?' 'Who d'you think you're talking to, you rascal?' 'To the house goblin, sir, in my sleep.' Well, then Pyotr Kirillich would go back to the dining hall and the drawing room again, he'd look out of the windows and into the garden to see whether a thunderstorm was gathering. It's true, though, thunderstorms broke out ever so often in the old days. And what terrible thunderstorms, too! Soon after dinner an oriole would start crying, and clouds would creep up from behind the garden. . . . The house would grow dark, the grass and dead nettle would start rustling, the turkey-hens and their chicks would all hide under the terrace. . . . Real sickening it was. And he, the master, would sigh and cross himself, climb a chair to light a wax candle before the icons and hang up the sacred towel left over from your great-grandfather's funeral—I was scared to death of that towel. Or he'd throw a pair of scissors out of the window. That's the first thing you do, scissors I mean, it's very good against a thunderstorm. . . ."

* * *

It had been jollier in the Sukhodol house when the French

people were staying there. At first it was a certain Louis Ivanovich, a gentleman with dreamy blue eyes and long mustaches, who wore exceedingly wide trousers narrowing down at the bottom and hair plastered across his bald pate from ear to ear. After that came an elderly Mademoiselle Suzie who was always shivering, and Louis Ivanovich's thundering voice could be heard in all the rooms as he yelled at Arkasha: "Go away and don't come back again!" From the classroom came: "*Maître corbeau sur un arbre perché,*" and Miss Tonya would be heard practicing on the piano. The French people remained at Sukhodol for eight years, staying on to keep Pyotr Kirillich company even after the children had been sent away to school in town, and they did not leave till the children came home for their third summer holidays. But after this, Pyotr Kirillich never sent either Arkasha or Tonya anywhere any more, for in his opinion it was enough if Petenka alone went to school. And so the children remained forever untutored and uncared for.

Natalia used to say:

"I was the youngest of them all, you know. And since Gervaska and your papa were almost the same age, they came to be the best of friends. But it's a true saying that you can't put the wolves in with the sheep. Well then, they came to be friends, they swore eternal friendship, they even exchanged baptismal crosses, but Gervaska soon went and cut a caper: he almost drowned your papa in the pond. He was just a dirty little brat, but already he was a great one for criminal pranks. He said to the young master one day, 'When you grow up are you going to flog me?' 'I am.' 'Oh no, you're not!' 'Why not?' 'Just because. . . .' And he went and thought something up: we had a barrel standing on top of the hill above the pond, and it gave him an idea. He told Arkady Petrovich to get into it and roll down the hill. 'You get first chance, master, I'll do it after you.' Well, the young master did what he said: he got into the barrel, shoved, and off he went clattering downhill and plopped straight into the water. . . . Oh, Holy

Mother of God! Nothing but dust whirling in a cloud. A good thing some shepherds happened to come along. . . ."

The house had still looked habitable as long as the French people remained in it. Before Grandmother died Sukhodol had masters and owners, rule and obedience, state rooms and family wings, holidays and weekdays. A semblance of this had been retained while the French people were there. But they went away and the house had no masters left at all. While the children were small, Pyotr Kirillich remained the head of the house to all appearances. But what could he do? Who ruled whom? Did he rule the servants or did the servants rule him? The piano was closed, the tablecloth vanished from the oaken table, they ate without one in a slapdash way, and the entry was always full of borzois. There was no one to look after the house, and the dark log walls, the dark floors and ceilings, the dark heavy doors and doorframes, the old icons with their Suzdal painted saints taking up a whole corner of the dining hall, soon grew quite black. The house was frightening at night, especially on stormy nights when the garden roared and droned in the wind and rain, when lightning flashed across the faces of the saints in the corner, when the sky burst apart and opened wide its tremulous rosy-gold heavens above the trees and the thunder crashed mightily in the blackness. In the daytime it was sleepy, empty and dreary. Pyotr Kirillich grew feebler and feebler as the years went by, more and more insignificant, while the house was managed by old Darya Ustinovna, Grandfather's wet nurse. But her power was almost equal to Grandfather's and the bailiff Demyan refused to interfere with the housekeeping. All he worried about was farm management, and he would sometimes say with a slow smile, "Why, I wouldn't wrong my masters!" My father, a youngster then, could not be bothered with Sukhodol: he was crazy about hunting, the balalaika, and about Gervaska who was supposed to be a footman, but who spent whole days with him duck shooting on the Meshchera Marshes somewhere, or in the coach house learning new tricks on the balalaika or the pipe.

"We got used to it," Natalia said. "He only came home to sleep. And if he didn't even do that, it meant he was either in the village, or in the coach house, or out shooting; hare in winter, fox in autumn, quail, duck or bustard in summer. He'd get on the racing droshky, sling his gun on his shoulder, whistle for Dianka, and off he'd go, to the Serednyaya Mill one day, the Meshchera Marshes the next, or out into the steppe. And Gervaska was always with him; he was always the ringleader, but he pretended it was the young master who dragged him into things. And Arkady Petrovich loved him, this enemy of his, truly, like a brother, but he made nastier sport of him as time wore on. Master would say, 'Come on, Gervaska, let's play our balalaikas. For heaven's sake teach me to play "The sun went down beyond the trees. . . ." And Gervaska would glance at him, blow some smoke out through his nostrils, and say with a smirk, 'First you kiss my hand.' Arkady Petrovich would turn deathly white, jump up and slap him on the cheek with all his might, but he'd only jerk his head and turn blacker still, scowling like some brigand. 'Get up, you scoundrel!' He'd stand up, stretching like a wolf-hound, his velveteen trousers hanging . . . and he'd say nothing. 'Beg my pardon!' 'Beg your pardon, sir.' But the young master almost choked with rage, he wouldn't know what to say next. 'Sir, that's right!' he'd shout. 'I'm trying to treat you like an equal, you scoundrel; at times I think I'd give my soul for you. . . . And you? Trying to enrage me on purpose, are you?' "

"It's a funny thing," Natalia would say. "The young master and Grandfather were flouted and mocked by Gervaska, and I was tormented by Miss Tonya. The young master and Grandfather too, if the truth be told, doted on him, and I on her . . . when I came back from Soshki and got my senses back a bit after my crime. . . ."

V

They did not begin to arm themselves with hunting crops for dinner until after Grandfather had died, Gervaska had fled, Pyotr Petrovich had got married, Aunt Tonya, her mind deranged, had dedicated herself to be a bride of Christ, and until Natalia had returned from Soshki. And the reason why Aunt Tonya's mind was deranged and why Natalia had been in exile was—love.

Now came the day of the young masters, to replace the dull, shut-in life of Grandfather's time. Pyotr Petrovich, retiring from the army to everyone's surprise, came back to Sukhodol. And his arrival proved fatal for both Natalia and Aunt Tonya.

They both fell in love. Neither knew how it had happened. It seemed to them at first that "life had simply become more exciting."

At the outset Pyotr Petrovich steered the life at Sukhodol on a new course of glitter and leisure as befitting the gentry. He brought with him his friend Voitkevich and a *chef*, a clean-shaven drunkard who squinted scornfully at the fluted jelly molds green with age, and the crude knives and forks. Pyotr Petrovich wanted to appear hospitable, generous and prosperous before his friend, and he went about it in an awkward, boyish way. But he was, indeed, little more than a boy, very gentle and handsome to look at, but harsh and cruel by nature, a boy who seemed self-assured, yet who was easily thrown into confusion almost to the point of tears, and nursed a grudge for a long time afterward against the person who had caused his confusion.

"I seem to remember, Arkady," he said at dinner the very day he arrived home. "I seem to remember we had some Madeira that wasn't at all bad."

Grandfather blushed and tried to say something but, his courage failing him, he only tugged at the neck of his coat nervously and said nothing. Arkady Petrovich asked in surprise:

"What Madeira?"

And Gervaska threw Pyotr Petrovich a brazen look and smirked.

"You've forgotten, sir," he said to Arkady Petrovich without even trying to conceal his smirk. "We really did have all kinds of this Madeira stuff, but it's all been pinched by us menials. It's a gentleman's wine, but we just guzzled it down instead of *kvas*."

"What's this I hear!" Pyotr Petrovich shouted, turning a dark red. "Silence!"

Grandfather joined in delightedly:

"That's the way, Petenka, that's the way! Bravo!" he cried joyfully in a thin voice and almost wept. "You can't imagine how he flouts me. If I've thought of it once, I've thought of it again and again. I'll steal up to him and crush his head with a bronze pestle. I swear I will! I'll stick a knife into his ribs to the very hilt!"

And Gervaska was quick to retort:

"I've heard the punishment for that is very severe, sir," he said with a frown. "Because I, too, can't drive the thought away that it's time the master went to heaven."

Pyotr Petrovich used to say that when he heard this unexpectedly insolent reply he only controlled himself because his guest was there. All he said to Gervaska was: "Get out this minute!" And afterward he actually felt ashamed of his outburst and, making his hurried excuses to Voitkevich, he smiled and looked at him with those beautiful eyes of his which no one who had known him could ever forget.

With Natalia, too, the memory of those eyes lingered too long.

Her happiness was extremely short-lived—and who could have thought that it would end in her going to Soshki, which was the most outstanding event in her whole life?

Soshki exists to this day, although a Tambov merchant has owned it for some time now. It is a long timber cottage standing in a barren plain. There is a granary, a well with a long arm to let down the bucket, and a barn with melon fields around it. All this was the same in Grandfather's time of course, and the town which lies halfway between Sukhodol and Soshki has not changed very much, either. The crime Natalia had committed came as a great surprise to herself: she stole Pyotr Petrovich's little folding mirror, framed in silver.

She saw the mirror and was so struck by its beauty (this, however, was the way she felt about all Pyotr Petrovich's things) that she could not resist the temptation of taking it. And for several days, until the mirror was missed, she lived dumfounded by her crime, spellbound by her dreadful secret and her treasure, like the girl in the tale about the little red flower. Before she went to sleep she prayed that the night would soon be over and that the morning would come quickly. There was a holiday atmosphere in the house which had come to life filled with something new and wonderful, brought to it by the handsome young master, smart and pomaded, with a high red collar to his tunic, and a face that was tanned but as delicate as a young lady's. Even the corridor where Natalia slept on a trunk had a festive air, and when she woke at dawn she instantly remembered that there was joy in the world, because the pair of top boots that stood waiting to be cleaned outside the door were so fine, they were fit for a king's son. But the most awesome and exciting place was beyond the garden, in the deserted bathhouse, where the folding mirror in its heavy silver frame was hidden—there, beyond the garden, where Natalia hurried stealthily through the shrubbery, wet with dew, while everyone was still in bed, so she could revel in her possession of this treasure, take it to the door, open it out in the hot morning sunlight, and stare at her reflection till her head reeled, and then hide it again concealing it carefully, and once more hurry back to the house to serve the one to whom she did not even dare to raise her eyes, and because of whom she stared at herself in the mirror with the mad hope that he might like her.

But the tale of the little red flower ended quickly, very quickly indeed. It ended in disgrace and shame which words could not describe, or so thought Natalia. It ended with Pyotr

Petrovich himself ordering her hair to be cropped, disfiguring her, while all the time she had been decking herself out, blackening her eyebrows in front of the little mirror, and creating some delicious secret, a fanciful intimacy between them. He had been the one to discover her crime and turn it into an ordinary case of theft, into the stupid escapade of a silly servant wench who, in a dress of ticking, her face swollen with tears, was put on a manure cart in view of all the servants and, disgraced, abruptly severed from all that was dear to her, driven to some strange and horrible farmstead, into the distant steppe. She knew beforehand: there, on the farm, she would have to tend the chickens, turkeys and melons; there, she would be scorched by the sun, forgotten by the whole world; there in the steppe, the days would seem like years, when a shimmering haze cloaked the horizon and all was so quiet, so sultry that you could sleep the sleep of the dead all day long if it were not that you had to listen to the gentle crackling of the dried-up peas, the busy fussing of the brood-hens in the hot sand, the placidly sorrowful cries of the turkeys, to watch the sudden approach of the eerie shadow of a hawk and leap up, shouting in a thin, drawn-out voice, "Shoo-oo!" To think of the terrible old Ukrainian woman who held Natalia's life and death in her hands, and who was certainly awaiting her victim with impatience, there at the farmstead. Natalia had but one advantage over those taken to their execution—she was free to hang herself. That was the only thought that sustained her on her way into exile—forever, she believed.

There was much to see on this journey from one end of the district to the other. But she was past that. All she thought of or, rather, felt was that her life was over, her crime and disgrace were much too great to leave her any hope of ever returning to it. So far she had one of her own people beside her, Yevsei Bodulya, but what was to come when he had handed her over into the keeping of the Ukrainian? He would sleep the night and depart, leaving her forever in a strange land. When she could weep no longer she began to feel hungry. And to her amazement Yevsei seemed to consider this very natural, and as they ate he talked to her as if nothing had occurred. And then she fell asleep and did not awaken until they had reached the town. And the town seemed to her bleak, dusty and oppressive, and something else that was vaguely terrifying and nostalgic, like a dream you could not relate. All the recollection she had of that day was that it was very hot in the steppe in summer, that there was nothing in the world more endless than a summer day, nothing longer than a highroad. She remembered that in the town a part of the streets was cobbled, making the cart rumble strangely. She remembered that from afar the town smelled of iron roofing, while in the center of the market square, where they took a rest and fed the horse, close to the eating-sheds which were empty at that hour, it smelled of dust, tar and rotting hay, for hay stalks stamped into the dung are always left behind at peasants' halts. Yevsei unharnessed the horse and brought it close to the cart to feed; he pushed his hot cap on the back of his head, wiped his sweating brow with a sleeve and, looking black from the heat, made for the tavern. He gave Natalia very, very strict orders to keep an eye on things, and to yell at the top of her voice if something happened. And Natalia sat without moving, never taking her gaze off the dome of the newly built cathedral, which shone like a great silver star far beyond the houses. She sat thus until Yevsei came back, looking merrier and chewing something. Holding a loaf of white bread in the crook of his arm, he began to lead the horse back between the shafts.

"We're a bit on the late side, my princess," he muttered happily, addressing either Natalia or the horse. "Let's hope they won't hang us for it. There's no fire, eh? And I won't break its wind on the way back either, the master's horse means more to me than your dirty mouth," he said, meaning Demyan now. "Bawling your mouth at me! 'Mind now! If you don't look sharp I'll see you get it in the pants. . . .' Oh you. . . ! I thought. I felt sick to my stomach with the insult of it. I'll have you know my masters never took my trousers down yet . . . and you're no match for them, you foul mug. . . . 'Look sharp!' he says. Why should I look sharp? I'm no more a fool than you are, I hope. If I feel like it, I won't come back at all. I'll deliver the wench and then I'll take to the open road and that's the last you'll ever see of me. I wonder at the wench too: what's the fool worrying about anyway? Has the end of the world come or something? There'll be wagoners or old folks coming past the farm—just say the word and you'll find yourself far beyond old Rostov in no time. . . . They can try and catch you then!"

And the thought "I'll hang myself" gave way in Natalia's sheared head to the thought of flight. The cart began to squeak and rock. Yevsei lapsed into silence and led the horse toward the well in the middle of the square. Over there, from where they had come, the sun was setting behind a large monastery garden, and the windows of the yellow prison, which stood across the road from the monastery, sparkled with gold. For a minute the sight of the prison stirred her thoughts of flight even more. "You can live even if you're a runaway. Only they say the old people blind the wenches and the children they steal by scalding their eyes with boiling milk, and then they make them beg for alms, and the wagoners whisk them away to the sea and sell them to the Nogais. . . . Sometimes it happens that the masters catch their escaped servants, too, put chains on them and throw them into jail. . . . But, as Gervaska was wont to say, let's hope the jailers are men and not beasts."

But the light reflected in the prison windows faded and her thoughts became confused—no, to run away was even more terrifying than to hang yourself. And then Yevsei, too, sobered up and grew silent.

"We're late, lass." He spoke uneasily now, jumping on to the edge of the cart.

And the cart, out on the highroad now, began to rock and jolt again, clattering loudly over the cobbles. . . . Natalia felt rather than thought: "Ah but anyway it would be better if the cart were turned back, if I could only fly to Sukhodol and fall at my master's feet." But Yevsei was whipping his horse on. She could no longer see the star beyond the houses. Ahead lay nothing but the bare white street, the white road and white houses—and all of it terminated in the huge white cathedral with its new white metal dome and the sky above it looked a bleak, bluish white. . . . Back home at this time the dew would already be falling, the garden would be sending up its cool fragrance and a warm smell would be coming from the kitchen. Far beyond the sea of grain, beyond the silvery poplars on the edge of the garden, beyond the old memorable bathhouse, the glow of the sunset would be dying away, while in the drawing room the terrace doors would be open, the crimson light merging with the shadows in the corners, and the sallow-skinned young lady with the black eyes, who looked both like Grandfather and Pyotr Petrovich, would be sitting with her back to the sunset, peering into her music, continually pulling down the sleeves of her light and loose gown of orange silk, striking the yellow keys and filling the drawing room with the solemnly melodious, sweetly despairing strains of Oginsky's polonaise and appearing to take no notice at all of the officer—a stocky, dark-skinned man, who stood behind her, his left hand on his waist, watching her swift hands with concentration and gloom. . . .

"She has hers, and I have mine," on evenings such as this Natalia felt rather than thought, with fluttering heart; and, running into the cool, dewy garden, deep into the wilderness of nettles and damp, strongly smelling burdock, she would stand poised, waiting for the impossible—for the young master to come down the terrace steps, go into the garden, catch sight of her and, turning abruptly, come close to her with quick strides—and she would not have made a sound, numbed by fear and joy. . . . But the cart clattered on. The town was all round them, hot and fetid, the same town she used to imagine as a place enchanted. And Natalia gazed in painful surprise at the elegantly dressed crowds, walking up and down along the stone paving in front of the houses, at the gates and the wide-open doors of the shops. . . . "And why did Yevsei have to go this way?" she mused. "How could he dare clatter along here with his cart?"

And now they were past the cathedral, driving down the bumpy and dusty road to the shallow river, past smithies and the tumble-down huts of the small tradesmen. . . . Once again there was a familiar smell of fresh warm water, of silt and the evening coolness of the fields. The first to light its flickering lamp was a lonely little house by the barrier, far away on the opposite bank. . . . Then they came to the open country, crossed the bridge, drove up to the barrier and saw, staring in their eyes, a stony desolate road, dimly white, that disappeared into the boundless distance, into the blue of the cool night. The horse began to jog along and once past the barrier it slowed down to a walk. And again you could hear how very, very still were the earth and the sky at night—only a tiny bell tinkled plaintively far away. The sound grew ever louder, ever more melodious, until at last it could be heard above the rhythmic thudding of a troika, the even beat of hoofs on the road, and the swish of carriage wheels. . . . A young freedman was driving the troika, while in the carriage, his chin thrust into the collar of his hooded army coat, sat an officer. He raised his head for a moment when they passed the cart—and suddenly Natalia saw a red collar, black mustache, and young eyes flashing at her from beneath the bucket-shaped helmet. . . . She cried out, paled and fainted.

She thought wildly that it was Pyotr Petrovich, and from the pain and tenderness which pierced her nervous servant's heart she suddenly understood what it was she had lost—his nearness. . . . Yevsei rushed to douse her cropped lolling head with water from his traveling can. And then a fit of nausea brought her back to her senses. She hastily thrust her head out over the edge of the cart. Yevsei quickly placed his palm beneath her icy forehead.

After that, relieved and shivering, the neck of her blouse wet, she lay on her back and gazed at the stars. The terrified Yevsei remained silent, thinking she was asleep—he merely shook his head and hurried his horse on and on. The cart jogged and sped away. And to the girl it seemed as though she had no body, that she had nothing but her soul. And this soul of hers felt as happy as though it were in heaven.

Her love was a little red flower blossoming in a fairy-tale garden. But it was into the steppe, into a remoteness even more forbidding than the remoteness of Sukhodol, that she carried her love, so that there, in silence and solitude, she could still its first sweet and poignant torments, and afterward for a long time to come, forever, until the day she died, bury it in the depths of her Sukhodolian soul.

VI

At Sukhodol they loved strangely. They hated strangely, too.

Grandfather, whose end was as ridiculous as that of his murderer or, for that matter, of anyone who met his end at Sukhodol, was killed that same year. The feast of the Intercession of the Holy Virgin was Sukhodol's patron saint's day, and Pyotr Petrovich invited a number of guests to dinner. He was very nervous, wondering if the Marshal of nobility, who had promised to be there, would come. Grandfather was happily excited too, for no apparent reason. The Marshal arrived and the dinner went off famously. It was both noisy and merry, Grandfather being the merriest of all. Early next morning, on the second of October, he was found dead on the drawing-room floor.

When he retired from the army, Pyotr Petrovich made no secret of the fact that he was sacrificing himself to save the Khrushchov's honor, the family and the family estate. He made no secret of being "forced" to take up the reins of management. He was also "obliged" to make ties, to associate with the most enlightened and useful noblemen in the district, and as for the others—to avoid breaking off all relations with them. In the beginning he did exactly what he had planned; he called on all the small-estate owners; he even visited Aunt Olga Kirillovna, a monstrously fat old woman who had the sleeping sickness and who cleaned her teeth with snuff. By autumn it did not surprise anyone any more that Pyotr Petrovich was ruling the estate like an autocrat. But then, he no longer looked the dandy young officer who had come home on leave, he was the master, a young landowner. He did not blush with embarrassment so easily now. He was perfectly groomed, he put on flesh, he wore expensive housecoats and pampered his small feet with soft red Tatar slippers, while his small hands were adorned with turquoise rings. Arkady Petrovich shrank from looking into his brother's black eyes, he did not know what to talk to him about, and at first he gave way to him in everything and spent his days out shooting.

At this dinner of his, Pyotr Petrovich wanted to charm each of his guests with his hospitality, and show them, besides, that he was indeed the master of the house. But Grandfather was a dreadful nuisance. Grandfather was blissfully happy, but he was tactless, garrulous and pathetic in his little velvet cap —a sacred relic—and his new and much too wide blue coat, made by the family tailor. He also fancied himself a good host and had fussed since early morning, inventing some stupid ceremony for receiving the guests. Only one side of the folding doors from the dining hall into the passage was ever opened. Yet he personally moved back the iron bars at the top and bottom, brought up a chair himself and, shaking all over, climbed on to it. When he had thrown the doors wide open, he took his stand on the threshold and, taking advantage of Pyotr Petrovich's silence, who was numb with shame and rage but resolved to stand anything, he never left his post until after the last guest had arrived. His eyes were glued to the front door, which had to be flung open too in conformity with some ancient custom or other—he shuffled his feet in his excitement, and as soon as he sighted the next guest coming in, he rushed out to meet him, hastily made a *pas*, skipping and throwing one foot out across the other, bowed low to him and said to one and all, gulping the words breathlessly:

"Oh, I am so glad! So glad! It's quite some time since you've been to see me! Come in, come in!"

It also maddened Pyotr Petrovich that Grandfather insisted on telling all and sundry that Tonya had gone to Lunevo to stay with Olga Kirillovna. "Tonya is ill with melancholy; she's gone to spend the autumn with her aunt." What would the guests think on hearing this uncalled-for announcement? Her affair with Voitkevich was now common property, of course. Perhaps Voitkevich had really had honorable intentions, sighing at Tonya's side, playing duets with her, reading *Lyudmila* to her in a muffled voice, or saying to her with a gloomy pensiveness: "The sanctity of vows betroth you to the dead. . . ." But Tonya had flared up wildly whenever he made an attempt to express his feelings, even when these attempts were of the most innocent sort, such as bringing her a flower, and, abruptly, Voitkevich left. And yet, when he had gone away, Tonya no longer slept at night. She took to sitting in the darkness beside her open window as if waiting for a moment that she alone knew, and then suddenly bursting into loud sobs, waking up Pyotr Petrovich. He would lie awake for a long time, listening to her sobs and the soft, sleepy murmur of the poplars in the dark garden which sounded like a never ending drizzle. Then he would go to comfort her. The sleepy housemaids trailed in to comfort her too, and sometimes Grandfather would hurry in anxiously as well. And Tonya would start stamping her feet and shrieking: "Leave me alone, you are my mortal enemies!"—and everything would end in an ugly brawl, almost a fight.

"Try to understand, you," Pyotr Petrovich hissed savagely, after he had driven out the housemaids and Grandfather and, slamming the door shut, stood holding on tightly to the handle. "Try to understand, you viper, what people may think."

"Oooh!" Tonya screeched in a frenzy. "Papa! He's abusing me, he says I'm pregnant!"

And, clutching his head in his hands, Pyotr Petrovich would rush out of her room.

The day of the party he was also very uneasy about Gervaska, afraid he might be insolent if they weren't careful.

Gervaska had grown terribly. Huge, awkward, but the best-looking and the most clever of all the servants, he, too, was dressed up in a blue coat, blue trousers and soft kidskin top boots with flat soles. A worsted mauve kerchief was knotted round his thin dark neck. His thick, brittle black hair was parted on the side; he had refused to have it cut short and had it trimmed in an even bob round his head. There was nothing for him to shave, for he only had two or three coarse black hairs curling on his chin and one each at the corners of his big mouth, "a slit from ear to ear," they teased him in the servants' hall. Lanky, very broad in his flat, bony chest, with a small head and deep eye sockets, thin ash-blue lips and large bluish teeth, this ancient Aryan, a Persian from Sukhodol, had already been nicknamed "borzoi." Looking at his grin, hearing his cough, many were struck with the thought: "Borzoi, you'll soon croak, you know." And yet to his face they called this youngster Gervasy Afanasyevich, thus setting him apart from the other servants.

His masters were afraid of him too. The masters and the serfs had this trait in common: they could either rule or cringe. To the amazement of all the servants, Gervaska got no punishment whatsoever for his insolent retort to Grandfather the day of Pyotr Petrovich's arrival. Arkady Petrovich told him curtly. "You're really a swine, brother," and the reply he received to this was as curt: "I can't stand him, sir." But to Pyotr Petrovich Gervaska came of his own free will; he stood in the door in his customary and unduly familiar pose, slumping his body backward on his disproportionately long legs in the widest of trousers, jutting his left knee forward, and requested to be flogged.

"I'm too hot-tempered and impertinent, sir," he said nonchalantly, flashing his great black eyes.

And Pyotr Petrovich sensing a hint in the words "hot-tempered," turned coward.

"Oh, we've plenty of time, old man! Plenty of time!" And he shouted with feigned sternness, "Leave the room! I can't stand the sight of a bold-faced chap like you!"

Gervaska stood a moment saying nothing. Then he spoke, "It's up to you."

He stood there a little longer, twirling a coarse hair on his upper lip and baring his bluish teeth in a doglike grin, his face empty of all feeling, and walked out. This instance convinced him firmly that the best way to act was to keep his face expressionless and to be as curt as possible in his replies. And as for Pyotr Petrovich, he not only began to avoid conversation with Gervaska, he actually avoided looking into his face.

On the day of the party Gervaska behaved with the same nonchalance and inscrutability. Everyone was run off their feet making preparations for the dinner, giving and taking orders, swearing, bickering, scrubbing floors, cleaning the dark, heavy silver of the icons with chalk that turned blue, kicking the dogs back as they tried to get into the entry, worrying that the jelly wouldn't set, that there wouldn't be enough forks to go round, that the sugar cakes and the pies would be burned. Gervaska alone smirked composedly and said to Kazimir, the drunkard *chef*, who was in a frenzy of excitement:

"Easy now, father deacon, your under-cassock might split."

"Mind you don't get drunk," Pyotr Petrovich said absently to Gervaska, his anxious mind on the Marshal.

"Never drank in my life," Gervaska threw back as to an equal. "It's no fun."

And afterward, with the guests there, Pyotr Petrovich shouted for all to hear, trying to ingratiate himself with Gervaska.

"Gervasy! Don't disappear, for heaven's sake. We're lost without you."

While Gervaska called back in the most polite and dignified voice:

"Don't worry, sir. I'm at your service."

He served as never before. He fully justified the words Pyotr Petrovich said to his guests in Gervaska's presence:

"You'd never believe how impertinent that huge chap is! But he's really got genius! Hands of gold!"

Could he ever have thought that he was adding the very drop that would overfill the cup? Grandfather heard his words. He started tugging at the neck of his coat and suddenly he cried to the Marshal at the other end of the table:

"Your Excellency! Lend me a helping hand! I appeal to you as to a father, and lodge a complaint against this servant of mine! This one here, this one—Gervasy Afanasyevich Kulikov! He flouts me at every turn! He—"

They did not let him finish, they comforted and pacified him. Grandfather's agitation reduced him to tears, but they all took to consoling him with such vigor and deference, which was a farce of course, that he succumbed and felt childishly happy again. Gervaska stood rigidly by the wall without looking up, turning his head away. Grandfather could see that the giant's head was too small, that it would have been smaller still if his hair had been cropped, that the back of his head was markedly sharp and his hair particularly thick on the nape—coarse hair, crudely trimmed, jutting out over his thin neck. Gervaska's face was peeling in spots from sunburn and from exposure to the wind when out shooting, and the spots showed pale mauve. And Grandfather darted frightened and uneasy glances at Gervaska, but he nevertheless went on shouting gleefully to the guests:

"All right, I'll forgive him, but only on one condition, my dear friends, that you will stay with me for at least three days. I positively refuse to let you go. I beg you particularly, do not leave me now that evening is nigh! When dusk falls I'm not myself at all: it's so melancholy, so sinister! Clouds are gathering in the sky now; they say two of Bonaparte's Frenchmen were caught in Troshin Wood again. . . . I'm sure to die at night, mark my words. Martin Zadeka, the book of dreams, says so. . . ."

But he died early in the morning.

He had his way after all: "to please him" a number of people stayed for the night. They drank tea all evening long, there was any amount of jam of so many different kinds that they could come up and taste one sort, come up again and taste another; and then more tables were laid, great clusters of spermaceti candles were lit. They were reflected in all the mirrors and lent the golden brilliance of a church to the rooms which swam in expensive, aromatic smoke, and came to life with noise and conversation. But to Grandfather the most important thing was that many of the guests were staying overnight. And therefore it did not only mean another pleasant day ahead but also a great deal of fuss and worry: why, if it had not been for him, for Pyotr Kirillich, the party would never have been such a success, the dinner so sumptuous and gay.

"Yes, yes," Grandfather was thinking excitedly that night as he stood in his bedroom with his coat off in front of the *prie-dieu* with thin wax candles burning on it, and gazed at St. Mercury's dark visage. "Yes, yes, evil shall slay the wicked. Let not the sun go down upon your wrath. . . ."

But then he remembered it was something quite different he wanted to think about; hunching his shoulders and whispering the fiftieth Psalm, he walked across the room and back, trimmed the pastille smoldering on his bedside table, picked up his psalter and, opening it, once again raised his eyes to the decapitated saint with a blissful sigh. And, suddenly, he came upon the thought that was escaping him and he beamed with a smile:

"Yes, that's it, that's it: if I had him I'd kill him, if I hadn't I'd buy him."

He hardly slept that night, worrying lest he should oversleep and fail to give the necessary orders. And early next morning, while the rooms, as yet untidied and unaired, stood hushed in the silence which is peculiar only to the morning after a party, he tiptoed cautiously in his bare feet into the drawing room, anxiously picked up some pieces of chalk lying on the floor beside the green card table, and gasped weakly in delight as he saw the garden through the glass doors: the clear brilliance of the cold azure skies, the silver of the morning frost covering the terrace and the balustrade, the brown foliage in the bare shrubs beyond. He opened the door and sniffed: the shrubs still had the bitter, fermenting smell of autumnal decay, but this smell was swallowed up in the wintry crispness. And everything was motionless, stilled and almost solemn. The sun, peeping from behind the village, lit up the tops of the half-bare birches lining the picturesque walk, and those white and gold tree tops, strewn with thin little golden leaves, transparent against the blue of the sky, had a lovely, joyous and elusively lilac tint. A dog ran past in the cold shadow of the terrace, and the grass, scorched by the frost as though it were sprinkled with salt, crunched underfoot. This sound was reminiscent of winter, and Grandfather, twitching his shoulders in pleasurable anticipation, turned back into the drawing room and, panting, started moving the heavy furniture, which rumbled when pushed about, and threw occasional glances at the sky reflected in the mirror. Suddenly Gervaska walked in quietly and quickly, without his coat, fuddled with sleep and "mad like hell," as he himself described it afterward.

He came in and shouted sternly in a loud hiss:

"Stop it, you! Why do you poke your nose into other people's business?"

Grandfather raised his excited face and whispered with the same kindliness he had been feeling all the previous evening and all night:

"Look what you're like, Gervasy! I forgave you last night, but instead of being grateful to your master, you—"

"I'm fed to the teeth with your sniveling," Gervaska cut him short. "Let go of that table!"

Grandfather threw a frightened look at the back of Gervaska's head that seemed to jut more than ever above the thin neck sticking out of the white shirt, but he flared up and stood between Gervaska and the card table which he was going to drag in a corner.

"*You* let go!" he shouted after a moment's thought, but his voice was not loud. "It's you who should give in to the master. You'll drive me too far: I'll stick a knife in your ribs."

"You will," Gervaska said angrily, flashing his teeth—and struck Grandfather hard across the chest.

Grandfather slipped on the polished oak floor, threw up his hands and as he fell struck his temple against the sharp corner of the table.

When Gervaska saw the blood, the senselessly slanting eyes and the gaping mouth, he tore from Grandfather's still warm neck the sacred golden plaque and the amulet on its grimy string. Looking over his shoulder, he pulled Grandfather's wedding ring off his little finger, too. Then he left the drawing room soundlessly and swiftly, and vanished into thin air.

The only person at Sukhodol who ever saw him again was Natalia.

VII

While she was at Soshki, two other major events took place at Sukhodol: Pyotr Petrovich got married and the brothers went to fight in the Crimean War.

She only came back after two years' exile: they had forgotten about her. And when she did come back, she did not recognize Sukhodol, just as Sukhodol did not recognize her.

That summer evening, when the cart that had been sent from the manor house to fetch her came squeaking up to the cottage and Natalia appeared in the door, Yevsei Bodulya cried in surprise:

"Can it be you, Natalia?"

"Who do you think it is?" Natalia replied with a barely perceptible smile.

Yevsei shook his head:

"You've grown mighty uncomely, you know."

But she only looked different, that was all. She was no longer the crop-haired, round-faced, bright-eyed girl; she was a young woman, lean, and slender, not tall, serene, reserved and gentle. She had on a Ukrainian checked wool skirt, and an embroidered blouse, and though her kerchief was dark, she wore it the way we do. She was somewhat sunburned and her face was sprinkled with little freckles the color of millet. But to Yevsei, a true Sukhodolian, the dark kerchief, the sunburn and the freckles looked ugly of course.

On the way to Sukhodol Yevsei asked:

"Well, lass, you're old enough to marry now. I suppose you want to get married, eh?"

She only shook her head and said:

"No, Uncle Yevsei, I'll never marry."

"What's come over you?" In his amazement Yevsei even took his pipe out of his mouth.

And unhurriedly she explained: marriage wasn't everyone's lot. They'd give her into Miss Tonya's keeping, probably, but since Miss Tonya had dedicated herself to God, that meant she wouldn't let Natalia marry either; and then she'd had many a dream that made it obvious enough. . . .

"What kind of dreams?" Yevsei asked.

"It wasn't anything really," she said. "Gervaska scared me to death that time he told me the news; I began to brood on it, so I had those dreams."

"Did he really stay and eat with you, Gervaska I mean?"

Natalia thought a little.

"Yes, he did. He came and said, 'The master sent me to you on a very important matter, but let me have something to eat first.' We set out the meal on the table thinking no ill of him. When he finished eating, he walked out of the cottage and beckoned me to follow. I ran out after him, and behind the cottage he told me everything and was off."

"But why didn't you call the people?"

"Not me. He had threatened to kill me if I did. He said I wasn't to tell before nightfall. And to them he said, 'I'll go and sleep under the shed.' "

All the servants at Sukhodol were very curious to see her when she got back; her old friends and the housemaids pestered her with questions. She answered them shortly, almost as though she gloried in the part she had taken upon herself to play.

"All was well," she repeated. And once she said in the tones of an old pilgrim woman, "God has many mercies. All was well."

And quietly, without delay, she took up her ordinary, humdrum duties about the house, as if she were not the least surprised that Grandfather was no more, that the young masters had gone to the war, that Miss Tonya was "touched" and wandered through the room imitating Grandfather, that Sukhodol was ruled by a new and utterly strange mistress—short, fat, very lively and pregnant.

The mistress called out imperiously from the dining hall:

"Tell her to come here . . . what's her name . . . Natalia."

And Natalia walked in swiftly and noiselessly, crossed herself, bowed to the icons in the corner, then to the mistress and miss, and stood still, waiting to be questioned and given orders. It was only the mistress, of course, who questioned her. Miss Tonya, who had grown very tall, thin and sharp-nosed, her unbelievably black eyes staring with a dull fixedness, did not say a word. It was the mistress who appointed her to Miss Tonya. Natalia bowed and said simply: "Yes, ma'am."

Miss Tonya, her gaze as fixedly indifferent, pounced on her that same evening and, squinting her eyes in a frenzy, tore at Natalia's hair with cruel delight because she had clumsily tugged at her stocking when helping her to undress. Natalia burst into childish tears but said nothing. Going into the maids' room, she sat down on the window seat, and, as she picked out her broken hairs, she actually smiled through the tears that hung on her eyelashes.

"My, she's fierce," she said. "I'm going to have a hard time."

Miss Tonya, awakening next morning, lay in bed for a long time, while Natalia stood by the door with lowered head, and cast sidelong glances at her pale face.

"Well, what did you dream about?" Miss Tonya asked with such apathy as if someone else were doing the talking for her.

Natalia replied, "Nothing, I think."

Whereupon Miss Tonya, as suddenly as the night before, jumped out of bed and in a savage fury hurled her cup of tea at Natalia, and then, falling across her bed, she started sobbing bitterly and screaming. Natalia dodged the cup, and soon she learned to duck with extraordinary nimbleness. When the stupid maids said, "Nothing, miss," in answer to Miss Tonya's question about their dreams the night before, she would sometimes shout at them, "Well, make up some lie then!" But since Natalia was not good at lying, she was obliged to train herself in the art of ducking, instead.

A doctor was brought to see Miss Tonya at last. He prescribed many different tablets and drops. Fearing that they wanted to poison her, Miss Tonya made Natalia try out the medicines first, and, submissively, she tasted them all, one after the other. Shortly after her return she learned that Miss Tonya had been waiting for her "like for a ray of sunshine"; it was, in fact, Miss Tonya who had thought of her, and had been straining her eyes to see if the cart was coming from Soshki, passionately assuring everyone that she would be perfectly well the minute Natalia came back. Natalia did come back—and was met with utter indifference. Could it be that Miss Tonya's tears were caused by her disappointment in Natalia? The girl felt a pang when this occurred to her one day. She went out into the passage, sat down on a trunk and cried again.

"Well, do you feel better for the medicine?" Miss Tonya asked when she came back into the room with her eyes swollen from weeping.

"Yes, Miss," Natalia whispered, though her heart beat faintly and her head spun from all the medicines, and, coming up to her, she kissed her mistress's hand with feeling.

And for a long time to come she went about with downcast

eyes, not daring to raise them to Miss Tonya, moved with pity for her.

"Oh, you Ukrainian snake, you!" Soloshka, one of the housemaids, once snapped at her. She, more than the others, had been striving to become Natalia's bosom friend and confidante of her thoughts and secrets, but all her advances had invariably met with curt, plain answers, which offered none of the delights of intimate friendship.

Natalia smiled sadly.

"Oh, well," she said pensively. "That's right too. You do get to be like the people you're with. Sometimes, you know, I miss my Ukrainians more than I do my own father and mother. . . ."

Her new surroundings had been quite lost on her when she had first arrived at Soshki. They got there early in the morning and the only thing that seemed strange to her then was that the cottage was very long and white, seen from afar amid the plains, that the woman who was lighting the stove greeted her pleasantly and the man did not stop to listen to Yevsei's gossip. Yevsei prattled on without a pause —of his masters, of Demyan, of the hot journey, of what he ate in town, of Pyotr Petrovich and, of course, of the theft of the mirror; while the Ukrainian, Shary by name but known as "badger" at Sukhodol, only shook his head and, when Yevsei had finished, glanced at him absently and with a very cheerful glint in his eye sang under his breath with a twang: "Whirl on, whirl on, snowstorm. . . ." Little by little Natalia came back to normal and began to marvel at Soshki, finding in it more and more charm and difference from Sukhodol. The cottage alone was worth seeing, with its snow-white walls, its smooth roof evenly thatched with reeds, and the way the interior was decorated—how rich it seemed in comparison to the slovenly wretchedness of the Sukhodol huts. Look at the sumptuous tinseled icons hanging in the corner, the lovely paper flowers wreathed round them, and the bright embroidered towels hanging above. And look at the flowered tablecloth. The rows of blue glazed pots and bowls on the shelves beside the stove. But the Ukrainian couple were the most amazing of all.

Natalia did not quite understand what was so amazing about them, but she was conscious of it all the time. Never before had she seen anyone as neat, unruffled and sound as Shary. He was not tall. He had a wedge-shaped head covered with cropped hair thickly threaded with silver; he did not wear a beard, but his mustache, scanty like a Tatar's, was also silver and his face and neck were burned black by the sun and lined with deep wrinkles, which were neat too, well defined and necessary for some reason. His gait was clumsy, for the top boots he wore over his bleached linen trousers were too heavy; the shirt he tucked into the trousers was of the same material, hanging loose under the arm, its collar turned down. He slouched a bit when he walked. But neither this, nor his wrinkles and gray hair aged him. There was none of our weariness or drowsiness in his face, and his somewhat small eyes had a keen look in them, with a hint of mockery. He reminded Natalia of the old Serbian who had once come to Sukhodol with a little boy who played a fiddle.

Marina, the Ukrainian woman, had been nicknamed "pike" by the Sukhodolians. This woman of fifty was tall and slender. A yellowish tan lay evenly on the fine skin—not a Sukhodolian skin—of her high-cheekboned face which if somewhat coarse was almost beautiful for its straight lines and the bright look in her stern eyes; these were either agate or amber-gray, changing color like a cat's. A kerchief of black and gold with red spots was wound round her head in a tall turban; a short black skirt, against which her white blouse looked even whiter, hung closely around her hips and legs. She wore hobnailed shoes on her bare feet, her calves were slim though rounded and the sunburn gave them a quality of brown polished wood. And when she sang at her work, her eyebrows drawn together, in a strong deep voice, the song about the infidels storming Pochayev

The evening glow
Went down below
Pochayev's walls . . .

and of the Mother of God herself defending the holy monastery, her voice rang with such melancholy and despair but, at the same time, with such majesty, power and menace, that Natalia could not tear her eyes away from her, looking on in awe-struck fascination.

They had no children, and Natalia was an orphan. Had she been staying with some Sukhodolian couple, they would have called her "daughter dear" at times and "dirty thief" at others, they would have fondled her one day and thrown it in her face the next. The Ukrainians, however, treated her almost coldly but fairly; they were neither inquisitive nor talkative. In the autumn a number of girls and women were brought from Kaluga, hired for the mowing and threshing, but Natalia shunned the company of these women dressed in bright, flowered *sarafans:* they were said to be dissolute and sick with foul diseases; they were large-breasted, brazen and insolent, swore lustily and dirtily, and simply scattered bawdy little couplets. They sat their horses like men and galloped them madly. Natalia's sorrow would have been dispelled in familiar surroundings, in confidences, tears and songs. But who was there for her to confide in or to sing songs with? These harsh-voiced women would start one of their songs but then the rest of them would join in too readily and raucously, with whooping and whistling. Shary sang nothing but his humorous dancing ditties. And as for Marina, she was stern, proud and pensively gloomy when she sang, even if it was a love song.

Willows I planted
Close to the water,
Rustling above,

she would recite in a plaintive, despondent voice, and pitching her voice low, she would add firmly and hopelessly:

Gone is my darling,
Gone now forever
Gone is my love. . . .

And in solitude Natalia slowly drank to the dregs her first cup of the bittersweet poison of unrequited love. She went through the agony of shame and jealousy, and the frightening and sweet dreams which often came to her at night, vain fancies and hopes which tormented her sorely through the silent days she lived in the steppe. Often the scorching pain in her heart would give way to tenderness, passion and despair, to submissiveness, and the desire for the most humble, insignificant existence close to *him,* for love that would forever be hidden from the whole world, love that expected nothing and demanded nothing. News and messages coming from Sukhodol would sober her for a while. But there was no news for a long time, she lost the sense of the humdrum side of Sukhodol life, and it began to appear so beautiful to her, her yearning for it was so strong, that she could hardly endure her loneliness and sorrow. . . . Then suddenly Gervaska came. He hurled all the news of Sukhodol at her with hasty brusqueness, and in half an hour told what another would not have managed to tell in a day. He told everything, including the fatal "shove" he had given Grandfather. He ended resolutely:

"Good-bye forever now."

And, with his enormous eyes burning through the dumfounded girl, he called back as he got to the road:

"It's time you, too, had your foolishness knocked out of you. He's getting married any day now, so even as a mistress you'd be no use to him. . . . Get some sense back."

And she did. She suffered this horrible news, pulled herself together and got her senses back.

After this her days dragged on bleakly and dully. They were like those pilgrim women who trailed on and on past the farm down the highroad and, stopping for a rest, held long conversations with her, teaching her to be patient and to rest her hopes in the Heavenly Father, whose name was pronounced with a dull plaintiveness, and above all the rule: not to think at all.

"Whether we think or not, it won't be the way we want it," the women would say, stopping to retie their bast shoes, wrinkling their wan faces and gazing ruefully into the vastness of the steppe. "The Lord has many mercies. . . . Pick us a few onions on the sly, there's a good girl. . . ."

There were others, of course, who put the fear of God into her, frightening her with her sinfulness, threatening her with hell-fire, and presaging calamities and horrors she had never known. And then she had two frightful dreams, almost one after the other. Her mind was constantly on Sukhodol—it was difficult not to think of it at first. She thought of Miss Tonya, of Grandfather, of her future, wondering whether she would get married and if so when and to whom. Her thoughts merged into a dream so imperceptibly one night that she saw with perfect clarity a sultry, dusty and alarmingly windy evening, and herself running with a couple of pails to fetch some water from the pond, when suddenly on the dry and loamy slope she saw a hideous, big-headed old dwarf in battered top boots, hatless, with his red straggly hair tousled in the wind and a fiery-red unbelted shirt streaming behind him. "Oh dear, is there a fire?" she screamed, alarmed and frightened. And the dwarf screamed too, his voice muffled by the hot wind: "Ruin, ruin, all is lost! A storm of untold horror is nigh! It comes, it comes. Think not of marriage!" Her other dream was even more horrible. She was standing in a hot, empty cottage at midday, with someone outside jamming the door tight, and was waiting breathlessly for she knew not what—and suddenly a huge gray goat leaped out from behind the stove, reared and made straight for her, obscenely excited, with eyes burning like coals, gleefully mad and beseeching. "I am your mate!" he shouted in a human voice, trotting toward her quickly and clumsily, his small rear hoofs clop-clopping rapidly, and with all his might he brought his front ones down on her breast. . . .

She jumped down from her bed in the passage, jolted awake, the hammering of her heart, her terror of the darkness and the thought that she had no one to run to, almost killing her.

"Oh, Jesus! Holy Mother of God! Oh, Holy Saints!" she whispered in a quick patter.

But because all the saints she could picture were dark brown and decapitated like St. Mercury, her terror increased.

And when she started thinking these dreams over, it occurred to her that her youth was past, that her fate was already sealed (no wonder something extraordinary, the love for the master, had fallen to her lot), that more trials were awaiting her, that she should try and imitate the Ukrainians' reserve and the pilgrim women's humility and simplicity. And since the Sukhodolians are fond of playing a part, of convincing themselves in the inevitability of something which they themselves have invented, so Natalia, too, chose a part to play.

VIII

Her knees gave way from happiness when, running out on to the porch on the eve of St. Peter's Day, she realized that Bodulya was there to fetch her, when she saw the dusty, shabby Sukhodol cart, when she saw Bodulya, a ragged cap on his tousled head, his matted beard bleached in the sun, and his face, tired and excited, old before its time and ugly, even strange with its mean and incongruous features, when she saw the old dog, shaggy, too, looking not only like Bodulya but like all of Sukhodol, its back a dingy gray, while its chest and the thick hair on its neck looked dark as though the black smoke of a chimneyless hut still clung to it. But Natalia soon took herself in hand. On the way home Bodulya rambled on in a desultory fashion about the Crimean War, happy about it one minute, complaining of it the next, while Natalia observed reasonably:

"Oh well, it seems we've got to give them a setback, the French that is."

She had an uncanny feeling all the long way to Sukhodol, looking with new eyes at things old and familiar, living her former self over again as she neared her old home, noticing changes, recognizing people. A two-year-old colt was running about the fallow land overgrown with cowslips, where the road forked off to Sukhodol. A youngster, holding the rope bridle down with his bare foot, was clutching at the colt's neck and trying to swing his other leg over its back, but the colt wouldn't let him—it jumped about and shook him off. And Natalia felt a wave of happy excitement on recognizing the youngster as Foma Pantyukhin. Next she saw the hundred-year-old Nazarushka, who no longer drove like a man but now sat in his empty cart like a woman—with his legs stretched out straight before him, his shoulders raised high, stiffly and weakly, his pitifully sad eyes faded, and his body so emaciated it was nothing but skin and bones dressed in a long, shabby shirt that had become a dusky blue, like the ashes on the floor of the stove where he was wont to lie. And her heart flinched again as she remembered how some three years before Arkady Petrovich, the most kindhearted and carefree man of all, had wanted to flog this same Nazarushka, who had been caught red-handed with a radish tail in the vegetable garden, and who stood weeping, dead with fright, among the servants who surrounded him and shouted through guffaws of laughter:

"Nothing doing, Grandad, no whimpering now! You'll have to take your trousers down, it seems! You can't get out of it!"

But how her heart began to throb when she saw the common, the row of cottages and the manor house, the garden, the tall roof, the rear walls of the servants' quarters, the barns and stables. Yellow rye fields, thickly dotted with cornflowers, came up close to the walls, to the tall grass and the thistles. Someone's calf, white with brown spots, stood deep in the oats, chewing away at the tassels. Everything was peaceful, simple and ordinary—all that was extraordinary and alarming remained in her mind alone, and her mind grew utterly dazed when the cart rolled briskly down the wide courtyard spotted with sleeping white borzois as a graveyard is spotted with tombstones, when, after an absence of two years, she walked into the cool house which smelled so dearly of wax candles and lime blossom, the pantry, Arkady Petrovich's Cossack saddle lying on a bench in the entry hall, the now empty quail cages at the window—and glanced timidly at St. Mercury who had been brought from Grandfather's rooms to the corner of the hall. . . .

The sun, streaming in from the garden through the little windows, lit up the gloomy hall as merrily as ever. A chicken, which had somehow got into the house, was clucking disconsolately as it wandered about the drawing room. Lime blossom, drying on the hot, bright window sills, sent up its fragrance. . . . It seemed to her that all the old things she was seeing about her had grown younger, and this you usually feel in a house where someone had just died. In everything, in everything, and particularly in the fragrance of the lime blossom, she felt a particle of her own self, her childhood, her adolescence, her first love. And she felt sorry for those who had grown up, died and changed—sorry for herself and Miss Tonya. Friends of her own age had grown up too. Many of the old men and women, whose heads used to shake with old age and who sometimes used to peep out dully at the world from behind the doors of the servants' rooms, had forever disappeared from this world. Darya Ustinovna was gone. Gone was Grandfather, who had been so childishly afraid of death, thinking that death would overpower him gradually, preparing him for the hour of doom, but which had mowed him down with its scythe so unexpectedly and swiftly. And it was hard to believe he was no more, that it was really his body that lay decaying under the mound of earth close to the church in the village of Cherkizovo. It was hard to believe that this black, gaunt, sharp-nosed woman, listless one moment, frenzied the next, nervously talkative and at times outspoken with her as with an equal, or suddenly tearing at her hair—was Miss Tonya. It was hard to understand why the house was being managed by some Klavdia Markovna, a short, shrewish little woman with a black mustache. . . . One day Natalia threw a timid look into her bedroom, and there she saw the fatal mirror framed in silver. A sweet pain wrung her heart and all her old terrors, joys, tenderness, anticipation of shame and bliss, and the smell of dewy burdocks in the twilight, overwhelmed her. . . . But all her feelings, all her thoughts she kept in secret and tried to suppress. Very, very ancient Sukhodol blood coursed through her veins. Too flat was the bread she had eaten, grown on the clayey soil that surrounded Sukhodol. Too flat was the water she had drunk from the pools which her forefathers had dug in the bed of the dried-up little river. She had no fear of the usual, exhausting workdays; she dreaded the unusual. She had no fear of death, but dreams, the darkness of night, storms, thunder and fire set her trembling with fright. And, as if it were a child under her heart, she carried the vague premonition of some imminent disaster. . . .

This premonition aged her. But then she also kept telling herself that her youth was past and she sought proof of this in everything. And before she had been back a year, that youthful feeling with which she had crossed the threshold of Sukhodol had vanished without a trace.

Klavdia Markovna was delivered of a boy. Fedosya, the poultry woman, was promoted to the post of nurse, and though a young woman, she put on the dark garb of old age, grew humble and pious. The young Khrushchov, blowing bubbles with his mouth, toppling over, helplessly overbalanced by the weight of his own head, and howling angrily, could hardly focus his milky, senseless eyes when he was already being called the young master, while from the nursery came the age-old muttered admonitions: "There he comes, there he comes, the old man with the bag. . . . Go away, old man, go away! Keep away from us, we won't let you take the young master, he won't cry, he's a good boy. . . ."

And Natalia copied Fedosya, considering herself a nurse too, nurse and companion to the sick young lady. Olga Kirillovna died that winter, and Natalia got permission to accompany the old women, who were ending their days in the servants' rooms, to attend the funeral. She ate frumenty there which nauseated her with its insipid and sickly sweet taste, and on returning to Sukhodol she gave a sentimental account of the old mistress "lying there in death as if she were alive," although even the old women had not ventured to look at the coffin holding that monstrous body.

And in the spring a wizard was brought to see Miss Tonya from the village of Chermashnoye, the famous Klim Yerokhin, prosperous small holder, a dignified and handsome man, with a large gray beard and curly gray hair parted in the middle, a very competent farmer, whose conversation was very reasonable and straightforward as a rule, until he transformed himself into a sorcerer at the sickbed. The clothes he wore were exceptionally strong and neat—a coat of coarse woolen cloth of steel gray; a red sash and top boots. His small eyes were sly and keen; they piously sought the icons when he walked into the house, stooping his well-made body a little, and started his businesslike talk. To begin with he spoke of the harvest, of rains and drought, after that he took a long time over his tea, drinking it very tidily, then he crossed himself again, and only after all this did he ask about the patient, changing his tone in a moment.

"Twilight . . . night is falling . . . the time has come," he would begin mysteriously.

Miss Tonya, shaking with fever, ready to collapse on the floor and writhe in convulsions, sat in her twilit bedroom and waited for Klim to appear at her door. Natalia, too, standing by her side, was numbed with horror from head to toe. The whole house grew still—even the mistress packed her room full of servant girls and talked to them in whispers. No one dared to put on a single light, no one dared raise a voice. Soloshka, the gay and carefree girl who stood on guard in the corridor in case she was wanted to carry out Klim's orders, felt everything grow dim before her eyes and her heart hammer in her throat: he walked past her, unwrapping a handkerchief with some magic bones in it. And then the funereal silence was rent by his loud, weird voice coming from the bedroom:

"Arise, my daughter!"

Then he thrust his gray head out of the door and uttered lifelessly: "The board."

And Miss Tonya, as cold as a corpse, her eyes bulging from terror, was stood on the board which lay on the floor. It was so dark by then that Natalia could hardly make out Klim's face. And suddenly he began to intone in a disembodied, uncanny sort of voice:

"Filat is coming. . . . Windows he'll open. . . . Doors he'll throw wide. . . . He'll cry and say: woe, woe!"

"Woe, woe!" he cried with sudden force and stern authority: "Begone, woe, into the dark forests below, that's where you belong, woe! Across the oceans and the seas," his muttering was rapid, gruff and ominous now, "the stormy Buyan Island rears, and on it lies a bitch obese, its monstrous back a thick gray fleece. . . ."

And Natalia felt there could never be words more hideous than these, which instantly whisked her soul away to the ends of some wild, fabulous and pristinely coarse world. There was no disbelieving the power of these words, just as Klim himself could not disbelieve it. With them he sometimes worked miracles over those sick in spirit—that same Klim who, his sorcery over, sat in the hall, talking so simply and modestly, wiping the sweat off his brow with his handkerchief and settling down to tea again.

"Well, two more nights left now. . . . God willing, perhaps she'll feel a little easier. . . . Have you sown any buckwheat this year, ma'am? The buckwheat's good this year, they say. Mighty good!"

The masters were expected back from the Crimea that

a thundercloud appearing behind the manor house, the moment the first whiff of wind whirled across the common and the first distant roll of thunder rumbled, the women would rush indoors to bring out their dark wooden icons and get bowls of milk ready, which, as everyone knows, is the quickest way to appease fire. And from the manor house scissors would come flying into the nettles, and the sacred and frightening towel would be taken out; curtains would be drawn across the windows and wax candles lighted with shaking hands. . . . Even the mistress was affected by the panic, perhaps sincerely or perhaps feigning sincerity. In the old days she used to say that a thunderstorm was a "natural phenomenon." Nowadays she, too, crossed herself, closed her eyes tight, and gasped at every flash of lightning, and in order to whet her own fear and that of the others she kept talking of some extraordinary thunderstorm that broke out in Tirol in 1771 and killed one hundred and eleven people outright. And her listeners capped her story and hastened to tell their own: of the willow tree on the highroad burned to the ground by lightning, of a woman struck down dead by a thunderbolt in Cherkizovo, of a troika hit so hard that all the three horses fell to their knees. . . . And finally a certain Yushka, an "erring monk" as he called himself, joined them in their morbid devotions.

IX

Yushka was a peasant by birth. But he had never done a stroke of work in his life, and he lived the life of a stray, paying for the temporary hospitality offered him with stories of his complete idleness and of his "misbehavior."

"I'm a peasant, brother, but I'm smart and I look like a hunchback," he would say, "so why should I work?"

And, indeed, he did look like a hunchback. His eyes were mocking and wise, his face hairless. He kept his shoulders raised high on account of his rickety chest; he bit his nails and kept brushing back his long copper-colored hair with fingers that were slim and strong. He thought it "indecent and boring" to till the land, and so went off to the Kiev Monastery, "matured" there and was eventually banished for his "misbehavior." And then, realizing that acting the part of a holy pilgrim, a man saving his soul, was too old a trick and might prove unprofitable, he tried another ruse: without taking off his cassock, he began to flaunt and brag about his idleness and lecherousness, to smoke and to drink as much as he could hold (he never got drunk), to make a mock of the monastery and explain with the aid of obscene gestures and movements exactly why he had been banished.

"Of course," he told the men with a wink, "of course, they threw me out for that right away. And so I turned back home to Russia. . . . I'd get along, I thought."

And get along he did. Russia gave the bawdy sinner as hearty a welcome as she gave those who were saving their immortal souls. She fed him, sheltered him at night and listened to him enraptured.

"And so you swore you'd never work, did you?" the men asked him, their eyes glinting with the expectation of thrilling confidences.

"The devil couldn't make me work now," Yushka replied. "I'm spoiled, brother. I've got more rut in me than a monastery goat. Those girls now—I have no use for married women at all—they're scared to death of me, but they love me. And why shouldn't they? I'm not bad myself—my feathers aren't pretty, but I've got what it takes."

When he arrived at Sukhodol, being a man of experience, he walked straight into the house, into the hall. There Natalia sat on a bench, humming: "I swept and swept the floor that day, and found a piece of sugar. . . ." When she saw him she started up, terrified.

"Who are you?" she cried.

"A man," Yushka replied, taking her in from head to toe in one rapid glance. "Tell the mistress."

"Who's that?" the mistress, too, cried from the drawing room.

But Yushka calmed her fears in a moment. He told her he was a monk and not an escaped soldier, as she must have supposed, and was on his way back home. He asked her to search him and then to permit him to spend the night there and rest a little. He so astonished the mistress with his outspokenness that the very next day he found he could move into the servants' quarters and become quite one of the family. Thunderstorms followed one after another, but he was indefatigable in amusing his hostesses with his stories. He thought of boarding up the dormer windows to protect the roof from lightning; he would dash out to the porch at the most frightening thunderclaps to show how little danger there was in them, and he helped the maids to light the samovars. The maids frowned upon him, conscious of his quick, lecherous looks on their bodies, but they laughed at his jokes, while Natalia, whom he had accosted in the dark corridor several times whispering rapidly: "I've fallen in love with you!" dared not raise her eyes to his. He was repulsive to her, with the smell of *makhorka* drenching the whole of his cassock, and frightening, so frightening. . . .

She knew quite definitely what would happen. She slept alone in the corridor close to her mistress's bedroom door, and Yushka had already hissed at her: "I'll come. I'll come even if you kill me for it. And if you start yelling, I'll burn the place to the ground." But what sapped her strength more than anything else was the realization that something "inevitable" was happening, that the horrible dream she had at Soshki about the goat was to come true shortly, that evidently it was preordained that she should perish together with Miss Tonya. It was clear to everyone now: the devil himself dwelled in the house at night. Everyone understood what it was, apart from the thunderstorms and the fires, that was driving Miss Tonya crazy, what made her moan voluptuously and wildly in her sleep, and then jump up with screams so terrifying that they drowned the most deafening of thunderclaps.

"The snake of Eden, of Jerusalem is strangling me!" she would shriek. And who could that snake be if not the devil, the gray goat that comes into the rooms of girls and women in the night? And was there anything more frightening in the world than his coming in the darkness, on rainy nights when thunder rumbled in incessant rolls and lightning flashed across the black icons? The passion, the lust with which he whispered to Natalia was inhuman too: then how could she struggle against it? Brooding on the fatal hour that would inevitably strike, sitting on her horsecloth on the floor in the corridor, peering into the darkness with beating heart, listening to the slightest rustle or creak of a board in the slumbering house, she already felt the first attacks of that grave illness which was to possess her for a long time to come: the sole of one of her feet would suddenly begin to itch, she'd feel a sharp, piercing cramp in it twisting and turning her toes inward, this spasm would run up her legs contorting her nerves cruelly and sweetly, right up to her throat, and in a moment she would want to shriek more madly and with more ecstasy and agony than Miss Tonya ever shrieked.

And the inevitable happened. Yushka came—on that ghastly night toward the end of the summer, on the eve of St. Elijah's, the ancient flame-thrower's day. There was no thunder that night, nor was there any sleep for Natalia. She fell into a doze and sudddenly she was startled awake as if she had been jolted. It was the dead hour of the night—she knew it by her madly beating heart. She jumped up, looked down one end of the corridor, down the other, and wherever she looked she saw the sky, silent and full of fire and mystery, flaring up, blazing and quivering with blinding flashes of gold and pale blue. Minute by minute the corridor grew light as day. She started running—and froze to the spot: the aspen logs, long since stacked in the yard, looked blindingly white in the flashes. She tried the dining hall: one of the windows was open, she could hear the steady swish of the trees; it was darker there, but the flash of lightning beyond the windows was the brighter for it. Darkness would envelop everything for a moment and instantly it would be all aquiver again, lightning would flash here and there, and the garden, with all its lacy tree tops, its ghastly pale green birches and poplars, would flicker, swell and tremble against the vast heavens of gold and pale violet.

"Across the oceans and the seas," she started whispering as she rushed back, aware that she was bringing on her ruin by repeating this devilish incantation, "and on it lies—" And just as she pronounced these primitively menacing words, she looked back and saw Yushka, his shoulders raised high, not two paces away from her. Lightning flashed across his face—pale with black hollows for eyes. He pounced on her soundlessly, grasped her with his long arms and, crushing her, brought her down to her knees in a moment, then on her back, on to the cold floor. . . .

Yushka came to her the following night too. He kept coming on many successive nights and she, faint with horror and disgust, meekly surrendered to him. It never even occurred to her to resist him or to seek protection with her mistress or the other servants, just as it never occurred to Miss Tonya to dare resist the devil who took his pleasure with her at night, or Grandmother herself, the imperious beauty who, they said, had not dared resist her serf Tkach, a desperate scoundrel and thief, eventually sent into exile in Siberia. . . . At last Yushka grew tired of Natalia, tired of Sukhodol, and he vanished as suddenly as he had appeared.

A month later she felt she was with child. And in September, on the day following the return of the young masters from the war, the manor house caught fire and blazed long and horribly. Her second dream had come true. It was twilight, rain was pouring down in torrents when the house was struck by lightning, by a golden ball which, according to Soloshka, leaped out of the stove in Grandfather's bedroom and sped bouncing through the rooms. And Natalia, who on seeing the smoke and the flames rushed for all she was worth from the bathhouse where she had been spending her days and nights in tears, used to relate afterward that in the garden she came upon someone dressed in a red coat and tall gold-braided Cossack hat, that he, too, had been running for all he was worth through the dripping shrubs and burdock. . . . Whether she had really seen all this or had only fancied it, Natalia could not tell for certain. All that was known for a fact was that the horror of it released her from her future child.

And that autumn she began to wilt. Her life got into a humdrum groove and never stirred out of it ever again. They took Aunt Tonya to Voronezh to kiss the holy relics of the saint. After that the devil no longer dared to approach her and she calmed down, took up her existence like everyone else —the derangement of her mind and spirit only manifesting itself in the brilliance of her wild eyes, her extreme untidiness and a savage irritability and despondency when the weather was bad. Natalia had accompanied her on this pilgrimage and she, too, had her peace restored to her on that trip where she found a solution to all that had seemed impossible to solve. How she used to tremble at the very thought of meeting Pyotr Petrovich! No matter how she tried to prepare herself for it she could never think of it calmly. And Yushka, her disgrace and ruin! But the very singularity of her ruin, the extraordinary depth of her sufferings, that element of doom in her downfall (for, surely, it had not been inadvertently timed with the horror of the fire!), her pilgrimage to the saint, gave her the right to look calmly and frankly into the eyes of Pyotr Petrovich, to say nothing of everyone else. The damning finger of the Lord had pointed at her and Miss Tonya—was it for them to be afraid of people now? When she returned from Voronezh and walked into the Sukhodol house, she was like a nun, a humble and simple servant to all, light and pure in heart as if she had partaken of the last Holy Sacrament on her deathbed, and she bravely came up to kiss Pyotr Petrovich's hand. And only for a moment, when her lips touched his small, dark hand with the turquoise ring, did her heart tremble youthfully, tenderly, and thrillingly. . . .

Life grew bleak at Sukhodol. There were definite tidings of liberty and this news actually alarmed the servants and the villagers. What would the future bring, they wondered. Would it be worse, perhaps? They were to begin living in a new way, and this was easier said than done. The masters, too, would have to live in a new way, and they had never even learned the old way. Grandfather's death, the war, the comet which had horrified the whole country, then the fire, and the tidings of liberty—all this wrought a swift change in the faces and the hearts of the masters, depriving them of youth and lightheartedness, of their former easily appeased irascibility, replacing it by malice, boredom and a rancorous fractiousness. They started having "differences," as Father put it, and ended by arming themselves with whips for dinner. . . . Need knocked at the door, reminding them of the dire necessity of somehow straightening out their affairs, which had been completely ruined by the Crimean War, the fire and debt. But in estate management the brothers only got in each other's way. One was ridiculously greedy, hard and mistrustful, while the other was ridiculously generous, kind and trusting. They managed to come to an understanding at last and agreed upon a venture that was bound to bring in a great profit. Mortgaging their property they bought about three hundred miserable horses. A certain Gypsy, Ilya Samsonov, helped to collect them from practically all over the district. They planned to feed the horses up during the winter and sell them at a profit in the spring. But, having devoured vast quantities of flour and hay, the horses began to sicken and die for some unknown reason one after the other, and by spring almost all of them were dead.

The discord between the brothers grew stronger. Their quarrels went so far that at times they snatched up knives and guns. And no one knows how it would all have ended if another calamity had not befallen Sukhodol. One winter day, four years after his return from the Crimea, Pyotr Petrovich drove to Lunevo where he had a mistress. He spent two days there, drinking heavily all the time, and he was drunk when he started back home. Snow was deep that winter; two horses were harnessed to the low, wide sledge, covered with a rug. Pyotr Petrovich ordered the off-horse, a spirited young mare, which sank belly-deep into the flaccid snow, to be unharnessed and tied to the rear of the sledge, while he lay down to sleep with his head toward it, so they said. Evening descended, misty and blue. Before he dropped off, Pyotr Petrovich shouted an order to Yevsei Bodulya, whom he was in the habit of taking along with him instead of the coachman Vaska Kazak, who, he feared, might kill him because feeling was running high against him for his maltreatment of the servants. "Get going!" he shouted, and kicked Yevsei in the back. And then, the powerful bay wheeler, already sweating, steaming and gurgling with its spleen, tore off along the difficult snowbound road, toward the misty haze of the desolate fields, into the darkening, gloomy winter night. . . . And at midnight, when everyone was sleeping the sleep of the dead at Sukhodol, someone rapped quickly and alarmingly on the window of the corridor where Natalia slept. She jumped down from her bench and ran out on to the porch in her bare feet. She saw the dim dark silhouettes of the horses and the sledge, and Yevsei standing with a whip in his hands.

"Trouble, there's trouble, lass," he started mumbling hollowly and strangely as though in sleep. "Master's been killed by the horse . . . the off-horse. . . . She ran up, stumbled and kicked him. . . . Crushed his face right in. . . . He's getting cold already. . . . It wasn't me, it wasn't me, I swear to God it wasn't!"

Without a word Natalia went down the porch steps, her bare feet sinking into the snow; she came up to the sledge, fell on her knees, clutched the icy, blood-clotted head to her breast, showered kisses on it and screamed at the top of her voice with a wildly joyous scream, choking with sobs and laughter. . . .

X

Whenever we happened to take a rest from city life in the quiet and destitute remoteness of Sukhodol, Natalia would tell us again and again the story of her wrecked life. And at times her eyes would darken and stare blankly, her voice would change to a stern, clear half-whisper. I kept recalling the crude image of the saint which had hung in the corner of the hall in our old home. Decapitated, the saint came to his people, bearing his dead head in his hands, to prove the truth of his story. . . .

Even those few material traces of the past which we had once found at Sukhodol were no longer there. Our fathers and forefathers had left us neither their portraits, nor their letters, nor even any of their ordinary household things. And whatever there had been, had perished in the fire. There was a chest in the corridor, which had stood there for many years, hung with tatters of the stiff, hairless sealskin that had once bound it almost a hundred years before. This was Grandfather's chest with drawers of speckled birch, filled with singed French dictionaries and prayer books, hopelessly spattered with wax. And then even this chest disappeared. The heavy furniture which had stood in the drawing room and the dining hall got broken and disappeared too. The house was getting old, it was subsiding more and more. All those long years it had weathered since the last events related here, were years of lingering death. . . . And its past became more and more legendary.

The Sukhodolians lived in a world that was remote and sinister, yet it had been a complex world with a semblance of stability and prosperity. Judging by the stagnancy of this life and the Sukhodolians' attachment to it, one might have thought it would never come to an end. But they were compliant, weak and "thin-skinned when it came to punishment," those descendants of the steppe nomads. And we witnessed the nests of the Sukhodolians disappearing swiftly without leaving a trace, just as the little mounds that top the underground channels and burrows of hamsters vanish one after the other when a field is ploughed. And the inhabitants of the Sukhodol nests perished and fled too, and those who somehow managed to survive, ended their days in some manner or other. So what we lived to see was not the Sukhodol world any longer, it was not life but only a memory of it, an existence that was semiwild in its simplicity. Our visits to our home in the steppe became rarer as the years went on. And we grew more and more estranged from it; we felt less and less our connection with the world and the class from which we were descended. Many of our countrymen were, like us, descendants of an illustrious, ancient lineage. The chronicles recorded our names: our ancestors were courtiers and army commanders and "eminent men," the closest associates and even relatives of tsars. And had they been called knights, had we been born in the West, how confidently we would have talked of them, how much longer we would have held on. A scion of the knighthood could not have said that a whole class had almost vanished off the face of the earth in as little as half a century, that so many of us had become degenerate, insane, had committed suicide, become out and out drunkards, had gone to seed, or had simply got lost somewhere. He could not have confessed as I am doing now that we have no clear conception, not even a slightly accurate idea of the life of our great-grandfathers, to say nothing of our earlier ancestors, that with every day we are finding it more difficult to picture things that took place a mere fifty years ago.

The spot where Lunevo had once been has been tilled and sown a long time ago, and so have the lands of many of the other estates as well. Sukhodol still held on by a miracle. But having cut down the last of the birches in the garden and sold practically all the arable land piecemeal, the owner himself, the son of Pyotr Petrovich, abandoned it—to take on the job of a railway guard. And the old inhabitants of Sukhodol —Klavdia Markovna, Aunt Tonya and Natalia—dragged out the last years of their lives in wretchedness. Spring gave way to summer, summer waned into autumn, and then came winter. . . . They lost count of the seasons. They lived in their memories and dreams, in wrangles and worries about their daily bread. In the summer the peasants' rye fields rolled over the acres where once the garden spread, and the manor house, standing amid these fields, was now visible from afar. The shrubs, which were all that remained of the garden, had become such a wild growth that you could hear the call of the quail right by the terrace. But summer was no problem. "It's heavenly in summer," the old women would say. It was the long rainy autumns and the snow-swept winters that were so depressing and tedious at Sukhodol. There was cold and hunger in the empty crumbling house. Blizzards drifted snow over it and icy winds pierced it through. And as for heating, they lighted the stoves very rarely. In the evenings a little tin lamp would shed its frugal light from the room of the old mistress—the only habitable room in the house. The mistress, wearing spectacles, a sheepskin coat and felt boots, would sit and knit a sock, bending close over the lamp. Natalia would doze on the cold stove ledge, while Miss Tonya, who looked like a Siberian *shaman,** sat in her cottage and smoked a pipe. When Aunt Tonya and Klavdia Markovna were not quarreling, the latter would place her lamp on the window sill instead of the table. And then a strange faint half-light would glow from the manor house into Aunt Tonya's icy cottage, crowded with pieces of broken furniture, cluttered with bits of smashed crockery, and obstructed by the piano which had collapsed on its side. This cottage was so ice-clad that the chickens, to whose care Aunt Tonya gave her remaining strength, had frostbitten feet from sleeping on these broken bits and pieces.

But there is no one left at Sukhodol at all now. All those mentioned in these annals, all their neighbors and contemporaries are dead. And sometimes you wonder if indeed they ever really lived.

* *Shaman*—witch-doctor of some Siberian tribes.—*Tr.*

You only feel that they did live in this world when you come to the graveyards, you even sense an eerie closeness to them. But even this requires an effort, you must first sit down and think a while beside one of the family graves, that is, if you can manage to find it. This is a disgraceful admission but it has to be made: we do not know the graves of our grandfather, our grandmother or Pyotr Petrovich. All we know is that they are not far from the altar of the little old church in Cherkizovo. You could never get there in the winter: snowdrifts are waist-deep there, with a few crosses and the tops of bare shrubs and branches sticking out of the snow. In the summer you walk down the hot village street, empty and quiet, tie your horse to the churchyard fence which has a dark-green wall of firs behind it darkening in the sultry heat. When you walk through the gate you see a whole grove of short spreading elms, ash and lime trees beyond the white church with its rusty cupola, and all will be shadow and coolness. You wander for a long time between the shrubs, over mounds and down hollows, covered with thin graveyard grass, you tread on stone slabs which have become spongy with rain, overgrown with black, crumbly moss and almost completely sunken into the ground. . . . You see two or three iron monuments. But whose are they? They have grown such a greenish gold that you can no longer read the inscriptions. Which of these mounds guard the bones of Grandmother, of Grandfather? God alone knows! All *you* know is that they are here somewhere close. And you sit there and think, trying to picture those Khrushchovs whom everyone has forgotten. And the world they lived in seems for a moment infinitely far, and then, suddenly, it seems so close. And then you say to yourself:

"It's not difficult to imagine, not difficult at all. All you've got to remember is that this gilded cross standing lopsidedly against the blue summer sky was the same in their time . . . that the rye ripened then as it does now in those desolate and sultry fields . . . that shade, coolness and shrubs have been here always . . . and a jaded mare roamed here and fed in this shrubbery just like that one over there, old and white with the thin greenish forelock and the pink battered hoofs."

Vasilyevskoye, 1911

The Last Rendezvous

I

THE MOONLIT autumn night was damp and cold when Streshnev ordered his horse to be saddled.

Moonlight fell in a streak of blue smoke through the narrow window of the dark stable, lighting up one eye of the saddle horse with the fire of a precious stone. The groom flung a headstall and a heavy, high Cossack saddle on the horse, pulled it out of the stable by the bridle, and tied up its tail in a knot. The horse was submissive. Only when it felt the saddle girth, did it blow out its ribs in a deep sigh. One of the girths was broken. The groom buckled it with an effort and pulled the end through with his teeth.

The stumpy horse looked sprucer now that it was saddled. The groom led it up to the front porch, wound the bridle round a rotting pole and walked away. For a long time the horse stood gnawing and biting at the pole with its yellow teeth. Now and then it blew out its ribs, whinnied, and let out a deep neigh. In a puddle beside it was the greenish reflection of the waning moon. A hazy mist was settling on the bare garden.

Streshnev appeared on the porch, hunting crop in hand. Hook-nosed, his small head thrown back, he looked tall and trim in his brown *poddyovka,* with a silver-chased leather belt gripping his slim waist, and a crimson-topped fur cap on his head. But even in the light of the moon, you could see that he had a worn and weather-beaten face, a coarse curly beard touched with gray and a stringy neck. You could see that his tall boots were old and the skirt of his coat showed dark spots of long-dried hare's blood.

A small, dark window beside the porch was pushed open, and a timid voice asked:

"Andrei dear, where are you going?"

"I'm not a child, Mother," Streshnev replied frowning, and took up the bridle.

The window was pulled to. But now a door banged in the hall. Pavel Streshnev, shuffling his slippered feet, came out on to the porch. His face was bloated and bleary-eyed, his gray hair combed back; he was in his underwear with an old topcoat thrown over his shoulders, half-drunk and talkative as usual.

"Where are you off to, Andrei?" he asked in a husky voice. "Please give my sincere regards to Vera Alexeyevna. I've always respected her most deeply."

"Can you respect anyone?" Streshnev replied. "And why do you always meddle in other people's business?"

"Sorry, sorry," said Pavel. "To a secret rendezvous rides the lovelorn gallant youth. . . ." he recited.

Clenching his teeth, Streshnev began to mount. The

moment his foot touched the stirrup, his horse came to life and started prancing clumsily. Seizing his opportunity, Streshnev mounted easily and sat back on the creaking saddle bow. The horse flung up its head and, smashing the moon in the puddle with a hoof, set off at a brisk pace.

II

The boundary strips in the damp, moonlit fields were blurred white with wormwood. Owls, spreading their large wings, soared suddenly and noiselessly from the boundaries, and the horse snorted and shied. The road passed through a thin wood, desolate and cold with moonlight and dew. The bright, wet-looking moon flashed through the bare tree tops, and the bare branches merged with its moist gleam and vanished into it. There was a bitter smell of aspen bark, of dead leaves in the gullies. . . . Now came the descent into the meadows which seemed bottomless, flooded with a thin white steam. The horse breathed white steam, too, as it threaded its way through bushes crystalline with dew. The snap of twigs under its hoofs was echoed on the opposite side, in the tall forest shadowing the mountain slope. . . . Suddenly, the horse pricked up its ears. Two wolves—sturdy, thick-necked and thin-legged—stood in the meadow's pale haze. They let Streshnev come up quite close, then they jumped round and loped clumsily up the hill across the radiantly glistening grass, white with rime.

"And if she stays for one more day?" thought Streshnev, throwing back his head and looking at the moon.

The moon hung to the right over the desolate, hazily silver meadows. . . . Oh, the melancholy beauty of autumn!

The saddle bow creaked as the horse, straining with all its might and whinnying, climbed up the side of a deep gully where the path had been washed away by streams, toward the tall, dense forest above. Suddenly, it missed its footing and almost crashed down the bank. Fury distorted Streshnev's features, he swung his crop and brought it down hard on the horse's head.

"You old dog!" his shout rang across the forest with a sort of dreary anger.

Stark fields stretched beyond the forest. On the hillside, amid dark buckwheat stubble, lay a poor estate with a few outbuildings and a thatched manor house. How mournful it all looked in the moonlight! Streshnev stopped. It seemed very, very late, it was so quiet here. He rode into the yard. The house was in darkness. Streshnev jumped down from the saddle. The horse remained standing with meekly drooping head. An old dog lay curled up on the porch, its nose between its paws. It did not move, but just looked at Streshnev, lifting its eyebrows and rapping its tail on the floor in welcome. He walked into the entry which had a stale privy smell in it coming from the closet. The hall was in twilight, the windowpanes in icy sweat gleamed golden. A small woman in a soft, light negligee ran in on soundless feet from the dark corridor. Streshnev bent down to her. She twined her bared arms round his thin neck in a quick and close embrace, and cried happily and softly, pressing her face against the coarse cloth of his coat. He could hear her heart beating like a child's, he could feel the little golden cross on her bosom, her grandmother's cross, all her remaining wealth.

"You'll stay till tomorrow?" she asked in a rapid whisper. "You will? Oh, it's too wonderful to believe!"

"I'll go and put the horse away, Vera," Streshnev said, freeing himself. "Till tomorrow, till tomorrow," he repeated, thinking the while: "Oh God, she's getting more rapturous with every day! And what a hard smoker she is, how immoderate in her caresses!"

Vera's face was sweet and velvety with powder. She rubbed her cheek against his lips, then kissed him hard upon them with her soft mouth. The cross gleamed on her uncovered breast. She had put on her sheerest nightgown, her cherished nightgown, the only one she possessed, saved for the most important occasions.

"How firmly I knew," Streshnev thought while trying to remember her as a young girl, "how firmly I believed fifteen years ago that I'd gladly give up fifteen years of my life, without a moment's hesitation, for just one rendezvous with her!"

III

Day would soon dawn. A candle was burning on the floor beside the bed. Streshnev lay on his back, the neck of his shirt undone, his long body stretched out, his small hook-nosed face turned haughtily away into the shadow, his arms flung above his head. Vera sat beside him with her elbows propped on her knee. Her brilliant eyes were red and swollen from weeping. She sat smoking and staring dully at the floor. She crossed her legs and found the sight of her small foot in its dainty, expensive shoe very pleasing. But the pain in her heart was too strong.

"I gave up everything for you," she said softly and her lips quivered.

Her voice held so much tenderness, so much childish grief! But, opening his eyes, Streshnev asked her coldly:

"What did you give up?"

"Oh, everything, everything. And above all my honor, my youth. . . ."

"You and I are not so terribly young."

"How rude you are, you don't understand me at all!" she said tenderly.

"All the women the world over always say the same thing. 'Understand' is a favorite word of theirs, only they put it differently. With delight and admiration at first: 'You are so clever, so understanding!' And later: 'How rude you are, you don't understand me at all!' "

Weeping softly, she went on as if she was not listening:

"Granted I am a failure. . . . But I have always loved music and I love it passionately still, and I would have achieved something, even if it wasn't much. . . ."

"Oh, it wasn't music! And the moment Padarsky—"

"That's rude, Andrei dear. . . . And now I'm a miserable dancing class pianist at a boarding school, and where, of all places? In the same cursed town I've always hated so! Yet even now, I could have found a man who'd give me a home and children, who'd love and respect me. But the memory of our love—"

Streshnev lighted a cigarette and answered her, letting the words drop slowly.

"Vera, we, the breed of noblemen, cannot take love simply. It's bane to us. And it's my life, not yours, that's ruined. Fifteen or sixteen years ago I used to come here every day, and I was willing to spend my nights upon your threshold. I was a mere youngster then, an emotional and sentimental fool. . . ."

His cigarette went out. He flung it away, dropped his arm down beside his body, and lay staring at the ceiling.

"The love stories of our ancestors, their portraits in the oval frames with a golden rim round the blue. . . . The images of Gury, Simon and Aviv, the patron saints of our ancient families. . . . Who if not you and I were destined to inherit it all? I even wrote poetry then:

And loving you, I dreamed of those who dreamed
And loved each other here a hundred years ago.
Beneath the stars that once for them had gleamed,
I thought of you and wandered to and fro. . . .

He glanced at Vera and changed to a harsher tone:

"Why did you go—and with whom! Did he belong to your race, your tribe?"

He sat up and fixed a hard, angry stare at her brittle black hair.

"I always thought of you with reverence and rapture, as my wife to be. But when did fate bring us together? And what did you become to me? My wife? And yet there had been youth, joy, innocence, a dark blush, a fine lawn shirt. . . . What it had meant to me to come here every day, to see your frock, of lawn too, light and youthful, your naked arms, browned by the sun and the blood of our ancestors, your flashing Tatar eyes—eyes that did not see me—the yellow rose in your black, black hair, your smile—somehow amazed and silly then, but a lovely smile—even your walking away from me down the garden path, thinking of someone else, and the way you hit your croquet ball pretending you were really in the game, and hearing your mother's insulting words to me from the balcony—to me it was. . . ."

"She is to blame for everything, not I," Vera brought out with an effort.

"No! Remember the first time you went away to Moscow; you were packing, singing something absently, without seeing me, engrossed as you were in your dreams, your certainty that you would find happiness? I went to see you off on horseback that clear, cold evening. The bright green grass, those rosy stubble fields, and that curtain in the open window of your train. . . . Oh, God!" he said with rancor and tears, and lay back on the pillow again. "Your hand was scented with verbena that left its fragrance on my hand, too. It got mixed up with the smell of the bridle, of my saddle, of horse sweat, but I could smell it still. I rode along the highroad in the dusk and wept. . . . So if there's anyone who has given up everything, sacrificed his whole life, it's I, old drunkard that I am!"

And, feeling on his lips the salty warmth of tears pouring down his cheeks and mustache. Streshnev swung his legs down on the floor and walked out of the room.

The moon was setting. White, spongy fog clung to the fields below the hill, tinged with deathly blue. A purple glow was rising far beyond. A cock was crowing in the forester's hut in the distant, cold, darkened wood.

Streshnev, in his stockinged feet, sat down on the porch steps and felt the waves of dampness chilling his very bones through the thin shirt.

"And afterward, of course, the roles were changed," he said quietly, with loathing. "Oh well, it doesn't matter now. It's all over. . . ."

IV

They had their morning tea served on a huge chest in the cold hall. The samovar was tarnished and covered with green mold; the fire in it had gone out long ago. The cold sweat beading the window had receded from the top panes and now you could see the sunny brilliance of the frosty morning and a crooked tree amid the colorless green which still survived here and there. A barefooted, red-haired servant girl, her face swollen from sleep, came in and said:

"Mitry's come."

"He can wait," said Streshnev without raising his eyes.

Vera did not raise her eyes either. Her face had become pinched overnight, brown smudges lay on her eyelids and under her eyes. Her black dress made her look younger and prettier, and her black hair gave her face powder a rosy tinge. Streshnev's lean, hard face was deathly pale. His head was thrown back and his prominent Adam's apple showed through his coarse, curly gray beard.

Though still low the sun was blinding. The whole of the front porch was white with frost. Rime lay sprinkled like salt on the grass and the bluish-green shells of cabbage leaves strewn in the yard. The man with leaden eyes who had driven up to the porch in his cart, filled with straw and also covered with frost, was now walking around stamping down the straw. He was holding a pipe between his teeth and a spiral of lilac smoke trailed back over his shoulder. Vera came out of the house wearing a fur coat that had once been expensive but was now shabby and old-fashioned; on her head was a summer hat of black straw trimmed with stiff, rusty satin flowers.

Streshnev took her as far as the highroad, riding behind the cart along paths on which the frost had melted. His horse strained toward the straw. He struck the horse across the nose with his crop and it flung its head and wheezed strenuously. They went on at a crawl and did not speak. The old dog had followed Streshnev from the house, and now it trotted behind him. The sun was warm, the sky gentle and clear.

When they were nearing the highroad, the driver suddenly spoke:

"I'll be sending my youngster to you again next summer, Miss. I reckon he'll help with the shepherding again."

Vera turned round with a shy smile. Streshnev took off his cap, leaned down from the saddle, took her hand and gave it a long kiss. Her lips clung to his graying temple, and she said softly:

"Take care of yourself, dearest. Don't think ill of me."

Once out on the highroad the driver changed to a trot and the cart clattered away. Streshnev turned back and rode straight across the fields without picking his way. The dog followed him at a distance, standing out clearly in the golden fields. He stopped now and again and shook his hunting crop at it. The dog would stop too and, sitting back on its haunches, it seemed to ask, "But where am I to go?" And the moment he rode on, the dog ambled unhurriedly after him again. His thoughts were on the railway station far away, on the gleaming rails, the smoke pouring from the southbound train. . . .

He rode down into the desolate fields, rocky in parts, that were almost hot. There was no sound in the dazzling autumn day beneath the clear blue skies. The stark fields, the gullies, the whole of this great Russian steppe was locked in silence. Puffs of cotton from the thistles and the dried-up burdock floated slowly in the air. Finches sat on the burdocks. Thus they would remain all day, only occasionally flying on to another spot, there to continue their quiet lives in beauty and happiness.

Capri, December 3, 1912

The Gentleman from San Francisco

> Alas, alas, that great city Babylon, that mighty city!
> For in one hour is thy judgment come.
>
> APOCALYPSE

THE GENTLEMAN from San Francisco—nobody in either Naples or Capri could remember his name—was on his way to the Old World with his wife and daughter, there to spend two whole years devoted entirely to pleasure.

He was firmly convinced that he was entitled to a rest, to pleasure, to a long and comfortable voyage, and to any number of other things. He had his own reasons for being so firmly convinced; first, he was a wealthy man, and secondly, he was only beginning to live, although he was already fifty-eight. Until then he had not lived, he had merely existed, not badly at all it must be said, but nevertheless it was nothing but existence, for he had centered all his hopes on the days to come. He had worked without a breathing spell—the Chinese, whom he imported in thousands to work for him, well knew what that meant! And at last he saw that he had achieved a great deal, that he had almost come up to the level of those he had once set up as an example to himself; and then he decided to take a holiday. It was a custom with the class of men to which he belonged to start off with a trip to Europe, India and Egypt when they were ready to enjoy life. He decided to do the same. Naturally, his chief concern was to reward himself for his years of toil; however, he was glad for the sake of his wife and daughter, too. His wife was never known to be particularly impressionable, but then all middle-aged American women are passionate travelers. And as for his daughter, a girl no longer young and rather sickly, the trip was an outright necessity for her. To say nothing of the good it would do her health, what of those happy friendships known to have been made on board ship? You sometimes actually find yourself sitting next to a multimillionaire at dinner or studying frescoes together in the lounge.

The route planned by the gentleman from San Francisco was an extensive one. During the months of December and January he was hoping to bask in the sun of southern Italy, to enjoy the ancient sights, the tarantella, the serenades of the wandering singers, and something that men of his age appreciate with a peculiar poignancy—the love of young Neapolitan girls, even if it isn't entirely disinterested. He proposed to spend Carnival week in Nice and Monte Carlo, where the most select society foregathers at that time, the society which rules and dispenses all the blessings of our civilized world—such as the latest cut of dinner jackets, the stability of thrones, the declaration of wars and the welfare of the hotels—where some of the guests plunge excitedly into automobile and yacht races or into roulette, others into what is customarily known as "light flirtation," and still others into shooting pigeons which, released from their cotes, soar beautifully over the emerald-green lawns, against the background of the forget-me-not sea, and then instantly flop on the ground like little white balls. He wanted to devote the first part of March to Florence and arrive in Rome for Passion Week in order to hear the *Miserere* sung there. His plans included Venice and Paris, bullfighting in Seville, bathing in the British Isles, then Athens, Constantinople, Palestine, Egypt, and even Japan—on the way back of course. . . . And everything began splendidly.

It was the end of November. Icy fogs and slushy snowstorms accompanied them all the way to Gibraltar, but they sailed on quite safely. There were many passengers on board. The famous *Atlantic* was like a huge hotel with so many facilities—an all-night bar, Turkish baths, a newspaper of its own, and life on board ran a scheduled course. They got up early, roused by the horns blaring shrilly in the corridors in that dusky hour of the morning when day was just breaking so slowly and glumly over the gray-green expanse of the sea, rolling heavily in the fog; they put on their flannel pajamas and had coffee, chocolate or cocoa; after that they bathed in marble bathtubs, did their exercises to work up a good appetite and a feeling of fitness, dressed and had their breakfast; until eleven they were supposed to walk briskly up and down the deck, breathing in the cool freshness of the ocean, or to play shuffleboard and other games in order to work up their appetites anew, and at eleven they fortified themselves with sandwiches and beef tea; thus fortified, they read the ship's newspaper with relish and calmly awaited lunch, which was even more nourishing with a greater variety of dishes than breakfast; the next two hours were devoted to rest: deck chairs were then ranged along all the decks, and the passengers lay back in them, wrapped in rugs, gazing at the cloudy sky and the frothy waves through the railing, or falling into a sweet doze; between the hours of four and five, refreshed and cheered, they had strong, fragrant tea and biscuits served to them; at seven, the bugles signaled the approach of the moment that formed the main purpose of this existence, its crowning glory. And, roused by the bugles, the gentleman from San Francisco, rubbing his hands in an access of life and vigor, hurried to his sumptuous cabin *de luxe* to dress for dinner.

At night the *Atlantic* seemed to gape into the darkness with countless blazing eyes, while a great number of servants worked busily in the kitchens, sculleries and wine cellars below. The ocean, moving beyond the walls, was awesome, but no one thought about it, firmly believing it to be in the hands of the Captain, a red-haired man of monstrous size and corpulence, who always looked sleepy and resembled an enormous idol in his black coat with gold-braid bands, and who very seldom emerged from his secret abode to be among the passengers. In the forecastle the siren kept wailing with infernal gloom or squealing in frantic fury, but not many of the diners heard the siren, for it was drowned by a splendid string orchestra, playing exquisitely and indefatigably in the two-storied marble dining room, which had deep pile carpets on the floor, was festively flooded with lights, thronged with ladies in low-cut evening gowns and gentlemen in tail coats or dinner jackets, with slender waiters, deferential *maîtres d'hôtel,* and a wine waiter who actually wore a chain around his neck like a lord mayor. The dinner coat and starched shirt made the gentleman from San Francisco look very much younger than he was. Lean and not tall, ungainly in build but well-knit, polished to a sheen and reasonably gay, he sat in the pearly golden halo of this room with a bottle of amber-colored Johannesburg in front of him, an array of glasses of the finest crystal, and a vase of curly hyacinths. His yellowish face with the neatly trimmed silver mustache had something Mongolian in it, gold fillings gleamed in his teeth, and his strong skull shone like old ivory. His wife, a large, broad and serene woman, wore clothes that were expensive but suitable to her age; while the daughter—tall and slim, with beautiful hair charmingly dressed, her breath sweetened with violet cachous, and with the faintest of little pink pimples, slightly dusted over with powder, around her lips and between her shoulder blades—wore a gown that was elaborate but light and transparent, innocently frank. . . . The dinner went on for over an hour, and after that there was dancing in the ballroom, during which the men—the gentleman from San Francisco among them of course—sprawled in armchairs with their feet up and decided the fate of whole nations on the basis of the latest stock exchange news, smoking themselves red in the face with Havana cigars and getting drunk on liqueurs in the bar attended by red-coated Negroes with eyeballs that looked like shelled hard-boiled eggs. The ocean roared, heaving black mountains on the other side of the wall, the storm whistled through the sodden, heavy rigging, the ship shuddered and shook as it struggled through the storm and the black mountains, cutting like a plough through their rippling mass which kept swirling into a froth and flinging high its foamy tails. The siren, suffocating in the fog, wailed in mortal agony; the watch up in the crow's-nest froze in the cold, their minds reeling from the unbearable strain on their attention, and the ship's belly below the water line was like the abyss of hell at its most sinister and sultry, its ninth cycle—the belly in which the giant furnaces roared with laughter as, with their blazing maws, they devoured ton after ton of coal, flung down them with a clatter by men drenched in pungent sweat, dirty, half-naked and purple in the glow of the flames. While up here in the bar, legs were flung carelessly over the arms of chairs, brandy and liqueurs were sipped at leisure, clouds of aromatic smoke hung in the air, and in the ballroom all was brilliance, radiating light, warmth and joy; couples whirled in a waltz or swayed in a tango, and the music, insistently and with a sadness that was voluptuous and shameless, sang its plea, always that one plea. . . . Among this brilliant crowd of people there was a certain well-known millionaire, a lanky, clean-shaven man in an old-fashioned dress coat, who resembled a prelate; there was a famous Spanish author, a world-celebrated beauty, and an elegant pair of lovers watched by all with curiosity, who made no secret of their happiness, for he danced with no one but her. And all this was so exquisitely and charmingly performed that no one but the Captain knew that the couple was hired by Lloyds to play at love for a good wage, and had been sailing on the company's ships for a long time.

Everyone was glad of the sun in Gibraltar, it seemed like early spring. A new passenger appeared on board the *Atlantic,* instantly drawing everyone's attention to himself. He was the crown prince of a certain kingdom in Asia, traveling incognito. A small man, perfectly wooden, broad-faced and narrow-eyed, wearing gold-rimmed spectacles, slightly unpleasant because the coarse black hairs of his mustache were stringy like a corpse's, but a nice, simple and unpresumptuous man on the whole. In the Mediterranean there was once again a breath of winter; the sea billowed in high varicolored waves like a peacock's tail, blown by the tramontane which came rushing toward the ship madly and merrily in the brilliant light of a perfectly clear day. And then, on the second day, the sky began to pale, the horizon was wrapped in mist: land was nearing, now there was a glimpse of Ischia and Capri, now if you looked through your binoculars you could see the lumps of sugar strewn at the foot of something dusky blue, Naples. Many of the ladies and gentlemen had already put on their light fur coats; the meek Chinese "boys," who never spoke above a whisper, bowlegged youngsters with pitch-black pigtails hanging down to their heels, with thick maidenly eyelashes, were quietly carrying rugs, canes, suitcases and dressing cases toward the companionway. The daughter of the gentleman from San Francisco stood on deck next to the prince, to whom she had been introduced the night before by a happy chance, and pretended she was following his pointed finger into the distance as he explained something to her hastily and softly. He was so short he looked like a little boy beside the others, seeming quite unprepossessing and odd—his spectacles, derby hat and English overcoat, the horsehair coarseness of his stringy mustache, the thin olive skin stretched tight across his flat face which might have been thinly coated with varnish—but the girl stood listening to him and she was so excited she could not understand a word he was saying; her heart was beating fast, strangely enraptured. Everything, every single thing about him was different from everyone else—his slim hands, his clear skin, beneath which coursed the blood of ancient kings, his very clothes—European and quite plain, but somehow exceptionally neat—held an extraordinary fascination for her. And meanwhile, the gentleman from San Francisco himself, wearing gray spats over his patent-leather shoes, kept glancing at the famous beauty who stood beside him, a tall blonde with a marvelous figure and eyes painted in the latest Parisian fashion, who was talking to a tiny, humpbacked hairless dog which she held on a thin silver chain. And the daughter, feeling vaguely discomfited, tried to take no notice of the father.

He was rather generous when traveling, and therefore he quite believed in the solicitude of all those who fed and waited on him from morning to night forestalling his slightest wish, who safeguarded his peace and kept him immaculate, who summoned porters for him and delivered his trunks to hotels. It had been like this everywhere, it had been so on board ship, it should be so in Naples, too. The city grew larger and nearer; the ship's band, with brass instruments flashing in the sun, was already crowded on deck and suddenly burst into a deafening and triumphant march; the gigantic Captain appeared on the bridge in his dress uniform and, like a merciful heathen god, waved to the passengers with an affable gesture. And, like everyone else, the gentleman from San Francisco fancied that the thundering strains of proud America's march were being played for him alone, and that the Captain was wishing him personally a happy landing. When at last the *Atlantic* entered the harbor and its many-storied mass, with people clustering at the rails, tied up to the pier and the chains of the gangplanks clattered—countless hotel porters and their assistants in gold-braided caps, all sorts of commissionaires, whistling urchins and hefty beggars with stacks of colored postcards in their hands, rushed forward offering their services. And he smiled at these beggars as he walked to the car of the hotel where the prince might also be putting up, and calmly spoke through his teeth first in English then in Italian:

"Go away! Via!"

Life in Naples instantly took on a clockwork regularity: in the morning there was breakfast in the gloomy dining room, an overcast sky that held little promise, and a crowd of guides at the lobby doors; then came the first smiles of the warm rosy sun, a view of Vesuvius from the high hanging balcony, the mountain cloaked entirely in the shimmering vapors of dawn, of the pearly silver ripples on the bay and the pale silhouette of Capri on the horizon, of tiny donkeys harnessed in dogcarts, tripping along the muddy quay below, and detachments of toy soldiers marching somewhere to the sounds of vigorous and challenging music. After that came the waiting car and a slow drive through the thronged, narrow gray corridors of streets, between tall, many-windowed houses, visits to the funereally stark and clean museums, lighted evenly and pleasantly but with a snowlike dullness, or to the churches, cold and smelling of wax, where the same thing was repeated over and over again: a stately entrance hung with a heavy leather curtain, and inside a vast emptiness and silence, the soft lights of the seven-branched candelabrum redly flickering in the depths upon the altar draped in lace, a solitary old woman among the dark wooden pews, slippery gravestones underfoot, and on the wall someone's *Descent from the Cross*—invariably famous. At one, there was lunch on the San Martin Hill, where quite a number of the very first-class people gathered toward noon, and where on one occasion the daughter of the gentleman from San Francisco had nearly fainted: she thought she saw the prince sitting in the room, whereas the newspapers said he was in Rome. At five, tea was served at the hotel in the beautiful drawing room which was so warm with its thick carpeting and blazing fires; and after that, dressing for dinner, once again the gong booming sonorously and masterfully through the whole building, once again the string of ladies in low-cut gowns, rustling down the stairs in their silks, reflected in the mirrored walls, once again the doors of the dining room flung open, wide and hospitably, and the red jackets of the musicians on their platform, the black crowd of waiters round the *maître d'hôtel* while he deftly ladled out the creamy pink soup into the plates. The dinners were so rich in food, wine and mineral waters, in sweets and fruit, that by eleven o'clock the maids were required to bring hot-water bottles to all the rooms for the guests to warm their stomachs with.

December, however, was not a very good month that year. When one talked to the porters about the weather they merely raised their shoulders guiltily and muttered that as far as they could remember, there had never been a winter like it, although it wasn't the first year they were obliged to mutter this and blame it on the fact that "something awful was happening all over the world." On the Riviera it stormed and rained as never before, in Athens there was snow, Etna, too, was covered with snow and cast a glow at night; and as for Palermo, the tourists were simply running away from the cold, helter-skelter. . . . The early-morning sun deceived them every day. At noon, the sky invariably turned gray and fine rain began to fall, becoming colder and harder as the day wore on; and then the palm trees at the hotel entrance would shine with a metallic sheen, the town appeared particularly dirty and cramped, the museums too monotonous, the cigar ends, thrown by the fat cabmen whose rubber capes flapped in the wind like wings, unbearably foul, the vigorous cracks of their whips over the heads of their skinny-necked nags too obvious a sham, the boots of the men sweeping the streetcar tracks dreadful, and the women, splashing through the mud in the rain with their black heads uncovered, disgustingly short-legged; but as for the dampness and the stench of rotting fish coming from the frothing water's edge, the least said about it the better. The gentleman and the lady from San Francisco began to quarrel in the mornings now. Their daughter either had a headache and went about looking wan and pale, or all at once she brightened up, was enthusiastic and keen on everything, and then she was both sweet and beautiful. Beautiful were the tender and complex feelings awakened in her by the homely man with the uncommon blood coursing through his veins, for after all, what awakens a girl's heart—whether it is wealth, fame, or an illustrious name—is not really of great consequence. Everyone assured them that it was quite different in Sorrento and Capri—there it was warmer and sunnier, lemon trees were in bloom, the people more virtuous and the wine better. And so the family from San Francisco decided to proceed to Capri, taking all their trunks along, with the intention of settling down in Sorrento after they had gone all over Capri, had trod the stones where once the palaces of Tiberius stood, visited the fabulous caves of the Azure Grotto, and listened to the Abruzzian bagpipers who, during the month before Christmas, roamed the island singing praises to the Virgin Mary.

On the day of departure—a very memorable day for the family from San Francisco—even the usual early morning sun was missing. A heavy fog completely hid Vesuvius, hanging in a low gray cloud over the leaden surface of the sea. There was no sight of Capri—as if it had never existed in the world at all. And the small ship making toward it lurched so heavily from side to side that the family from San Francisco had to lie prone on their sofas in the wretched saloon of this poor ship, their feet wrapped in rugs and their eyes closed from nausea. The lady thought she suffered more than the others; nausea gripped her again and again and she believed she was dying, while the maid who came running to her with a basin, and who had for many years been sailing this sea day in, day out, in all weathers, hot or cold, but was indefatigable nevertheless, merely laughed. The daughter was dreadfully pale and she held a slice of lemon between her teeth. The father, who lay on his back dressed in a loose overcoat and a large cap, never unclenched his jaws once during the voyage; his face had grown dark, his mustache seemed whiter, and his head was racked with pain: what with the miserable weather, he had been drinking too heavily and enjoying too many "living tableaux" in certain haunts during the last nights on shore. And meanwhile the rain lashed at the rattling portholes, water dribbled down on to the sofas, the wind tore through the masts with a howl, and now and again came together with the onslaught of the swell to lay the little ship on its side, and then something could be heard rolling and rumbling below. It was a little quieter at the stops in Castellammare and Sorrento, but even there the swell was dreadful and the shores with all their precipices, gardens, pineries, pink and white hotels and dusky curly green hills, flew up and down as though on swings. Boats kept knocking against the side of the ship, the third-class passengers were shouting heatedly, somewhere a child was choking with screams as if it had been crushed, a damp wind blew in at the door with never a moment's pause, from a boat tossing on the waves, flaunting a flag of the Royal Hotel came the sound of a boy's shrill lisping voice shouting incessantly as he tried to entice the passengers with his "*Kgoyal! Hôtel Kgoyal!*" And the gentleman from San Francisco, feeling very old—which was what he should have felt—now thought with boredom and anger of all these "Royals," "Splendids" and "Excelsiors," and of those greedy, garlic-stinking little wretches called Italians. Once, during a stop, he opened his eyes and, sitting up on the sofa, saw a pile of such miserable little stone hovels, moldy through and through, stuck one on top of the other at the foot of a sheer rock close to the water's edge beside some boats, heaps of rags, empty tins and brown fishing nets, that a feeling of despair seized him as he remembered that this was the real Italy which he had come to enjoy. . . . At last, when it was already dusk, the black mass of the island, shot through with the little red lights at its foot, began to bear down on them; the wind abated, becoming warmer and more fragrant, and golden snakes, gliding away from the lampposts on the quay, came floating on the subdued waves which gleamed like black oil. Then, suddenly, the anchor began to rumble and with a clatter of chains flopped into the water with a splash, the furious cries of boatmen, vying with one another, came from all sides; and instantly one felt one's spirits lifting, the cabin lights shone more brightly, one wanted to eat, drink, smoke and move about. Ten minutes later the family from San Francisco boarded a roomy barge; in a quarter of an hour they disembarked on the quay, and then they were sitting in a bright little car and whirring up a sheer mountainside past vine poles, crumbling stone walls and wet, gnarled orange trees protected here and there with matting, their bright-colored fruit and thick shiny leaves flashing past the open windows of the car and gliding downhill. In Italy the earth smells sweetly after rain, and every one of the islands has its own peculiar smell.

The Island of Capri was damp and dark that night. But now it came to life for a moment and put on lights here and there. A crowd of those whose duty it was to give the gentleman from San Francisco a fitting welcome, were already waiting at the top of the hill on the funicular platform. There were other arrivals, too, but they deserved no attention—a few Russians who had settled down in Capri, absent-minded and untidy men wearing spectacles and beards, the collars of their threadbare overcoats turned up; and a party of long-legged, round-skulled young Germans in Tyrolese suits with canvas rucksacks slung on their shoulders, who were in need of no services from anyone and felt at home wherever they happened to be and were not at all generous with their money. As for the gentleman from San Francisco, who calmly shunned both the Russians and the Germans, he was instantly marked down. He and his ladies were hurriedly helped out of the car; men started running ahead of him to show him the way; he was again surrounded by urchins and those stalwart Capri peasant women who carry on their heads the suitcases and trunks of decent tourists. Their wooden sandals clattered down the small square which was like an opera set with its globe of light swinging above in the damp breeze, and its crowd of urchins breaking into birdlike whistling and turning somersaults. And the gentleman from San Francisco strode in their midst as though he were making a stage entrance, through a kind of medieval archway formed by the houses, merging together overhead, beyond which lay the noisy little street, climbing up toward the brilliantly lighted hotel entrance, with a tuft of palm leaves showing above the flat roofs on the left and a black sky studded with blue stars above and ahead. And once again it seemed that it was in honor of the guests from San Francisco that this damp little stone town on the rocky island in the Mediterranean had come to life, that it was they who had made the owner of the hotel so happy and hospitable, that for them the Chinese gong was waiting to boom all through the building, summoning everyone to dinner the minute they entered the lobby.

The owner, who welcomed them with a polite and courtly bow, an exceedingly elegant young man, gave the gentleman from San Francisco a momentary start, for when he saw him he suddenly remembered that among all the other muddled dreams which had thronged his sleep the previous night he had seen the replica of this gentleman, wearing the same roundly cutaway morning coat, his hair plastered down to the same mirrorlike gloss. Amazed, he all but stopped in his tracks. But since his soul had been cleansed of any so-called mystical feelings years ago, to the last mustard seed, his amazement instantly faded away; he jokingly mentioned this strange coincidence between dream and reality to his wife and daughter as they walked down the hotel corridor. His daughter, however, looked up at him in alarm when she heard it; her heart suddenly cringed with a feeling of sadness, of frightening loneliness on this strange, dark island. . . .

A person of exalted rank—Rais XVII—who had been visiting Capri, had just left. And the guests from San Francisco were allotted the suite he had occupied. They had the prettiest and smartest maid appointed to them, a Belgian girl whose waist was drawn hard and thin by her corset, and whose starched cap perched on her head like a small toothed crown. They were given the most imposing of valets, a black-haired fiery-eyed Sicilian, and the nimblest of "boots," a small, plump man called Luigi, who had held many such jobs in his time. And a minute later, the gentleman from San Francisco heard a light knock on his door, followed by the appearance of the French *maître d'hôtel* coming in to inquire if the new guests would be dining, and to inform them, should their answer be in the affirmative (of which, however, there was no doubt), that there was lobster, roast beef, asparagus, pheasants, and so on, on the menu. The gentleman from San Francisco still felt the floor rising and falling under him—that's how seasick the rotten little Italian ship had made him—but he calmly went and rather clumsily closed the window which had burst open at the *maître d'hôtel's* entrance, and through which came the smells of a kitchen far away and wet flowers in the garden below. He replied with unhurried precision that they would be dining, that their table was to be placed well back in the room, a good distance away from the doors, that they would be drinking a local wine, and every word he uttered was echoed by the *maître d'hôtel* in tones of the most varied pitch, all of which, however, had but one meaning: that the rightness of the gentleman's wishes could not be doubted, and that everything would be carried out to the letter. Finally he inclined his head and asked tactfully:

"Will that be all, sir?"

And, hearing a thoughtful "y-yes" in reply, he volunteered the information that after dinner that night a tarantella would be danced in the lounge by Carmella and Giuseppe, well-known all over Italy and to all the "tourist world."

"I've seen her on postcards," said the gentleman from San Francisco in a voice that expressed nothing. "And that Giuseppe fellow—is he her husband?"

"Her cousin, sir," the *maître d'hôtel* replied.

And after a moment of hesitation, thinking of something

but saying nothing, the gentleman from San Francisco dismissed the man with a nod.

After that he started dressing for dinner with as much care as if he were preparing for his wedding. He switched on all the lights, flooding all the mirrors in the room with brilliance, glitter and the reflection of furniture and open trunks. He began to shave and to wash, ringing the bell incessantly, while other impatient rings, coming from the rooms of his wife and daughter, clashed with his and assailed the corridor with peals. And Luigi, in his red apron, distorting his face with a grimace of horror which reduced the maids, who were running past with jugs of water, to tears of laughter, bounded along to answer the gentleman's bell with the lightness inherent in so many fat men. Rapping on the door with his knuckles, he asked with feigned humility, exaggerated to inanity:

"*Ha sonato, signore?*"

And from the other side of the door came a drawling, rasping and pointedly polite voice:

"Yes, come in. . . ."

What did the gentleman from San Francisco feel, what did he think about on that night that was to be so momentous for him? Like anyone else who had just had a rough crossing, he wanted nothing but his dinner and dreamed with relish of his first spoonful of soup, his first sip of wine; he was actually somewhat flurried as he performed his customary ritual of dressing for dinner, so he had no time for thought or feeling.

When he had shaved and washed and neatly fitted his false teeth back into place, he stood before the looking glass and wielding a pair of silver brushes vigorously put the strands of sparse pearly white hair into place on his dark yellow skull. Then he pulled his cream-colored underwear on his aged but still strong body, its waistline thickened from overeating, put his black silk socks and pumps on his lean flat feet; then bending his knees he adjusted the silk braces that held up his black trousers, tucked in his snow-white shirt with its bulging starched front, fixed a pair of shining links into his cuffs, and began the struggle to force the collar stud into the stiff collar. He still felt the floor was heaving, the tips of his fingers hurt dreadfully, the stud pinched the sagging skin under his Adam's apple, but he was adamant and at last he got the better of the job. His eyes shining from exertion, his face livid because the tight collar was strangling him, he sank down exhausted on the stool in front of the dressing table and faced his full-size reflection which was repeated in all the other mirrors in the room.

"Oh, it's dreadful!" he muttered, dropping his strong bald head, without trying to understand, without thinking what it was he found so dreadful. Then, from habit, he keenly inspected his short fingers with their gout-hardened joints, his large almond-shaped, almond-colored fingernails, and repeated with conviction, "It's dreadful. . . ."

But just then the dinner gong boomed for the second time, sonorously as in a heathen temple. And, getting up hurriedly, the gentleman from San Francisco tightened his collar still more with a tie, drew in his stomach with a waistcoat, put on his coat, straightened his cuffs, and looked himself over in the glass once more. "That Carmella girl, olive-skinned with artifice in her eyes, like a mulatto, in her flowery orange dress, must be an exceptionally good dancer," he mused. And briskly walking out of the room, he followed the carpeted corridor to his wife's room next door and asked in a loud voice if they would be ready soon.

"In five minutes!" his daughter's voice, lilting and already gay, called back.

"Fine," said the gentleman from San Francisco.

And with leisurely steps he started down the corridors and red-carpeted stairs in quest of the reading room. The servants he met flattened themselves against the wall when they saw him, while he strode by, apparently unaware of them. There was an old lady, who was late for dinner, hurrying along the corridor in front of him as quickly as she could—an old lady with milky-white hair and a back that was already stooped, but who wore, despite this, a low-cut gown of pale-gray silk. Her gait was funny, like an old hen's, and he had no difficulty in catching up with her and leaving her behind. At the glass doors leading into the dining room, where everybody was already seated and had begun to eat, he stopped in front of a table loaded with boxes of cigars and Egyptian cigarettes and, choosing a large Manila, he threw three lire down on the table. As he passed through the winter garden he glanced casually out of the open window. A gentle breeze wafted from the darkness, he fancied he saw the top of the old palm tree spreading its gigantic-looking branches from star to star, he heard the steady wash of the sea in the distance. In the quiet, cosy reading room, unlighted but for the lamps shining over the tables, was an old gray-haired German who stood reading some rustling newspapers, a man who looked like Ibsen, with crazy, bewildered eyes behind round silver-rimmed spectacles. Eyeing him coldly up and down, the gentleman from San Francisco settled himself in a deep leather armchair in a corner, beside a green-shaded lamp, put on his pince-nez and, twitching his head because the collar was choking him, he disappeared entirely behind his newspaper. He quickly ran through some of the headlines, read a few lines about the never-ending war in the Balkans, turned the page over with a customary gesture—and suddenly the lines blazed up before him with a glassy brilliance, his neck strained forward, his eyes bulged, and the pince-nez slipped down his nose. He jerked forward, he tried to take a breath—and gave a bestial wheeze. His lower jaw sagged open, gold fillings gleamed in his mouth, his head fell back on his shoulder and lolled helplessly, the hard front of his shirt jutted out, and his whole body began to slip down to the floor, while he kept struggling with someone and kicking up the carpet with his heels.

If it had not been for the presence of the German in the reading room, they would have managed to hush up this horrible occurrence quickly and neatly, instantly whisking away the gentleman from San Francisco by his head and his feet down the back alleys, as far away as possible, and never a soul from among the hotel guests would have known what he had been up to. But the German rushed screaming out of the reading room, raised a commotion in the dining room, and roused the whole place. Many of the guests jumped up from their dinner, overturning chairs, many went pale and ran to the reading room, crying, "What's happened, what's it all about?" in different languages, and no one gave them an answer. No one could make out what had happened because to this day people find death the most amazing thing in the world, and they flatly refuse to believe in it. The hotel-owner dashed from one guest to the other in an effort to hold back the rout and to calm them with hurried assurances that it was nothing, a mere trifle, a little fainting fit that had seized a certain gentleman from San Francisco. But no one was listening to him, for many had seen the waiters and valets tearing off the gentleman's tie, waistcoat and crumpled dinner jacket, and even, for some unknown reason, dragging the pumps off his black, silk-clad flat feet. But he was still writhing. He doggedly struggled with death, he refused to give in to the thing that had borne down on him so unexpectedly and rudely. He jerked his head from side to side, he wheezed as though his throat had been cut, he rolled his eyes drunkenly. When they had hastily carried him in and laid him on the bed of room No. 43—the smallest, poorest, dampest and coldest room at the end of the ground floor corridor—his daughter came running in with her hair streaming, her dressing gown gaping open to reveal the bare bosom lifted high by her corsets, and after that came his wife, big and heavy, quite dressed for dinner, her mouth round with horror. But by that time he had even stopped jerking his head.

Within a quarter of an hour everything more or less settled down to normal at the hotel. But the night was irreparably ruined. Some of the guests came back into the dining room and finished their dinner, but in silence and with injured expressions, while the owner went from table to table, shrugging in helpless and seemly annoyance, feeling that he was blamelessly guilty, assuring everyone that he understood perfectly "how unpleasant it all was" and promising to do "everything in his power" to remove this unpleasantness. But the tarantella had to be canceled, nevertheless. Extra lights were put out, most of the guests left for the beer hall, and everything grew so quiet that you could hear the clock ticking in the lobby which was deserted except for the parrot who muttered woodenly, fussing in its cage before settling down to sleep and finally doing so with one claw flung ridiculously over the top perch. The gentleman from San Francisco lay on a cheap iron bed, covered with coarse woolen blankets, in the dim light of a single bulb close to the ceiling. A rubber ice bag hung down on his cold, wet forehead. His livid and already dead face was cooling gradually, the hoarse rattle, breaking through his open mouth with its glitter of gold, was growing weaker. It was no longer the gentleman from San Francisco who was wheezing—he was no more—it was someone else. His wife, his daughter, the doctor and the servants stood and looked at him. Suddenly, the thing they had been waiting for, the thing they dreaded, happened—the wheezing ceased. And slowly, very slowly, before the eyes of all of them, a pallor spread over the face of the deceased, his features grew finer and lighter, with a beauty that would have befitted him long ago.

The owner came in. "*Già è morto,*" the doctor told him in a whisper. The owner shrugged, his face impassive. The lady came up to him with tears trickling down her cheeks, and timidly suggested that the deceased should now be taken up to his room.

"*Mais non, madame,*" the owner objected hastily and politely but with no gallantry whatsoever now, and he spoke to her in French and not in English, for he had no further interest at all in those trifles which the visitors from San Francisco might now leave behind in his cashbox. "It's quite impossible, madame," he said and added, in explanation, that he valued the suite most highly and that if he agreed to her request, the whole of Capri would come to know of it and tourists would refuse to stay in the rooms.

The daughter, who had been looking strangely at him all

this time, dropped into a chair and, smothering her mouth with her handkerchief, burst into sobs. The mother's tears dried instantly and her face flushed red. She raised her voice, she became insistent, stating her demands in her own language and still unable to believe that all respect for them had been irrevocably lost. The owner rebuked her in politely dignified tones: if madame disapproved of the hotel's rules, he dared not hold her there; and he declared firmly that the body was to be removed by morning, that the police had been notified and a representative was due immediately to carry out the necessary formalities. Was it possible to get a coffin, even if it was only a plain ready-made one on Capri, madame asked? No, he was sorry, it was quite impossible and the time was too short to have one made. Some other way would have to be found. His English soda water, for instance, was shipped out to him in large, long packing cases . . . the partitions from one of the cases could be taken out. . . .

The hotel was plunged in sleep. They opened the window in room No. 43—which faced a corner of the garden where a sickly banana tree grew in the shadow of the tall stone wall with broken glass stuck on top. They switched off the light, left the room and locked the door. The dead man remained in the darkness. Blue stars gazed down upon him from the sky. A cricket in the wall began to chirp its melancholy, carefree song.

Two maids were sitting on the window sill in the dimly lit corridor, darning. Luigi came in with a pile of clothes in his arms and shoes on his feet.

"*Pronto?*" (Ready?), he asked anxiously in a loud whisper, rolling his eyes at the frightening door at the end of the corridor. And, waving his free hand lightly in that direction, he hissed loudly, "*Partenza!*" which is the usual shout in Italy when a train steams out of a station, and the maids clung closely together, choking down their soundless laughter.

And then he ran up to the door with soft leaps, rapped upon the panel lightly and with his head inclined asked in an undertone, in a most deferential manner:

"Ha sonato, signore?"

Now, constricting his throat, jutting his lower jaw forward, in a voice that was rasping, sad and drawling, he spoke the answer, as if it was coming from the other side of the door:

"Yes, come in."

At daybreak, when the sky grew light beyond the window of room No. 43 and the damp breeze rustled in the ragged leaves of the banana tree, when the blue sky of morning awakened and spread its cloak over the Island of Capri, and the pure, clear-cut top of Monte Soliaro turned golden in the reflection of the sun, rising beyond the distant blue mountains of Italy, when the road menders started out on their way to work, repairing the island's paths for tourists to tread, then a long soda-water packing case was brought to room No. 43. Shortly afterward it became very heavy and pressed painfully against the knees of the junior porter who was taking it in a one-horse cab at a brisk pace along the white highroad that wound down the mountain-side. The driver, a flabby man with bloodshot eyes, in a shabby old coat, short in the sleeves, and down-at-heel boots, had a hangover, for he had been playing dice all night long at the inn. He kept whipping his sturdy young horse, which was decked out in the Sicilian fashion with briskly jingling, clamoring bells of different shapes on the bridle, adorned with red wool pompons, and on the tips of the high copper ridge of the pommel, and with a quivering, yard-long feather sticking up from its trimmed forelock. The cabman was silent, crushed by his own dissoluteness and his vices, and the fact that the night before he had lost all those coppers with which his pockets had been crammed. But the morning was crisp and with air as fresh as this, the nearness of the sea and the blue skies above, a head is soon cleared of its drunken haze, and lightheartedness is quickly recovered; and then the cabman also found consolation in the unexpected fee he had earned from some gentleman from San Francisco, who was rolling his dead head about in the packing case behind his back. The small ship, lying like a beetle on the bright and delicate blue that filled the Bay of Naples so generously, was already sounding the last hoots and these were eagerly echoed over the whole of the island whose every bend, every mountain ridge and every stone was so clearly visible, as if there were no atmosphere at all. At the quay the cab was overtaken by the car in which the senior porter was bringing the mother and daughter, both of them pale, with eyes sunken from tears and a sleepless night. And ten minutes later, the little ship was again chugging away in a swish of water to Sorrento and Castellammare, taking the family from San Francisco away from Capri forever. And once again peace and quiet was restored to the island.

On that island, two thousand years ago, there lived a man who got hopelessly entangled in his foul and cruel deeds, who for some reason rose to power over millions of people and who, losing his head from the senselessness of this power and from his fear that someone might thrust a knife into his back, committed atrocities beyond all measure. And mankind remembered him forever, and those who with combined effort are now ruling the world with as little reason and, on the whole, with as much cruelty as he did, come here from all over the world to take a look at the remains of the stone house on one of the sheerest sides of the island, where he used to live. That beautiful morning, all those who had arrived in Capri for this particular reason were still asleep in their hotels, although a string of little mouse-gray donkeys with crimson saddles were already being led up to the hotel entrances, for the Americans and Germans—men and women, young and old—to clamber on to when they got out of bed and had stuffed themselves with food, to be followed at a run along the rocky paths, all the way to the very top of Monte Tiberio, by old Capri beggarwomen with staffs in their gnarled hands. The travelers slept in peace, comforted by the thought that the dead man from San Francisco, who had been planning to go with them but had instead just frightened them with a reminder of death, had already been shipped to Naples. And the island was still wrapped in silence, the shops were still shut. The fish and vegetable market in the small square was the only place open to business, and there was no one there but the common people. Among them idling his time away as usual, stood the tall boatman Lorenzo, a care-free old rake so unusually handsome that he was known all over Italy, where he had often sat for painters. He had brought along a couple of lobsters he had caught in the night and he had already sold them for next to nothing, and now they were rustling in the apron of the cook from the same hotel where the family from San Francisco had spent the night. Lorenzo was now free to stand there till evening if he so wished, glancing about him with a regal air and cutting a figure with his tatters, his clay pipe and his red flannel beret, worn over one ear. Two Abruzzian mountaineers came down the steep Monte Soliaro from Anacapri, down the ancient Phoenician path, with steps hewn out of the rock. One of them had a bagpipe under his leather cloak—a large goatskin bag with two pipes—while the other carried something that looked like a wooden flute. They were coming downhill, and the whole country lay below, joyous, beautiful and fulgent: the rocky humps of the island, almost all of which lay at their feet, the fabulous azure in which it floated, the vapors of morning rising from the sea toward the east, shimmering in the blinding sun which was already hot as it rose higher and higher in the sky, the dimly blue mass of Italy with its mountains near and far still vague in the morning haze, the beauty of which man has no words to express. Halfway down the mountain they slowed their pace. There, above the path, in a niche in the rocky wall of Monte Soliaro, stood the Mother of God, bathed in sunlight, warmth and brilliance, clad in snow-white plaster robes, wearing the crown of a queen, rustily golden from the rains, meek and merciful, with eyes raised heavenward to the eternal and blissful abode of her thrice blessed Son. They bared their heads and raised their flutes to their lips—and praises poured forth, naïve and humbly joyous, to the sun, to the morning, and to her, the Immaculate Intercessor for all the suffering in this wicked and beautiful world, and to the One who had been born of her womb in a cave at Bethlehem, in the poor shepherds' shelter, in the far land of Judea.

And in the meantime, the body of the old man from San Francisco was returning home to its grave on the shores of the New World. After suffering much humiliation, much carelessness at the hands of men, traveling from one harbor warehouse to another for about a week, it found itself at last on board the same famous ship which had only such a short while ago brought it to the Old World in so stately a manner. But now they were hiding him from the living—they lowered him in his tarred coffin into the blackness of the hold. And once again the ship sailed off on its long voyage. That night it passed the Island of Capri and its lights, slowly vanishing in the dark sea, seemed sad to those who were watching it from the island. But there, on board, in halls flooded with light and gleaming with marble, a great ball was being held that night, true to custom.

A ball was held on the second and the third night out too—once again a furious storm was raging over the ocean, making it drone like a dirge and roll in mountains that were somber and black like a funeral pall, edged with a silvery fringe. To the Devil watching from the rock of Gibraltar, the stony gateway between the two worlds, the countless, blazing eyes of the ship were hardly visible behind the curtain of snow, as the ship sailed away into the night and the storm. The Devil was as vast as a rock, but the ship was even vaster than he was, many-tiered and many-funneled, created by the arrogance of a New Man with an old heart. The storm tore at its rigging and its wide-mouthed funnels, white with snow, but it was firm, stalwart, majestic and—frightening. On the very top deck, lonely amid the whirling snow, rose the cozy, dimly lighted apartments, where the corpulent Master, so like a heathen god, presiding over the whole ship, slept lightly and fitfully. He heard the deep howls and the furious squeals of the siren choking in the storm, but he sought reassurance in the proximity of something in the next room that was, in reality, the thing he could understand least of all: that large cabin, armor-clad it seemed, which every now and again was filled with a mysterious roar, a flickering and a dry sputtering of blue lights, which flared up and burst around the pale-faced radio operator with a half circle of metal round his head. At the very bottom, in the underwater depths of the *Atlantic* where the twenty-ton steel bulks of the boilers and other machinery shone dimly, hissed out steam and dripped boiling oil and water, in that kitchen where the motion of the ship was being cooked over infernal fires heated from below, power was churning, power frightening in its concentration, transmitted to the very keel, to the endlessly long vault, into the rounded and dimly lighted tunnel, where a colossal shaft rotated slowly in its oily bed with an inexorability that was crushing to a man's soul, as if it were a live monster stretched out in the muzzlelike tunnel. But the middle part of the *Atlantic*, its dining rooms and ballrooms, radiated light and joy; they hummed with the voices of a well-dressed crowd, sang with string orchestras and emanated the fragrance of flowers. And again there was the slender and graceful couple of hired lovers, swaying sinuously or clinging together convulsively, among the crowd, amid the brilliance of lights, silks, diamonds and women's naked shoulders: the pretty girl with downcast eyes that were depraved and modest, with innocence in her coiffure, and the tall young man with black hair that seemed glued down, his face pale with powder, dressed in a narrow long-tailed dress coat and graceful patent-leather pumps, a beautiful man who looked like a huge leech. And no one knew that it had long been nothing but drudgery for this couple to writhe in their sham bliss to the strains of the lewdly sad music, nor did anyone know that a coffin stood on the floor of the dark hold, far, far below them, close to the gloomy, sultry depths of the ship fighting against the darkness, the ocean and the storm. . . .

Vasilyevskoye, October, 1915

Light Breathing

OVER A FRESH mound of earth in the cemetery stands a new cross of oak—strong, heavy and smooth.

It is April, the days are gray. Through the bare trees the tombstones in this spacious provincial cemetery are visible from afar, and the wind rings on and on in the porcelain wreath at the foot of the cross.

There is a rather large convex glass medallion set in the cross, bearing the photograph of a schoolgirl with happy and amazingly eager eyes.

This was Olya Meshcherskaya.

As a little girl she was indistinguishable from the crowd of brown-frocked schoolgirls. What could one say of her, except that she was one of those pretty, rich and fortunate girls, that she was quick to learn but was naughty and quite unimpressed with the sermons preached to her by her grade supervisor? And then she began to blossom out and to develop very rapidly. By the time she was fourteen—slim-waisted and slender-legged—her breasts and all those curves whose fascination man has found no words to express, were already well outlined. By fifteen, she was known as a beauty. To think how carefully some of her schoolmates did their hair, how meticulous they were about their persons, how they watched their every controlled movement! But she was afraid of nothing—neither inkstains on her fingers, nor a reddened face, nor tousled hair, nor a knee suddenly bared if she fell when running. Without any effort at all she gradually came to possess all that set her so far apart from the rest of the girls in the last two years—grace, elegance, cleverness, and a clear brilliance in her eyes.

No one danced at balls as beautifully as Olya did, no one skated as well as she, no one was more popular at the dances and, for some reason, no one was adored by the junior grades more than she was. And then she was no longer a child, and imperceptibly she got a reputation for herself at school, and talk started and spread that she was frivolous, that she could not live without being courted, that a boy called Shenshin was madly in love with her, that she was supposed to love him too but was so fickle in her treatment of him that he once tried to end his life. . . .

During this last winter of hers, Olya quite lost her head in a whirl of gaiety, so they said at school. The winter abounded in snow, sun and frost: the sun sank early beyond the tall fir trees in the snow-swept playground; it was invariably clear and radiant, bringing promise of frost and brightness for the morrow, of strolls along Sobornaya Street, skating in the city park, a rosy glow in the evening sky, music, and the crowd of skaters gliding this way and that, among whom no one seemed more carefree and happy than Olya Meshcherskaya. And then one day, during the midday break, as she raced about the assembly hall, running away from a flock of happily squealing first-grade girls, she was suddenly summoned to the headmistress. Abruptly she stopped in her flight, took just one deep breath, smoothed her hair with a quick and already typically feminine gesture, hitched up the corners of her apron on her shoulders, and with radiant eyes ran upstairs. The headmistress, young-looking but gray-haired, sat knitting tranquilly at her desk with the tsar's portrait on the wall behind her.

"Good morning, Mademoiselle Meshcherskaya," she said in French, without raising her eyes from her knitting. "I'm sorry to say it's not the first time that I have been obliged to call you here in order to talk to you about your conduct."

"Yes, madame, I am listening," Olya replied, coming closer to the desk. She looked at the headmistress with bright and candid eyes but with no expression whatsoever on her face, and dropped a curtsey as lightly and gracefully as she alone could do.

"You will not listen well, I'm certain of it unfortunately," the headmistress said and, with a tug at the wool which made the ball spin on the polished floor, drawing Olya's curious glance to it, she looked up and said: "I shall not repeat myself, nor shall I speak at great length."

Olya liked this large and scrupulously clean room very much, with the gleaming tiles of the stove breathing warmth on a frosty day, and the bunch of lilies of the valley on the desk sending up a cool fragrance. She looked up at the young tsar, painted full height in some brilliant hall or other, then she turned her gaze to the even parting in the headmistress' neatly marcelled hair and remained expectantly silent.

"You are no longer a child," the headmistress said ponderously, her irritation growing.

"No, madame," Olya replied simply and almost merrily.

"But you are not a woman either," the headmistress said even more ponderously, and the lusterless skin on her face crimsoned slightly. "To begin with, how dare you do your hair like that? It is the style of a grown-up woman!"

"It's not my fault that I've got nice hair, madame," replied Olya and raised both hands to touch her beautifully dressed hair.

"Oh, so it's not your fault!" the headmistress said. "Your hair style is not your fault, the expensive combs are not your fault, it's not your fault that you're ruining your parents with those twenty-ruble shoes you're wearing! But I repeat, you are quite losing sight of the fact that you are a mere schoolgirl still. . . ."

At this, Olya Meshcherskaya, retaining all her simplicity and composure, suddenly interrupted her politely:

"Excuse me, madame, but you are wrong. I am a woman. And do you know whose fault it is? It was Alexei Mikhailovich Malyutin, my father's friend and neighbor and your brother. It happened last summer in the country. . . ."

And a month after this conversation, a Cossack officer, unattractive and plebeian-looking, who had no connection at all with the society to which she belonged, shot Olya Meshcherskaya on the station platform in full view of a great crowd of people who had descended from the train. Olya's unbelievable confession, which had dumfounded the headmistress, was confirmed. The officer made a statement to the examining magistrate that Meshcherskaya had lured him on, had been intimate with him, had promised to marry him and then, on the day of the murder, had suddenly told him at the railway station, where she had come to see him off to Novocherkassk, that she had never even thought of loving him, that she was only making sport of him with all this talk of marriage, and showed him a page of her diary where she had written about Malyutin.

"I read those lines while she strolled up and down the platform, waiting for me to finish them, and there and then I shot her," the officer said. "Here is the diary, see what she wrote in it on July 10 last year. . . ."

This is what they read:

"It's almost two in the morning. . . . I fell into a sound sleep but instantly I awoke. . . . Today I have become a woman!

. . . Daddy, Mummy and Tolya, all went away to town and I was left alone. I was so happy to be alone! In the morning I walked in the garden and the meadow, I went into the forest, and I fancied I was alone in the whole world, and never in my life did I have such fine thoughts as I had then. I had dinner alone, too, and then I played the piano for a whole hour, and the music made me feel that I would live forever and be happier than anyone in the world. After that I fell asleep in Daddy's study, and at four Katya woke me up and said that Alexei Mikhailovich had come to call. I was very glad to see him, I so enjoyed receiving and entertaining him. He arrived in a carriage drawn by a pair of very handsome horses, and they remained in front of the porch all the time. He did not go at once because it had been raining and he hoped the road would dry a little toward evening. He was sorry he had missed Daddy; he was very cheerful and behaved like a young man with me, joking and pretending he had been in love with me for a long time. When we were walking in the garden before tea, the weather turned lovely again, the whole of the dripping garden was pierced with sunlight, though it had turned quite cold, and he held my arm and said that we were Faust and Margaret. He's fifty-six, but he's still very good-looking and he's always well turned out. The only thing I didn't like about him was that he came wearing a cape. He smelled of English toilet water, and his eyes were quite young and black, though his beard, elegantly parted in two long strands, was perfectly silver. We had tea on the glass veranda; I felt a sort of faintness and lay down on the sofa, while he sat and smoked in his chair, and then he came and sat beside me; he spoke pleasantries to me again, then he started examining my hand and kissing it. I covered my face with my silk handkerchief, and he kissed me on the lips through the silk, again and again. . . . I can't understand how it could have happened; I must have gone out of my mind; I never thought I was like that! There's only one way out for me now. . . . I feel such loathing for him, I can't endure it. . . ."

The town becomes so clean and dry in these April days and the cobblestones so white, that it is easy and pleasant to walk along them. Every Sunday, after church, a little woman dressed in mourning with black kid gloves and an ebony-handled umbrella, starts down Sobornaya Street on her way out of town. She follows the paved road across the dirty square, surrounded by a great many smoke-blackened smithies and swept by the crisp wind blowing in from the fields. Farther on, between the monastery and the prison, there shows a white line of clouds in the sky and a gray patch of fields; after that the way lies through the puddles, close to the monastery wall, a turn to the left and then there is a big, low garden, fenced in with a white wall, with the Assumption of the Holy Virgin over the gate. The little woman crosses herself discreetly and rapidly and walks down the main alley with sure steps. When she reaches the bench facing the oaken cross, she sits down and stays there for an hour, or perhaps two, in the wind and the coolness of spring, until her feet in their light shoes and her hands in their thin gloves become completely chilled. Sometimes, listening to the spring birds singing sweetly even in the cold, and to the wind ringing in the porcelain wreath, she thinks she would give anything in the world, half a lifetime, so that this dead wreath before her need never have been. The wreath, the mound, the oaken cross! Could it really be that beneath the cross lay the one whose eyes shone so immortally from the medallion above? How could one reconcile the purity in those eyes with the horror now associated with Olya Meshcherskaya's name? But in her heart of hearts the little woman is happy, like all who passionately cherish a dream.

This woman is Olya Meshcherskaya's form mistress, a spinster no longer young, who has long been living in dreams that took the place of life for her. Her brother was the first of these fanciful dreams—a poor and in no way remarkable junior officer—and she put all her hopes in him, in his future which for some reason she thought would be brilliant. After he was killed in action at Mukden, she tried to convince herself that she was working for an idea. The death of Olya Meshcherskaya carried her away on a new dream. And now the girl was the object of her persistent thoughts and feelings. She visited her grave every holiday, she sat gazing for hours at the oaken cross, she called up Olya's pale little face as she lay in the coffin among the flowers, and she remembered the words she had once overheard. Walking in the playground during the midday break, Olya Meshcherskaya had been saying them very, very quickly to her best friend, the tall and plump Subbotina.

"I read in one of Daddy's books—he has plenty of funny old books—I read what a woman should possess in order to be beautiful. . . . You know, the things it said, I simply can't remember them all! Well, naturally, she had to have black eyes, eyes like boiling pitch—word of honor, that's exactly the way it was put: like boiling pitch! Eyelashes, black as night, a gentle blush caressing the cheeks, a slender body, arms longer than ordinary—can you believe it, longer than ordinary?—small feet, a moderately large bosom, well-shaped legs, knees the color of sea shells, sloping shoulders—I learned a lot of it by heart it's all so true!—but the main thing, d'you know what the most important thing is?—light breathing! And I've got that, you know—listen to the way I breathe! I do it lightly, don't I?"

And now this light breathing is dispelled in vapor over the world, in the clouded sky, in the cold spring wind.

1916

Sunstroke

After dinner they came up on deck and stood close by the rail, leaving the bright, hot lights of the dining room behind them. She closed her eyes, pressed the back of her hand to her cheek and laughed a frank, charming laugh—everything was charming about that small woman—and said:

"I'm quite drunk. . . . And anyway, I've gone quite mad. Where did you come from? Three hours ago I didn't even know you existed. I don't even know when you came on board. Was it in Samara? But it doesn't matter. . . . Am I dizzy or are we turning round somewhere?"

Ahead lay darkness and lights. A soft steady breeze blew into their faces from the darkness, and the lights rushed away from them in an arc. With the dash of a Volga craft, the boat swung in a wide curve as it ran up to a small pier.

The lieutenant took her hand and raised it to his lips. The hand, small and strong, smelled of sunburn. And his heart came to a blissful and frightening standstill when he thought how strong and tanned her whole body must be under that light linen dress, after lying on the hot sand beneath a southern sky for a whole month (she told him she was on her way from Anapa).

"Let's get off. . . ." he muttered.

"Where?" she asked surprised.

"At this stop."

"What for?"

He said nothing. She pressed the back of her hand to her hot cheek again.

"You're mad. . . ."

"Let's get off," he repeated dully. "Please."

"All right, as you wish," she said turning away.

Coming on at full speed, the ship thudded softly against a dimly lit pier, and they almost fell on top of one another. A cable flew over their heads, the ship was driven back, water churned noisily and gangplanks rumbled. . . . The lieutenant rushed for their luggage.

A minute later they passed the sleepy little office, came out on the beach, sinking ankle-deep in the sand, and silently got into a dusty carriage. The drive up the long slope, soft with dust and marked by infrequent crooked lampposts, seemed endless to them. But now they topped the rise and the wheels clattered on the cobblestones: here was a market square or something, now came the government buildings, the fire tower, and the warmth and scents of a provincial town on a summer night. The driver stopped before a lighted doorway beyond which they could see a steep old wooden staircase and an old, unshaven porter in a pink shirt and a frock coat, who took their suitcases with a disagreeable air and led the way upstairs on his shambling feet. He brought them to a large but dreadfully stuffy room, searingly heated by the day's sun, with white curtains at the windows and a couple of new candles on the dressing table. And the minute they walked in and the porter had left them, closing the door behind him, the lieutenant rushed to her so impetuously, and desire so vehement smothered them both when they kissed, that this moment was to remain in their memories for many years to come: neither he nor she had ever experienced anything like it in all their lives.

At ten o'clock in the morning—a sunny, hot and joyous morning with church bells pealing, with the noise and bustle of the market in front of the hotel, with the smells of hay, tar and again all those strong mixed scents of a Russian provincial town—she, that small nameless woman who had not told him her name after all, but, laughing, had called herself a fair stranger, went away. They had not had much sleep, but in the morning, when she left the bed and came round the screen, washed and put on her clothes in five minutes, she looked as fresh as a girl of seventeen. Was she feeling embarrassed? Only very slightly. She was as simple and cheerful as ever, and her common sense was already asserting itself.

"No, no, dearest," she said in answer to his plea that they continue their voyage together. "No, you must stay behind until the next boat. If we go on together everything will be spoiled. It would be very unpleasant for me. I give you my word of honor that I'm not at all what you might have thought me to be. Nothing even remotely like this has ever happened to me before, nor will it ever happen again. I must have lost my senses. . . . Or, rather, we both had something like a sunstroke. . . ."

And the lieutenant agreed with her with a certain lightheartedness. He took her as far as the pier with a light and happy heart, arriving there just as the pink *Samolyot* was ready to sail. He kissed her in front of everyone on deck and barely managed to jump down the gangplank before it was hauled up.

He got back to the hotel feeling as lighthearted and carefree as before. However, he found that some change had already occurred there. Without her the room somehow looked quite different. It was still filled with her presence, but empty! That was odd! The room still smelled of her good English *Eau-de-Cologne,* her unfinished cup of tea was still standing on the tray, and yet she was no longer there. . . . And the lieutenant's heart was suddenly wrung with such tenderness that he hastened to light a cigarette and began pacing up and down the room.

"What a strange adventure!" he said aloud with a laugh, conscious of the tears welling up in his eyes. " 'I give you my word of honor I'm not at all what you might have thought me to be. . . .' And now she's gone. . . ."

The screen had been moved back, the bed not yet made. And he felt he simply could not bear to look at that bed now. He put the screen back to hide it, closed the windows to shut out the noise of the market crowd and the squealing of wheels, he let down the white, puffed-up curtains, and sat down on the sofa. Well, that was the end of his "shipboard adventure"! She was gone and by now she was far away, probably sitting in the white glass lounge or lying back in a deck chair, gazing at the vast river gleaming in the sun, at the timber rafts moving downstream, at the yellow shoals, at the bright vista of water and sky, at all this infinite expanse of the Volga. . . . And good-bye now, forever. . . . For where could they ever meet again? "After all," he thought, "how could I, for no reason at all, suddenly appear in the town where she lives with her husband, her three-year-old daughter, all the rest of her family and her whole everyday world!" And this town seemed to him different somehow, a sacred town, and the thought that she would just go on living her lonely life there, perhaps thinking of him often, remembering their chance meeting and those fleeting hours, while he would never see her again—this thought staggered him. No, that could not be! It would be too mad, too unnatural and incredible! And he felt a pain so poignant, such futility in all the life that stretched before him without her that terror and despair gripped him.

"What the hell!" he thought, getting up and starting to

pace the room again, trying not to look at the bed behind the screen. "What's come over me? After all, this isn't the first time. . . . And what's so wonderful about her? What did happen? It's really like a sunstroke! But the main thing is how on earth am I going to get through the rest of the day without her in this miserable town?"

He still remembered everything about her, all the slightest details that singled her out. He remembered the smell of her sunburn and her linen dress, her strong body, and the lilting, frank and cheerful sound of her voice. He still felt with extraordinary vividness the ecstasy he had experienced from all her feminine charm, and yet this other, this quite novel feeling was the more important now, this peculiar, strange feeling which he did not have at all when they were together, of which he had never suspected himself capable when he began the affair the night before, thinking it would be an amusing experience, this feeling which he could tell to no one, no one now! "And the worst of it is, I'll never be able to tell her!" he thought. "What am I to do? How can I live through this endless day with these memories, this agony that cannot be appeased, in this Godforsaken little town on the same gleaming Volga that has carried her away in the pink ship?"

He had to seek salvation, to find something to distract his mind, to go somewhere. He resolutely put on his cap, picked up his cane, briskly walked down the empty corridor with a jingle of spurs, and ran down the steep staircase to the front door. Yes, but where was he to go? A cab stood by the entrance, and the driver, a young chap, smartly dressed, sat calmly smoking a cigarette evidently waiting for someone. The lieutenant threw a perplexed and amazed look at him: how could he sit on his coachbox so calmly, smoke a cigarette and altogether be so ordinary, carefree and indifferent? "I expect I'm the only one in this whole town who's so dreadfully unhappy," he thought as he started out toward the market place.

The market was already thinning. He walked aimlessly between carts loaded with cucumbers, stepping on the fresh manure, and strolled among new pots and bowls, while the women sitting on the ground vied with one another to offer him their wares. They picked up their pots and tapped them with their fingers making them ring to show their quality, while the men deafened him with their shouts: "Here, the best cucumbers ever, your honor!" It was all so stupid and preposterous that he fled from the market. He dropped into the cathedral toward the end of the service, where the singing of the choir was already loud, joyful and deliberate, with the consciousness of duty done; and after that he walked for a long time, round and round the little neglected garden perched on the cliff above the boundless, steel-gray expanse of the river. . . . The shoulder straps and buttons on his tunic were too hot to touch. The band inside his cap was sticky with sweat, his face was flaming. When he got back to the hotel he was delighted and relieved to walk into the large, empty, cool dining room on the ground floor, to take off his cap and sit down at a table close to an open window which let in hot air, but it was air anyway, and to order iced beetroot soup.

Everything was fine, everything held immeasurable happiness and great joy; even in this very heat, in the market smells, in all of the strange, wretched little town and in this old provincial hotel, there was joy, and yet his heart was breaking. He drank several glasses of vodka and while he ate his dill pickles he was thinking he would be willing to die on the morrow, without a moment's hesitation, if only she could be brought back by some miracle, if only he could spend one more day with her—spend it with her just so that he could tell her, convince her, prove to her somehow that he loved her desperately and rapturously. . . . But why prove it? Why convince her? He did not know why, but it was more necessary than living.

"My nerves are all shot to blazes!" he muttered, pouring out his fifth glass of vodka.

He pushed his soup away, ordered some black coffee and sat smoking and thinking hard: what was he to do now, how to shake off this sudden and unexpected love? But to shake it off was impossible. All at once he quickly got up again, took his cap and cane, and, having asked where the post office was, hurried off toward it, already framing the wording of his telegram in his mind: "From now and forever my life is in your power until death." But when he got to the old, thick-walled building of the post office and telegraph, he stopped, horrified: he knew the town where she lived, he knew that she had a husband and a three-year-old daughter, but he did not know her name! He had kept asking her to tell him at dinner the night before and afterward at the hotel, but every time she merely laughed and said:

"But why do you want to know my name? I'm Marya Marevna the fairy-tale princess. Isn't that good enough for you?"

There was a photographer's window on the corner, next to the post office. He stood staring for a long time at a large photograph of an officer with thickly fringed epaulets, protuberant eyes, a low forehead, amazingly sumptuous sideburns and the broadest of chests completely covered with decorations. . . . How mad, how absurd and horrible was all that was ordinary and trivial when your heart was smitten—yes, it was smitten, he knew it now—with that frightening "sunstroke," with a love that is too strong, with happiness that is too great! He looked at a wedding group—the young bridegroom in a long frock coat and white tie, with cropped hair, standing rigidly at attention, arm in arm with a girl in a bridal veil—he brought his eyes to rest on a picture of a pretty and saucy-looking girl wearing a student's cap at a rakish angle. . . . And then, tormented by distressing envy for all these people he did not know, people who were not suffering, he looked with strained attention down the street.

"Where shall I go? What shall I do?"

The street was quite empty. The houses were all alike, white, two-storied, middle-class homes with large gardens, and there did not seem to be a soul in any of them; the street was carpeted with thick white dust, and all of it blinded one, all of it was flooded with sunlight, passionate and joyous, but somehow out of place. In the distance the street humped uphill and butted into the cloudless, grayish and shimmering sky. There was a hint of the south in this, reminding him of Sevastopol, Kerch . . . Anapa. . . . This was particularly unbearable. And with drooping head, squinting in the glare, his eyes fastened anxiously on the ground before him, staggering and stumbling, getting tangled in his spurs, the lieutenant made his way back.

He felt so shattered with weariness when he got to the hotel that he might have traversed great spaces somewhere in the Sahara Desert or in Turkestan. Mustering his remaining strength he entered his large and empty room. It had already been tidied, deprived of all trace of her, and only a hairpin she had dropped lay on the bedside table. He took off his tunic and looked at himself in the mirror: his face—an ordinary officer's face, dark-gray with sunburn, with a colorless mustache bleached in the sun and bluish eyeballs which looked whiter still against his tan—now held an agitated, frenzied expression. There was something youthful and profoundly unhappy in his thin white shirt with its starched turned-up collar. He went to the bed and lay down on his back, putting his feet in their dusty top boots on the rail at its foot. The windows were open, the curtains down, and a gentle breeze puffed them out now and again, bringing into the room the heat of the sweltering iron roofs and all that brilliant and now utterly desolate and soundless world. He lay with his hands behind his head, staring fixedly before him. Then he clenched his teeth and closed his eyes, feeling the tears rolling down his cheeks, and at last he fell asleep. When he opened his eyes, the reddish-yellow sunset was already aglow behind the curtains. The breeze had died down, the room was stuffy and as hot as an oven. And he recalled the previous day and that morning as if they had been ten years ago.

Unhurriedly he got up, unhurriedly he washed, drew the curtains, rang, asked for a samovar and his bill, and then he leisurely drank his lemon tea. After this he ordered a cab, had his suitcases taken down and as he got into the carriage and settled on its seat of faded, rusty brown, he tipped the porter a whole five-ruble note.

"Looks to me, your honor, it was I who brought you here last night," the driver said cheerfully as he picked up his reins.

When they came down to the pier, the blue summer night had already spread over the Volga, and many little lights of different colors were already scattered down the river, and lanterns hung suspended from the masts of the ship as it swung up to the pier.

"Got you here on time!" the driver said ingratiatingly.

The lieutenant tipped him with a five-ruble note too, bought his ticket and went down to the pier. . . . Just like the night before, there was the soft thud against the mooring block, a slight dizziness because of the heaving floor, and then a flying cable, the noise of water churning and rushing forward beneath the wheels of the boat which was driven back somewhat. And this crowded ship, already fully lighted and smelling of the kitchen, gave him a feeling of extraordinary friendliness and contentment.

A minute later they were on their way, upriver, the same way that she had gone off earlier that morning.

The dark glow of the summer sunset died away far ahead casting its gloomy, drowsy and varicolored reflection upon the water that still quivered and glimmered here and there with ripples far below the glow, and the lights, scattered in the darkness about them, floated far, far away. . . .

The lieutenant sat on deck under an awning feeling as though he had aged ten years.

Maritime Alps, 1925

Lika

I

Those spring days of my first wanderings were also the last days of my youthful asceticism.

When I awoke on my first morning in Orel, I was still the person I had been on my way there—solitary, free and serene, a stranger to the hotel and to the town—and I even woke up at an hour unusual for the town, when it was just becoming light. But already the next day I woke up later, like everybody else. I dressed with care and studied my reflection in the mirror. . . . Already the day before, at the newspaper office, I had felt self-conscious of my Gypsy tan, the weather-beaten gauntness of my face, and my unkempt hair. I had to make myself look decent, especially since my circumstances had improved quite unexpectedly the day before: not only had I received an offer of a job but also an advance, which I took —blushing painfully, it's true, but take it I did. And so I started down the main street, dropped in at a tobacconist's and bought a box of expensive cigarettes, then I went into a barber's, walking out afterward with a nicely diminished and fragrant head and with that peculiar manly vigor with which one always leaves the barber's. I would have liked to go back to the office at once to pick up as quickly as I could the joyful thread of all those impressions which fate had showered so generously upon me the day before. But I could not possibly go back right away. "What? Has he come again? And in the morning, too!" they would say. And so I took a stroll instead. At first I followed the route I had taken the day before— down Bolkhovskaya Street, then on to Moskovskaya, a long shopping street leading to the railway station. I walked as far as some dusty triumphal arch beyond which the street grew empty and poor. I left it for the even poorer Pushkarskaya suburb, and then came back to Moskovskaya Street. And when I had gone down to the Orlik River, crossed the old wooden bridge which shook and rumbled under the cart wheels, and had walked up to the government buildings, I heard bells pealing in all the churches and, coming down the avenue toward me, in a carriage drawn by a pair of tall black horses, their step brisk but measured in befitting contrast to the clamoring bells, I saw the Archbishop himself, who with a benevolent wave of his hand distributed blessings right and left to all the passers-by.

The office was crowded again. Avilova, a small woman, was busy at her large desk; she only flashed me a kind smile and instantly bent over her work once more. Lunch was again a long and jolly affair, and after lunch I listened to Lika playing the piano stormily, and then she, Obolenskaya and I went into the garden to sit on the swing. After tea, Avilova showed me the house, she took me through all the rooms; on her bedroom wall I saw the portrait of a hairy, bespectacled individual with broad bony shoulders looking down in displeasure. "My late husband," Avilova said casually, and I was slightly taken aback, because the absurdity of uniting this consumptive old man and the lively, pretty woman who had suddenly called him her husband, struck me forcibly. And then she went back to her work again. Lika was dressed for the street and, in that peculiar way she had of talking, which I had already noted with a feeling of embarrassment, she said, "Well, my children, I must fly!" and went away, while Obolenskaya took me shopping. She suggested that I should go with her to Karachevskaya Street, saying that she had to call on her seamstress there, and I felt pleased with the intimacy which she had suddenly established between us with her informal suggestion. I walked beside her and listened to her crisp voice with a feeling of pleasure; at the seamstress's I stood and waited with peculiarly pleasurable patience for her to finish her discussions and consultations. It was already twilight when we came out into the street again. "Are you fond of Turgenev?" she asked. I found it difficult to answer: because I am country born and bred, people have always asked me this question, invariably suspecting me of a fondness for Turgenev. "Well, never mind," she said. "You'll find it interesting anyway. There's a house not far from here which is supposed to have been described in *A Nest of the Gentlefolk*. Would you like to see it?" We walked to the outskirts of the town and came to a deserted street of dark gardens, where on a cliff above the Orlik, in an old park full of young April foliage, stood a gray house, long since empty, with tumble-down chimneys where jackdaws were already making their nests. We paused there a while and looked at it over the low wall, through the garden which was still thin and lacy against the clear evening sky. . . . Liza, Lavretsky, Lemm. . . . And I passionately desired love.

We all went to the city park that night. I sat beside Lika in the semidarkness of the summer theater, and together with her delighted in all that noisy nonsense that was being performed by the orchestra and the actors on a stage which depicted a square of sorts, lighted from below, with pretty town wives and king's cuirassiers tapping their feet in time to the blaring dance tunes and clinking their empty tin mugs. After the show we had supper in the park; I sat with the ladies on the big crowded terrace with a bottle of wine before me in an icebucket. Their friends kept coming up, they presented me to all of them, and everyone was very nice to me except one, who nodding carelessly in my direction took no further notice of me whatsoever; this man who had later caused me very much torment—quite carelessly too—was a tall officer with a long, dark lusterless face, black motionless eyes, and black sideburns, dressed in a well-fitting frock coat which came down below his knees, and narrow trousers with foot straps. She talked and laughed a lot, showing her beautiful teeth, well aware that everyone was watching her in admiration, and I could no longer look at them calmly, my blood froze when I saw the officer hold her small hand in his large one for a moment longer than necessary as he said good-bye to her.

The first thunderstorm of the year broke out the day of my departure. I remember the roll of thunder, the light carriage taking me to the station with Avilova, my feeling of pride in the carriage and in my companion, the odd sensation of my first parting with *her*, my fanciful love for whom I quite believed in already, and that feeling which was predominant over everything—a feeling that I had made an exceptionally fortunate acquisition of something in Orel.

At the station I was struck with the greatness and the size of all those solemnly gorgeous, select people thronging the platform expectantly, and with the plebeian appearance of the clergy in spite of all the brilliance of their garb, as they stood in front of everyone, silver crosses and censers in their hands. The moment the royal train came bearing down upon the station with all its ponderous force, and the scarlet cape of the carrot-haired giant who jumped down from the train dazzled everyone, things seemed to grow muddled and incoherent—after that I remember nothing but the somber and sinister solemnity of the requiem mass. And then, the greasy-steel bulk of the steam engine with its coal-black flags began to rumble with the mighty, regal jolts of its funnel's resumed breathing, the connecting rod moved back slowly in a gleam of white steel, and the blue train—plate glass and golden eagles—floated past. . . . I gazed at the steel wheels as they turned faster and faster, at the brakes and springs, and the only thing I saw was that all of it was thickly covered with white dust, the wonderful dust gathered on the long journey from the south, from the Crimea. Rumbling and roaring, the train disappeared from view, continuing its mournful royal journey across Russia, toward the capital, while I was already carried away entirely into the bewitching Crimea, into Pushkin's enchanting Gurzuf days.

My modest provincial train was there, on a distant side line, and I was already looking forward to the solitude and rest it would give me. Avilova stayed with me until it steamed out of the station, chatting gaily all the time, saying that she hoped to see me in Orel again soon, and giving me to understand with a smile that she was well aware of the comic grief that had befallen me. At the third bell, I kissed her hand warmly and she touched my cheek with her lips. I jumped into the train, it gave a jerk and started moving while I thrust my head out of the window and watched her growing smaller and smaller as she stood there, waving to me gently. . . .

After that everything seemed touching to me: the short little train, hardly dragging along one minute and suddenly beginning to rock and rumble ominously, the desolate stations and halts where the train stood endlessly for unaccountably long moments, and all that which was already dear and familiar to me, that was once again all about me—the fields flying past the windows in slanting humps, still bare and therefore particularly unattractive, coppices of bare birches meekly waiting for spring, doleful horizons. . . . The evening was doleful too, with a springlike coolness in the air and a pale, low sky.

II

When I left Orel I took one dream with me—that I might somehow manage to continue all that had begun in Orel as soon as possible. But as I sat by the window gazing into the fields, at the slow April sunset, I forgot my dream for longer and longer spells the farther I left the town behind me. And then twilight deepened in the train; it was twilight beyond the window, too, in that thin oakwood, moving to the left of the train—that bare, crooked oakwood carpeted with last year's russet leaves that had just emerged from the layer of snow. And now I was on my feet, clutching my bag and growing more and more excited, for there was Subbotin Wood, and soon we would come to Pisarevo. The train gave a sad, warning cry into the emptiness; I hurried out on to the platform at the end of the carriage. It was primordially raw somehow, chilly and drizzly; I saw a solitary freight car standing in front of the station; we skirted it, and I jumped down while the train was still moving. I ran across the platform and through the dimly lighted, infinitely sad station building, trampled with many muddy peasant feet, and came out into the dark front driveway. There was a flower garden in the circular courtyard, miserable and dirty with melting snow, and a wretched cart horse barely discernible in the dusk. The driver, who would sometimes spend weeks in vain expectation of a fare, dashed eagerly toward me, delightedly agreeing with every word I said and willing to rush me to the ends of the earth for anything I would give him—"I suppose you'd be fair, sir,"—and a minute later I was jolting along submissively in his shallow little cart, first through a dark, stark village, and then—more and more slowly—across dark, silent fields, lost to the whole world, across a black sea of soil beyond which something shimmered greenly in the boundless distance toward the northwest, beneath flimsy clouds. A night breeze, thin and rainy—an April breeze—blew into my face, and far away a clucking quail seemed to be continuously changing its position in the wind. Rare stars twinkled amid the clouds in the low Russian sky. . . . Quail again, spring and earth again—and my erstwhile, dull poor youth again.

The journey was tormentingly long: ten versts across open country with a Russian muzhik for company is no short trip! The driver grew silent and inscrutable; he smelt of his stuffy hut and of the brittle leather of his worn-out sheepskin coat; he silently ignored my requests to hurry, and whenever we had to go up a gentle slope he jumped down from his seat and walked with measured strides beside his wretched old mare which could hardly stagger along, the rope-plaited reins in his hands and his face turned away. When we drove into Vasilyevskoye it seemed to be the dead of night: no sign of life, not a light anywhere. My eyes were accustomed to the darkness and I could clearly make out each cottage, every bare branch in that broad street along which we drove into the village, and then I felt and saw the descent into the April rawness of the riverside, the bridge across the river to my left and, to my right, the road up the slope toward the house that loomed uninvitingly above. I felt everything very keenly again: how dreadfully familiar everything was, and at the same time how new in its rustic darkness, its wretchedness and indifference to the rest of the world! As he toiled uphill my driver gave no sign of life at all. Suddenly ahead of us a light flashed up in a window behind the pine trees in the front yard. Thank goodness they were not asleep yet! Happiness, impatience and a boyish shame overwhelmed me when at last the cart stopped in front of the porch and I had to climb down, open the front door, walk into the hall, and see the smiling scrutiny they gave me.

The following morning I left Vasilyevskoye and rode through the bare fallow and the ploughed fields in a gentle, bright, early morning drizzle, which stopped one minute and started up again the next. Ploughing and sowing was underway. A barefooted man walked with swaying gait behind the wooden plough, his splayed white feet slipping down into the soft furrow loosened up by the hunching and straining horse; behind the plough hobbled a blue-black rook which kept snapping up dark-red worms in the furrow, and behind the rook came an old hatless man with wide, measured strides, a seed bag hanging on a shoulder strap across his chest, and with a sweeping and nobly generous gesture of his right hand, he scattered the seed over the ground in regular semicircles.

In Baturino I actually felt a pang from the affection and delight with which I was welcomed home. What impressed me most was not so much the delight of my mother as that of my sister: I never expected or hoped for that beautiful expression of happiness and love when, having caught sight of me from the window, she rushed out to meet me on the porch. She was so sweet altogether with her sincerity and her youthfulness; even her new frock which she was wearing for the first time that day in honor of my arrival looked innocent and young. I thought the house charming too, with its ancient and beautiful crudeness. My room was exactly the way I had left it that winter; everything was in its old place, and even the half-burned tallow candle in its metal candlestick was still there on my desk. I walked in and looked about me: black icons in the corner, glimpses of trees and of the sky through the old-fashioned windows with the top panes of colored glass (mauve and garnet), the sky turning blue here and there and sprinkling the greenly budding branches and twigs with a thin rain. Everything in the room was somewhat somber, spacious and profound . . . the ceiling of dark, smooth wood, the walls of the same dark, smooth panels . . . smooth and ponderous the rounded posts of the oak bedstead. . . .

III

A matter of business served as a good pretext for my next trip to Orel. We had to pay our interest into the bank, and so I took it there, but I only paid a part of it in, squandering the rest of the money. This was a grave lapse on my part, but something odd was happening to me—I did not attach very much importance to it. All that time my actions were guided by a senselessly blissful resolve. I missed the passenger train to Orel and managed to get taken on the engine of a freight train. I remember climbing a high metal step into something that was coarse and dirty, and standing there watching. The engineer and his mate were dressed in some sort of clothes greasy beyond description and gleaming with a metallic sheen; their faces were just as greasy and shiny, their eyeballs as white as a Negro's and their eyelids blackened as though they were wearing stage make-up. A young chap, wielding an iron shovel with a mighty clatter, scooped up coal heaped in a corner, slammed back the furnace door from which fiendish red tongues of flame licked out, and, swinging back his shovel, doused the hell-fire with coal. The older man wiped his fingers on a hideously greasy rag and, flinging it away, gave something a pull and then a turn. . . . A whistle rent the air, splitting your eardrums, blinding steam enveloped you in its hot breath, a roar deafened you suddenly—and slowly you were pushed forward. . . . And afterward this roar became a savage rumbling, our strength and vigor grew and grew, everything began to shake and rock and leap about us. Time stood still, stony in its concentration, while the fire-breathing monster flew over the hillocks with a rhythmic tremor, and each lap came to an end too soon. And then, in the peaceful silence of the night, when the train stopped, the fragrance of the woods at night wafted toward us, and songs of nightingales, blissful and triumphant, trilled from every tree and bush. . . .

When I got to Orel I bought some outrageously gorgeous clothes: soft, foppish top boots, a sheer black *poddyovka,* a red silk shirt and the sort of cap that is worn by the upper classes—black with a red band. I bought an expensive cavalry saddle which was so marvelous with its strong-smelling creaking leather, that as I traveled home with it that night, I could not sleep for joy that it was there, lying beside me. I went through Pisarevo again on my way back because I wanted to buy myself a horse, and a fair was being held at the village. There I made friends with some chaps of my own age, also dressed in *poddyovkas* and caps like mine; they were old habitués of horse fairs and with their help I bought a young thoroughbred mare (although the Gypsy made frantic efforts to foist on me an old gelding, a run-down Don horse, saying: "Buy Misha, your honor, you'll never stop thanking me for Misha!").

After that, the summer became one long holiday for me—I never spent more than three days running at Baturino; I stayed with my new friends most of the time, and when *she* came back from Orel, I couldn't keep away from the town at all. The moment I got her laconic note: "I'm back and counting the hours," I rushed to the station, in spite of the fact that the silly jocosity of her tone struck me unpleasantly and that it was already late and clouds were gathering in the sky; but once in the train, I felt a drunken delight in its fast pace which seemed even faster with the thunderstorm already raging, the clamor of the wheels merging with the claps of thunder, and the rain falling noisily on the roof—all this amid the blue flashes of lightning that flooded the black windowpanes and the rain that lashed them with frothy, fragrant water.

I believed there was nothing more to it than the pleasure of gay meetings. But then—it was toward the end of the summer—one of these friends of mine who lived with his sister and his elderly father on a small estate close to the town, on the steep bank of the Ista, and who was also a frequent caller of hers, invited quite a number of people to his birthday party. He called for her himself, she rode in his charabanc with him while I followed on horseback. I gloried in the brilliant, dry expanse of the fields—the spreading acres which looked like yellow sand dotted with hayricks as far as the eye could see. Everything in me clamored for something desperately daring. I lashed my horse to the pitch of excitement, held it back and then let it go to leap madly over a hayrick, grazing its pasterns with its sharp horseshoes and drawing blood. The birthday dinner on the rotting wooden terrace lasted till evening, and imperceptibly it merged with the darkness, lamps, wine, songs, and there I sat beside her, holding her hand, no longer embarrassed, and she did not pull her hand away. Late at night we left the table, as if by agreement, and walked down the terrace steps into the darkness of the garden. She paused in its warm blackness and, leaning back against a tree, held her hands out to me, and though I could not see in the darkness I instantly divined her gesture. . . . The skies turned gray soon after that, young cocks started crowing huskily with hopeless blissfulness, and in another minute the whole of the garden emerged against the vastness of the golden dawn breaking behind it over the yellow fields across the river in the valley. . . . We stood on the cliff above the valley, and she, gazing at the skies unfolding in a blaze of sunlight and no longer seeing me, sang Tchaikovsky's "Morning." Breaking off at a note that was too high for her to take, she picked up the pretty flounces of her cambric skirt, the color of a quail, and ran toward the house.

I stood still, feeling lost, but then simply keeping my feet was already more than I could do, to say nothing of coherent thinking. I lay down under an old birch tree which grew on the edge of the cliff in a wealth of dry grass. It was already light, the sun was high, and, as usual toward the end of summer in fair weather, the day immediately became hot and brilliant. I put my head on the roots of the tree and fell fast asleep. But the sun blazed hotter and hotter, it was so sultry and dazzling when I awoke a little later, that I got up and, staggering, went in search of shade. The house, bathed in piercing blinding sunrays, was still asleep. Our host alone was awake. The window of his study, framed in a wild growth of lilac, stood open, and you could hear his cough in which you sensed an old man's delight in the first pipe of the day and the first cup of strong tea with cream. The sound of my footsteps and the noise made by the startled sparrows streaking away from me off the lilac bushes, gleaming in the sun, made him look out of the window as he drew his shabby old dressing gown of Turkish figured silk together over his chest, and showed his face—frightening with its swollen eyes and huge gray beard—and then he smiled with extraordinary kindness. I bowed guiltily, slipped across the terrace and through the open drawing-room doors. The room was perfectly lovely with its early-morning stillness and emptiness, with butterflies flitting about, with its old-fashioned blue wallpaper, its armchairs and small sofas. I lay down on one of them—its curves were exceptionally uncomfortable—and once again fell fast asleep. But then, it seemed to me it was a moment later, though in reality I slept for a long time, someone came up to me and, laughing, started saying something and tousling my hair. I woke up—before me stood my young hosts, brother and sister, both of them dark, fiery-eyed and handsome in a Tatar way, he in a yellow silk shirt, and she in a blouse of the same yellow silk. I sat up with a start: they were telling me in a very nice way that it was time to get up and have breakfast, that *she* had already gone, not alone but with Kuzmin, and then they handed me a note from her. I instantly remembered Kuzmin's eyes—quick, bold, and speckled, the color of a bee—I took the note and went into the old "housemaids" room where I found a little old woman all in nondescript black, a jug of water in her thin freckled hand, humbly waiting for me beside a stool with a basin on it. I read the note: "Don't try to see me again," it said, and then I began to wash. The water was icy and biting—"Ours is spring water, from a well," the old woman said, and handed me a mile-long linen towel. I quickly made for the hall, picked up my cap and crop and ran across the hot yard to the stables. . . . At my approach my horse neighed softly and sorrowfully from the darkness—it had not been unsaddled the night before and now stood beside an empty manger with its belly drawn in—I seized the bridle, leaped into the saddle, still controlling myself, though strangely and wildly excited, and galloped away through the gates. When I rode out of the grounds I cut sharply across the fields, flying blindly over the rustling stubble, bringing my horse up short at the first hayrick I came to and, bounding down from the saddle, flopped down beside it. The horse seized clusters of stalks scattering glasslike grain and tugged at it noisily; grasshoppers ticked busily in the stubble and the hayricks like hundreds of tiny clocks; the bright fields spread in a sandy desert about me, but I saw and heard nothing, I only kept repeating to myself: she must give me back this night, this morning, herself, her cambric flounces swishing as her feet flickered in the dry grass, or both of us will die!

I galloped toward the town obsessed by this mad idea, filled with a mad conviction that it must be so.

IV

After that I stayed on in the town for a long time, spending days with her in the dusty little flower garden at the back of her widowed father's house. Her father, who was a carefree man, a physician with liberal ideas, let her do whatever she liked. Ever since I had come rushing to her from the Ista and she, seeing my face, had pressed both her hands to her heart, it could no longer be said whose love was the stronger, the happier, the sillier, mine or hers (for hers, too, had sprung up suddenly and unexpectedly). At last we decided to part for a while to give each other a short breathing spell at least. Another thing which made this parting a dire necessity was that I had fallen hopelessly in debt by staying at the Noblemen's Hotel on credit. And then the rainy season started, too. I did all I could to put off our parting, but at last I pulled myself together and left the town in pouring rain. During my first days at home I only slept, wandered desultorily about the house, doing nothing and thinking of nothing. Then I began to pause for thought: what was happening to me anyway, and how would it all end? One day my brother Nikolai came into my room, he sat down without taking off his cap and said:

"And so, my friend, your romantic state continues undisturbed. Nothing's changed: 'The magic vixen bore me off beyond dark forests and tall mountains,' the story says, and what lies beyond those forests and mountains, nobody knows. I know everything, you see; I've heard something and the rest I can guess—all these stories are more or less the same, you know. I am also aware that you can't reason sensibly now. But still, what are your plans for the future?"

I replied half-jokingly:

"Everyone is borne away by some magic vixen or other, but where to and what for remains unknown, of course. It even says so in the Bible: 'Go, young man, in your youth wherever your heart leads you and wherever your eyes bring you.' "

My brother remained silent, staring at the floor and apparently listening to the rain whispering in the dismal autumn garden, and then he said sadly:

"Oh well, go, then. . . ."

I kept asking myself what I should do. And the answer was quite clear. But the harder I tried to convince myself that the decisive, farewell letter had to be written immediately—I could still do it, for we had not broken the last barrier yet—the deeper I was moved with tenderness and admiration for her, for the loveliness of her eyes, her face, her laughter, her voice, and a sentimental gratitude to her for loving me. . . .

And a few days later, in the evening, a rider, dripping with rain, suddenly appeared in our yard and handed me a rain-soaked envelope: "I can bear it no longer. Come." The thrilling thought that I would see her, hear her voice a few hours hence, kept me awake till dawn. . . .

And this is how I spent the autumn months—either at home or in town. I sold my saddle and horse and, when in town, no longer put up at the Noblemen's Hotel but stayed at Nikulina's boardinghouse on Shchepnaya Square. The town was quite different now, not at all like the town where I grew up. Everything was plain and humdrum, and only sometimes, walking down Uspenskaya Street, past my old school and grounds, I recaptured something of my old sentiments, something to which my soul responded. I was a regular smoker by that time; I also dropped into the barber's for a shave quite casually, where once I had sat with such childish meekness, stealing wary glances at the rapidly clicking scissors which snipped my silky hair. From morning to night we sat on the Turkish divan in the dining room, and were almost always alone: her father left the house early and her brother went to school, and after lunch the doctor had a nap and then went off somewhere again, while the schoolboy was busy playing a mad game, running about with his ginger dog Volchok who, shamming fury, barked and spluttered with rage as it raced up and down the wooden staircase to the second floor. Then came a period when the monotony of sitting on the divan and perhaps my immoderate and ever-present sensitiveness bored her, and she started going out on different pretexts, calling on her girl friends and acquaintances, while I went on sitting on the divan alone, listening to the screams, laughter and stamping feet of the schoolboy and to Volchok's affected barks on the staircase. I sat looking through a mist of tears at the window with the half-drawn curtains and the dull gray skies beyond, and smoked one cigarette after another. . . . And then something happened to her again: she took to staying at home, she grew so tender and kind to me once more that I could no longer make out what sort of a person she really was. One day she said to me: "Oh well, my sweet, I suppose it's fate!" and wrinkling up her face happily, she burst into tears. This happened after lunch at an hour when everyone in the house trod on tiptoe lest they disturb the doctor's sleep. "I'm only terribly sorry for Daddy, he's the most precious thing in the world to me!" she said, amazing me as usual with her excessive love for her father. And as luck would have it, the schoolboy came running in at that precise moment and mumbled absently that the doctor wanted to see me. She turned pale. I kissed her hand and left the room with resolute strides.

The doctor met me with the kindly cheerfulness of a man

who had just had a very good sleep and a refreshing wash; he was humming a song and lighting a cigarette.

"My young friend," he said, offering me a cigarette. "I've been wanting to talk to you for a long time—you know what it's about. You know perfectly well that I'm not given to prejudice. But I want my daughter to be happy; I feel very deeply for you, too, and so let us have a frank, man-to-man talk. Strange as it may seem, I don't know you at all. Tell me then: who are you?" he said with a smile.

Blushing and paling, I drew hard on my cigarette. Who was I? I would have liked to answer proudly like Goethe (I had just read Eckermann then)—"I do not know myself, and God forbid that I should ever do so!" But I answered modestly:

"I write, as you know. . . . I shall continue writing and perfecting myself. . . ." And unexpectedly I added: "Perhaps I'll study and enter the university. . . ."

"Enter the university? That's splendid, of course," the doctor replied. "But it's no joke preparing for the entrance exams. And then, exactly what do you want to train for? Just a literary career or social work as well, the civil service?"

And once again my mind was thronged with nonsensical thoughts—Goethe again: "I live through the ages with a feeling of the disgusting instability of all things worldly. . . . Politics may never become a matter for poets. . . ."

"Social work is not a matter for poets," I answered.

The doctor glanced at me with faint surprise:

"In other words, Nekrasov, for example, was no poet according to you? But you do at least follow the trend of contemporary life, don't you, even if it's with half an eye? Do you know what inspires and moves every honest and intelligent Russian just now?"

I thought for a moment and pictured all that I knew: everyone talked of reaction, of elective councils, Zemstvo officers, of "all the happy undertakings which marked the era of great reforms razed to the ground" . . . of Tolstoi propagating a "cell in the dell" . . . that we were indeed living in Chekhov's

"Twilight" . . . I remembered the booklet of Marcus Aurelius' sayings advertised by Tolstoi's followers: "Fronton has taught me how hard are the hearts of the men known as aristocrats. . . ." I recalled the sad old Ukrainian with whom I had sailed down the Dnieper in the spring, a sectary who kept repeating to me the words of St. Paul in his own peculiar manner, ending with "For we wrestle not against flesh and blood, but against principalities, against powers, against the rulers of the darkness of this world, against spiritual wickedness in high places." I felt anew my old leanings for Tolstoi's gospel which liberated one from all and every social obligation and which at the same time was directed against the "rulers of the darkness of this world" who were hateful to me too—and I started off on a homily on Tolstoi's teachings.

"In other words, you believe that the sole means of salvation from all evil and misfortune lies in this notorious nonaction and nonresistance, do you?" the doctor asked with exaggerated nonchalance.

I hastened to reply that I was all for action and resistance but "of quite a different sort." My adherence to Tolstoi's teachings came to be formed of all those strong and contradictory feelings which were roused in me by Pierre Bezukhov and Anatoly Kuragin, Prince Serpukhovsky in *Kholstomer* and Ivan Ilyich, by *What Are We To Do?* and *Does a Man Need Much Land?*, by gruesome pictures of the town's filth and poverty painted in the article about the census-taking in Moscow, and a romantic dream of life close to nature, among the people, inspired in me by *The Cossacks* and my own impressions of the Ukraine; how wonderful it must be, I thought, to shake the dust of all our iniquitous life and instead to enter upon a clean life of work somewhere on a farm in the steppes, in a little white mud house on the shores of the Dnieper. Something of all this, skipping the mud house, I told the doctor. He listened to me carefully, I thought, but rather too patronizingly. There was a moment when his sleep-laden eyes dimmed and his hard-clenched jaws quivered with a suppressed yawn, but he mastered his drowsiness, the yawn merely distending his nostrils, and said:

"Yes, yes, I'm listening. . . . You mean to say that you are not striving for any, so to say, of the usual blessings of this world, for yourself personally? But not all blessings are personal, you know. I, for one, am far from being an admirer of the people; I know them too well unfortunately and hardly believe in their being the well and fount of all wisdom; neither do I believe it my duty to uphold the world on its three whales in a joint effort with the people; but surely it's wrong to assert that we are under no obligation to them at all and owe them nothing. However, I would not venture to preach to you on this subject. I am very glad anyway that we have been able to talk about it. Now then, I'll go back to what I set out to say. I shall speak briefly and, you must forgive me, quite uncompromisingly. Regardless of what you and my daughter may feel for one another, regardless of what the present stage of development of that feeling may be, I'll say this to you now: she is altogether free to act, of course, but if for example she wished to bind herself to you with any sort of permanent ties and asked me for my blessing, so to say, she'd get a flat refusal from me. I like you very much; I do wish you every possible sort of luck, but that is that. Why? you will ask. I'll answer this quite like a lower middle-class father: I don't want to see the two of you unhappy, wallowing in misery, leading an insecure existence. And then, allow me to speak with absolute frankness: what have you got in common? Lika is a pretty girl and—why conceal it—rather fickle. She's carried away with something one day, and the next it's another infatuation—and of course it's not Tolstoi's cell in the dell she's dreaming of—just look at the way she's dressed although this is only a dull small town! Far be it from me to say that she is spoiled. I only want to say that I think she's not your sort at all, so to say. . . ."

She was waiting for me at the foot of the stairs and met me with eyes that were questioning and prepared for a shock.

I quickly told her the doctor's last words. Her head drooped.
"No, I'll never go against his will," she said.

V

When staying at Nikulina's boardinghouse, I would sometimes go out and walk aimlessly across Shchepnaya Square, then through the desolate fields behind the monastery, past the large cemetery fenced in with ancient walls. There was nothing there but the wind, sorrow and desolation, the eternal peace of crosses and gravestones, neglected and forgotten by the world, there was a feeling of emptiness there, like a lonely, vague thought. Over the cemetery gates was a fresco of a boundless blue-gray plain pitted with gaping graves and toppling gravestones, from under which rose toothy, bony skeletons and primordially ancient men and women in pale green shrouds. And over this plain flew a huge angel holding a trumpet to his lips, his faded blue robes streaming behind him, his bare maidenly legs bent at the knee and the chalk-white soles of his long feet turned up. . . . A provincial, autumn peace reigned at the boardinghouse too; there were hardly any arrivals from the villages. When I got back I walked into the yard and saw the cook wearing men's top boots coming toward me from the sheds carrying a rooster. "I'm taking him to the house now," she said, laughing at something. "He's gone quite crazy with old age, let him room with me for a change." I mounted the steps up the wide stone porch, passed the dark entry, then the warm kitchen with its plank beds, and entered the front rooms—the bedroom of the proprietress and the room in which there were two large sofas rented out to the infrequent guests, either tradesmen or clergymen, but mostly to me alone. Stillness, and in the stillness the alarm clock ticking peacefully in the bedroom. . . . "Did you have a nice walk?" my hostess asked with a smile of sweet sympathy as she came out of her room. What a charming, melodious voice she had! She was plump and round-faced. There were times when I could not look at her calmly, especially on those evenings when, flushed all over, she came back from the bath-house and sat drinking tea for a long time, with her hair still damp and dark, a soft and languid gleam in her eyes, her clean body relaxed loosely and comfortably in an armchair, while her cat, silky white with pink eyes, purred on her plump and slightly spread knees. A rapping would be heard outside: this was the cook fastening the heavy shutters, the iron bolts of the elbow-shaped levers rattling as she pushed them into place through round openings on both sides of the window (this brought back to mind the dangerous times of old). Nikulina would then get up, thrust little iron wedges into the holes on the end of the levers and once again settle down to tea, and then the room would be cosier still. . . . Crazy thoughts and feelings overwhelmed me: to give everything up and stay there forever, in this boardinghouse, and sleep in her warm bed to the sound of the peacefully ticking alarm clock. On the wall above one of the sofas there was a picture of a bright green forest, standing like a long wall, a log cabin and beside the cabin a little old man, humbly bent, his feeble hand resting on the head of a brown bear, also humble, meek and soft-pawed. On the other wall was an utterly incongruous picture, considering that someone would have to sit or sleep on the sofa under it. It was a photograph of an old man in his coffin, a white-faced, important man in a black frock coat, Nikulina's late husband. A rhythmical tapping and a monotonous chant came from the kitchen, well in harmony with the long autumn evening: "In front of the church stood a carriage, a wedding resplendent within. . . ." The song was sung by girls hired from the suburbs to chop the crisp, taut cabbage heads to be salted for the winter. And in everything—the banal song, the rhythmical homely tapping, the old cheap print, and even in the dead man whose life seemed to continue in the senselessly happy world of the boardinghouse, there was a sadness, delicious and bitter. . . .

VI

In November I went back home. We arranged to meet in Orel: she would take the train on the first of December and I would come later, if only a week later for the sake of decorum. But on the first, on a frosty, moonlit night, I drove like mad to Pisarevo so that I could board the train which she was to take from town. I can still see and feel that night, that fabulously beautiful night. I can see myself in the level, snow-clad field, halfway between Baturino and Vasilyevskoye, my pair of horses flying, the wheeler seeming to shake the shaftbow always on the same spot, beating time at a round trot, the off-horse rhythmically flinging up its croup, kicking up clots of snow with its hindlegs, the horseshoes flashing whitely . . . and then, suddenly losing its footing, it would plunge into the deep snow on the side of the road, grow flustered and hurried, floundering in the snow, tangled in its fallen traces, and when it found a foothold, jump on to the road and fly on again, pulling hard at the shaft. . . . Everything flew by at a great speed and at the same time seemed to stand still and wait: the scaly crust of snow shone motionless and silver far away beneath the moon which hung low and still blurred in the frost, a mystical sadness in the radiantly misty ring around it, and I was stiller than anything else, benumbed by the gallop into stillness, resigned to it for the moment, bemused with waiting, and yet gazing wistfully into some memory: there was another night like this and the same road to Vasilyevskoye, only it had been my first winter at Baturino, and I was still pure, innocent and joyful with the joy of my first days of youth, when I was first poetically enraptured with the world unfolded for me by those old little volumes brought from Vasilyevskoye, their stanzas, messages, elegies and ballads:

Horsehoofs thudding. All is stark,
Desolate steppe around them. . . .

"And now, where is it all?" I was thinking without, however, for a minute coming out of my predominant state, that of benumbed waiting. "Horsehoofs thudding. All is stark. . . ." I said to myself in time to the galloping horses (in time to the rhythm of motion which has always held me so powerfully in its spell), and I felt I was someone else, a dashing man of the old days, galloping somewhere in a shako and a bearskin greatcoat; the only reminder of reality was the driver standing in the front, covered with snow, with a cloth coat worn over his sheepskins, and the frozen, fragrant oat straw mixed with snow dust, stuffed under the box seat at my frozen feet. . . . When we had left Vasilyevskoye behind, the wheeler, skidding into a snowdrift, turned over and broke the shaft and I, while the driver was binding it together, sat dying of fear that I should miss the train. The moment we arrived I spent all my money on a first-class ticket—she always traveled first—and rushed to the platform. I remember the light of the moon, misty from frozen steam which swallowed up the yellow lights of the platform lamps and the lighted windows of the telegraph office. The train was already steaming in. I stared into the dim, snowy distance, feeling as if I were made of glass because of the frost and my inner icy shivering. A bell suddenly clanged loudly and hollowly, doors banged and squeaked shrilly, the quick footsteps of people coming out of the station creaked sharply and firmly—and then the engine appeared in the distance like a black shaggy mass, the awesome triangle of dimly red lights came forward slowly to the sound of its labored breathing. . . . The train toiled up to the station strenuously, covered with snow, frozen through and through, creaking, squealing and whimpering. . . . I leaped up the steps, threw the door wide open—and there she was, her fur coat thrown over her shoulders, sitting in the dusk under a lantern screened by a dark-red curtain, all alone in the whole carriage, staring straight at me. . . .

The carriage was old, tall, and mounted on three pairs of wheels; as it sped on in the cold, it shook and rumbled, it seemed to be falling all the time, rocking and heaving, the doors and walls creaked, the frost-covered windows glittered like gray diamonds. . . . We were already far away; it was the middle of the night. . . . Everything happened without our volition, or our consciousness. . . . She got up with a flaming face that saw nothing, smoothed her hair and, closing her eyes, sat unapproachably in a corner. . . .

VII

We lived in Orel that winter.

There are no words to express the feelings with which we came out of the train that morning and walked into the newspaper office, secretly united by this new and frightening intimacy.

I put up at a small hotel, and she stayed with Avilova as before. There we spent most of the day, and our cherished hours at my hotel.

Our happiness was not lighthearted, it was exhausting both mentally and physically.

I remember one evening: she was at the skating rink, and I sat working in the office. I was already beginning to get work there that brought in a small revenue. The house was empty and silent; Avilova had gone to attend some meeting or other; the evening seemed endless; the lamp in the street beyond the window sorrowful and unwanted, and the footsteps of the passers-by—coming and going, crunching on the snow—seemed to take something away from me, to deprive me of something. Loneliness, hurt and jealousy weighed heavily upon my spirit—there was I sitting all alone, doing some stupid work, unworthy of me, to which I had stooped for her sake, while she was out having a good time, there on the ice-bound pond, surrounded by white snow hills with black firs, loud with a military brass band, flooded with mauve gaslight and dotted with flying black figures. . . . Suddenly the bell rang and she walked in swiftly. She had on a gray suit, a gray squirrel cap, in her hands she held her shining skates, and everything in the room was instantly and joyously filled with her young, frosty freshness and the beauty of her face, flushed with the cold and with the exercise. "Goodness, I'm tired," she said and went into her room. I followed her; she threw herself on the sofa, fell back with smiling exhaustion, still holding the skates in her hands, while I, with a feeling that was tormenting and already habitual, gazed at her ankle laced into the tall boot, at her gray-stockinged leg revealed by her short gray skirt—even the sight of that thick woolen cloth alone tormented me with desire—and then I started reproaching her because we had not seen each other all day. But suddenly, with heart-rending tenderness and pity, I saw that she was asleep. . . . On awakening, she said gently and sadly: "I heard almost all you said. Don't be angry with me, I'm very tired. You know, I've gone through too much this year."

VIII

She wanted an excuse for staying on in Orel, and so she took up music. I found a pretext too: working on the staff of *The Voice.* I actually enjoyed it at first: I enjoyed the semblance of order that had now taken place in my existence; I was comforted by a certain responsibility which had now entered my utterly irresponsible life. Then the thought began to flit through my mind more and more often: was this the sort of life of which I had dreamed? Here was I living what might be the best years of my life, when I should be owning the world, and yet I did not even own a pair of galoshes! Did all this exist only for the moment? Then what lay ahead? I began to imagine that in our intimacy, too, things were far from well, in the harmony of our emotions, thoughts, tastes, and therefore in her faithfulness as well: this "everlasting contradiction between dream and reality," this everlasting intangibility of love in its fullness and entirety, as I had experienced it that winter with all the force of novelty and with a feeling that it was hideously unfair to me.

I suffered most of all when I attended receptions and balls with her. When her partner was handsome and a good dancer, and I saw her pleasure, her animation, her quickly flickering skirts and feet, the music lashed painfully at my heart with its vigorous rhythm, its waltz tunes, and made me want to weep. Everyone looked on with delight when she danced with Turchaninov, that unnaturally tall officer with black side-burns, long dark face and motionless dark eyes. She was rather tall, but he was a couple of heads taller, and as he held her close, whirling her gracefully and endlessly in a waltz, he looked down at her with something like insistence, and in her upraised face there was both happiness and misery, something beautiful and at the same time infinitely hateful to me. How hard I prayed to God then, that something quite inconceivable should happen, that he should suddenly bend down and kiss her, thereby instantly confirming and relieving my tormented expectation, the sinking feeling in my heart!

"You think of no one but yourself, you'd like everything to be the way you want it," she told me once. "I expect you'd gladly deprive me of all private life, of all my friends, you'd cut me off from everyone the way you yourself are cut off. . . ."

And indeed, in keeping with the mysterious law whereby an element of pity and compassionate tenderness has to be present in any love and particularly love for a woman, I hated her moments of gaiety—in society especially—her animation, her desire to shine and to be admired; and I passionately loved her simplicity, quietude, meekness, help-lessness, and the tears which made her lips swell at once like a child's. At social gatherings I really kept apart most of the time, behaving like an unkind observer, actually and secretly glorying in my isolation and malevolence which sharply whetted my impressionability, vigilance and insight into all the shortcomings in the others. But then, how I yearned for true intimacy with her, and how I suffered when I failed in this!

I would often read poetry to her.

"Listen to this!" I would exclaim. " 'Take my soul afar

where sorrow broods, like the moon above the hills and woods.' "

But she was not impressed.

"Yes, that's very nice," she said as she lay curled up snugly on the sofa, both hands tucked under her cheek, her glance slanting up at me vaguely and indifferently. "But why 'like the moon above the hills and woods'? Is it Fet? He's altogether too fond of describing nature."

I was indignant: "describing," she said. And I would plunge into tirades trying to prove to her that there was no nature that was not part of us, that every slightest movement of the air was a movement of our own lives; but she would merely laugh and say:

"It's only spiders who live like that, my sweet!"

Then I would read on:

How sad to see the path no more,
Again it's hid beneath the snow,
Again the slith'ring silver snakes
Across the snowdrifts crawling go.

She would ask: "What snakes?"

And I would have to explain that it was a blizzard, with snow whirling close to the ground. And, turning pale, I read:

The hoary night peeps moodily,
Under the hood of my sleigh,
O'er hills and woods, through smoky clouds,
Glimmers the wraith of the moon.

"Darling," she said, "I've never seen anything at all like that, you know!"

Then I read with concealed resentment:

Between the clouds the sun shone high and hot and fine,
And in the sand you drew a shimmering design.

She listened approvingly, but probably only because she imagined that it was she who was sitting in the garden, drawing designs in the sand with a dainty little parasol.

"That's really sweet," she said. "But enough poetry, come nearer. . . . You are always cross with me!"

I often told her about my childhood, my early adolescence, the romantic charm of our estate, about my mother, my father and my sister; she listened with ruthless indifference. I wanted her to be moved and saddened by the stories of my family's occasional spells of poverty, of the time, for instance, when we had had to take all our icons out of their frames and send the antique silver to town to pawn with Meshcherinova, a solitary old woman, who looked frighteningly oriental with her hooked nose, mustache, bulging eyes, her silks, shawls and rings, in whose empty house, cluttered with all sorts of museum pieces, a parrot screeched all day long in a shrill, dead voice. But instead of being moved and saddened she would say absently:

"Yes, it's dreadful."

The longer I lived in the town, the more I felt out of place there, even Avilova's manner toward me had changed for some reason; she became cool and mocking. The duller and drearier my life in town grew, the more I was drawn to be alone with *her*, to read to her, to tell her things and to pour out my heart to her. My hotel room was narrow and drab. I felt terribly sorry for myself, for the miserable suitcase and the few books that were all my wealth, for my lonely nights in this room, nights so wretched and cold that I could be said to conquer them, rather than sleep, aware through my somnolence that I was awaiting dawn, and the first peal ringing out in the frosty morning from the belfry nearby. Her room was cramped too; it was at the end of the corridor beside the attic stairs, but its windows faced the garden, it was quiet, warm and cozy. A fire was lit in the evenings, and she had a way of curling up so nicely on the sofa against the cushions, drawing up her feet in their exceptionally pretty slippers. I would recite:

A snowstorm howled when midnight came
Across the woods so deep and far,
The twigs were crackling in the flame
As we sat close around the fire.

But all these snowstorms, forests, fields, the savage and poetic joys of home, coziness and fire, were particularly alien to her nature.

For a long time I believed I could excite her admiration if I just said: "Do you know those beaten autumn roads, rolled smooth like lilac rubber, spiked with horseshoes and gleaming in a blinding, golden streak in the setting sun?" I told her of that day, late in the autumn, when my brother Georgy and I had gone to buy some birch timber in the woods: the ceiling had suddenly caved in in the kitchen, almost killing our former cook, a very old man, who was always warming himself on the stove ledge, and so we had had to go into the forest to buy a birch tree for the beam. It had rained all the time—tiny, swift drops falling across the sunlight; we had ridden in the cart with the workmen, driving at a brisk pace first along the highway and then through the grove of trees glistening with raindrops in the sunlight, strikingly picturesque, unrestrained and yet submissive, standing in a glade still green but already dead and waterlogged. I told her how dreadfully sorry I had been for that spreading birch, sprinkled from top to bottom with tiny, auburn leaves, when the men, walking around it in their uncouth way, had examined it rudely and then, spitting in their great ridged palms, had raised their axes and struck together at its trunk, motley with white and black. . . . "You can't imagine how terribly wet everything was, how iridescent and brilliant!" I said to her, and ended by confiding in her that I wanted to write a story about it. She shrugged and said:

"But, darling, what's there to write about? Why keep on describing nature?"

Music was one of my most complex and tormenting delights. I adored her when she played something beautiful. My heart ached with a rapturously self-sacrificing tenderness for her. I wanted to live on and on. I often thought as I listened to her playing: "If we ever part, how shall I be able to listen to this without her? Will I ever be able to love anything at all and to delight in anything without sharing this love and delight with her?" But I was so brusque in my criticism of things I disliked, that she would flare up and shout to Avilova in the next room, breaking off her music and sharply facing about:

"Nadya! Nadya, listen to the rubbish he's talking!"

"And I'll go on, too," I cried. "Three-quarters of every one of these sonatas is nothing but banality, din and chaos! Oh, that's the gravedigger's spade striking the coffin, you say. Oh, I see the nymphs dancing in the glade, and there I hear the roar of waterfalls! Nymphs—that's one of the most loathsome words I know! It's even worse than the newspapers' pet word 'fraught'!"

She tried to convince herself that she was passionately fond of the theater, while I hated it, with growing certainty that the brilliance of most actors was nothing but their comparatively greater skill in being vulgar, in pretending better than the others—according to the most vulgar standards—that they were artists and creators. All those everlasting matchmakers in their silk kerchiefs the color of onionskin and their Turkish shawls, grimacing servilely and purring sweetly as they fawned upon some Tit Titich, who would throw back his shoulders with that inevitable proud earnestness, and, as inevitably, would press his left hand with widespread fingers to his heart, or rather the breast pocket of his long-skirted frock coat. Those hoglike Mayors and flippant Khlestakovs, those Osips with their abdominal, glum wheezes, those nasty little Repetilovs, foppishly indignant Chatskys, those Famusovs gesticulating with their beringed fingers and pushing out their actors' lips like fat, purple plums; those Hamlets dressed in undertakers' cloaks and hats with curly feathers, with their lewdly languid, painted eyes, black velvet thighs and plebeian splay feet—all of it actually made me shudder. And the opera!

Rigoletto, hunched up, with his spindly legs straddled contrary to all aesthetic rules, and close together at the knees; Susanin rolling his eyes heavenward blissfully and mournfully and intoning with a rumble: "You will arise, my dawn!" The miller in "Mermaid" with arms as thin as twigs, wildly flung out and trembling wrathfully (still wearing a wedding ring, however), and dressed in shirt and trousers so tattered and ragged as though a whole pack of mad dogs had been at them. We never got anywhere in our arguments about the theater: we just lost all give and take, all understanding for one another. For instance, there was that famous provincial actor on tour in Orel, playing in *Notes of the Madman*, and everyone watched him eagerly, enraptured with him as he sat on the hospital bed in his dressing gown, his effeminate face too deliberately unshaven, saying nothing for a long, painfully long minute, benumbed with some inanely happy and ever-growing amazement, raising his finger at last very, very slowly, and, finally, with unbelievable slowness and unbearable expressiveness, bringing out syllable after syllable, hideously twisting his mouth: "On this day . . ." And the following night he was even more splendid in pretending he was Lyubim Tortsov, and the next—Marmeladov, grimy and purple-nosed, saying: "May I venture, my kind sir, to approach you with my respectful conversation?" There was that famous actress writing a letter—she had suddenly decided to write something momentous and, quickly sitting down at her desk, she dipped her dry pen into a dry inkwell, in a flash drew three long strokes across the page, thrust it into an envelope, jingled the bell, and said curtly and drily to the pretty housemaid in the white little apron who answered the bell: "Have it delivered at once!" And every time we came back from the theater we would shout at one another until three in the morning, keeping Avilova awake, and by then I would be cursing not just the madman, Tortsov and Marmeladov, but Gogol, Ostrovsky and Dostoyevsky too. . . .

"But even supposing you're right," she would scream, pale now, her eyes quite dark and exceptionally lovely for that reason. "Why must you get so furious about it? Nadya, ask him!"

"Because," I would shout in reply, "because it's enough for me to hear an actor pronounce the word 'aroma' as 'aromàh' to make me want to strangle him!"

We began the same quarrel after every venture of ours into Orel society. I passionately wanted to share with her the delights of my powers of observation, my keenness and subtlety in exercising them. I wanted to infect her with my cutting criticism of everyone and everything about me, but I saw with despair that my wish to make her a participant in all my thoughts and feelings brought just the opposite results. I said to her one day:

"If you only knew how many enemies I have!"

"What enemies?" she asked. "Where are they?"

"All sorts, everywhere: at the hotel, in the shops, in the street, at the station. . . ."

"But who are they?"

"Why, everyone, everyone! What a lot of horrid faces and bodies! You know, even St. Paul said: 'All flesh is not the same flesh: but there is one kind of flesh of men, another flesh of beasts. . . .' Some are simply hideous! The way they plant their feet, the way they bend their bodies forward, one might think they'd only just stopped walking on all fours! Yesterday, for instance, I walked behind a broad-shouldered and altogether thick-set policeman for a long way down Bolkhovskaya Street. I kept my eyes glued to his fat back in the greatcoat, his shins in shiny, heavily bulging top boots. Ah, how I gloated over those bulging top boots, their strong smell, the cloth of that gray, solid greatcoat, the buttons on his belt strap, and the whole of that powerful, forty-year-old animal in all his military harness!"

"Have you no shame!" she said with aversion and chagrin. "Can you really be so horrid and mean? I don't understand you at all. You're made up of the most extraordinary contradictions!"

IX

And yet when I arrived at the office of a morning, I welcomed the sight of her gray fur coat on the peg with increasing warmth and joy, for it seemed to be herself, or at least a very graceful part of her, and her dear gray overshoes standing underneath the coat—a most touching part of her. In my impatience to see her I would be the first to arrive at the office; I would take up my work, glancing through and editing our provincial articles, reading the leading newspapers, compiling "our own telegrams" from them, all but writing anew some of the stories sent in by our local novelists, while all the time I would be waiting and listening until at last I heard her quick steps, her swishing skirts. She seemed like a new person, with her cool perfumed hands, a youthful light in her eyes which were especially bright after a good night's rest; she would run across the room to me, throw a look over her shoulder and kiss me. She sometimes dropped in to see me at the hotel too, a smell of winter and the cold fur of her coat clinging to her. I would kiss her apple-cool face, put my arms inside her coat and hug all that warmth and sweetness that was her body and her dress, and she would struggle free, laughing, "Let me go, I've come on business," and, ringing for the servant, she would tell him to put my room in order while she supervised and helped him herself.

Once I happened to overhear her conversation with Avilova: they were sitting in the dining room one evening discussing me frankly, thinking that I was in the print shop. Avilova was saying:

"Lika dear, but what of the future? You know the way I feel about him, he's very nice of course, I quite understand your infatuation. . . . But then, what next?"

I was plunged into an abyss. So I was "very nice." Was that all? Was it nothing but "infatuation"?

The answer I heard was even more horrible:

"But what can I do? I see no way out. . . ."

A rage so vehement welled up in me that I was about to rush into the dining room, shouting that there *was* a way out, that within the hour I would leave Orel, when suddenly she spoke again:

"Oh, can't you see, Nadya, that I love him truly? And then you don't really know him—he's a thousand times better than he seems. . . ."

That was true. I may have seemed much worse than I was. I lived tensely and fitfully, I often treated people harshly and arrogantly, I easily fell into melancholy and despair; but my mood changed quickly when I saw that nothing threatened our peace and harmony, that no one was trying to claim her, and then my innate readiness to be kindhearted, frank and happy came back to me at once. If we were going to a party and I was sure that it would bring me neither injury nor hurt, how gladly I made ready for it, how I preened myself before the mirror, admiring my eyes, the dark spots of my youthful flush, and the snow-white starched shirt, which freshly laundered stuck hard together and crackled delightfully when I ripped it open. I simply loved those balls when my jealousy did not torment me! Every time I got ready for a ball I went through some cruel moments. I was obliged to put on the dress coat which had belonged to Avilova's late husband, a perfectly new coat, it's true, never worn once, I believe, but it seemed to pierce me through and through nevertheless. But I forgot those pangs the moment I went out into the street, breathed the frosty air, saw the speckled starry sky, and got into a droshky. Heaven alone knows why they used to put red-striped canopies over the brilliantly lighted front doors when there was a ball on, and why it was necessary for the policemen controlling the passage of the carriages and sledges to give a performance of such dashing ferocity! But no matter, such were the balls with those bizarre entrances casting their bright, white-hot lights on the trampled snow, with all that show of efficiency and speed, the sharp commands of the policemen, their frozen wirespun mustaches, their polished top boots stamping in the snow, their hands in white knitted gloves hidden in their pockets, their elbows turned outward in a peculiar way. Practically all the guests were in uniform—there were plenty of uniforms in Russia once upon a time—and every one of the men was arrogantly excited by his rank and his uniform. I have noticed that even if a man possessed the highest of titles and held the most eminent of posts all his life long, he could never take them for granted. The guests stirred me too as they arrived, at once becoming the object of my instantly sharpened, antagonistic vigilance. But almost all the women were sweet and desirable. They looked charming as they emerged from their fur wraps and hooded cloaks in the hall, and became indeed the ones for whom the wide, red-carpeted stairs were intended, and who should be reflected again and again in the mirrors in bewitching bevies. And then the magnificent emptiness of the ballroom before the ball—its fresh chilliness, the ponderous cluster of the chandelier pierced with a diamond play of lights, the huge curtainless windows, the gloss and sweep of the still empty parquet floor, the smell of flowers, powder, perfume, white kid gloves, and all the excitement of watching more and more guests coming in, waiting for the first roll of the orchestra, the first couple to suddenly fly across the expanse of this virgin floor—always the most self-assured couple, the best dancers.

I invariably set out for a ball before *they* did. When I arrived the guests would still be driving up, the footmen downstairs would be struggling with armfuls of topcoats, fur coats and military coats, fragrant with frost, and everywhere the atmosphere would be too chilly for my thin dress coat. And I—dressed in someone else's coat—my hair brushed smooth, slender but appearing even thinner than I really was, grown weightless, strange to all and lonely (a strangely haughty young man, doing some strange sort of job on the newspaper staff)—I was so soberly and clearly conscious of myself in the beginning, and so apart from the rest, that I might have been an icy mirror reflecting it all. The gathering grew larger and noisier; the thundering music sounded more familiar now; the doors of the ballroom were already crammed; there were more and more women; the air became thicker and warmer, and I got drunk with it, began to look at the women with more daring and at the men with more arrogance, gliding through the crowd with smoother steps, my "beg your pardon" as I collided with some dress coat or uniform sounding more and more polite and haughty. . . . Suddenly I would see them—there they were, half-smiling, slowly making their way through the crowd—and my heart came to a standstill with a pang of intimacy, but also with embarrassment and wonder: they seemed the same and yet different. She, especially, was quite unlike herself. At such moments I was invariably struck by her youth and slenderness: her slim waist tightly laced into a corset, her charming gown so light and so chastely gay, her arms, bare from the top of the gloves to her shoulders, chilled and purple like the arms of adolescents, the expression on her face that still lacked self-assurance . . . only her hair piled high was like a society belle's. There was a peculiar appeal in this, but something which at the same time seemed ready to escape me, to betray me and even to entertain a secret desire for depravity. Soon afterward someone would hurry up to her, drop her a low bow with the haste peculiar to balls, she would hand her fan to Avilova and absently, as it were, put her hand gracefully on his shoulder and, whirling, gliding on her toes, disappear into the waltzing crowd, in the noise and the music. And I would look on with a feeling of finality, with what had already become an icy hostility.

Avilova, small, lively, always cheerful and poised, struck me, too, with her youthfulness and radiant prettiness. It was at one of these balls that I realized that she was only twenty-six and for the first time, afraid to believe my own thoughts, I suddenly understood the reason for the queer change in her attitude to me that winter, divining her love and jealousy.

X

And then came a long separation.

It all began with the sudden arrival of the doctor. As I walked into the office one cold, sunny morning, I suddenly caught the strong smell of some very familiar brand of cigarettes, and heard excited voices and laughter in the dining room. I paused, wondering what it could mean. But it was the doctor who had filled the whole house with smoke; it was his voice I heard talking loudly with the eagerness peculiar to the type of men who, having reached a certain age, go through the years without changing at all, enjoying perfect health, constant smoking and incessant garrulity. I was dumfounded—what was behind this unexpected visit? Was it something he wanted from her? And how was I to walk in, how should I behave? Nothing frightening happened at first, however. I quickly took myself in hand, went into the dining room and was "pleasantly surprised. . . ." The doctor, in his kindness, was actually somewhat confused; he smilingly hastened to tell me with an air of apology that he had come to have a change from the provinces for a week or so. I saw right away that she was keyed up too, and so was Avilova for some reason. However, I still had hopes that the cause of this was the doctor, an unexpected guest, a man who had just arrived from his small town and was therefore drinking his hot tea in someone else's dining room with exceptional relish after a night in the train. I was already beginning to calm down, and this was when the blow was dealt me: I suddenly understood from all the doctor was saying that he had not come alone but with Bogomolov, a young, rich and even famous tanner in our town, who had long been wanting to marry her. And then I heard the doctor laugh and say:

"He says he's head over heels in love with you, Lika; he's come with the most deliberate intentions! And so the fate of this unfortunate young man is entirely in your hands: you'll have mercy on him if you wish, if you don't you'll wreck his life forever. . . ."

And wealth was not Bogomolov's only attraction: he was clever, he had a bright and pleasant disposition, he had a university education, he had been abroad, he spoke two foreign languages. He was quite a hideous sight the first time you saw him: his carrot-red hair was sleekly brushed with a part in the middle, his face delicate and round, and his body monstrously, inhumanly fat, like that of an infant fantastically well-nourished and grown to a supernatural size, or like a huge young Yorkshire pig, a gleaming mass of fat and blood. And yet everything about this pig was so magnificent, so clean and healthy that you actually felt a surge of happiness when you were with him: his blue eyes were as clear as the skies, his complexion unbelievably fine, and there was something shy and endearing in the whole of his manner, his laugh, the tone of his voice, the play of his eyes and lips. His hands and feet were touchingly tiny, his suit was made of English cloth, his socks, shirt and tie were all of silk. I darted a quick look at her and saw her embarrassed smile. . . . And all at once I felt like a stranger; it suddenly seemed to me that I was unwanted and disgracefully *de trop* in this house, and a hatred for her welled up in me.

After that we never had an hour alone together, she was always with her father or Bogomolov. Avilova kept smiling mysteriously and gaily. She was so nice and pleasant to Bogomolov that from the outset he felt perfectly at home there; he would make his appearance in the morning and stay till night, only going back to his hotel to sleep. Moreover, the amateur dramatic society of which Lika was a member began to rehearse a play which was to be staged in carnival week, and through Lika they got both Bogomolov and the doctor, too, to take small parts in it. She told me she was only letting Bogomolov court her for her father's sake, so as not to hurt him with too churlish an attitude toward his friend, and I kept a tight hold on myself pretending that I believed her. I even forced myself to attend their rehearsals, thus trying to conceal my painful jealousy and all those other torments which I had to suffer there, for her pathetic attempts at "acting" made me burn with shame. Altogether this utter and general want of talent was a horrible spectacle to behold.

The play was directed by a professional, an unemployed actor, who naturally fancied he had the spark of genius and reveled in his foul theatrical experience, a man of uncertain age on whose putty-colored face the lines were so deep that they might have been cut there on purpose. He kept losing his temper while shouting instructions as to how this or that part should be played; he swore so coarsely and vehemently that cordlike veins swelled on his temples. He would play a male and then a female part for them, and everyone would wear themselves out trying to copy him, torturing me with every note of their voices, every movement of their bodies: abominable though the actor was, his imitators were even more so. And then why did they act at all? What for? Among the company there was a "lady of the regiment," a character found in every small town, a bony, self-confident and bold woman; there was a garishly dressed spinster, always uneasy, always waiting for something, with a habit of biting her lips; there were two sisters known to the whole town for their inseparability and their extraordinary likeness: both were tall, with coarse black hair and black eyebrows meeting across the bridge of their noses, both were sternly taciturn—a proper pair of black shaft horses. There was the governor's confidential secretary, quite young though already growing bald, a fair-haired man with goggling blue eyes and red eyelids, very tall, in a very tall starched collar, tediously polite and tactful; there was the famous local lawyer, an immense bulk of a fat-breasted and fat-shouldered man with ponderous feet —I invariably mistook him for the butler at the balls in his dress coat; there was a young artist—black velvet blouse, long Indian hair, a goat's profile tapering to a goatee, effeminate perversion in his half-closed eyes and in his soft, bright red lips which you felt ashamed to look at, and a woman's hips.

Then came the night of the play. I thought I would go backstage before the curtain went up. It was a madhouse there, everyone was dressing, making up, shouting, quarreling, rushing in and out of the dressing rooms, colliding and not recognizing each other—so queer was their dress (one was actually wearing a brown dress coat and mauve trousers), so lifeless were their wigs, beards and staring faces daubed with paint, with patches of pink plaster stuck on their foreheads and noses, painted, shining eyes with eyelashes blackened so heavily and crudely that they blinked slowly like a manikin's eyes. When I ran into her I did not recognize her either, astounded as I was with her likeness to a doll in her pink, daintily old-fashioned frock, her thick flaxen wig and the cheap prettiness and childishness of her chocolate-box face. Bogomolov played the part of a yellow-haired yard man, and so they spared no effort in dressing him up, as befitted the creation of a "true-to-life" character. The doctor had the part of an old uncle, a retired general. The play opened with a scene in his country house with him sitting in a wicker armchair under a green tree made of planks nailed to the bare floor; he was dressed in a brand-new raw silk suit; he, too, was painted pink all over, with huge milky mustaches; he sat leaning back in his chair, his eyes fixed resentfully on the newspaper he held spread wide in front of him, and although the scenery represented a fine summer morning, the footlights illuminated him brightly from below so that, in spite of his white mustache and hair, he looked surprisingly young. After reading the newspaper for a moment he was supposed to say something in a grumpy growl, but he just kept staring at the paper unable to bring out a word, although a desperate hiss was heard coming from the prompt-box. And only when at long last she came running from behind the scenes (with a childishly playful, charmingly boisterous laugh) and jumped on him from behind, pressing her hands to his eyes and shouting, "Guess who?" did he give voice, shouting too, and spacing the words: "Let go, let go, you naughty girl, I know perfectly well who it is."

The hall was in semidarkness, the stage was sunlit and

bright. Sitting in the front row, I glanced up at the stage and then at those about me: the row was made up of the richest citizens, smothering in fat, and the highest ranking and most imposing police and army officers, and all of them looked spellbound with what was going on on the stage; there was tension in their postures and smiles were frozen on their faces. . . . I could not even endure it to the end of the first act. The moment something banged on the stage—a sign that the curtain was due—I quickly left the hall. By then the actors were on their mettle, and their immoderately lively ejaculations sounded particularly unnatural when they reached the ordinary lighted vestibule where the old attendant, who was used to anything, helped me on with my coat. I rushed out into the street at last. An odd sensation of disastrous loneliness mounted in me to a state of ecstasy. The streets were deserted and clean, the street lamps cast a dead light. I did not go home but went to the office instead, for my narrow hotel room was too frightening. I walked past the government buildings, turned into the empty square where the cathedral stood, its faintly glistening gilt dome vanishing into the starlit sky. . . . There was something profound and awesome in the very crunch of my boots on the snow. . . . The house was warm, still and peaceful with the slow ticking of the clock in the lighted dining room. Avilova's little boy was asleep, his nurse opened the front door to me, gave me a sleepy look and shuffled away. I went into the room beside the stairs, a room I already knew so well and which meant so much to me. I sat down in the dark on the old sofa which now seemed so fateful. I both wanted and dreaded the minute when they would all drive up, walk into the house noisily, all talking at once, laughing, settling down to tea, sharing their impressions—but more than anything else I dreaded the moment when I should hear her laughter, her voice. . . . The room was full of her, her absence and her presence, and all her smells —herself, her gowns, her perfume, her soft dressing gown lying beside me on the arm of the sofa. Cold, blue night looked wrathfully in through the window, stars flashed brilliantly behind the black branches of the trees. . . .

In the first week of Lent she left with her father and Bogomolov (having refused him). But I would not so much as speak to her long before that. She cried all the time she packed, hoping that I might suddenly hold her back, refuse to let her go.

XI

It was Lent, a fast that is strictly observed in provincial towns. In the evenings the droshky-drivers stood idly on the corners freezing in the cold and warmed themselves up by violently swinging their arms back and forth across their chests; only if an officer walked past would they venture to call out timidly: "Your honor! How about a fast one?" The jackdaws chatted nervously and gaily, sensing spring's approach, but the crows went on croaking harshly and sternly.

Our separation seemed especially dreadful at night. Waking up in the middle of the night I was struck with the thought: how could I live now, and why should I live at all? Was it really I—this man who for some reason lay in the darkness of this senseless night, in a strange provincial town peopled with thousands of strangers, in this hotel room with a narrow window which all night long I had fancied was a tall, gray, speechless devil. Avilova was the only friend I had in the town. But was she really an intimate friend? This intimacy was ambiguous and awkward. . . .

I was no longer an early arrival at the office. When Avilova saw me coming in she gave me a smiling welcome. She was nice and sweet to me again, she no longer sneered at me, and now all I saw in her was her steady love for me, her constant sympathy and care. I often spent my evenings alone with her; she played the piano for me while I lay back on the sofa, blinking away the tears that welled up in my eyes from this musical bliss, the heartache music made more poignant, and from an all-forgiving tenderness. When I came into the general office, I always kissed her small firm hand, and proceeded into the staff room. There was never anyone there but the editorial writer, smoking a cigarette. He was a stupid, pensive man, exiled to Orel under police surveillance; a rather queer-looking man: he wore his beard like a peasant, a dingy brown homespun *poddyovka* and tarred top boots which reeked strongly but pleasantly. He was left-handed, for half of his right hand was missing, and he held down the paper on the desk with the stump hidden in his sleeve, and wrote with his left hand. He used to sit and think for a long time, smoking hard, and then suddenly he would bring the stump down more deliberately on the paper and be off, writing quickly and energetically, with the agility of a monkey. The next to arrive was usually the foreign news editor, an old man, small, with short legs, who wore glasses that gave him a surprised look; in the hall he took off his short jacket lined with rabbit fur and his Finnish cap with the ear flaps down, and then when he was left in his small top boots, trousers and flannel shirt, girt with a narrow leather belt, he looked as short and puny as a ten-year-old boy. His gray hair stood up very ferociously, sticking up high and wide like a porcupine's, and his glasses gave him a ferocious look too. He always brought two boxes with him to the office, one held cigarette wrappers and the other tobacco, and while he worked he kept making himself cigarettes. While he ran his experienced eye down the columns of the newspapers, he would stuff pale, stringy tobacco into a thin copper tube, grope absently for a wrapper, press the handle of the contraption into his soft shirt front, the tube into the paper wrapper, and deftly shoot the cigarette on to the table. The make-up man and the proofreader came in next. The make-up man walked in with an unruffled, independent air; he was amazing in his politeness, taciturnity and inscrutability; he was unusually lean and gaunt, with Gypsy black hair, a greenish-olive complexion, a small black mustache, and dead ash-gray lips; he was always neat and immaculate in his black trousers and blue smock with a large starched turndown collar—all of it dazzlingly fresh and clean. I would sometimes speak to him in the print shop, and then he would break his silence, fix his dark eyes on me with a steady, hard stare, and talk without raising his voice, as if he had been wound up, always on the same subject: the unfairness of the world in everything, everywhere and always. The proofreader was always in and out; he invariably found things he could not understand or did not approve of in the article he was reading, and would come in to ask the author for explanations or alterations: "I'm sorry but there's something here that's not very well put," he would say. He was fat and clumsy with frizzy hair that looked slightly wet, he hunched his shoulders from nervousness and fear that people might see he was dead drunk, he bent over you when he asked for an explanation, holding in his alcohol-laden breath, stretching out his shiny, swollen and shaking hand to point out the line he did not understand or considered unfortunate. I sat in the room and absently edited the manuscripts of others, but most of the time I looked out of the window and thought what I myself would write and how I would do it.

Now I had another secret torment, another bitter and elusive dream. I had taken up writing again, prose for the most part, and again my work was being published. But my thoughts were not on what I had written and published. I was tormented by the desire to write something different, not at all what I could and did write: something that I could not write. I thought what rare happiness it must be, what spiritual endeavor to develop within yourself, from sources life had given you, something truly deserving of being a writer. And so my life became more and more a struggle with this elusive desire, a search and capture of that new and equally elusive happiness, pursuit of it and incessant brooding on it.

The mail arrived at noon. I would come out into the general office and once again see Avilova's beautifully and carefully done hair as she bent over her work, and everything about her seemed so dear: the soft sheen of her shagreen leather shoes under the table, the fur cape on her shoulders which also gleamed with the light of the bleak winter day that fell through the window beyond which crows dotted the gray, snowy sky. From the mail I would pick out the latest of periodicals from the capital and cut the pages hurriedly. . . . A new Chekhov story! The sight of that name alone affected me so that I could not even read the opening lines—the ecstasy I could foresee blinded me with such poignant envy! In the meantime more and more people came and went: there were some advertisers among them, and a great variety of people who were also possessed by the lust for writing; there was an imposing old man in an angora muffler and mittens who had brought along a whole stack of large sheets of cheap paper with the words "Songs and Thoughts," written on the title page in all the clerical splendor of the quill-pen days. There was a very young officer, flushing crimson with embarrassment, who handed in his manuscript with a curt and politely clear request that we should look it through and if we published it be sure not to disclose his real name—"Only my initials, please, if your rules allow it." After the officer came an elderly priest, sweating with excitement and the warmth of his topcoat, who wanted to publish his *Village Scenes* signed *Spectator;* the priest was followed by the district attorney, an extremely spick-and-span man; he removed his new overshoes, his new fur-lined gloves, new greatcoat lined with polecat, and his new tall fur hat in so leisurely a manner it seemed quite queer, and when he had emerged from these top clothes he appeared exceptionally thin, tall, toothy and well-scrubbed; it took him almost half an hour to wipe his mustache with an immaculate handkerchief, while I sat hungrily watching his every movement, exulting in my writer's perspicacity.

"Yes, yes, he naturally has to be so well-scrubbed, so neat, unhurried and careful of his own person if he's got those gat-teeth and thick mustache, a hairline already receding from his forehead which bulges like an apple, eyes so brilliant, cheekbones showing bright feverish spots, feet large and flat, and hands large and flat with large, round fingernails!" I thought.

The nurse brought the little boy in from the garden to lunch. Avilova would run out into the hall, nimbly kneel on the floor before the child and take off his white sheepskin cap, unbutton his tiny dark-blue *poddyovka* lined with white fleece, and kiss his cool, glowing cheeks, while his gaze wandered absently as he stood thinking some thought of his own, indifferently letting her undress him and kiss him—and I caught myself envying all this: the blissful senselessness of the boy, the happiness of Avilova's motherhood and the aged stillness of the nurse. I now envied anyone whose life was occupied with ready-made worries and duties and not with anticipation, with fanciful preparation for the strangest of all human occupations called "writing." I envied everyone who had a simple, precise and definite job to do in life, so that when he had finished it he could be absolutely easy in his mind and free till the next day.

I usually went out after lunch. The town was shrouded in a thick snowfall, those large, drowsy flakes of Lenten snow which were so misleading with their delicate, peculiarly sheer whiteness, making you believe that spring was really near. A droshky flew past soundlessly, the driver had a carefree air, he had probably just had a quick drink and was looking forward to something pleasant and good . . . what could have been more commonplace? But now everything stung me, even if it was the most momentary of impressions, and having stung me it instantly gave me an impetus to retain the impression, not to let it go to waste and vanish without a trace, in a flash of avarice I had to seize the impression at once for my own, and make something out of it. There he streaked past, and everything about the moment and the driver streaked across my heart too, and, lingering with a strange and vague memory, it weighed upon me long and vainly. Next I came to a rich mansion, I saw in front of it a highly varnished carriage looming darkly through the snowflakes, the greasy-looking tires of the large rear wheels sinking in the old snow and softly powdered with the new. I walked on and as I glanced at the back of the thick-shouldered driver towering on the box seat in a velvet mortarboard cap as thick as a cushion, his sash wound high under his armpits the way children are belted in winter, I suddenly saw a sweet little dog with ears sticking up like a bow, sitting behind the glass door of the carriage, amid beautiful, pale satin cushions, shivering and staring so intently as if it were about to say something. And joy pierced me like a flash of lightning again—I must remember it—"ears like a bow."

I dropped in at the library. It was old and rare in wealth. But what a dismal and unwanted air it had! An old, neglected building, a vast, bare hall, a cold staircase to the first floor, a felt-padded door faced with torn oilcloth. There were three rooms lined from floor to ceiling with tattered, dog-eared books, a long counter, a small desk, a short, flat-chested, sullenly quiet woman in charge, dressed in something dark and dull, with pale skinny hands, an inkstain on the third finger; there was an unkempt youth in a gray smock with a soft, mouse-gray head of hair badly in need of cutting, to carry out her orders. I used to go into the reading room, a circular room smelling of fumes, a round table in the center with the *Parish News* and the *Russian Pilgrim* on it. I never failed to find another reader there—a haggard youngster, a schoolboy in a short, shabby topcoat, slumped over the table, leafing through a thick book with an air of secrecy, a youngster who kept furtively wiping his nose with a handkerchief he had rolled into a little ball. . . . Who if not we two should be sitting there, both of us queer in our loneliness in this town and in our choice of books? The youngster was reading something quite ridiculously unsuitable for a schoolboy: *Soshnoye Pismo.** And I, too, would often get a puzzled look from the librarian when I asked her for the *Northern Drone, Moscow Herald, Pole Star, Northern Flowers,* Pushkin's *Contemporary.* . . . I read new books, too, the biographies of famous people, but only in an effort to find some support in them and to draw an envious

* A cadastre of arable land.—*Tr.*

comparison between them and myself. Oh, famous people! What an infinite number of poets, novelists and story writers the world has known and how few of them have survived! The same names are famous now and forever! Homer, Horace, Virgil, Dante, Petrarch . . . Shakespeare, Byron, Shelley, Goethe . . . Racine, Molière. . . . The same old *Don Quixote*, the same *Manon Lescaut*. . . . I remember reading Radishchev for the first time in that room with profound admiration—"I cast my eyes about me and my soul was fraught with anguish for the sufferings of mankind!"

Leaving the library toward the end of the day, I slowly strolled along the darkening streets. The sound of the church bells tolling softly, lingered in the air. Feeling sorry for myself, nostalgic for *her*, homesick, I went into a church. Here, too, there was this feeling of unwantedness: emptiness and dusk, a few flickering candles, some old men and women in prayer. The churchwarden with gray hair parted in the middle like a peasant's stood motionless behind the candle counter in a religious fervor, while he ran his eye over the congregation with a tradesman's acumen. The splay-footed sexton shuffled about with difficulty, straightening a slanting and too quickly melting candle, or snuffing out another that had burned down, sending up a smell of burning wax; he took out the candle end and kneaded it in his old hand into one lump of wax together with all the other candle ends, and you could see how infinitely bored he was with all this worldly and strange existence of ours, all the sacraments of baptism, communion, nuptials and burials, all the feast days and fast days following each other unendingly, year after year. The priest, strangely thin in his cassock without the chasuble, his uncovered hair hanging loosely in a casual and womanly way, stood facing the closed altar doors, dropping such low bows that his stole fell away from his chest and swept the floor, his voice raised in a sigh:

"O Lord in Heaven, dispenser of life and death. . . ." echoing in the wistful, repentant twilight, in the sorrowful emptiness. I quietly left the church and once again breathed the wintry air which had a promise of spring in it, watching the darkening smoky sky. A beggar bowed his head of thick gray hair low before me with sham humility, his hand cupped ready to receive the five-kopek piece I would drop in it, but the moment he had closed his fingers tightly over it he looked up and gave me a sudden jolt with his watery, turquoise-blue eyes of an inveterate drunkard and his huge strawberry of a nose made up of three large, lumpy and porous strawberries. And oh, I felt such an agony of joy again: imagine, a three-lump, strawberry nose!

I walked down Bolkhovskaya Street gazing into the darkening sky, the silhouettes of the old roofs against the sky, and the incomprehensible, soothing charm of these silhouettes tormented me. The roof of an old home—who has ever written of it? Lights went on in the streets, shop windows glowed warmly, black shapes walked the pavements, the skies turned a darker, deeper blue, the town grew sweeter and cozier . . . . Like a detective I followed first one of these shapes and then another, staring at their backs, at their overshoes, trying to understand, to capture something of them, to get right into them. I wanted to write! It is these roofs, these overshoes and backs we ought to write about, we should not write "to struggle against arbitrary rule and violence, to defend the downtrodden and destitute, to portray vivid characters, to paint embracing pictures of the contemporary world, public sentiments and trends!" I quickened my steps, going down to the Orlik. Evening gave way to night, the gaslight on the bridge was already burning brightly, and under that light stood a wretched sewer-cleaner with a bloated, pimply face and pale bleary eyes, his red bare feet in the snow, and nothing on him but a torn cotton shirt and short pink drawers. He stood reeling, his hands thrust inside his shirt, hugging himself, looking at me with dog's eyes and shivering all over like a dog. "Your honor! Your honor!" he muttered woodenly. Thieflike I quickly seized and secreted within myself my impression of him, and for that I thrust a whole ten-kopek piece at him. . . . What a horrible life! But was it really horrible?

Perhaps "horror" was not the word for it at all, but something quite different? The other day I had thrust a five-kopek piece at another poor devil like that and cried naïvely: "But it's really horrible your living like this!" and you should have seen the sudden insolence, firmness and anger at my stupidity with which he threw back huskily: "There's nothing horrible about it, young man!" And once past the bridge, I saw the blinding lights of the plate-glass window of a pork butcher's on the ground floor of a large building. The window was so thronged with every conceivable sort of sausage and ham, you could hardly see the white, brilliant interior of the shop itself, also hung closely with sausages and hams. "Social contrasts!" I thought spitefully as though trying to sting someone, as I walked past bathed in the light and radiance shed by the window. I would go into the hackney-coachmen's tearoom in Moskovskaya Street and sit there in the din, the stuffiness and steamy warmth, looking at the fleshy, purple faces, the red beards, and the rusty peeling tray before me with two white teapots on it, their lids tied to the handles with dripping strings. Do you think I was observing the people's way of life? Not at all—only the tray, the dripping string!

XII

Sometimes I walked toward the railway station. Beyond the triumphal arch the streets were plunged in darkness, in the murk of a small-town night. And then I saw a wretched little provincial town, unbeknown, existing only in my fancy, but existing with such vividness as if my whole life had been spent in it. I saw its wide, snow-swept streets, hovels darkening in the snow, a tiny red light in one of the windows. . . . Enraptured, I kept saying to myself: that's it, that's it, that's the way it should be written, just four words: snow, hovel, sanctuary lamp—and nothing else! The cold wind blowing from the fields brought the shriek and hiss of steam engines, and the delicious smell of coal that stirred you to the depths of your soul with a sensation of distance and open spaces. I saw the black shapes of droshkys rushing their fares along the street toward me, and I wondered if the Moscow mail train had come in. Indeed it had, for the station restaurant was hot and stuffy with people, lights, kitchen smells and samovars being kindled. The Tatar waiters rushed about with flying coattails, all of them bow-legged, dark-faced, with high cheekbones, equine eye hollows and shaven, bluish skulls as round as cannon balls. There was a whole party of merchants at the big table, eating cold sturgeon with horse-radish: all of them members of the sect of "skoptsi" with large, solid female faces the color of saffron, narrow eyes, great-coats lined with foxskins. . . . The station bookstall always held a great fascination for me, and so I wandered round it like a ravenous wolf, straining to see the titles on the yellow and gray backs of Suvorin's editions. And all of this would rouse to such a pitch my everlasting yearning for travel and trains, develop it into such longing for her, with whom I could have been so ineffably happy traveling, that I hurried out into the open, fell into a sledge and dashed back to town, to the office. Heartache and speed are always a wonderful combination! Sitting in the sledge, which jolted and dipped into the holes, I would look up and suddenly see that there was a moon in the sky, a pale face peeping whitely behind the dark blur of floating wintry clouds. How high in the sky and how indifferent to everything it was! The clouds sailed along, revealing it for a moment and shrouding it again, but it did not care; it cared nothing for them. I kept my head thrown back until my neck began to hurt, I never took my eyes away from the moon, straining to understand what it resembled when the whole of it, gleaming, rolled free of the clouds. Was it the white mask of the dead? I knew it was lighted from within, but what was it made of? Paraffin? Yes, yes, of course that was it! I must mention it like that somewhere.

In the hall of the office I ran into Avilova, who, surprised and pleased, said to me: "Oh, how nice! Come to the concert with me!" She was dressed in something black and lacy, something lovely that made her look even smaller and slimmer, leaving her shoulders, arms and the gentle curve of her throat uncovered, she had been to the hairdresser's, her *coiffure* was perfect, her face was dusted with powder which made her eyes seem darker and brighter. I wrapped her fur coat round her shoulders, with difficulty checking my impulse to kiss suddenly this terribly close bare flesh and this fragrant, waved hair. . . . Well-known performers from the capital were giving a concert at the Club of the Nobility where the hall blazed with all its chandeliers. There was a beautiful soprano and a huge, dark baritone who, like all singers, was a striking figure of amazing fitness and the crudely magnificent power of a young stallion. He was dazzling in his enormous patent-leather shoes, his beautifully fitted dress coat, white shirt front and white tie, with challenge and heroic valor in his thundering voice, virile and ominously insistent. She, withdrawing from him or merging her song with his again, responded to him hurriedly, breaking in with tender reproaches and complaints, with passionate sorrow and rapturous joy, laughing in hastily blissful grace notes. . . .

XIII

I often woke up at the break of dawn. A glance at my watch told me it was not yet seven. I wanted dreadfully to dive under my blanket again and stay in my warm bed a little longer. The light in the room was coldly gray and the silence of the slumbering hotel was only disturbed by a very early sort of sound—the swish of the clothesbrush and its knocks against coat buttons at the farther end of the corridor. But I was so frightened of wasting another day, so anxious to settle down to my writing as soon as possible, and really in earnest that day, that I pounced on the bell rope and sent an insistent, plaintive peal quavering down the corridor. How alien and disgusting it all was—this hotel, this grimy servant swishing the clothesbrush, this miserable tin washstand which spurted a slanting jet of icy water into your face! How pathetic was my youthful gauntness in the thin nightshirt, how sad the pigeon frozen into a little ball on the coarse-grained snow of the window ledge outside! My heart would suddenly be aflame with a joyful and daring resolve: to get out of here at once, that very day, back to Baturino to my own dear home! But when I had gulped down my tea and given a semblance of tidiness to my few books on the battered little table which stood beside the washstand, pushed up against the door which led into the next room occupied by a faded, wistfully beautiful woman with an eight-year-old child, I became engrossed in my usual early-morning occupation—that of preparing myself for writing, straining to analyze what it was I had in me, searching within myself for something that was on the point of becoming defined, of taking shape. . . . I waited for that moment, but now I was afraid that once again there would be nothing but this waiting, this growing excitement turning my hands icy-cold, and then utter despair and flight into the street, into the office. My thoughts became confused, my mind again tormenting me with its spontaneity, its desultoriness, thronged with the most diverse feelings, thoughts and fancies. . . . The central theme was always myself, my personality, for if the truth be told I was not really interested in others, no matter how keenly I studied them. Well then, I thought, perhaps I should simply write a story about myself. But how? Something like "Childhood, Boyhood"? Or simpler still: "I was born in such and such a place in such and such a year. . . ." But, heavens, how dry, how paltry and how false! That's not what I felt at all. Though I would be ashamed and embarrassed to say it, this is what I felt: I was born in the universe, in timelessness and infinity, where once upon a time a certain solar system was formed, then something called the sun and then the earth. . . . But what did it mean? What did I know about all this except mere words? In the beginning the earth was a shimmering gaseous mass. . . . Then, after millions of years, this gas became a liquid, then the liquid hardened and, I think it was two million years later, protozoa appeared on the earth: algae and Infusoria. . . . And then the invertebrates: worms and mollusca. . . . And then amphibia. . . . And after the amphibia, monstrous reptiles. . . . And then some caveman or other and his discovery of fire. . . . After that came Chaldea, Assyria and Egypt which I don't remember doing anything except building pyramids and embalming mummies. . . . A certain Artaxerxes who ordered the scourge of the Hellespont. . . . Pericles and Aspasia, the battle of Thermopylae, the battle of Marathon. . . . However, long before all this, there were those legendary times when Abraham arose with his flock and went into the promised land: "By faith Abraham, when he was called to go out into a place which he should after receive for an inheritance, obeyed; and he went out, not knowing whither he went." No, he knew not whither he went. And neither did I. "By faith . . ." Faith in what? The loving kindness of God's will? ". . . not knowing whither he went." No, he did know: toward happiness, that is, something that would give him joy and contentment, in other words, love, life. . . . But then this was the way I had always lived, too, living only for whatever inspired love and joy. . . .

On the other side of the door behind my little table I could hear the voices of the woman and the child, I could hear the washstand pedal banging, water splashing, tea being made, and the child being urged to eat: "Kostya, dear, do eat your bun!" I would get up and start pacing the floor. Now there was this dear little Kostya! When she had given him his breakfast, his mother usually went out till about noon. When she got back she cooked something on her kerosene burner, gave the boy his dinner, and went out again. What agony it was to watch this little Kostya who had become a sort of hotel child, wandering from room to room all day, peeping into the room of anyone who happened to be at home, timidly starting a conversation, trying to ingratiate himself with his host, to say something pleasing, but no one would listen to him and some would even chase him away muttering: "Off you go, my lad.

Do leave me alone." There was a little old lady in one of the rooms, a very grave and respectable woman, who considered herself above all the other hotel guests, who walked down the corridor without vouchsafing anyone a look and who would very often, much too often, lock herself into the bathroom and noisily splash about. This lady owned a large, broad-backed pug dog, so overfed that there were rolls of fat at the back of its neck; it had goggling glassy eyes the color of gooseberries, an ugly nose, obscenely dented in the middle, a lower jaw thrust forward conceitedly and contemptuously, and a tongue like a toad's caught between its two canine teeth. The dog usually wore the same expression which showed nothing but alert insolence, and yet it was extremely high strung. And so, if little Kostya, driven out of someone's room, happened to cross its path in the corridor, one would immediately hear the pug choking savagely, making a rattling and wheezing sound in its throat, quickly growing into a rage of indignation and ending in loud and furious barks which made Kostya break out into hysterical wails.

Settling back in my chair again, I felt depressed with life's wretchedness and its painful complexity in spite of all its banality. Now it was little Kostya I wanted to write about, or something of the sort. Take that elderly seamstress, for example, who had once stayed at Nikulina's boardinghouse for about a week, continually cutting something on the table heaped with snippings, putting the tacked pieces together and running them through on the sewing machine. It was worth remembering the way she twisted and screwed up her large thin mouth to follow the course of her cutting scissors, how she enjoyed sitting down to tea and always tried to say something nice to Nikulina, to keep the conversation going, shamming animation while her large, workworn hand went out absently, as it were, to the platter of sliced white bread, and her eyes darted sidelong glances at the glass jam dish. And that lame girl on crutches I met the other day in Karachevskaya Street? All the lame and the hunchbacks walk with arrogance and defiance. But this girl came limping toward me shyly; she held a black crutch in each hand and supported her weight on them as she made her measured dips, jerking up her shoulders, the black crutch handles jutting out under her armpits. She looked at me intently. Her coat was short, like a child's, her dark brown eyes were intelligent, pure and bright, like a child's too, and yet with the wisdom of the world in them, a knowledge of its sorrows and mysteries. . . . Oh, the beauty of some of these unfortunate people, with their very souls reflected in their faces, in their eyes!

I would again make an effort to concentrate in order to decide how to begin the description of my life. How, indeed! After all, I really had to begin by saying something if not of the universe as such, where I had been born at a given moment, then at least of Russia. I had to give the reader some conception of the country to which I belonged, of the world which brought me into being. But this was another thing I knew very little about. The ancient tribes of Slavs, the discord between these tribes. The Slavs were known for their tall stature, fair hair, bravery and hospitality; they worshiped the sun, thunder and lightning, revered wood and marsh goblins and mermaids, "in all, the forces and phenomena of nature. . . ." What else? Inviting the princes, the emissaries of Tsargrad at Prince Vladimir's, precipitating the dethroned god of thunder Perun into the Dnieper while the people wept. . . . Yaroslav the Wise, dissensions between his sons and grandsons. . . . I remembered Vsevolod of the Big Nest. . . . But what was much worse, I did not know a thing about contemporary Russia! Of course there were the landowners, threatened with ruin, and the starving peasants, there were the rural officials, gendarmes, policemen and village priests who, according to the writers, were invariably burdened with large families. . . . What else? There was Orel, one of the oldest towns in Russia. At least I could have learned something of its life, its inhabitants, but what did I know? Its streets, droshkys, rutted snow, shops and signboards, signboards everywhere. . . . The archbishop, the governor . . . the colossal and handsome Rashevsky, a police inspector of bestial cruelty. . . .

There was Palitsin too, the glory of Orel, one of its pillars, one of those eminent oddities Russia has been famous for since time immemorial. He was old and highly born, a friend of Aksakov and Leskov, he lived in something that resembled an ancient Russian palace, the timber walls of his rooms hung with rare icons. He always wore a queer loose coat trimmed with colored morocco, his hair was cut in an even bob, he was solid-faced, narrow-eyed, very sharp-witted and well-read, so they said. But did I know anything else about this man Palitsin? No, not a thing!

At this I suddenly felt indignant. After all, why did I have to know anyone or anything perfectly? Why could I not simply write about things as I knew them and felt about them? I would jump up again and start pacing the room, glad of my indignation, clutching at it as if therein lay my salvation. And all at once I would see before me the Svyatogor Monastery, where I had been in the spring. I saw the congregation of men from many parts standing before its walls on the shores of the Donets, the lay brother I had followed about the courtyard in a vain effort to talk him into putting me up for the night, the way he had shrugged and scuttled off, all of him streaming as he ran—arms, legs, hair and the skirts of his cassock—and what a slim, supple body he had, the face of a freckled youngster, frightened green eyes and quite an exceptional wealth of fine, pale-gold hair in springy, fluffy curls. . . . Then I saw those spring days when I sailed down the Dnieper, a journey without end, it had seemed. Dawn in the steppe and then the hard train bench where I had awakened, stiff and frozen with the hardness of my bed and the cold, and, looking up, I had seen that nothing was visible through the white frozen windows, I could not tell where we were, and I had felt that this uncertainty was the most wonderful thing of all. My senses keen with early-morning alertness, I had jumped up, opened the window and leaned out: the morning was white, shrouded in a thick white mist, it smelled of spring and mist, and as the train sped on it had flailed my hands and face with white wetness.

XIV

One day I overslept for some unknown reason. And when I awoke I did not stir but remained gazing in front of me at the window, at the serene white light of a winter day, feeling unusually calm, unusually sober in my mind and spirit, and sensing a strange smallness and simplicity in all my surroundings. I remained thus for a long time; my room did not oppress me, I felt it was so much smaller than I and entirely separate from me. I got up, washed and dressed, made my customary obeisance before the small icon hanging on the headpost of my cheap iron bedstead—that same icon which, strangely enough, is hanging in my bedroom now, a smooth dark-green piece of wood hardened with time, ornamented crudely in silver, the humps being the robes of the three angels at Abraham's board, their markedly oriental, glazed faces eyeing me darkly from the round holes in the silver. This icon had been handed down from generation to generation in my mother's family; it was her blessing to me as I set out on my journey into the world, leaving behind the somewhat ascetic life of my childhood, boyhood, the first years of youth, and all that obscure and secretive period of my worldly existence which now seems to me to have been quite exceptional, hallowed and fabulous, transformed with the years into a life apart, to which even I was a stranger. . . . Having made my obeisance, I went out to buy something I had thought of while lying in bed. On my way I remembered a dream I had the night before. It was carnival week, I was staying with the Rostovtsevs again, and my father and I were in the circus watching a little group of black ponies, as many as six of them, come running out into the arena. They all wore small fancy saddles bright with copper and jingling bells, they were tightly bridled, their red velvet reins were tautly secured to the saddles, they arched back their thick, short necks, on which the trimmed manes stood up like a black brush, while red feathers stuck up from their forelocks. They kept time running round well abreast at a trot, their bells jingling, their black heads inclined stubbornly and angrily, all of them perfectly matched in color and size, all with the same broad flanks and short legs. They stopped short suddenly and obstinately, champing at their bits and shaking their feathers. The dress-coated trainer had to shout repeated commands and crack his whip again and again until at last he succeeded in making them fall on their knees and bow to the public, after which the band, suddenly breaking out into a relieved and jolly gallop, sent them racing in a file round the arena, pursuing them as it were. I went into the stationer's and bought myself a thick copybook with black oilcloth covers. When I was back in my room, I sat drinking tea and thinking: "Enough. From now on I'll just read and sometimes jot things down—different thoughts, feelings and observations, without any claims to anything . . ." And, dipping my pen in the ink, I wrote on the front page neatly and clearly: Alexei Arsenyev. Notes.

After that I sat still for a long time thinking what I should write down in the book. I smoked hard but I felt no torment, nothing but sadness and stillness. At last I began:

"Prince N., the well-known disciple of Tolstoi, called at the newspaper office and asked us to print his report on collections and expenditures made in the cause of the starving in Tula. Short, rather fat. Strange soft Caucasian-looking top boots, astrakhan cap, topcoat with lamb collar—all old and worn, but expensive and neat—soft gray shirt, belted with a leather thong, outlining his rounded stomach, and golden pince-nez. Very unassuming. But I took an instant dislike to his imposing appearance, his well-groomed milk-white face and cold eyes. I hated him at once. I'm no disciple of Tolstoi's of course, nonetheless I'm not what everybody thinks I am. I want the world and the people in it to be beautiful, to inspire love and joy, and I hate anything that prevents this.

"I was walking along Bolkhovskaya Street the other day and this is what I saw: the setting sun, the frosty skies clearing up in the west, and a pure evening light streaming from this green, transparent, cold sky, flooding the whole town; the strange wistfulness of this light cannot be expressed in words. And on the pavement stood an old organ-grinder, livid with cold in his tatters, and the frosty evening resounded with the flutelike whistling, trilling and wheezing of his decrepit organ, a romantic melody breaking through, a faraway, old-fashioned foreign melody tearing at your soul with strange dreams and regrets. . . .

"Wherever I go I am either horrified or hurt. Something I saw a fortnight ago is still vivid in my memory. It was evening too, but dark and overcast. I casually walked into a little old church, I saw the lights of candles flickering in the darkness close to the pulpit, very low down, and coming closer I froze to the spot: three wax candles on the edge of a bier shed their faint and melancholy light into the little pink coffin that was trimmed with paper lace on the sides, and illumined the dark, round-faced child lying in it. You might have thought he was asleep but for the porcelain glaze on his face, the tinge of lilac on his round, closed eyelids and the triangle of his mouth, but for that infinitely calm, eternal alienation from everything in the world that was imprinted on his features.

"I wrote and published two stories, but everything in them is false and unpleasant. One is about some starving peasants, whom I have never seen and really cannot pity, the other follows the trite theme of a landowner faced with ruin which is equally unreal, whereas all I wanted to write about was the huge silvery poplar growing in the front garden of Mr. R., a poor landowner, and the motionless stuffed hawk which stands on the bookcase in his study, spreading its speckled brown wings and staring down at you with its shining yellow glass eyes, staring, staring all the time. . . . If I were to write of impoverishment, I would only describe the romance of it. The poor fields, the poor ruins of a manor house and garden, poor in servants, horses and hounds; the old men and women, that is, the "old masters" ending their days in the cramped back rooms, letting the young ones take the front—all this is sad and touching. And I would like to describe what these "young masters" are like—illiterate idlers and beggars, who still imagine that theirs is the true blue blood, theirs the highest and only class of gentlemen. Their caps, satin shirts, Cossack trousers and top boots. . . . Drinking, smoking and bragging, whenever they get together. Drinking vodka out of fine old champagne glasses. Loading their rifles with blanks to shoot out the lighted candles amid roars of laughter. A certain Mr. P., one of these "young gentlemen," abandoned his ruined estate altogether and moved to a long unused water mill, and there he lived in a log cabin with his mistress, a peasant woman with hardly any nose at all. He slept with her on a plank bed spread with straw, or out "in the garden," that is under an apple tree beside the cabin. A bit of broken mirror hung from a branch of the apple tree, reflecting the white clouds. For want of anything better to do he would sit and sling stones at the peasants' ducks on the pool beside the mill, and every time he hit the water the whole flock would whirl up and, making the most frightful noise, dart away across the pool.

"Our former serf Gerasim, old and blind, walked like all other blind people with his face turned up as though he were listening while he felt his way along with his stick. He lived in a little cottage on the outskirts of the village all by himself, with no one for company but a quail which beat about in its bast-woven cage, the top of its head worn bald from hitting it against the linen cover day after day, trying to jump out. Blind though he was, Gerasim never missed a summer's day to go out at dawn and catch quail, delighting in the way their calls were borne across the fields on the mellow breeze that wafted into his blind face. He used to say that there was nothing sweeter in the world than those thrilling moments when the quail, coming closer to the net, clucked at regular intervals louder, more passionately, and more excitingly for the catcher. He was a true, genuine poet!"

XV

I did not feel like going to lunch at the office. I went instead to a tavern in Moskovskaya Street. I drank a few glasses of vodka and ate a herring, and as I looked at its flattened head on the dish I thought: I must jot this down too—"The cheeks of the herring are mother-of-pearl." After that I had some sizzling *selyanka.** The place was quite crowded, a smell of pancakes, fried fish and burning fat hung in the low room; white-coated waiters ran about, dancing and bending backward, flinging their heads high, while the owner—the Russian spirit personified—followed each of them with a keen, slanting eye, as he stood behind his counter in a picturesque pose, acting the part he had practiced so well of a stern and pious man. Little black nuns, who looked like jackdaws, their feet in heavy shoes with tabs, shuffled between the tables occupied by tradesmen, bowing low and silently holding out their little black books with silver braid crosses on the covers, and the tradesmen, frowning, picked out the dirtiest kopeks from their purses. All this seemed a continuation of my dream, and I, feeling slightly heady with the vodka, the *selyanka* and my childhood memories, was on the verge of tears. . . . I went back to my hotel, lay down and fell asleep. I woke up in the twilight, filled with sorrow and vague repentance. I stood in front of the mirror, combing my hair, and noticed with displeasure that it was too long and much too artistic. I went to the barber's. There I saw, swathed in white, a stocky man with a hairless scalp and jutting ears—a bat, on whose upper lip and cheeks the barber was working up the lather to an amazing thickness and frothiness. Deftly removing all this whiteness with his razor, he soaped the face lightly once more and shaved it again, this time with careless, short upward jerks. The bat started up, straddle-legged, pulling his white wrapping along with him, he held it to his chest with one hand and washed his purple-red face with the other.

* *Selyanka*—a highly flavored dish of cabbage and fish, or sausage.—*Tr.*

"A whiff of Eau-de-Cologne, sir?" the barber asked.

"Go ahead," said the bat.

The scent spray hissed, and then the barber patted the bat's moist cheeks lightly with a towel.

"There you are, sir," he said smartly, sweeping away the wrapper. The bat got up to reveal a hideous appearance: a large big-eared skull, a broad, lean face the color of red morocco, the eyes in this clean-shaven face beaming like an infant's, and a black hole for a mouth; he was short, broad-shouldered, with a spiderlike short body and thin legs, as crooked as a Tatar's. Slipping a tip into the barber's hand, he put on a superb black overcoat and derby hat, lighted a cigar, and walked out. The barber turned to me and said:

"D'you know him? He's Yermakov, the merchant, the richest man here. D'you know how much he usually tips me? Take a look!"

He opened his fingers and showed me the money, saying with a cheerful laugh: "Two kopeks!"

After that I went wandering through the town in my usual way. I saw a church and went in. From my loneliness and melancholy I had already got into the habit of going into churches. Inside it was warm and the brilliance of candles gave it a wistfully festive look; they burned brightly in clusters in their tall candlesticks around the lectern on which lay a brass cross, inset with imitation rubies, and in front of which stood the priests and deacons intoning plaintively: "Our homage to Your cross we bring, O Lord in heaven." In the dusk beside the door stood a large old man in a long cloth coat and leather overshoes; a man as strong and rugged as an old horse, who seconded the priests in a stern drone for general edification it seemed. And in the crowd close to the lectern stood an old pilgrim, bathed in the warm, golden light of the candles. He was ascetically gaunt, his face—dark and finely drawn like an ancient icon—was almost hidden by the strands of his long, dark, womanish hair, hanging down his cheeks with pristine chasteness. He held a tall wooden staff, polished to a sheen through long years of use, firmly in his left hand, and a black leather bag was hitched on his back. He stood apart, immobile, estranged from everyone. I looked at him and once again tears welled up in my eyes, and awareness of my country, of Russia, with all its ancient darkness, overwhelmed me nostalgically and mournfully. Someone tapped me lightly on the shoulder with a candle, I turned round and saw a bent old woman in a cloak and shawl, one good tooth sticking out of her naked gums. "For the cross, my dear." Eager to oblige, I took the candle from her cold, dead hand with its bluish fingernails, stepped toward the blinding candlestick awkwardly, and ashamed of my awkwardness somehow managed to stand the candle among the others, and suddenly thought: "I'll go away." Stepping back from the lectern and bowing to the cross, I quickly and quietly walked toward the darkness of the door, leaving behind me the lovely cozy light and warmth of the church. Sullen darkness and a moaning wind awaited me outside. "I'm going," I said to myself, putting on my hat, and suddenly resolving to go to Smolensk.

Why Smolensk? It was my old dream of the Bryansk woods, of Bryansk outlaws. . . . I came to a tavern in a side street and went in. At one of the tables sat a nasty sort of chap, who yelled a song as he sprawled across the table, pretending to be drunk and acting the role the Russians love so much of maudlin delight in their own ruin. "By a fatal mistake I got locked into chains!" he bawled. He was watched with disgust by the man sitting at the next table, his head thrown back and black mustache straggling; a thief he must have been, judging by his long neck and the sharp, large and mobile Adam's apple, working under the thin skin. A tall, tipsy woman, who was evidently a laundress, in a shabby dress that clung to her skinny legs, stood swaying by the bar: she was trying to prove someone's baseness to the bartender, stressing her words by slapping down her hand, the fingers gleaming glassily from so much washing. A glass of vodka stood before her; she would pick it up and hold it without drinking, then put it down again and go on with her tirade, banging on the counter. I wanted some beer, but the air was too dank and foul, the light of the lamp was too wretched, and melting snow, seeping into some dirty rags rotting on the sills of the small frozen windows, dripped down on the floor. . . .

Unfortunately, Avilova was entertaining some guests in the dining room. "Oh, it's our dear poet!" she said. "Do you know everyone?" I kissed her hand and was presented to the guests. Next to her sat an old, wrinkled gentleman, dressed in a black morning coat with a white silk waistcoat; his well-trimmed mustache was dyed brown and a brown wig covered his bald pate. He got up smartly and bowed with great courtesy and a nimbleness amazing for his age. The skirts of his morning coat were edged with black braid, something I have always liked. I envied others who had such coats and dreamed of having one myself. Next to him sat a lady who carried on an unstemmed and very clever flow of talk; she offered me her solid, plump hand with the ragged imprint of the seam of her glove showing on its glossy cushioned surface, holding it as if it were a seal's fin. She talked well, hastily and somewhat breathlessly; she had no neck at all, she was rather fat, especially behind, about the armpits, her waistline was rounded and hardened like stone, gripped by her corset; she wore a smoky-gray fur round her shoulders, and its smell, mingling with the sweet smell of her perfume, her wool dress and her warm body, was very musty.

At ten the guests rose to go; they said a lot of pleasant things to their hostess and left.

"Oh, what a relief!" Avilova said with a happy laugh. "Let's go and sit in my room. We ought to open the window here. . . . But, my dear, what is the matter with you?" she said with tender reproach, stretching both her hands out to me.

I pressed them and said:

"I'm going tomorrow. . . ."

She threw me a frightened look:

"Where to?"

"To Smolensk."

"What for?"

"I just can't go on like this. . . ."

"But why Smolensk? Let's sit down. . . . I don't understand a thing."

We sat down on the sofa which had a summer loose cover of striped ticking on it.

"Now this ticking here," I said. "It's like the covers in a railway carriage. I can't even look at the material calmly, I want to go so badly."

She settled back deeper on the sofa and I saw her legs before me.

"But why Smolensk of all places?" she asked, looking at me with puzzled eyes.

"And then to Vitebsk, to Polotsk. . . ."

"What for?"

"I don't know. First of all, I love the sound of the names: Smolensk, Vitebsk, Polotsk."

"No, but seriously?"

"I *am* serious. Don't you know how wonderful some words sound? Smolensk was always being burned down in the old days, it was always being besieged. . . . I actually feel bound to it in some way; you know, once upon a time some ancient documents belonging to our ancestors perished in one of those horrible fires, and as a result we lost some important rights of inheritance and some privileges. . . ."

"Goodness, what next! Do you miss her very much? Doesn't she write to you?"

"No, she doesn't, but that's beside the point. Life in Orel as a whole goes against my grain. 'The wandering deer knows his grazing ground. . . .' My literary attempts are quite hopeless, too. I sit there the whole morning through, and there's nothing but drivel in my head, as if I were mad. And what keeps me alive? You know, at home in Baturino there's a shopkeeper's daughter who has given up all hope of ever getting married, and so she is only kept alive by her shrewd and malevolent perspicacity. That's the way it is with me, too."

"What a child you are," she said gently, and stroked my hair.

"It's only the lowest organisms that develop quickly," I said. "And then, who isn't a child? Once I traveled up to Orel with a member of the Yeletsk District Court, a respectable, serious man, who looked like the King of Spades. . . . He sat there reading the *New Times,* and then he got up, left the compartment and vanished. It worried me, and so I went out too, and opened the door on to the platform at the end of the carriage. He neither saw nor heard me against the roar of the train, and what do you think he was up to? He was dancing a jig, doing the most intricate steps with his feet in time to the wheels."

She looked into my eyes, and suddenly said softly, meaningfully:

"Would you like to come to Moscow with me?"

A thrill of terror ran through me. I blushed, stammered and mumbled my refusal and my thanks. . . . To this day I recall that moment with the anguish of a great loss.

XVI

The following night I was already on my way, traveling in a bleak third-class compartment. I was all alone; it even frightened me a little. The dim light of a lantern quivered dismally, wavering across the wooden benches. I stood in front of the black window—raw, chilly air coming in through its invisible chinks—and, shielding my face from the light with my hands, I stared tensely into the night, into the forests. Thousands of fiery red bees swarmed past, they flew and broke apart and mingled with the chill of winter, in which there was a smell of incense and the wood burning in the engine. How enchantingly dark, majestic and stern was the forest at night. The endless narrow road cut through the woods, the great, dark ghosts of century-old pines thronging it on both sides in closed ranks. The lighted rectangles of the windows fell slantwise on the white snowdrifts along the line, telegraph poles flashed past from time to time, and above and beyond all was steeped in darkness and mystery.

Next morning I woke up suddenly with an access of vigor: all was quiet and light, the train had stopped, we had reached Smolensk, a large station. I jumped out of the train and greedily gulped the fresh air. Close to the station building a crowd of people stood round something in a close ring. I hurried up: it was a wild boar, killed in the hunt, huge and powerful, stiff and frozen through, frightfully rough even to look at, its whole body spiky with the long, gray needles of its thick bristles powdered with dry snow; it had little pig's eyes and two white fangs jutting from its tightly clenched mouth. "Shall I stay?" I wondered. "No, on to Vitebsk!"

I arrived there on a frosty, clear evening. Everything was deep in snow, silent, clean and virginal, the town struck me as ancient and foreign with its tall houses, merging into their pointed roofs, with their small windows and rough semicircular gates, cut deeply into the ground floor. Now and then I came across some old Jews in long frock coats, white stockings and laced boots, with sideburns which looked like twisted hollow sheep's horns, bloodless faces and sadly questioning black eyes. The principal street was the promenade—a dense throng of plump girls dressed up with the showiness of provincial Jews in thick velvet coats, pale blue, mauve or garnet red, moved slowly along the pavments. They were followed at a discreet distance by young men who, though wearing bowlers, still kept their long sideburns; there was a maidenly softness and roundness in the oriental beauty of their faces with the silky young growth on their cheeks, and their languid doe's eyes. . . . I walked as though spellbound in this crowd, in this town which seemed so ancient to me in all its beautiful novelty.

It grew darker; I came to a square with a yellow Roman Catholic church, two belfries towering up in the center. I walked in and saw rows of benches in the half-light, and up in front a semicircle of little lights on the communion table. And all at once I heard the slow and pensive sounds of the organ overhead, flowing smoothly and softly, gaining volume, growing higher, harsh and metallic; there was a quavering and grinding noise as though the sounds were fighting free of something that was smothering them, and, suddenly, they tore away and swelled in glorious, heavenly canticle. In front of me, where the lights were flickering, a muttering rose and fell, voices intoned in Latin with a nasal twang. In the dusk I made out some armor-clad figures on pedestals, ranged like black ghosts on both sides of the stone pillars that vanished into the darkness overhead. High above the altar a large stained-glass window was gloomily fading away. . . .

XVII

That same night I left for Petersburg. When I walked out of the church, I went back toward the station to take the train to Polotsk. I wanted to settle down there in some old hotel; I don't know why, but I wanted to live there a while in complete solitude. The Polotsk train was to leave late that night. The station was empty and dark. The restaurant was lighted by a single sleepy lamp on the counter, the wall clock ticked with such long pauses, it seemed that time itself was coming to an end. I sat there for ages all alone in the heavy silence. At last there came the smell of a samovar being kindled; the station began to come to life and light; I got up quickly and without knowing what I was doing, bought a ticket for Petersburg.

There, at the Vitebsk railway station, in that endless waiting for the train to Polotsk, I had felt my frightening estrangement from everything about me; I had felt amazed and puzzled—what was all this, and why, why was I there among it? There was the silent, dusky restaurant with the lamp burning drowsily on the counter, the gloomy expanse of the dining room, its width and height, the table which took up most of the floor in the center, laid with the banality of all railway stations, the old sleepy waiter with a bent back and limp, badly cut coattails, who crawled out from behind the counter, sagging on his legs, when the spicy smell of the samovar kindlings floated into the room, and with the resentful clumsiness of the old began to climb up on the chairs ranged along the walls, and, with shaking hands, light the wall bracket lamps in their pearly glass globes. . . . Then there was the tall gendarme officer who, jingling his spurs disdainfully, walked through the restaurant out to the platform, and the slit in his floor-length army coat reminded me of the tail of an expensive stallion. What was the meaning of it? Why? What for? And there was nothing to compare with the freshness of the cold, snowy night which the officer let into the room as he opened the door to go out. That was when I came out of my bemused state and suddenly and inexplicably decided to go to Petersburg.

Wintry rain was falling in Polotsk, the streets were wet and wretched. I only looked in between trains and was glad of my disappointment. As I traveled on, I wrote down: "An endless day. Endless snow-clad, wooded country. Nothing but the bleakness of sky and snow outside. When the train enters a dense forest it grows dark inside, and then it comes out into the dismal expanse of snow-clad plain again, and you can see on the far horizon above the mass of forests, something dimly leaden, hanging low in the sky. All the stations are built of timber. . . . It's the North!"

Petersburg seemed like the extreme north to me. The driver rushed me in the gathering blizzard through streets that impressed me with their unusual harmony and similarity toward Ligovka and the Nikolayevsky Station. It was no more than three in the afternoon, but the round clock in the conventional bulk of the station building was already alight and shining through the blizzard. I stopped just before it, on the other side of the Ligovka which goes along the canal. It was horrible there—lumberyards, droshky-drivers' quarters, tearooms, taverns and beer shops. I sat for a long time without taking off my overcoat in the hotel, recommended to me by the driver, and gazed down from the height of the sixth floor through the hopelessly dismal window into the twilight turbidness of snow, my head reeling with fatigue after my journey in the rocking train. So this was Petersburg! I felt it very forcibly: I was in this city, hemmed in with its dark and ominous grandeur. The room was very hot and stuffy with the smell of the old woolen draperies and matching sofa cover, and with a strong stench of that reddish stuff they polish the floors with in cheap hotels. I left the room and ran down the steep staircase. Out in the street the impenetrable, whirling snow dealt me an icy blow. I got hold of a sledge I had glimpsed through the blizzard and flew to the Finland Station to get the feel of the border. There I fast got drunk, and suddenly sent her a telegram: "Arriving the day after tomorrow."

Moscow, huge, old, and teeming with life, welcomed me with brilliant spring sunshine, melting snows, streams and puddles, the roar and clamor of the horse-drawn street cars, the noisy confusion of pedestrians and vehicles, an amazing number of carriers' sledges, heavily loaded with goods, dirty, narrow streets, the Kremlin, looking like a popular print with its palaces and buildings, and the golden domes of the cathedrals shining in a cluster. I marveled at St. Basil's, I went into the Kremlin cathedrals, and had lunch at Yegorov's famous restaurant on Okhotny Ryad. It was wonderful there: downstairs it was somewhat drab and noisy with trading commoners, but in the two low rooms upstairs it was clean, quiet and decorous—even smoking was prohibited—very cozy with the sun peeping into the little windows from the yard, and with a trilling canary in a cage; a sanctuary lamp glimmered whitely in a corner; the top half of one of the walls was taken up by a dark picture, covered with a tan varnish: it showed a scaly roof curving upward, a long terrace and on it some unnaturally large figures of yellow-faced Chinese, drinking tea—they wore golden robes and green hats which looked like the shades of cheap lamps. In the evening of the same day I left Moscow.

In our town the sledges had already been replaced by carriages, the station was swept by a raging wind from the Sea of Azov. She was waiting for me on the platform, which was dry and cleared of its burden of snow. The wind tore at her spring hat and made it difficult for her to see. I saw her from afar; she looked lost, screwing up her eyes in the wind as she tried to catch sight of me in one of the moving carriages. There was that touching and pathetic something in her which always strikes us in our dear ones after a separation. She had grown thinner, her clothes were simple. When I leaped down from the train, she tried to free her lips from the veil she wore tied under her chin, but she could not do it, and kissed me through it awkwardly, turning deathly pale.

During the drive she silently bent her head in the face of the wind and only repeated several times in a bitter, flat voice:

"What were you doing to me, what were you doing to me!"

And then she said in the same flat voice:

"Are you going to the hotel? I'll come with you."

When we were inside the room—a large one on the second floor with an anteroom—she sat down on the sofa and watched the porter stupidly dumping my suitcase in the middle of the room on the carpet. He then asked me if there was anything else I wanted.

"No, nothing," she said for me. "You may go." And began to unpin her hat.

"Why are you so silent? Why don't you say something?" she asked nonchalantly, tightening her quivering lips.

I knelt down before her, hugged her knees, kissed them through the cloth and wept. She lifted my head, and once again I felt her dear, inutterably sweet lips on mine, and heard our tremulous hearts dying to a blissful standstill. I jumped up, turned the key in the door, with icy hands drew the white puffed-up curtains down on the windows—outside a black, leafless tree swayed in the wind, and a rook screamed in alarm and swung on a branch drunkenly. . . .

"All Father asks is that we put off our wedding for six months," she said to me softly afterward, as she lay languidly resting. "Wait, my life is yours now anyway, it's yours completely, to do with as you like."

There were tall white candles on the dressing table, the stiff curtains gleamed a lusterless white, and the strange patterns of the plaster ornament looked down on us from the chalk-white ceiling.

XVIII

We went to a town in the Ukraine where my brother Georgy had moved from Kharkov to take charge of the Rural Board statistics office, and where both of us were to work. Passion Week and Easter we spent at Baturino. My mother and sister adored her, my father addressed her fondly, and willingly gave her his hand to kiss in the mornings, and only my brother Nikolai was reserved and overpolite to her. She was quietly and timidly happy with the novelty of being a part of our family, our house, estate, my room where I had spent my youth and which now seemed beautiful and touching to her, my books which she looked through in that room with timorous joy. And then we left.

One night going to Orel. Changing to the Kharkov train at dawn. On a sunny morning we stood in the corridor of the train in front of a hot window.

"How very strange, I've never been anywhere except Orel and Lipetsk," she said. "Is Kursk next? It's the South to me already."

"Yes, and to me too."

"Are we going to have lunch at Kursk? Do you know, I've never had lunch in a station restaurant. . . ."

After Kursk, the farther we went, the warmer and prettier

the country became. Grass was already lush on the banks of the line, there were flowers and white butterflies, and the butterflies meant summer.

"It will be awfully hot there in the summer!" she said smiling.

"My brother says the town itself is a garden."

"Yes, the Ukraine. I would never have guessed. . . . Look, look what huge poplars! And quite green too! Why so many windmills?"

"Windpumps, not windmills. We'll be able to see the chalk hills now, and then Belgorod."

"I understand you now. I couldn't endure it either, living in the North without this wealth of sunshine."

I pulled down the window. The sunny wind blew in warmly, the engine smoke smelled of coal and brought with it a whiff of the South. She half-closed her eyes, the sun moved over her face in hot streaks, over the dark young hair fluttering about her forehead, and over her simple cotton frock, dazzling it blindingly and warming it.

The valleys near Belgorod wore the unpretentious sweetness of joyfully blossoming cherry orchards and whitewashed cottages. At Belgorod Station, there was the cooing patter of Ukrainian women selling rolls.

She bought some, haggling over the price, enjoying her domesticity and her use of Ukrainian words.

We changed trains again at Kharkov that night.

It was dawn when we arrived.

She was asleep. The candles in the carriage were burning low, in the steppe it was still night, a dark half-light rather, but beyond it lay a distant, low, greenish line of the secretly breaking day. How unlike ours was this country, this bare, boundless plain with its humped burial mounds. A slumbering halt flashed past—not a shrub, nor a tree beside it, and the stone cottage itself looked bare and bluish-white in this mysteriously breaking day. . . . How dismal were the little stations here!

Now day was seeping into the train as well. Dusk lay

close to the floor, but higher up it was half-light. In her sleep she hid her head under the pillow and drew up her legs. Softly, I covered her with the old silk shawl my mother had given her.

XIX

The station was on the outskirts of the town, in a broad valley. It was small and pleasant with smiling waiters, soft-spoken porters and benevolent drivers sitting on the boxes of their capacious coaches, drawn by a pair of horses.

The town, lush with gardens, with a cathedral on a cliff, looked down from its mountaintop to the east and south. In the eastern valley there was a solitary steep hill, crowned with an ancient monastery, beyond it all was green, rolling plain, the valley gradually merging into the steppe. In the south, beyond the river and its bright meadows, the vista vanished in the dazzling sunlight.

Many of the town streets seemed cramped by the gardens that hemmed them in and the poplars growing in rows along the wooden walks where you could often meet a haughty, big-breasted wench, her skirt clinging tightly to her hips, a heavy yoke with a couple of pails on her shoulders. We admired the poplars which were extraordinarily tall and powerful; it was May, thunderstorms and heavy rains were not infrequent, and the firm green leaves were shiny, and gave out a fresh, pitchy fragrance. The spring was always bright and cheerful here, the summer sultry, the autumn long and clear, and the winter mild with moist breezes, charming with the muffled tingling of tiny bells, hung on the bow shafts of the sledges.

We took a house in one of these streets. Kovanko, our landlord, a large, bronzed old man with bobbed gray hair, was quite an estate owner: he had a house, a lodge and a garden. He lived in the lodge, while the house—whitewashed and shady from the garden just behind it, with a large glassed-in veranda running across the front—he leased to us. He had a job somewhere, and when he came home from work he had a good dinner, a nap, and then without bothering to dress sat in front of the open window smoking his pipe and humming songs.

The rooms in the house were low and plain. There was a very old chest in the corridor, covered with a piece of unbleached cloth hemstitched with colored thread. We had a young Cossack girl for a servant, whose beauty had something Nogaian in it.

My brother had grown even nicer and kinder. My hopes were justified; he and Lika soon became the closest of friends; whenever I quarreled with her or with him, they always took each other's side.

Our circle of friends and colleagues (doctors, lawyers and Board officers) was like my brother's Kharkov circle. I fell into their ways easily and was very glad to see Leontovich and Vagin, who had also moved there from Kharkov. The only thing which made this circle different from the Kharkov one was that it was made up of people of more moderate views, who maintained an almost urban mode of life with its small-town prosperity, and were sociable not only with anyone coming from another town, but even with the local chief of police.

Our social gatherings were mostly held in the house of one of the Rural Board members. He owned five thousand acres of land and ten thousand sheep, his house was rich and hospitable, maintained solely for the sake of his family, while he himself was a small, modest and poorly dressed man who had been to Yakutsk in his time, and who looked like a sorry guest in his own home.

XX

There was an old stone well in our yard; two white acacias grew in front of the lodge, and beside the porch of the house a chestnut tree flung up its dark crown shadowing the right side of the veranda. By about seven in the morning, all this would already be hot, bright and sunny, resounding with the monotonous, worried calls of the hens from the poultry yard, but in the house, especially in the back rooms which faced the garden, it would still be cool, and the bedroom where she stood splashing in front of the washstand in her little Tatar slippers, her breasts taut with cold, smelled of fresh water and toilet soap. In embarrassment, she would turn her wet face to me, with soap on her neck underneath her hair, stamp her foot and say: "Go away!" After that the fragrance of freshly made tea came from the room opening on to the veranda; the Cossack girl was busy there, her steel-shod heels tapping smartly; she wore her half-boots on her bare feet, her ankles were as slim as a thoroughbred filly's, and gleamed below her skirt with an oriental sheen; her rounded neck with its amber necklace gleamed too, her face framed in black hair was animated and sensitive, her slanting eyes flashed eagerly, and her hips swung with every movement she made.

My brother appeared at breakfast with a cigarette in his fingers, with Father's smile and manner: short and running to fat he did not look like Father, but he had inherited something of his patrician manner; he affected elegant clothes, held his cigarette and crossed his legs in a very stylish way now. There had been a time when everyone had firmly believed his future would be brilliant; he had been convinced of it too, but now he was perfectly satisfied with the position he held in this remote Ukrainian town. He appeared at breakfast with a twinkle in his eye: he felt perfectly fit and strong —we made up his family which he loved dearly, and his daily attendance at the office, where, as in Kharkov, most of the time was passed in smoking and chatting, was a pleasure to him. And when, breakfast over, she joined us, all ready to go, dressed with summer gaiety, he beamed all over and kissed her hand.

We walked past beautiful poplars, shining richly in the sun, along the hot wooden walks close to the heated walls of the houses and sun-warmed gardens; her pale silk parasol swelled roundly against the deep-blue sky. We had to cross a parched square and go into the yellow Board building. Downstairs it smelled of the caretakers' top boots and the leaf tobacco they smoked. All sorts of secretaries and clerks in black lustring coats—a cunning breed and much experienced for all their apparent simplicity—hurried busily up and down the stairs with papers in their hands and a Ukrainian way of inclining their heads. We would go past the staircase into the depths of the first floor to the low rooms taken up by our section—a very nice place because of the people who worked there—bright and animated intellectuals casual in manner and dress. It seemed strange to see her in these rooms, sorting various questionnaires which she put into envelopes ready for dispatch to the rural districts.

At noon the caretakers served us tea in cheap glasses with slices of lemon on cheap saucers, and at first the impersonal touch in all this actually gave me a certain pleasure. And then all our friends from the other sections would come in for a chat and a smoke. Sulima, the Board's secretary, would be there too. He was a handsome, somewhat round-shouldered man in gold-rimmed glasses, with a velvety sheen to his magnificently black hair and beard. He had a soft, ingratiating walk, an ingratiating smile, and the same manner of talking; he always had a smile on his face and always affected this softness and graciousness; he was very much the aesthete, he called the monastery crowning the hill in the valley "a frozen chord." He often came in, and the glances he gave her became more and more benign and mysterious; walking up to her desk, he would bow low over her hands, look up at her and, smiling sweetly, gently say: "And what are you sending out now?" At this she would pull herself up and try to make her reply as charming and candid as possible. It did not worry me at all, I was now immune to jealousy.

Once again, with no effort on my part, I came to hold a unique position in the office, the same as I had in Orel, and as a worker I was looked upon with kindly mockery. I sat there compiling reports in a leisurely way, calculating the amount of tobacco or sugar beet planted in such and such a *volost** of such and such an *uyezd*,** noting the measures taken there to combat beetles harmful to this crop, or sometimes I would just sit and read a book, taking no heed of the conversation about me. I enjoyed having my own desk and the fact that I could order any quantity of new nibs, pencils and excellent writing paper from the office stores.

We worked till two in the afternoon. Then my brother would get up from his chair and call out with a smile: "Break up the meeting!" and everyone would eagerly rush to get their summer caps or hats. We would pour out into the bright square in a crowd, shake each other's hands, and go our different ways, swinging our canes.

XXI

Until about five the town was deserted, the gardens lay baking in the sun. My brother slept, while we two just lolled on her large bed. The sun moving round the house shone into the bedroom windows through the pale-green foliage of the trees in the garden, which was reflected in the mirror over the washstand. Gogol had been a student in this town, and had known all the neighboring districts—Mirgorod, Yanovshchina, Shishaki, Yareski. We often recited, laughing: "How delightful, how resplendent, a summer day in the Ukraine!"

"It's too hot, anyway," she said, sighing happily and turning over on her stomach. "And all these flies! How does it go on about the vegetable gardens?"

"The emeralds, topazes, rubies of those ethereal insects scattering over the many-colored vegetable patches."

"There's magic beauty in it!" she sighed. "I'd love to see Mirgorod. We really must go there one day, mustn't we?

* *Volost*—a division for local government consisting of a group of village communities.
** *Uyezd*—soviet county congress.

Please, let's go! But what a queer man he was, how disagreeable. He was never in love with anyone, not even in his youth. . . ."

"True, the only senseless thing he did in all his youth was take that trip to Lyubek."

"Like yours to Petersburg. . . . Why are you so fond of travel?"

"And why are you so fond of getting letters?"

"But who ever writes to me now?"

"You like getting them anyway. We're all of us forever waiting for something pleasant or interesting to happen, dreaming of some happy surprise, of some adventure. Well, that's the lure of travel. And then, the feeling of freedom, release, the novelty which always puts you in a holiday mood and heightens your enjoyment of life! That's just what all of us want, what we seek in every strong emotion."

"Yes, it's quite true."

"You talk of Petersburg. If you only knew how horrible it was, and how instantly I realized, once and for all, that I belonged to the South, body and soul. Gogol once wrote from Italy: 'Petersburg, snow, scoundrels, the office—all this I dreamed of: when I awoke I found I was at home.' And I, too, woke up here. It thrills me to hear the words: Chigirin, Cherkasy, Khorol, Lubny, Chertomlyk, Dikoye Polye; it thrills me to see these roofs, thatched with reed, the men's cropped heads, the women in their yellow and red boots, and even the baskets in which they carry their plums and cherries on yokes across their shoulders. 'Circling, in anguish, the gull bewails her young with a cry; winds over steppe unfurl, the sun is hot and high'—that's Shevchenko, a perfect genius! There's no country in the world more beautiful than the Ukraine. And the main thing is that it no longer has any history, it ended its history forever, long ago. There's only the past, the songs and legends of the old days—a sort of timelessness. This fascinates me more than anything else."

"You use the word 'fascinate' very often, don't you?"

"But life should be fascinating. . . ."

The sun began to go down; it poured generously in through the open windows, fell on the polished floor, played with the mirror's reflection on the ceiling; the window sills grew brighter and hotter, and flies buzzed on them in gleeful swarms. They stung her cool naked shoulders. A sparrow suddenly alighted on the window sill, looked about with a quick, keen eye and, soaring up again, vanished in the bright green of the trees, lacy now against the afternoon sky.

"Now, tell me something else," she said. "Tell me, shall we ever go to the Crimea? If you only knew my dreams! I dream that you'd write a story—I think you'd write it beautifully—and then we'd have some money, we could take a holiday. . . . Why have you given up writing? You're a wastrel, really, squandering your talents!"

"You know there used to be some Cossacks once called 'roamers' because they roamed. Well, I suppose I'm a roamer too. 'The Lord makes noblemen of some and homeless beggars of the others. . . .' What I like best in Gogol is his notebook: 'A steppe gull with a bracket-shaped crest soared up from the road. A barrier across the whole road, green with holy thistle, and beyond it nothing but the boundless plain. . . . Sunflowers over the wattle fences and ditches, the thatched foreroof of a freshly whitewashed cottage, and a line of red painted round the pretty window. You are the ancient root of Russia, where feeling is more genuine and Slav nature softer!' "

She listened keenly, and then she suddenly said:

"Tell me, why did you read me that part in Goethe? The part where he left Friederice and suddenly, in his imagination, saw a horseman riding somewhere in a gray coat, sewn with gold braid. How is it put there?"

" 'This horseman was myself. I wore a gray coat, sewn with gold braid, which I had never possessed.' "

"Yes, of course, and it's all so wonderful and eerie. And then you said that everyone had his own dream coat in his youthful fancies. . . . Why did he desert her?"

"He used to say that he was always driven by his demon."

"Yes, and you too will stop loving me soon. Be honest, tell me, what do you wish and dream of most?"

"My dream? To be some ancient Crimean khan, and live with you in the Palace of Bakhchisarai. The whole of Bakhchisarai is in a stony gorge of burning heat. But in the palace it's always shady and cool, with fountains splashing and mulberry trees growing outside the windows. . . ."

"Do you really mean it?"

"I do. My mind is always cluttered with some dreadful nonsense, you know. Take that gull now, this combination of sea and steppe. I remember Nikolai used to laugh and say that I was a born simpleton, and it hurt me horribly until one day I happened to read that Descartes himself used to say that in his spiritual life clarity and reason occupied the most insignificant place."

"Go on about the palace, is there a harem there? It's very important. Remember you tried to prove to me that a man's love was a mixture of many different loves, that you felt that way about Nikulina and then Nadya. . . . D'you know, at times you're very cruelly frank with me. The other day you said something of the sort about our Cossack girl too."

"I only said that when I look at her I terribly want to go into the saline steppes somewhere and live in a tent."

"There you are, you admit it yourself that you'd like to live with her in a tent."

"I didn't say with her."

"Who else? Oh, a sparrow's flown in again! I hate it, it's such bad luck when they fly into a room and beat against a mirror."

And, jumping up, she clapped her hands quickly and awkwardly. I caught and kissed her naked shoulders, her legs. . . . The contrast in the hot and cool parts of her body moved me most of all.

XXII

It got cooler toward the evening. The sun was behind the house, we had tea on the veranda, by the windows that opened on to the yard. She read a lot now, and after tea she usually asked my brother questions, and he was very pleased to enlighten her. The evenings were perfectly still and quiet; only the swallows flitted about the yard and, soaring, vanished into the fathomless sky. They would be talking, while I sat listening to someone singing:

Away upon the hill
Men are making hay. . . .

The song told of men harvesting on the hill; it flowed smoothly and slowly with the sadness of separation, then it grew in volume and firmness and rang with freedom, valor, the spirit of battle and the lure of distances:

Down below the hill
Riding fast away
Are the Cossacks bold. . . .

The melody rang with a wistful pride in the Cossack troop riding away down the valley, with the heroic Doroshenko leading it and Sagaidachny following:

Would you choose a pipe
Rather than a wife,
Cossack strange and bold?

There was a pause of admiration for a man so strange, and all at once the song burst forth triumphantly with joyful abandon:

Let the others marry,
We've no time to tarry,
But my pipe will be a comfort
And a friend upon the road. . . .

I listened, feeling sadly and sentimentally envious.

When the sun set, we sometimes went to town, or to the garden on the cliff behind the cathedral, or out into the open country. There were several paved streets in town where Jewish shopkeepers sold their wares; there was a bewildering number of watchmakers, apothecaries and tobacconists. The houses in these streets were of white stone, they gave out warmth after the day's heat, there were booths on the corners selling syrups of different hues with fizzing water, and all this spoke of the South, made you want to go even farther south, and I remember I often thought of Kerch at the time—why Kerch, I do not know. As I gazed down into the valley from the cathedral garden, I would imagine I was going to Kremenchug or Nikolayev. When we went out into the open country, we had to go through the western outskirts of the town that were still quite rustic. The cottages, cherry orchards and melon fields ran down into the plain, facing the arrow-straight Mirgorod highway. Far away upon this road, which was marked by telegraph poles, you could see a sluggishly moving cart, drawn by a pair of oxen swaying in the yoke, their heads drooping; the cart trailed on and disappeared together with the telegraph poles, as if they had been swallowed up by the sea. And in the hazy distance you could hardly discern the last poles which looked like tiny matchsticks. This was the road to Yanovshchina, Yareski, Shishaki.

We often passed an evening in the city park. A band played there and the lighted terrace of the restaurant was like the stage of a theater, you could see it from afar, bright against the surrounding darkness. My brother would make straight for the restaurant, while we would sometimes stroll to the end of the park, out to the edge of the cliff. The nights were deeply black and warm. There were little lights in the darkness below somewhere, and voices, joined in harmonious, hymnlike song, floated up to us, falling and dying away. This was the young lads of the suburbs singing. The melody merged with the darkness and the stillness. When a train with lighted windows rumbled past, the depth and the blackness of the valley struck you particularly, and gradually the rumbling would fade away and the lights dim, as if the whole train had vanished into the ground. And once again songs would be heard, and the sweep of the horizon beyond the valley would quiver with the incessant croaking of frogs, which seemed to hypnotize this silence and this darkness, keeping it forever spellbound and bemused.

The crowded terrace of the restaurant was pleasantly cramped and blinding after the blackness of the valley. My brother, already tipsy and sentimental, sitting at a table with Vagin, Leontovich and Sulima, would instantly get up and wave to us. There would be a noisy welcome, and more white wine, glasses and ice would be ordered. And then the band would be gone, the park empty and dark, a breeze would start up and worry the candle flames in their pointed glass shades, scattered with moths, but everyone said it was too early to go and we sat on. At last we would admit that it was time to go, but it was difficult to make a move. We went home in a crowd, talking in loud voices, our feet clattering on the wooden walks. The gardens were asleep, mysteriously dark, bathed in the soft light of the low moon. When at last the three of us entered our yard, the moon would be shining into it, gleaming on the black windows of the veranda; a cricket chirped quietly; each tiny leaf, every twig of the acacias was etched with amazing and exquisite clearness in a motionless shadow on the white wall of the house.

The moments before we fell asleep were the best. A single candle burned on the bedside table. A cool breeze wafting from the garden brought in a breath of happiness, pure, young and healthy. She sat in a dressing gown on the edge of the bed, her dark eyes on the candle flame, and braided her softly shining hair.

"You're always wondering at the change in me," she said. "But if you only knew how *you* have changed. You're taking less and less notice of me, especially when we are not alone. I am afraid I'll soon be just like the air for you: you can't live without it and yet you don't notice it. It's true, isn't it? You say that this is real love. But I think it means that you want more than me now."

"Yes, I want more, more," I answered laughing. "Nothing is enough for me now!"

"That's just what I keep saying: you're always drawn somewhere. Your brother told me that you asked him to let you go with the traveling statisticians. Why did you do that? Why do you want to go jolting in a carriage in the heat and dust, to sit in a stuffy office afterward for days on end, filling in the very same questionnaires that I send out. . . ." She looked into my eyes, threw her pigtail over her shoulder and said: "What do you find so attractive in it?"

"Only that I'm happy, that nothing seems really enough for me now."

She took my hand in hers.

"Are you really happy?"

XXIII

My first trip took me down the very road where she so wanted to go—the Mirgorod highway. Vagin, who had some business in Shishaki, took me along with him.

I remember how nervous we were lest we should oversleep that day—we had to start out early before it began to get hot—how tenderly she woke me up, having risen before daybreak to get my breakfast, fighting down her disappointment that she was not coming with me. The morning was overcast and cool; she kept looking out of the window, worrying that the rain might spoil my trip. To this day I can feel the tenderness and the excitement with which we got up nervously when we heard the carriage bell jingling outside, embraced impetuously, and ran out to the gate where Vagin, dressed in a long duck dustcoat and a gray summer cap, sat waiting for me in the hired carriage.

I remember how the bell seemed to be muffled by the tremendous airy spaces of the steppe, how the day became dry and hot, how the cart ran smoothly through the deep dust on the road, and everything about us became so monotonous that soon you found it unbearable to gaze into the drowsy, pale distance, tensely waiting for something. At noon we saw in that hot sea of ripening wheat something that took us back to the days of the nomads: Kochubey's endless sheepfolds. "Noon, sheepfolds," I wrote down between the jolts. "Skies gray with heat, hawks and rollers. . . . I am completely happy!" At Yanovshchina I noted down: "Yanovshchina, the old inn, its black interior and cool half-light; the Jew told us he had no beer, nothing but a drink. What kind of a drink? Why, just a drink! A violet drink! The Jew, a skinny man, was dressed in a long frock coat in the orthodox way, but his son, who fetched the drink from the back room, wore a school uniform with a brand-new leather belt high on his pale gray tunic. He was an exceptionally fat youngster, but very handsome with a Persian cast to his face." When we left Shishaki I immediately recalled Gogol's notes: "And suddenly there was a chasm in the middle of the road—a precipice into the deep. And in the depths there were forests, and beyond them more forests, the nearer ones green and the distant ones dark-blue, and beyond that a stretch of sand, a silvery-straw color. . . . A creaking windmill flapped its sails over the precipice. . . ." In the depths of the valley, below the precipice, the River Psyol swerved in an arc, and there was a large village there, green with gardens. We spent a long time in this village looking for a certain Vasilenko, with whom Vagin was to do business, and when we had found his house we discovered that he was out; and so we stayed and waited, sitting under a lime tree, close to his cottage, with the dampness of willow herb and the croaking of frogs all around us. When Vasilenko arrived, we all sat there the whole evening long, eating and drinking homemade liqueurs; the lamp on the table threw up its light to the leaves of the lime tree, while the impenetrable gloom of a summer night closed in around us. Suddenly a gate banged in this darkness and a young woman, her face powdered to the paleness of lead, made a picturesque appearance at the table. She was the local Board's feldsher, a friend of Vasilenko's, who had of course quickly found out that he was entertaining some visitors from town. She felt very embarrassed at first, she did not know how to behave and blurted out the first thing that came into her head, but then she got over it, drinking with us glass for glass, and squealing louder and louder at every joke I made. She was a very nervous sort of woman, with broad cheekbones, sharp black eyes, sinewy hands that smelled strongly of Chypre, and jutting collarbones; her breasts lay heavily under her thin blue blouse, her waist was slim and her hips broad. I saw her home in the middle of the night. We walked in the impenetrable blackness into an alleyway over ruts dried to a hard crust. She stopped beside a wattle fence and dropped her head on my chest. I hardly managed not to let myself go. . . .

Vagin and I came home late the following day. Lika was already in bed with a book. When she saw me, she sat up, glad and surprised. "What, back already!" she cried. When I gave her a hasty account of my trip and, laughing, told her about the feldsher woman, she cut me short:

"Why must you tell me this?"

And tears gathered in her eyes.

"How cruel you are to me!" she said, quickly groping for her handkerhief under the pillow. "It's bad enough that you left me all alone here. . . ."

How often in my later life was I to remember those tears! I remembered them one day twenty years later. I was on holiday at a seaside resort in Bessarabia. I came back after a swim and lay down in my study. It was a hot, windy day, the trees around the house murmured with a loud, silky-hot swish, that died down only to grow into a furious tumult, patches of shadow and sunlight quivered on the trees, the softly pliant branches swayed to and fro. . . . When the wind blew up louder and stronger, it suddenly rent the green veil of the trees in front of my window and disclosed a sultry, enameled sky; the shadow on my white ceiling was torn asunder too, and as the shadow receded it paled to a faint mauve. Then everything became calm again, the wind vanished into the depths of the garden, away to the cliff jutting over the sea. I looked and listened, and suddenly I thought: somewhere, twenty years ago, in that long-forgotten town in the Ukraine where we were just starting out on our life together, there had been a day like this, too. I had awakened late; she had already gone to the office—the windows into the garden had also been open, and beyond them the trees had droned and swayed, darkening and flashing in just the same way, and the room had been filled with the happiest wind in the world which brings promise of breakfast and the fragrance of frying onions. I had opened my eyes, taken a gulp of the wind and, propping my pillow up higher, had lain gazing at the other pillow, to which still clung the faint violet perfume of her beautiful dark hair and of her flimsy handkerchief which she had clutched for a long time in her hand after we had made up. And when I remembered all this, when I remembered that I had since then lived half a lifetime without her, had seen the whole world and was still seeing it and living in it, whereas she was no longer in this world, had not been for an eternity, the blood froze in my veins, I threw my legs down from the sofa and went out, unconscious of the path leading to the cliff, gazing down the clearing at the vitriol-green slab of sea, which suddenly appeared awesome and wonderful to me, timeless and primordial. . . .

That night I swore to her that I would never go away again. A few days later I was off once more.

XXIV

When we were at Baturino, my brother Nikolai used to say:

"I'm dreadfully sorry for you. You've written yourself off much too early."

But I did not feel that I had written myself off at all. Once again I looked upon my job as a passing thing, and I could not consider myself a married man. I would have been horrified at the very thought that I should have to live without her, but at the same time the thought that we may be bound for life puzzled me; could it really be that we had become united forever and would go on living like this to a ripe old age, with a home and children like everyone else? The last—home and children—appeared particularly unbearable to me.

"We'll get married one day," she said to me, dreamily. "After all I do so want to be married, and then there's nothing more beautiful than a church wedding! And perhaps we'll have a child . . . wouldn't you like that?"

I felt a sweet and secret pang, but I laughed it off saying:

"The immortal create, the mortal produce their like."

"And what about me?" she asked. "What will there be for me when our love is over and our youth too, and you no longer need me?"

This had a very sad sound, and so I declared passionately:

"Nothing will ever pass. I'll never stop needing you!"

Now it was I who wanted to be loved and to love while retaining my liberty and supremacy in everything—just as she had felt in Orel.

She appeared most touching to me at bedtime when, having braided her hair, she would come up to me to kiss me good night, and I saw how much shorter she was without her high heels, and how she had to raise her head to look into my eyes.

But my love for her was strongest in those moments when she demonstrated her loyalty to me, when she waived her own desires and recognized my claims to a certain peculiarity of feelings and actions.

We often recalled our winter in Orel, the way we had parted when I went off to Vitebsk, and I would say:

"Polotsk, now, what was the attraction it had for me? The word Polotsk, you know, has for a long time been associated in my mind with a legend about Prince Vseslav of ancient Kiev, which I had read somewhere when I was at school. He was dethroned by his brother, and he fled into the 'dark lands of the Polotskites' where he ended his days in 'frugal poverty' in self-denial, prayer, toil and 'entrancing memories.' He invariably awoke an hour before dawn in sweet and bitter tears, with a fanciful dream that he was in Kiev once more in his true and princely state, and that the bells ringing for matins came from St. Sophia's Cathedral in Kiev and not from Polotsk at all. And ever since I had read that, the Polotsk of that period has always appeared perfectly wonderful to me in all its antiquity and barbarism. I imagined a dark, wild winter day, a Kremlin built of logs with timber churches and smoke-blackened huts, the snow trampled down by the hoofs of horses and the feet of men in sheepskins and bast shoes. . . . And when at last I found myself in the real Polotsk, I naturally saw not the slightest resemblance to the one I had imagined. But still, there are two Polotsks for me even now—the Polotsk of my fancy and the Polotsk of reality. And I can also see the real one through a veil of romance today: the town is dull, damp and cold, it's a gloomy town, but at the railway station, the large hall with its huge arched windows is warm, the chandeliers already lighted although day is just beginning to wane, the room is thronged with men in uniform and in civilian clothes, hastily filling themselves up before the train for Petersburg comes in, all is loud with voices and knives knocking against plates, waiters rushing to and fro carrying with them the smell of cabbage soup and sauces on their trays. . . ."

Whenever I talked like that she listened to me with rapt attention, and when I stopped she would say in tones of conviction: "Yes, yes I understand!" And I, eagerly grasping my chance, would preach to her:

"Goethe said: 'We are dependent upon what we ourselves have created.' There are emotions which I just cannot resist; I am helpless before them. At times a picture I imagine of something stirs in me such tormenting yearning to go there, to the place I imagined, that is, to something that lies beyond that fancy—beyond it, you understand—and I simply lack words to express this yearning!"

Vagin and I made a trip to Kazachyi Brody one day, an ancient village in the Dnieper Valley, where we saw off the settlers who were moving to the Ussuri district. We came back by train one early morning. When I got home from the station she and my brother had already left for the office. Feeling fit and virilely sunburned, very pleased with myself, I was keyed up with impatience to tell them about the extraordinary scene I witnessed: I had seen crowds of people setting off for those fabulous parts, seven thousand miles away from Kazachyi Brody! I quickly walked through all the rooms, empty and tidy, went into our bedroom to wash and change, looked at her knickknacks on the dressing table and at her little pillow in its lace-inset cover lying on top of the large one, with a strange sort of joyous pain—all of it appeared to me so infinitely dear and lonely, it stung my heart so piercingly with the bliss of being guilty toward her, when suddenly my glance fell on an open book lying on the bedside table. It was Tolstoi's *Family Happiness*, and the following passage was underlined: "At that time none of my thoughts, none of my feelings were mine, they were his thoughts and feelings, which had suddenly become my own. . . ." I turned over a few pages and saw more lines marked: "That summer I often went into my bedroom and I no longer felt my old tormenting desire and dreams of the future but, instead, apprehension for my present happiness. . . . Thus passed the summer and I began to feel my loneliness. He was always away on business, he was neither sorry nor afraid to leave me alone. . . ."

I stood stock-still for a few minutes. It struck me that it had never even occurred to me that she could have any hidden feelings unknown to me, and what was more, sorrowful feelings and thoughts which were already expressed in the past tense! *At that time* none of my thoughts . . . *That summer I often went* . . ." But the last words were the most amazing: "Thus passed the summer, and I began to feel my loneliness. . . ." In other words, her tears that night I came back from Shishaki were not spontaneous?

I walked into the office with exaggerated brightness, kissed her and my brother gaily, and chatted and joked. Secretly anguished I carried on in this strain until the moment we were alone, and then I said to her harshly, without preamble:

"So you've been reading *Family Happiness* while I've been away, have you?"

She blushed and said:

"Yes, why?"

"The lines you've marked have quite amazed me!"

"Why?"

"Because they make it quite clear that you are already unhappy with me, that you are already feeling lonely and disappointed."

"You always exaggerate so," she said. "Why disappointed? It was only that I felt rather sad, and really I did find a certain resemblance. . . . But I assure you it's not at all as you imagine it."

Who was she trying to convince—me or herself? But I was nevertheless very glad to hear her say what she did; I very much wanted to believe her; it suited me perfectly to believe her. "A steppe gull with a crest soars up from the road . . . she hurries on, a sash of blue drawn tight around her waist, her tremulous breasts quivering under her linen blouse, her feet without shoes, her legs, bare to the knee, are alive with young blood and vigor. . . ." How strong was my attraction to all this! How could I deprive myself of it! And, besides, I believed I could have all this and keep her too. I preached to her on every pretext that she should live for me and in me alone, that she should not deprive me of my liberty and willfulness, and for this I should love her even more. I believed that my love for her was so great that anything should be permitted me, forgiven me.

XXV

"You've changed a lot," she said. "You are more manly, kinder and sweeter now. You're more cheerful, too."

"You see! And my brother Nikolai and your father as well were always harping that we'd be very unhappy."

"It's because Nikolai took an instant dislike to me. You can't imagine what I went through at Baturino because of his icy politeness to me."

"You're wrong, he spoke of you very tenderly. He said to me: 'I'm terribly sorry for her as well, she's so young too and to think of what you two are in for! In what way will your existence be any different from that of any provincial exciseman a few years from now?' Remember how I used to laugh and paint my future? A wretched three-room flat, a fifty-ruble salary . . ."

"It was only you he was sorry for."

"He could keep his pity. He used to say that all he hoped for was that my 'wantonness' would save the two of us, that even a job like this would be too much for me, and that we should soon come to a parting of the ways. 'You'll either leave her in your cruelty,' he used to say, 'or she'll leave you after she's had a taste of those precious statistics and has come to appreciate the life you have doomed her to.' "

"He needn't have rested his hopes in me. I shall never leave you. I shall only leave you if I see that you no longer need me, that I'm in your way, a hindrance to your freedom, to your calling."

When a calamity befalls a man he keeps coming back to the same tormenting and useless thought: how had it begun? When? What were all those little things and how could I have swept aside all those warning signals? 'I shall only leave you if. . . .' But why did I not see the significance of those words, why did I not see that there was a certain 'if' which she did not exclude?

I valued my "calling" too highly. I used my liberty more and more wantonly—Nikolai had been right. I found it harder and harder to stay at home: whenever I had a day off I'd take a trip somewhere or just go out on a ramble.

"Where did you get so sunburned?" my brother asked me at dinner. "Where have you been tramping again?"

"I've been to the monastery, to the river, the station. . . ."

"And always by himself," she said with reproach. "How often he's promised to take me to the monastery. I've only been there once in all this time, and it's so beautiful there, such thick walls . . . swallows . . . monks. . . ."

It hurt me and shamed me to look into her eyes. But, dreading any encroachment upon my liberty, I merely shrugged and said:

"What are all those monks to you?"

"And to you?"

I tried to change the conversation.

"I saw something awfully queer at the cemetery there today: it was an empty grave! One of the brothers had it dug for him in advance, he even had a cross put up at the head, the inscription was on it too, his name, the date of birth; he even had the word 'died' written in, with a space left for the future date. It's all so neat there, so well kept, with pretty walks and flowers, and suddenly this waiting grave."

"There you are, you see?"

"What is there to see?"

"You're trying to misunderstand me on purpose. But never mind. It's true what Turgenev said—"

I interrupted her:

"It seems to me that all your reading now boils down to an effort to find something about you and me. However, all women read like that."

"Well, granted I'm only a woman, I'm not as selfish as you—"

"Do stop it, now," my brother would break in with a fond smile.

XXVI

Toward the end of the summer my position in the office became even more advantageous: whereas I had been merely "attached to it" before, I was now put on the staff and given a new job, which could not have suited me better: I was put in charge of the Board's library, that is, an assortment of administrative publications which had accumulated in the cellars. This new job, devised for me by Sulima, required me to sort out these publications and install them in proper order in a room cleared specially for the purpose—a long, vaulted room in the basement, equipped with the required number of shelves and bookcases—and thereafter, to look after the books and lend them out to the members of the Board if and when they should be needed by one or another of the departments. I sorted them out, put them in good order on the shelves and made ready to look after them and lend them out. But since I never had to lend out anything, except for a few publications in the autumn before the Board's annual meeting, all that I had to do was look after them, in other words just sit idle in this basement room, which I came to love for its unusually thick, fortresslike walls and vaulted ceiling, its profound silence—not a sound ever penetrated it—and its small window far up from the floor with the sun coming in through the top; I could also glimpse the stems of various shrubs and grasses growing in the waste plot behind the building. I had even greater freedom of action: all day long I sat in this tomb in complete solitude, reading and writing, and whenever I felt like it I could stay away for a week, lock the low oaken door and go out, or take a trip anywhere I fancied.

I went to Nikolayev; I don't know why. I often walked to a

farmstead in the suburbs rented by two brothers, followers of Tolstoi, so they could lead a godly life there. For a time I spent every Sunday evening in a large Ukrainian village beyond the next station from town, and would come home on the late train. . . . What were all these walks and trips for? She sensed that secret something which, besides everything else, lay at the bottom of my wanderings. My account of the feldsher woman at Shishaki had impressed her much more than I thought. Jealousy began to prey upon her; she tried to suppress it but sometimes it got the better of her. For instance, about a fortnight after I had told her of my Shishaki adventure, she suddenly did something that was quite contrary to her generous, noble and still maidenly nature, and was more in the spirit of any ordinary "mistress of the house." She found some excuse or other and with a harsh firmness discharged the young Cossack girl who had been serving us.

"I'm well aware that you're hurt," she said nastily to me. "I should think so, this 'filly,' as you call her, taps so smartly with her heels across our rooms, she has such fine, slim ankles, such slanting, flashing eyes! But you are forgetting that this filly is insolent and willful, and that there are some limits to my patience after all. . . ."

I replied in all sincerity, from the bottom of my heart:

"How can you be jealous of me? Here I am looking at your incomparable hand and thinking: this hand alone I would not exchange for all the beauties in the world! But I am a poet, an artist, and all art, Goethe says, is sensual."

XXVII

One August evening I set out for the cottage of the two Tolstoi followers when day was almost over. The town was deserted at this still sultry hour, and besides it was Saturday. I walked past the closed Jewish shops and rows of old stalls. The bells rang out for vespers. Although the shadows of the trees and houses were already long, the air was still sultry with the late afternoon sultriness peculiar to southern towns at the end of summer, when everything is parched in the parks and front gardens, baking in the sun day after day, and everything everywhere—in the town, the steppe and the melon fields—is languidly drowsy with the long summer heat.

In the square, beside the town well, a statuesque Ukrainian girl stood like a goddess, her bare feet in steel-shod boots; she had brown eyes and that peculiar purity of brow found in Ukrainian and Polish women. The street, going downhill from the square into the valley, faced the eventide expanse of the steppe with the barely visible hillocks on the southern horizon. I went down the street, turned into a quiet alleyway running between the middle-class houses in the suburbs, and came out into the meadow to go up the hill and then down into the steppe. In the fields, on the threshing floors, amid the blue and white mud huts, hand flails flickered in the air: the same young lads who whooped so wildly and wonderfully or sang their hymnlike songs so solemnly on summer nights, were threshing now. From the top of the hill the whole steppe, as far as the eye could see, looked golden with a thick stubble. The wide road was so deep in soft dust that you seemed to be walking in velvet-soled boots. And the country around—the wide steppe and the very air—was blindingly brilliant in the setting sun. To the left of the road, on the cliff over the valley, stood a cottage with peeling whitewashed walls: this was where the two brothers lived. I turned off the road and walked toward it through the stubble fields. But when I got there I found it empty. I looked into the open window—myriads of buzzing black flies swarmed on the walls, the ceiling and in the pots on the shelves. I looked into the open doors of the cowshed—nothing but the evening sun casting a red glow on the dry manure. I went into the melon field and saw there the wife of the younger brother, sitting on the edge balk. I walked up, but she did not notice me or pretended not to; she sat sideways, motionless, small and lonely, her bare feet trailing, one hand propping her up, while in the other she held a bit of straw which she was nibbling.

"Good evening," I said when I was close. "Why do you look so sad?"

"Good evening, sit down," she said with a little smile and, flinging away the straw, offered me her sunburned hand.

I sat down and looked at her: she was just like a little village girl watching the watermelons. Sun-bleached hair, a peasant's blouse with a low-cut neck, a shabby black skirt tight over her mature hips. Her small bare feet were dusty and looked dry and dark with sunburn. How could she walk barefooted over manure and all those prickly grasses, I wondered. Because she belonged to our circle where bare feet are not shown in public, I always felt both embarrassed and drawn to look at her feet. Conscious of my stare, she pulled them up.

"Where's everyone?" I asked.

She smiled again.

"They've gone somewhere. One of the saintly brothers has gone to the fields to thresh, he's helping some poor widow or other, and the other one's gone to town to post his letters to the great teacher: his weekly report about all our iniquities, temptations, and weaknesses of the flesh. And also, one of our current 'trials and tribulations' which has to be reported too: brother Pavlovsky has been arrested in Kharkov for distributing leaflets—denouncing military service, of course."

"You seem to be very much out of sorts."

"I'm fed up," she said, tossing her head and throwing it back. "I can't stand it any more," she added softly.

"What can't you stand?"

"Can't stand anything. Give me a cigarette."

"A cigarette?"

"Yes, yes, a cigarette!"

I gave it to her and struck a match, she puffed quickly and awkwardly to get her cigarette started. Inhaling jerkily and, like all women, blowing through her lips to let out the smoke, she lapsed into silence, staring into the valley and beyond. The low sun was still hot on our backs and on the heavy long melons which lay beside us, denting the dry soil with their sides, their parched stems tangled like snakes all about them. All of a sudden she threw away her cigarette, dropped her head in my lap and sobbed hungrily. And from the way I comforted her, kissed her hair, which smelled of the sun, caressed her shoulders and looked at her legs, I clearly understood what I found so attractive about these disciples of Tolstoi.

And Nikolayev? Why did I go there? I wrote notes on my way:

"We've just left Kremenchug; it's evening. Crowds of people at the Kremenchug Station, on the platform, in the restaurant, southern stuffiness, southern jostling. The same in the train. Ukrainian women for the most part, all of them young, sunburned, sprightly and excited with the journey and the heat—on their way to the South, to work. They stir you so with the hot smell of their bodies and their peasants' clothes, they prattle so, drink and eat, flashing their nut-brown eyes and flirting with their rapid speech, that it's quite a strain. . . .

"A long, long bridge across the Dnieper, a crimson blinding sun shining into the windows on your right, swelling yellow waters below and beyond. Lots of women nonchalantly taking off all their clothes on the sandy beach and bathing in the river. There's one flinging away her chemise, running and falling clumsily on her breast in the water, kicking up a storm with her feet. . . .

"The Dnieper is far behind us now. Evening shadows in the dismal mountains covered with tufts of cut grass and stubble. For some reason I thought of Svyatopolk the Cursed: I can see him riding on an evening like this down that valley in front of a small company. Where is he going? What is he thinking? And this was a thousand years ago, and today everything in the world is as beautiful. But no, it isn't Svyatopolk, it's some savage-looking peasant riding his exhausted horse at a walk in the shadow between the mountains, and behind him there's a woman with her hands tied behind her back, her hair tousled, her young knees bared, her teeth clenched, her eyes glaring into the back of his head, while he peers into the distance. . . .

"A wet moonlit night. Flat steppe beyond the window, black mud on the roads. The whole train is asleep, a stub of thick burned-down candle in the dusty lantern. The window is down and the wind brings in the dampness of the fields which mixes incongruously with the fetid air inside the train. Some of the Ukrainian women sleep flat on their backs with arms flung out, lips parted, breasts outlined under their blouses, heavy hips in tight skirts. . . . One of them has just awakened and lies there staring at me. Everyone is asleep—I keep fancying that she is about to call me in a mysterious whisper. . . ."

The village where I used to spend my Sundays was not far from the station, lying in a wide, low valley. I took the train there one day, got off and started toward the village on foot. It was late. In the distance I saw the white blurs of cottages surrounded by orchards, nearer on the common loomed the dark shape of a tumble-down windmill. There was a crowd about it, a fiddle squealed a catchy dance tune and I heard the tap of dancing feet. After that I spent several Sunday evenings standing in this crowd, listening to the fiddle, the dancing feet or the chorus of voices chanting monotonously until midnight; I would come close and stand beside a red-haired wench with a high bosom, thick lips and a strangely bright look in her yellow eyes, and we would instantly, taking advantage of the crowd, quietly grope for each other's hands. We stood there calmly, trying not to look at one another, realizing that I would be in for it if the village lads guessed the reason why this gentleman from town had started frequenting their gatherings. It was sheer accident that brought us together the first time, but after that, as soon as I appeared, she would at once throw a look over her shoulder and, sensing my closeness, take my hand in hers and hold it for the rest of the evening. And the darker it grew the harder she clenched my hand and the closer she pressed her shoulder to mine. Late at night, when the crowd began to thin, she would make her stealthy way to the other side of the windmill and hide behind it, while I would slowly start down the road to the station, wait until there was no one left beside the windmill and, bending low, run back. We had never put this arrangement of ours into words. We would stand close to the windmill without speaking, and torment ourselves silently and blissfully. One night she walked with me to the station. The train was not due for half an hour; the station was plunged into darkness and silence, only the crickets chirped their comforting song and the moon rose slowly in a purple glow above the black gardens, far away above the village. A freight car with open doors stood in the siding. Impulsively, horrified at what I was doing, I pulled her toward this carriage and climbed into it; she followed me and twined her arms hard round my neck. I struck a match to see where we were, and recoiled in horror: the light of the match revealed a long cheap coffin in the center of the floor. She streaked out like a wild goat, I sprang out after her. Once out of the car she kept falling down in the darkness, choking with laughter, and kissing me with a wild abandon, while all I wanted was to get away from there. After that, I never showed myself in the village again.

XXVIII

In the autumn we went through that festive period which always took place in the town toward the end of the year—it was the time of the Board annual meeting, attended by the members of the town councils from all over the province. The winter was gay, too: we had the Ukrainian theater with Zankovetskaya and Saksagansky on tour, concerts given by the capital's celebrities: Chernov, Yakovlev and Mravina; there were quite a few balls, masquerades and receptions. After the annual meeting was over I made a trip to Moscow to see Tolstoi, and on my return I gave myself up to worldly joys with particular relish. And these worldly joys worked a great outward change in our life. I do not think we ever spent an evening at home. They also worked an imperceptible change for the worse in our private life.

"You've changed again," she said to me one day. "You're quite a man in his prime now. And that French beard you're wearing too—"

"Don't you like it?"

"Of course I do, why shouldn't I? Only, everything is so transient!"

"Yes, it is. You, too, are growing to look like a mature young woman. You're thinner and more beautiful than ever."

"And you've begun to be jealous again. And now I'm afraid to confess something to you."

"What is it?"

"I'd like to wear a fancy dress to the next masquerade. Something that's not expensive and quite simple. A black lace mask and something black, flowing and long. . . ."

"And what will you be?"

"Night."

"So you're back to your Orel ways, are you? Night! That's rather vulgar."

"I see nothing vulgar or bad in it," she retorted dryly and independently, and I, with sinking heart, sensed in this dryness and independence of hers something that really brought back the old Orel days. "You're simply jealous again."

"But why am I jealous again?"

"I don't know."

"Yes, you do. Because you are drawing away from me again, you want to be admired again, to have the men courting you again."

She smiled spitefully.

"You've no right to talk. You've never left Cherkasova's side all the winter."

I blushed.

"Never left her side—that's too much! Is it my fault that she goes to the same places that we do? What hurts me most is that you've grown less unreserved with me, as if you're harboring some secret. Tell me honestly what is it? What secret are you nursing?"

"What secret?" she said. "Just sorrow that our old love is no more. But what's the use of talking about it. . . ." And after a pause she added: "And as for the masquerade, I'm quite prepared to forego it altogether if it's so disagreeable to you. Only you're much too exacting with me, calling every dream of mine vulgar, depriving me of everything while you deny yourself nothing. . . ."

* * *

I did quite a lot of traveling that spring and summer again. I met Cherkasova again in early autumn (there had really been nothing between us until then) and learned from her that she was moving to Kiev.

"I'm leaving you forever, my friend," she said looking at me with her hawk's eyes. "My husband is waiting for me impatiently. Would you like to take me as far as Kremenchug? In absolute secrecy, of course. I have to spend a whole night there, waiting for the boat. . . ."

XXIX

It happened in November. To this day I can see and feel those motionless, bleak and somber days in that dull Ukrainian town, its deserted streets with the wooden planks laid along the narrow walks, its black gardens behind the fences, the tall, bare poplars lining the boulevards, the stark city park with the windows of the summer restaurant boarded up, the moist air, the graveyard smell of decaying leaves, and myself wandering dully and aimlessly through the streets and the park, my obstinate unchanging thoughts and memories. . . . Memories—they are so oppressive and frightening that there is even a special prayer to save one from them.

At a certain fatal hour her secret torments, of which she

had dropped hints occasionally, possessed her with madness. My brother Georgy came home late from work that day; I came even later; she knew that we should both be late, for the Board was getting ready for the annual meeting. She stayed at home all by herself, she had not been out for several days, as usual every month, and as usual, too, in that period she was not quite herself. She must have lain for a long time on the sofa in our bedroom, her legs drawn up as usual, smoking hard—she had taken up smoking some time ago, ignoring my pleas and demands that she give up this habit which suited her so badly. I imagine she lay staring in front of her for a long time, then she suddenly got up, wrote me a few lines on a scrap of paper in a steady hand—my brother found the note on her dressing table when he got back from the office—and hurriedly packed a few things, the rest she just left behind, and for a long time I did not have the courage to pick up all these things strewn carelessly about the room and hide them away. That night she was already far on her way home to her father. . . . But why did I not immediately rush after her? Perhaps it was because I felt ashamed and also because I well knew that she was adamant at certain moments of her life. At last I got a few words in reply to all my telegrams and letters: "My daughter has gone away, forbidding me to make her whereabouts known to anyone at all."

I do not know what would have happened to me if it had not been for my brother, even though he was so confused and helpless. He did not give me the note she wrote in explanation of her flight right away, he tried to prepare me for the blow, very clumsily too, and at last he resolved to brave it, shed a bitter tear and handed it to me. A steady hand had written on the scrap of paper: "I can no longer stand your going farther and farther away from me. I cannot bear to let you go on trifling with my love all the time, more and more frequently now; I cannot kill the love in my heart but neither can I help knowing that I have sunk to the pit of mortification, to the limit of disappointment in all my foolish hopes and dreams, and I pray to God that He may give you the strength to live through our separation, to forget me and be happy in your new life which is now completely free. . . ." I read all this at a glance and said rather brutally, feeling the ground caving in under my feet and the skin on my face and head freezing and tightening:

"Oh well, it was only to be expected, these disappointments —the usual story."

After that I had the courage to go into our bedroom and with a nonchalant look lie down on the sofa. At dusk my brother peeped in cautiously, but I pretended I was asleep. Completely at a loss when faced with any sort of crisis and, like Father, loathing them, he was anxious to believe that I was really asleep, and glad that he was duty bound to attend a Board meeting again that night. He quietly dressed and left. I think the only reason that I did not shoot myself that night was because I had firmly decided to do it on the morrow anyway. When the room grew lighter with the milky moonlight flooding the garden, I went into the dining room, put on the lamp and, standing by the sideboard, drank a glass of vodka, then another. . . . I left the house and wandered through the streets; they were frightening: mute, warm and damp, everything, all the bare gardens and the poplars in the avenues were shrouded in a thick white mist mingled with the moonlight. But it was even more frightening to go back, to light the candle in our bedroom and in its faint light see all those scattered stockings, shoes, summer frocks and that pretty little dressing gown in which I embraced her body before going to sleep, feeling her warm breath, kissing her face raised up to mine with surrender in it. An ecstasy of tears alone could save me from this horror, tears shed with her, before her, but she was no longer there!

Then came another night. The same faint glimmer of the candle in the stark silence of the bedroom. Beyond the black windows, deep autumn rain pattered steadily in the darkness of the night. I lay staring into the corner—there was the old icon to which she used to pray every night. An old piece of wood, hard as though cast in steel, painted with vermilion and on this varnished red background, the image of the Holy Virgin in robes of gold, stern and sorrowful, with large black eyes gazing beyond the hereafter. Eyes in a dark rim. This rim was awesome! And awesome was the sacrilegious association in my thoughts: she and the Holy Virgin, this image and all those feminine things which she had strewn about in her mad haste to flee.

A week passed, another week, a month. I had long since given up my job, I never went anywhere, I tried to overcome one memory after another, day after day, night after night, and I kept thinking: this was the way the Slav men, once upon a time, hauled their heavily laden boats across the forest roads, towing them over the ruts.

XXX

I went through the agony of her presence everywhere in the house and the town for another month. At last I felt I could not endure this torture any longer and decided to go to Baturino, to stay there a while, without making any plans for the future.

I hugged my brother quickly for the last time in parting and got into the carriage of the moving train—it seemed very odd to get in and say to myself: there you are, free as a bird again! The night was dark, wintry and snowless, the train rumbled loudly in the dry air. I took my suitcase and found a seat in a corner close to the door. I sat and remembered how fond I was of repeating the Polish proverb in her presence: "Man is made for happiness as a bird is made for flight." I stared hard at the black windows of the roaring train so that no one should see my tears. It was a night's journey to Kharkov . . . and that other night from Kharkov, two years ago; a spring dawn, and how soundly she had slept in the train as day seeped in. . . . I sat tensely in the poor light of the lantern, in the cramped, fetid carriage, and waited for morning to come, for the sight of people, movement, and a glass of hot coffee at Kharkov. . . .

Then came Kursk, another town of memories; a spring noon, lunch with her at the station, her delight: "It's the first time in my life I'm having lunch at a railway station!" And now, at the close of this gray and rigorously cold day, our excessively long and unusually humdrum passenger train stood in front of this station, an endless line of large, ponderous third-class cars for which the Kursk-Kharkov-Azov railway was famous. I got out and looked at it. The engine loomed so far ahead that you could hardly see it. There were people with kettles in their hands jumping down from the train and hurrying to the restaurant for boiling water, all of them equally horrid. My train companions appeared on the platform too—an apathetic merchant, fatigued by his unhealthy corpulence, and a frightfully eager and highly inquisitive young chap, the common sharpness of whose features kept revolting me all day.

He darted a suspicious glance at me—I had been attracting his attention all day too. "There he's sitting," he must have thought, "this gentleman, or whoever he is, saying nothing!" However, he cautioned me with a friendly and rapidly uttered remark:

"You know, they've always got roast geese here, dirt cheap!"

I stood and thought of the restaurant which I could not enter, for there we two had once had lunch. There was a strong scent of the harsh Russian winter in the air, although there was still no snow. What boredom awaited me at Baturino! My father and mother growing old, my poor sister fading away, the poverty-stricken estate, the poverty-stricken house, the bare low garden swept by the icy wind, the dogs barking in a peculiar wintry way that always sounds unwanted and dismal when there is a wind like this. . . . The tail of the train stretched endlessly away. Across the platform barrier one could see the soaring crowns of the bare poplars, and beyond the poplars the provincial hackney coaches waiting on the frozen cobblestones. The very sight of these coaches spoke without words of the boredom and bleakness of this place, called Kursk. There on the platform, under the poplars, stood the women, their heads wrapped closely in their shawls with the ends crossed over their breasts and tied round their waists, their faces blue with cold, their voices inviting and obsequious as they called out offering their "dirt cheap" geese, tremendous and frozen stiff with pimply skins. Those who had managed to fill their kettles were briskly tripping back to the train into the warmth of the carriage; they now shivered happily in the cold, and with rakish humor haggled with the women as they hurried past. At long last the distant engine let out a howl of infernal gloom, threatening me with a still longer journey. . . . What made my plight so hopeless was that I did not know where she had gone. Had it not been for this I would have overcome all shame and ferreted her out long ago, bringing her back no matter what the cost—her crazy flight had certainly been a fit of madness, and it was only because she was ashamed of herself that she showed no signs of repentance.

My homecoming was quite different from what it had been three years before. I saw everything with different eyes. And everything about Baturino was even more miserable than I had pictured it on my way there: the wretched hovels in the village, the savage, shaggy dogs, the barbaric ice-clad water carts in front of the doors which had grown into the hard mud, humps of this mud on the driveway to the house, the empty yard in front of the glum house with its sad windows, its ridiculously tall and ponderous roof dating back to the day of our grandfathers and great-grandfathers, the two porches shadowed with the low roofs, the logs grown ash-blue from old age—everything was old, neglected and senseless, and the icy blasts of wind were senseless too, bending the top of the precious fir tree, which was higher than the roof, sticking up over the rest of the garden pathetic in its winter bareness. I saw that life at home had already become one of undisguised poverty—the cracks in the brick stoves were patched up with clay, the floors were carpeted with rough horse-cloth for warmth. Father alone tried to outweigh all this with his manner: he had grown thin and small and quite gray, he was always well shaved nowadays, his hair was smoothly brushed, he no longer affected his old carelessness in dress—it hurt to watch these valiant efforts of old age and poverty—he was more vigorous and cheerful than anyone else (evidently for my benefit, because of my disgrace and disaster). He said to me once, holding a cigarette in a shaking and already shriveled hand, and looking at me with tender wistfulness:

"Oh well, my dear boy, it all follows a law—the excitement, the sorrows and joys of youth and the peace and quiet of old age. How does it go?" he said, laughter in his eyes, " 'peaceful joys'—drat and blast them all!—

Alone in this our humble cottage,
Away from glitter, crowds and noise,
We breathe the freedom of the meadows,
And taste the bliss of peaceful joys. . . ."

When I think of Father, I invariably have a feeling of remorse; it always seems to me that I did not appreciate him and love him enough: I always feel guilty of being too poorly acquainted with his life, his youth especially, of having cared too little to learn more of it when I had the chance. And I keep trying and failing to understand exactly what sort of man he was—a man of quite another age and race, his whole nature amazing in its sterile talent, the perfectly wonderful ease with which he exercised his various gifts; his amazingly warm heart and quick mind which understood everything, grasped everything at a hint, combining a rare straightforwardness and reserve, an outward simplicity with an inner complexity, a sober perspicacity with a romantic heart. That winter I was twenty and he was sixty. It is hard to believe now that there had been a time when I was twenty and the youthful forces in me had only just been developing in spite of everything. And his life was already done. And yet no one had understood so well what I had been through that winter, and I do not think that anyone had felt this combination of sorrow and youthfulness in my soul as he had.

We were sitting in his study. It was a quiet and serenely sunny day, the yard, already covered with snow, glistened kindly through the low window of the room, which was warm, smoky, untidy and dear to me since my earliest childhood for this very untidiness and coziness, its never altered plain furnishings which seemed to me so inseparable from all Father's habits and tastes, from all my early memories of him and of myself.

When he spoke about the "peaceful joys" he put aside his cigarette, took his guitar down from the wall, and played one of his favorite songs, a folk song. The look in his eyes grew steadfast and cheerful, secreting something within itself at the same time, in tune with the soft gaiety of the guitar murmuring with a bitter and wistful chuckle about something that was precious and lost, of everything passing in this life of ours anyway, and nothing being worth the tears. . . .

Soon after my arrival, my feelings got the better of me, I tore off and rushed madly to town. I came back empty-handed the same day, for I had simply not been admitted to the doctor's house. With the daring born of despair I sprang from the sledge in front of the familiar and now frightening door; I threw a horrified look at the dining-room windows with the curtains half drawn, where once I had passed so many days sitting with her on the sofa—those autumn days, our first days—and I tugged at the bell. The door swung back, and I found myself face to face with her brother who, turning pale, said to me brusquely:

"Father does not wish to see you. And as you know she has gone away."

It was the same schoolboy who used to race so madly up and down the stairs with his dog Volchok that autumn. And now I saw before me a morose, very dark-skinned youth in a white shirt cut like an officer's, in tall boots, with a young black growth on his upper lip, a malignantly adamant look in his small black eyes, his tanned face greenish in its pallor.

"Please go away," he added in a low voice and I could see his heart hammering through the thin shirt.

And yet all winter long, every day, I obstinately waited for a letter from her, I could not believe that she was so stonily cruel.

XXXI

In the spring of that year I learned that she had been ill with pneumonia when she came home, and had died within a week. I also learned that she had willed it that I should be kept in ignorance of her death as long as possible.

* * *

I still have that notebook bound in brown morocco, the present she had bought me with her first salary, a day that was perhaps the most touching one in all her life. I can still make out the few words she had written on the front page when she gave me the book, with two mistakes made in her excitement, her haste and embarrassment. . . .

I dreamed of her a few nights ago—for the first time in all my long life without her. She was as young as she had been then, at the time when we shared our lives and our youth, but her face already held the charm of faded beauty. She was thin, she wore something that looked like mourning. I saw her vaguely, but with a love and joy so much stronger and closer in spirit and body, so much more poignant than anything I had ever felt for anyone else.

Maritime Alps, 1927-29, 1933

Dark Paths

ONE COLD rainy day in autumn, a mud-spattered coach with the hood half up, drawn by three rather ordinary horses abreast, their tails tied up out of the slush, came rolling along one of the Tula highways that was awash with rain and cut with numerous deep, black ruts. The troika stopped in front of a long timber building, one section of which was occupied by the stagecoach station, and the other by a one-room inn, where travelers could rest or spend the night, have dinner or order a samovar. On the box sat a large, sturdy man, tightly belted in his peasant's overcoat, with a dark, grave face and a thin pitch-black beard which made his look like an outlaw of old. And in the coach was a slender old man in a large cap and a gray officer's cloak with an upturned beaver collar, a man whose eyebrows were still black but whose mustache was already gray, its tips touching his sideburns of the same gray. His chin was clean-shaven, and all in all his appearance was not unlike that of Alexander II, a style that was very much in vogue among the officers during his reign. His eyes, too, had the same look—questioning, stern and yet weary.

When the coach came to a stop, he threw out a leg encased in a closely fitting military boot, and, holding his cloak together with chamois-gloved hands, ran up the porch steps.

"To your left, Your Excellency," the driver called roughly from his box, and the man, stooping a little in the doorway because of his great height, walked into the entry and then into the room on his left.

The place was warm, dry and neat; a new gilded icon glistened in the left-hand corner, under it stood a table covered with a clean, unbleached linen tablecloth, with well-scrubbed benches ranged around it; the stove, which took up the right-hand corner of the room, was newly whitewashed; nearer the door stood a kind of couch draped in different colored horse-cloths, the arm pushed up against the side of the stove; a delicious smell of soup—well-cooked cabbage, beef and bay leaf—came from behind the oven door.

The newcomer threw his cloak down on the bench—appearing even more erect and slender in his tunic and top boots—then he took off his gloves and cap and with a weary gesture passed his pale thin hand over his hair—his gray hair, brushed forward from the temples toward the corners of his eyes, had a soft curl in it, and his handsome, long, dark-eyed face showed tiny pockmarks here and there. There was no one in the room and, pushing the door slightly ajar, he shouted querulously:

"Hey, is anyone there?"

Whereupon a dark-haired woman came into the room. Her eyebrows were black like the man's and, like him, she still retained a beauty that was not in keeping with her years. She resembled a middle-aged Gypsy woman in that her upper lip and the sides of her face were shadowed with a soft down, she was light on her feet though her body was heavy, with large breasts under her red blouse, and her stomach, triangular like a goose's, outlined by a black woolen skirt.

"Welcome, Your Excellency," she said. "May I offer you something to eat or would you rather have a samovar?"

The newcomer threw a cursory glance at her rounded shoulders and her slim feet in their shabby red Tatar slippers, and answered carelessly and brusquely:

"A samovar. Are you the innkeeper or the servant?"

"The innkeeper. Your Excellency."

"You mean you run the place yourself?"

"That's right."

"How's that? Are you a widow or something that you're all alone in business?"

"I'm not a widow, Your Excellency, but I've got to make a living somehow. And I like being in business."

"I see, I see. That's good. And your room is so clean and pleasant."

The woman kept her slightly narrowed eyes fastened on him with a searching look.

"I like cleanliness too," she said. "After all, I was brought up in the gentry's service, I ought to know how to keep my place decent, Nikolai Alexeyevich."

He drew himself up at once, opened his eyes wide and blushed.

"You can't be Nadezhda?" he said hurriedly.

"Yes, Nikolai Alexeyevich," she replied.

"Good God! Good God!" he said, sitting down on the bench and staring hard at her. "Who ever would have thought it! How many years is it since we last saw each other? About thirty-five, I should imagine?"

"It's thirty, Nikolai Alexeyevich. I'm forty-eight now and you're close on sixty, I think?"

"Something like that. . . . Good God, how strange!"

"What's strange, sir?"

"Why everything, everything. . . . Surely you must understand!"

His weariness and his indifference vanished. He got up and started pacing the room with resolute strides, his eyes upon the floor. Then he stopped and, with a blush creeping through his gray sideburns, began to speak:

"Since then I have heard nothing about you at all. How do you come to be here? Why didn't you stay on with your masters?"

"They gave me my liberty after you left."

"And where did you go then?"

"It's a long story, sir."

"And you say you were never married?"

"No, never."

"But why? A girl as beautiful as you were then?"

"I couldn't do it."

"Why not? What are you trying to say?"

"What is there to explain? I expect you remember how much I loved you."

He blushed so hard that tears welled up in his eyes, and with a scowl he resumed his pacing.

"Everything passes, my friend," he muttered. "Love, youth, everything, everything. It's an ordinary, sordid story. Everything passes with time. What does it say in the Book of Job? 'Thou shalt remember it as waters that pass away'?"

"It's all God's will, Nikolai Alexeyevich. Youth does pass for all of us; but love—that's a different thing."

He raised his head and, stopping in front of her, asked with a strained smile:

"But surely you couldn't have loved me all your life?"

"I did, you see. I lived by that alone and the passing years made it no different. I knew that you had changed long ago, that it meant as little to you as if it had never been, but still. . . . It's too late for reproaches now, but it's true you abandoned me very heartlessly then. At times I wanted to lay hands upon myself from the hurt of it alone, to say nothing of the rest. You know there was a time, Nikolai Alexeyevich, when I used to call you Nikolenka, and you called me—do you remember? And you were always reciting poetry to me about all sorts of 'dark paths,' remember?" she added with a grim smile.

"Ah, how lovely you were then!" he said, nodding in reminiscence. "How passionate! How beautiful! What a body, what eyes! Remember the way everyone gazed at you?"

"I remember, sir. You were exceptionally handsome too. And it was to you that I gave my beauty and my passion, you know. That's something that can never be forgotten."

"Ah! Everything passes. One forgets everything."

"Everything passes, but one does not forget everything."

"Go," he said, turning away and walking to the window. "Please go."

And pulling out a handkerchief, he pressed it to his eyes and added in a quick patter:

"I only hope God forgives me. You have, I see."

She went toward the door and paused there:

"No, Nikolai Alexeyevich, I have not forgiven you. Since we have begun to talk about our feelings, I'll be frank with you. I have never been able to forgive you. I never had anything more precious in this world than you—either then or afterward. And that is why I cannot forgive you. Oh well, what's the use of remembering, you don't bring the dead back from the graveyard."

"Yes, yes, there's no sense in it, tell them to get the horses ready," he replied walking away from the window, and now his face was stern. "I'll only say this to you: I have never been happy in my life, please don't think I have. Forgive me, I may be wounding your pride, but I'll tell you frankly—I loved my wife to distraction. Yet she deceived me, she abandoned me with much more insolence than I abandoned you. I adored my son while he was a child—what hope I placed in him! But he grew up to be a scoundrel, a rake and a cad without a heart, without honor or conscience. . . . However, that too is the most ordinary and sordid of stories.

I wish you luck, my dear. I think that in you I too lost the most precious thing I ever had in my life."

She came up to him and kissed his hand, and he kissed hers.

"Tell them I'm ready to go. . . ."

As he drove away he was thinking glumly: "How sweet she used to be! How bewitchingly lovely!" He remembered with shame his parting words to her and the kiss he had given her hand, and, instantly, he felt ashamed of his shame. "Isn't it true she gave me the best moments of my life?"

A pale sun appeared low in the western sky. The driver kept his horses at a trot, changing from one black track to another, choosing those that were less muddy, and he, too, was engrossed in his own thoughts. At last he said with grave brusqueness:

"She kept looking from the window, Your Excellency, when we were driving away. You've known her long, I suppose?"

"Yes, Klim."

"That's a very wise woman. And she's getting richer all the time, they say. She lends money out to folks."

"That doesn't mean a thing."

"Oh, doesn't it! Don't we all want to better our lot? And if you're decent about the interest, there's little harm done. And they say she's fair on that score. But she's hard too! If you don't pay back on time—you've only yourself to blame."

"Yes, yes, you've only yourself to blame. . . . Hurry, please, I'm afraid we'll miss the train. . . ."

The sun, sinking low, cast a yellow light over the desolate fields, the horses splashed steadily through the puddles. He drew his black eyebrows together and mused, absently following the flickering horseshoes before him:

"Yes, you've only yourself to blame. Yes, of course, the best moments of my life. And not only the best, the truly wonderful ones! 'Around us bloomed the sweet brier red, and paths with lime trees tall were shadowed. . . .' But, good heavens, what would have happened then? Supposing I hadn't left her, what then? Heavens, what rubbish! This Nadezhda woman—not the owner of a wayside inn, but my wife, the mistress of my house in Petersburg, the mother of my children?"

And, closing his eyes, he shook his head.

October 20, 1938

The Raven

My father looked like a raven. It had occurred to me when I was a child. One day I saw a picture in the *Niva* showing a rock with Napoleon standing on it, pot-bellied, in buckskins and short black boots, and suddenly I laughed joyfully as I recalled a picture in Bogdanov's *Travels to the Pole* because Napoleon looked just like a penguin, and then the sad thought struck me: "And Papa looks like a raven."

My father held a very prominent post in our town, which was a district center, and this had an even more ruinous effect on his character. I do not suppose that even in that society of civil servants to which he belonged, there was any man more overbearing, gloomy, taciturn and coldly cruel in his unhurried words and actions, than he. He really was like a raven—short, thickset, slightly round-shouldered, with coarse black hair and a long big-nosed face, clean-shaven and dark-skinned—and he looked particularly like one when, in his black dress coat, he attended one of the charity balls sponsored by the Governor's wife and stood hunched and immobile close to a booth, decorated to look like a Russian cottage, moving his large raven's head, staring obliquely with his bright raven's eyes at the dancing couples, at the people who came up to the booth, and at the lady in the booth who, with a charming smile and with diamonds sparkling on her large hand, served the cheap yellow champagne in shallow glasses. She was a tall woman, wearing a boyar headdress and a gold brocade gown, and her nose was so pink and white with powder that it looked like a false one.

Father had been a widower for a good many years. He only had us two children—my eight-year-old sister Lilya and myself—and the huge, highly polished rooms of our apartment which gleamed with cold, unlived-in splendor. The apartment was on the first floor of one of the buildings belonging to the Department where my father was employed, and its windows faced the poplar-lined avenue between the cathedral and the main street. Fortunately, I spent most of the year in Moscow, where I was a boarder at the Katkov Lycée, and only came home for Christmas and the summer holidays. But something quite unforeseen awaited me on my arrival home for the summer when I had finished my schooling.

When I got home from Moscow I was simply astounded. It seemed as though the sun had suddenly come to shine in our apartment which was so funereal before. It was aglow with the sunny presence of a gay young girl, who had just been taken on to replace my sister's old nurse, a tall, flat old woman who looked like a medieval wooden statue of a saint. Being a poor girl, a daughter of one of Father's subordinates, she was exceedingly happy at the time that she had found such a good position immediately upon leaving school, and that now I had arrived she would have someone of her own age in the house. But goodness, how timorous she was. How shy in my father's presence at our formal dinners as she anxiously watched our black-eyed Lilya, who was taciturn like Father. But this very taciturnity of hers was surly, as was her every movement, for she sat twisting and turning her black head about with an air of defiance, as if she was forever on the lookout for something. Father was quite unrecognizable at dinner now; he no longer threw heavy looks at old Gury, serving at the table in white knitted gloves. He talked a little now and then—dragging out the words, it's true, but it was talking anyway—addressing no one but her, of course, calling her "dear Yelena Nikolayevna" most ceremoniously—and he even attempted to joke or smile. And this so embarrassed her that she merely smiled miserably in reply and blushed, her delicate thin face crimsoning in spots—the face of a slight, fair-haired girl in a soft white blouse, dark under the arms with hot young sweat, with small, barely outlined breasts. At dinner she never dared raise her eyes to mine, for then I was even more frightening to her than Father. But the harder she tried to avoid looking at me, the colder became the oblique looks Father darted at me. I felt we both realized that her painful efforts to ignore me and listen instead to my Father or attend to the ill-natured, restless though silent Lilya, concealed quite another fear—tremulous fear for the happiness we both felt in being together. Father always used to have his evening tea served to him in a large gold-rimmed cup on his desk in the study, but now he had it with us in the dining room, and she poured it out for us, presiding at the samovar. Lilya would already be in bed by then. He would come out of his study dressed in a long, loose smoking jacket, lined with red, settle down in his armchair and pass his cup to her. She would fill it to the brim, the way he liked it, and hand it to him with shaking fingers. Then she poured mine and hers and, dropping her eyes, took up her sewing, while he talked, taking his time, of things that were very strange indeed:

"Women with fair hair, dear Yelena Nikolayevna, look their

best in either black or crimson. . . . Now, for instance, a black satin gown with a high pointed collar like Mary Stuart's, sewn with small brilliants, would become your face very well . . . or a medieval gown of crimson velvet with a small *décolleté* and a little cross of rubies worn with it. . . . A fur-lined wrap of blue Lyons velvet and a Venetian beret would suit you too. . . . All this is daydreaming, of course," he would say, smiling. "We only pay your father 75 rubles a month, and he has five children besides you to support, all of them young—therefore, it's more than likely that you'll have to live in poverty all your life. But then I always say—what's the harm in daydreaming? It cheers you up, it gives you strength and hope. And then again, it does happen sometimes that a dream suddenly comes true, doesn't it? Very rarely, of course, very rarely indeed, but it does. Take that cook at the Kursk railway station, for instance, the one who drew a two hundred thousand lottery ticket—an ordinary cook, too!"

She tried to pretend she was taking all this for kindly banter; she forced herself to look up at him and smile, while I sat playing patience as if I weren't listening to any of it. As for Father, he went even further on one occasion. He suddenly said, indicating me with a nod:

"Now this young man here probably has his dreams too. He's thinking his dear papa will die one day and then he'll have more gold than he can count. And, indeed, he won't be able to count it, for there will be nothing for him to count! It goes without saying that his papa does have certain holdings—that little estate, for instance, of a thousand acres of black soil in Samara Province—but I very much doubt that the son will inherit it, he's not overaffectionate with his papa, and then, as far as I can judge, he'll develop into a first-class wastrel. . . ."

This last conversation took place on the eve of St. Peter's Day, a very memorable day for me. Father started off early the following morning, to attend services at the cathedral and then afterward to lunch with the Governor whose birthday it was that day. But Father never had lunch at home except on Sundays anyway, and so the three of us were alone as usual. Toward the end of the meal, when Lilya was given some cherry jelly instead of her favorite sugar cakes, she started screaming at Gury at the top of her voice, banged her fists on the table, flung her plate on the floor, her head began to jerk and shake and angry sobs choked her. We carried her to her room with some difficulty because she kept biting our hands and kicking, but we entreated her to calm down, promising her we would punish the cook severely for this, and at last we managed to placate her and lull her to sleep.

And even this alone—our hands touching as we carried Lilya to her room—was like a tremulous caress, filling us with untold tenderness for one another. Rain was falling heavily outside, lightning pierced the darkening rooms again and again, and the windowpanes rattled with the thunderclaps.

"It's the thunderstorm that has affected her so," she said in a happy whisper when we had come out into the passage, and suddenly she stopped, listening.

"Oh, there's a fire somewhere!" she said.

We ran to the dining room, threw open the window and saw the fire brigade rushing past our house, rumbling down the avenue. Rain was pouring down swiftly on the poplars—the thunderstorm was over, just as though the rain had put it out—and we heard the firemen's bugle sounding a soft and impishly playful warning amid the clamor of the rushing long-shafted wagons loaded with hoses and ladders, with brass-helmeted firemen standing up in them, amid the jingling of the bells fixed on the bows above the manes of the black draught horses; and the metallic clatter as the horses drew the carts over the cobblestones at a gallop. Then came the very, very rapid peals of the alarm bell, clanging in the belfry of St. John the Warrior's. We stood close to each other at the window, breathing in the fresh smell of water and the rain-beaten street dust, and we seemed to be straining, with all our senses stirred to a pitch of excitement, only to see and to hear. And then the last of the wagons, with a huge red tank on it, rumbled past. My heart beat faster, the skin felt tight on my forehead. I took her hand as it hung limply at her side and I gazed at her profile beseechingly, and she, too, blanched, parted her lips, and took a deep breath that raised her breast. There were tears and a plea in the eyes she turned to me. I caught her shoulder with my hand and for the first time in my life fainted in the exquisite coolness of a girl's lips. . . .

After this not a day, not a single hour passed without our meeting, accidentally as it were, either in the drawing room or in the ballroom, or in the passage and even in Father's study—he never came back until late. They were short meetings with desperately long, insatiable kisses, already unbearable in their inconclusiveness. And Father, sensing something, again stopped coming to the dining room for evening tea with us, and grew morose and taciturn once more. But we no longer took any notice of him, and her manner at the dinner table became more serene and poised.

In the beginning of July, Lilya fell ill from eating too many raspberries, and was in bed recuperating slowly, spending all her days drawing pictures with colored crayons of some fabulous cities on large sheets of paper tacked on a board. Therefore she had no choice but to stay beside Lilya's bed, embroidering a Ukrainian blouse for herself—she could not possibly leave her post because Lilya demanded constant attention. And I, alone in the empty, silent house, was tormented with a ceaseless desire to see her, kiss her and hold her in a close embrace. I would go and sit in my father's study trying to read, picking books at random from his bookcases. And that is what I was doing on that particular day too. It was already close on evening. Suddenly I heard the sound of her light, swift footsteps. I threw down my book and jumped up.

"Has she fallen asleep?"

She made a hopeless gesture.

"Oh no! You don't know her—she doesn't care if she stays awake two nights running, like all mad people! She made me come here to hunt for some yellow and orange pencils on her father's desk. . . ."

And, bursting into tears, she came up to me and dropped her head on my breast:

"Oh God, when will it all end? Tell him at last, tell him that you love me, that nothing in the world can keep us apart!"

Raising her face, wet with tears, she threw her arms about me impetuously and clung to me in a breathless kiss. I pressed her whole body to mine, I drew her toward the sofa—could I remember or think of anything at a moment like that? But then I heard someone coughing softly in the doorway: I looked over her shoulder and saw Father standing there, watching us. Then he turned about and, hunching his shoulders, walked away.

We none of us appeared at dinner that night. Later, Gury knocked on my door and said: "Your father requests you to go to his room." I went into the study. He was sitting in the armchair facing his desk and, without turning round, he began to speak:

"Tomorrow, you will leave for my Samara estate and stay there for the rest of the summer. In the autumn you are to go to Moscow or Petersburg and look for a post. If you dare disobey me I shall disinherit you forever. But that is not all: tomorrow I shall ask the Governor to have you banished into the country immediately and taken there under escort. Now go, and don't let me see you again. Your train fare and a certain amount of pocket money will be delivered to you by my man in the morning. I shall write to my estate office in due course to give you a sum of money for your first days in the capitals. You need entertain no hopes of seeing her before you leave. That is all. Go."

That same night I left for the province of Yaroslavl and remained there all the summer, staying with one of my school friends. With the help of his father I secured a post that autumn at the Ministry of Foreign Affairs in Petersburg, and wrote to my father telling him that I not only renounced my rights to his inheritance forever, but also refused any assistance from him. The same winter I learned that he had retired and had also moved to Petersburg "with his charming young wife," I was told. And one night, as I walked into the stalls of the Mariinsky Theater, a few minutes before the curtain went up, I suddenly saw them. They were in a box close to the stage, sitting in the front seats with her mother-of-pearl opera glasses lying on the barrier before them. Looking like a raven in his dress coat, hunched and squinting with one eye, he sat reading his program intently. And she, gracefully poised, her fair hair piled up on top of her head, looked eagerly about her at the warm, brilliantly lighted, softly murmuring house below, at the evening gowns, dress coats and uniforms of the people in the boxes. A little cross of rubies glowed darkly on her breast, her slender but already rounded arms were bare, and something like a peplum of crimson velvet was caught with an agraffe of rubies on her left shoulder. . . .

May 18, 1944